Ace Books by Glenda Larke

THE AWARE
GILFEATHER
THE TAINTED

The TAINTED

BOOK THREE OF THE
ISLES OF GLORY

GLENDA LARKE

ACE BOOKS, NEW YORK

THE BERKLEY PUBLISHING GROUP
Published by the Penguin Group
Penguin Group (USA) Inc.
375 Hudson Street, New York, New York 10014, USA
Penguin Group (Canada), 90 Eglinton Avenue East, Suite 700, Toronto, Ontario M4P 2Y3, Canada
(a division of Pearson Penguin Canada Inc.)
Penguin Books Ltd., 80 Strand, London WC2R 0RL, England
Penguin Group Ireland, 25 St. Stephen's Green, Dublin 2, Ireland (a division of Penguin Books Ltd.)
Penguin Group (Australia), 250 Camberwell Road, Camberwell, Victoria 3124, Australia
(a division of Pearson Australia Group Pty. Ltd.)
Penguin Books India Pvt. Ltd., 11 Community Centre, Panchsheel Park, New Delhi—110 017, India
Penguin Group (NZ), Cnr. Airborne and Rosedale Roads, Albany, Auckland 1310, New Zealand
(a division of Pearson New Zealand Ltd.)
Penguin Books (South Africa) (Pty.) Ltd., 24 Sturdee Avenue, Rosebank, Johannesburg 2196,
South Africa

Penguin Books Ltd., Registered Offices: 80 Strand, London WC2R 0RL, England

This is a work of fiction. Names, characters, places, and incidents either are the product of the author's imagination or are used fictitiously, and any resemblance to actual persons, living or dead, business establishments, events, or locales is entirely coincidental. The publisher does not have any control over and does not assume any responsibility for author or third-party websites or their content.

THE TAINTED

An Ace Book / published by arrangement with HarperCollins Pty. Ltd.

PRINTING HISTORY
Voyager Books edition / 2004
Ace edition / July 2006

Copyright © 2004 by Glenyce Noramly.
Maps copyright © by P. Phillips.
Cover art by Scott Grimando.
Cover design by Annette Fiore DeFex.
Interior text design by Stacy Irwin.

ISBN: 0-441-01419-4

ACE
Ace Books are published by The Berkley Publishing Group,
a division of Penguin Group (USA) Inc.,
375 Hudson Street, New York, New York 10014.
ACE and the "A" design are trademarks belonging to Penguin Group (USA) Inc.

PRINTED IN THE UNITED STATES OF AMERICA

10 9 8 7 6 5 4 3 2 1

*Selina, this one is for you,
with love and pride always,
in this, a productive year for us both.*

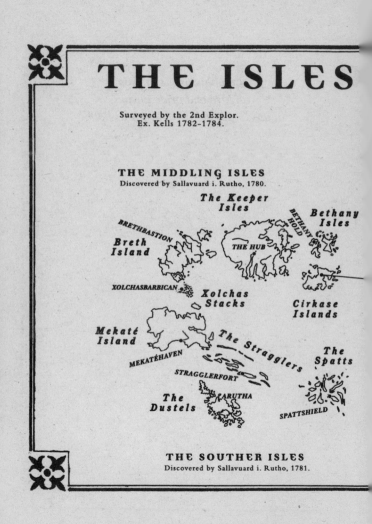

THE ISLES

Surveyed by the 2nd Explor.
Ex. Kells 1782-1784.

THE MIDDLING ISLES
Discovered by Sallavuard i. Rutho, 1780.

The Keeper Isles

Bethany Isles

BETHANY HOLD

BRETHBASTION

Breth Island

THE HUB

Cirkase Islands

XOLCHASBARBICAN

Xolchas Stacks

Mekaté Island

The Stragglers

The Spatts

MEKATÉHAVEN

STRAGGLERFORT

The Dustels

FARUTHA

SPATTSHIELD

THE SOUTHER ISLES
Discovered by Sallavuard i. Rutho, 1781.

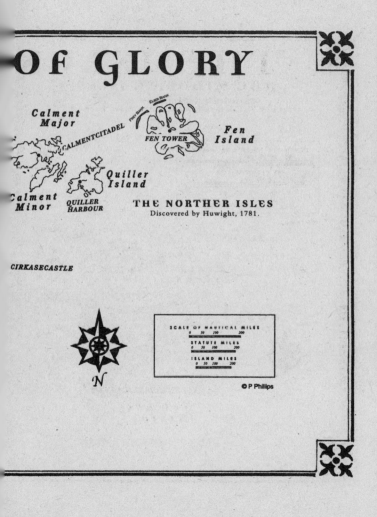

OF GLORY

Calment
Major

CALMENTCITADEL

Calment
Minor

QUILLER
HARBOUR

Quiller
Island

ELVER BANK

FISH BANK

FEN TOWER

Fen
Island

THE NORTHER ISLES
Discovered by Huwight, 1781.

CIRKASECASTLE

SCALE OF NAUTICAL MILES
0   50   100   200

STATUTE MILES
0   50   100   200

ISLAND MILES
0   50   100   200

© P Phillips

N

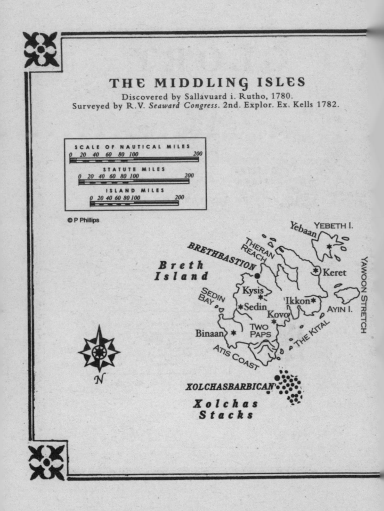

THE MIDDLING ISLES

Discovered by Sallavuard i. Rutho, 1780.
Surveyed by R.V. *Seaward Congress*. 2nd. Explor. Ex. Kells 1782.

SCALE OF NAUTICAL MILES
0   20   40   60   80   100   200

STATUTE MILES
0   20   40   60   80   100   200

ISLAND MILES
0   20   40   60   80 100   200

© P Phillips

YEBETH I.
Yebaan

THERAN
REACH

BRETHBASTION

*Breth
Island*

Keret

YAWOON STRETCH

SEDIN
BAY

Kysis

'*Ikkon*

Sedin

AYIN I.

Kovo

Binaan

TWO
PAPS

THE KITAL

ATIS COAST

N

XOLCHASBARBICAN

*Xolchas
Stacks*

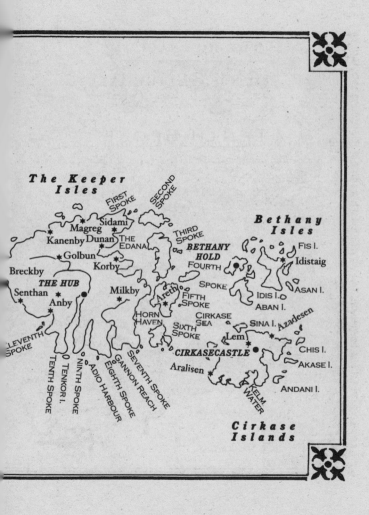

The Keeper Isles

FIRST SPOKE
SECOND SPOKE
THIRD SPOKE

Magreg
Sidami
Kanenby Dunan THE EDANA
Golbun Korby
Breckby
THE HUB
Senthan
Anby Milkby
ELEVENTH SPOKE
TENTH SPOKE
NINTH SPOKE
TENKOR I.
ADIO HARBOUR
EIGHTH SPOKE
GANNON REACH
SEVENTH SPOKE

Bethany Isles

BETHANY HOLD
FOURTH SPOKE

FIS I.
Idistaig
ASAN I.
IDIS I.O
ABAN I.

FIFTH SPOKE
Areth
CIRKASE SEA
SIXTH SPOKE

HORN HAVEN

SINA I. Azadesen
Lem
CHIS I.
CIRKASECASTLE
AKASE I.
Aralisen
HELM WATER
ANDANI I.

Cirkase Islands

THE HUB RACE

CAPE HAY

OUTER

TENKOR

THE TONGUE

TURTLE POINT

TENTH SPOKE

HIGH

Tenkorport-
Tenkorhaven

LOW

Low Sands

BENDERBY FLATS

THE ROCKS

SERRATED SPIT

ROWLE

RORKI

NINTH SPOKE

SLOUGH

ADIO HARBOUR

ADIO SANDS

N

© P Phillips

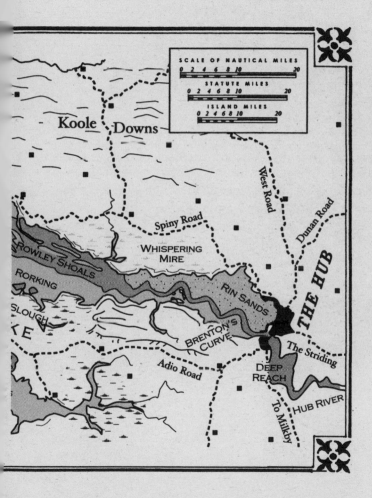

ACKNOWLEDGMENTS

Once again a number of people, from all corners of the world, have helped to get me and this final book of the trilogy to this point, and my thanks go out to you all:

To all the team at HarperCollins Publishers Australia and Stephanie Smith in particular. (And not forgetting Theresa, one of the HC reps in Perth, because she looked after me so well at Swancon.) To Kim Swivel, for being a great copy editor.

To my agent, Dorothy Lumley in the UK, as always.

To fellow Voyager authors who took the time—in spite of their own heavy schedules—to read the manuscript and who provided invaluable comments, as always: Russell Kirkpatrick over in New Zealand (author of The Fire of Heaven trilogy) and Trudi Canavan in Victoria (author of The Black Magician trilogy).

To Fiona McLennan in Sydney and Davina MacLeod in Melbourne who also made time to read the manuscript and offered insightful comments and ideas. I don't know how you do it, guys.

To everyone on the Voyager message board (www.

voyageronline.com.au) who offered advice on the title for this volume, and thanks for all the interesting conversations and laughs.

To Perdy Phillips in Fremantle for producing the wonderful maps.

To Colin in Scotland, webmaster, for his time and humour.

To Steve Rowley in the UK who answered all my inane questions about the Severn bore. (If anyone is interested in following up on this topic, try this website: www.boreriders. com.)

To Mark Hickey in Perth who tried to impart some of his knowledge about surf skis. (Any idiocies in this book about riding waves should be attributed to the author, not Mark—or better still, blame the sylvmagic.)

It wasn't easy being a girl sometimes. Especially not when you were just sixteen, and hauling in wet fishing nets over a deck slippery with scales and slime. It was even harder when you were also a Dustel Islander, without a proper home, and the only fishing grounds you were permitted to fish were those of the Reefs of Deep Sea.

It isn't fair, Brawena Waveskimmer thought. The reefs were several days' sail away from South Sathan Island in the Stragglers where most of the Dustel fisher folk lived, and that meant all the fish had to be cleaned and salted on board before returning to port. Then, of course, they didn't fetch the higher prices of fresh fish sold by the local Stragglermen.

"It's a circle," she muttered under her breath. A horrible endless circle keeping them poor. They worked harder than most people and yet earned less. And all because they were Dustels, not Stragglermen. Because they were citizens of a place that no longer existed.

"Watch what you are doing," her grandfather growled. "You almost lost that fish."

She hooked the flopping tunny from the deck and dropped it into the holding area. Her grandfather resumed winching in the net. I shouldn't be doing this at all, she thought resentfully. It's a man's work. If only Da hadn't drowned at sea. If only I had brothers instead of a pack of sisters.

For that matter, if only Morthred hadn't sunk the Dustel Islands beneath the sea almost a hundred years ago . . .

She'd heard the story often enough. Her grandfather's father was alive then. From the deck of the family fishing boat, he actually saw the distant islands sink beneath the horizon. No one had believed it at first. The fishermen pulled up their nets and set sail for Arutha Port, expecting the islands to appear out of a sea mist any moment—but they weren't there to find any more. A couple of shocked Awarefolk clung to the wooden wreckage of someone's home, now gently bobbing in an expanse of floating debris that stretched for miles in all directions. And there were birds . . . disoriented birds everywhere, flying aimlessly, keening their distress. Among them—although her great-grandfather had not known it just then—were all that remained of the non-Aware citizenry of the port. Many of them flew clumsily down to his boat, calling and crying out to him to help them, save them, didn't he know who they were . . . *Look here, I'm your cousin, Etherald; look at me, I'm your neighbour Lirabeth . . .* But he didn't know what they were saying. He hadn't understood then what they were trying to tell him as they came and settled on the mast of the boat, as they crowded the rigging and clung to the gunwale. They chirped and chittered and cried, and they had made no more sense to themselves than they had to him.

No one understood until much, much later. And now it was the best kept secret of the Isles of Glory, kept by all people who claimed Dustel ancestry: the knowledge that their closest relatives were sentient birds. Not the same ones who had suffered the spell, of course, but their descendants. Small, dark birds with a purplish sheen and a maroon band across their breasts, who spoke their own avian language and yet could understand human speech.

Brawena took the last fish out of the net and straightened her aching back. And saw something that shouldn't have been.

"Grandda, what's that?"

The old man stared out in the direction of her gaze. There was a disturbance in the water, a sudden swirl about fifty paces astern. Even as they watched, it began to spread, sending out tentacles of movement through a gentle swell.

"Must be a school of something," he said gleefully. "Get the foresail up, lass."

She moved to do his bidding as he raised the anchor, but she kept an eye on the swirling water while she worked. "It doesn't look like fish," she said, as he edged the boat around and the canvas gathered up a puff of wind. "It can't be a whale . . . or a sea-dragon, can it?"

He frowned and eased off on the tiller so that the canvas hung limply. There was something odd about the disturbance. It looked almost as if the water was boiling, or as if some great leviathan of the deep was pushing its way upwards. The water was *heaving*. A school of frightened fish swept past the boat and for once neither Brawena nor her grandfather took any notice.

"I think we had better leave," the old man said suddenly. "Get the mainsail up, girl, and quickly." The urgency of his tone made Brawena dive for the halyard without taking time to ask why. It was one thing to suggest leaving, of course, and quite another to do so when there was only the lightest of breezes. Until the underwater upheaval, the ocean had been almost flat, and the wind playfully fickle, dancing up ripples here and there, then fading into stillness.

Once the sail was up, Brawena looked back over the stern.

In the middle of the boiling ocean, something thrust its way upwards like a huge skeletal hand reaching for the sky. Water poured away from it, leaving the bare fingers standing red and naked and shining in the sun. She still hadn't had time to make sense of that when the sea surface seemed to rip open in a jagged line, as if a giant had torn it asunder from underneath. Everywhere she looked shapes reached up out of the water, shedding the sea in torrents. A school of porpoises leapt away in panicked curves of silver and gray.

A gust hit the sails of the boat, and it heeled sharply. Brawena clutched the gunwale, her mouth dropping open as she gazed wide-eyed on the scene astern. Scarlet trunks, leafless ebony trees, round seaweeded knobs, pillars of purple and green and gold sprang from beneath the ocean and were pushed skywards. Waterfalls cascaded foam from between them all as water rushed back to the sea.

And still the things from the depths pushed up from the sea floor. The scarlet and black trees—corals she realized—were now ten paces up in the air and still rising, thrust upwards on a base of seaweed-covered rocks and sand. And the welling up of water came closer and closer to the boat, as more reefs appeared from beneath the waves. The last mass to appear, covered in weed and oyster shells and anemones, seemed strangely angular, the corners too regular to be natural. There were towers and steps and walls of rock, lines of them . . . Streets of coral-encrusted buildings. Fish caught in the ruts of bygone roadways flopped and gulped, hot and helpless.

Doomed, she thought, and sadness cut through her

like a flensing knife. All that life, it's all doomed in the
sunlight . . .

She clutched at her grandfather.

He wiped away tears and whispered, "Child, it's
happened. It's finally happened." Their boat, caught
on the outward flow of waves, slid away from the
broiling seas.

"*What* has?" she whispered, knowing she should
be able to make sense of this, but was shocked into a
state from which sense seemed to have vanished.

"Don't you understand, lass?" He waved at the
land behind them. "Those are the Dustel Isles!" His
face glowed with joy even as his tears runnelled down
the creases of his cheeks. "There was once a town,
right there—see the buildings? Perhaps it was even
Port Arutha. Brawena, Morthred is dead! *We can go
home again . . .*"

Postseaward, 1797.

Anyara isi Teron: Journal entry
23/1st Double/1794

As I pen this in my cabin aboard the R. V. Seadrift, I
find myself wondering: is this really I, Anyara isi
Teron, here on board a ship bound for the Isles of
Glory? Freckled, prosaic, undistinguished Anyara,
embarking on an adventure most men could only
dream about—it's not possible, surely! And yet I, an
unmarried woman, find myself untrammelled by
family, with the shores of Kells rapidly dwindling on
the horizon and empty ocean ahead . . . adventure
indeed.

True, there is Sister Lescalles isi God sitting
opposite me as I write, reading her religious tracts
and praying for my godless soul. My parents would
only countenance my journey if I was chaperoned by a
senior missionary sister of the Order of Aetherial
Nuns, and Lescalles is nothing if not senior. She must
be close to seventy. Far too old, surely, to embark on a
journey like this one, yet her eyes shine with the zeal
of a proselytiser as she contemplates the Glorian
souls she will save.

And true, too, somewhere on board is Shor iso
Fabold, who is charged with "keeping an eye on
Anyara to make sure she comes to no harm in this
madcap venture of hers." Poor Shor. He has grown to
hate me, and we would avoid each other if we could.
But alas, how is it possible to avoid someone on a
ship smaller than our townhouse garden back in
Postseaward? We dine at the same table, share the
same companionways and walk the same decks. We
nod politely and bid one another good morrow, but
underneath he seethes. And to think there was a time I
would have wed him, had he asked, and been joyous in
the union.

That was before he found out I was determined

to set sail for the Glory Isles. Before he found out I
was reading copies of all the translations of his
conversations with Blaze Halfbreed and Kelwyn
Gilfeather. (I asked the young clerk who worked in the
library of the National Society for the Study of non-
Kellish Peoples to secretly copy them for me; in return
I promised to procure him a job as librarian on my
cousin's country estate. We both kept our side of the
bargain. There, I have written down my wickedness . . .
I am quite without conscience.)

There is an irony in the antipathy with which Shor
now regards me, of course. The seeds of all he now so
dislikes about me were sown by what I learned of
Blaze Halfbreed, and it was he who—by his interviews
with Blaze—unwittingly showed me that other
possible future. Through her, I learned there can be
another life for a woman, a life beyond that of
obedience and piety and "taking a turn around the
garden" for fresh air and health. Poor Shor indeed.
He admired both my intelligence and my independence, but ended by hating my exercising of either.
The idea that I have obtained official royal sanction of
my journey—I am bidden by Her Excellency the
Protectoress to report to her on the position of
Glorian women in Isles society—is anathema to him.

And so we tread carefully around each another, and
pretend indifference to our shared past. It is awkward,
but I have no regrets for what I have done. My deception
was regrettable, I know, but he would not let me read the
text of his conversations with Blaze, so what was I to
do? He titillated my imagination with his stories of her,
but tried to hide her actual words from me. Am I
the brazen jade he named me in our final argument?
Probably. But I will let nothing stop me from searching
for this woman, born half a world away from me, whose
life has been so different from my cosseted existence—
and yet who has the power to speak to my soul.

I have more of the copied conversations with me on
board: I had not time to read them all before we left.

I have yet to find out if Ruarth Windrider—whose impossible love for Flame, the Castlemaid of Cirkase, brought tears to my eyes—survived the death of the dunmagicker Morthred. I desperately want to know if Flame rose above her contamination with dunmagic. Did she give birth to the child, Morthred's heir, who was the source of her contamination? Did Blaze ever marry, and if so, then whom? And I want to know just what this mysterious Change is that Blaze has spoken of so often. I want to know what happened to the ghemphs: why and how they vanished. Shor told me Glorians were still receiving citizenship tattoos from the ghemphs as late as the year the first Kellish explorers arrived, 1780, but then they abruptly stopped. He said he never found a child born later than that who had an ear tattoo.

And, most importantly of all, I want to know what happened to magic. Is Shor right and it was all a figment of the collective imagination born of superstition: some kind of mass hallucination experienced by the Glorian peoples?

I could probably find an answer to most of these questions were I to read the rest of the copied documents I have. From where I sit, if I glance over to the wall under the porthole, I see my two sea chests, now stacked on top of each other to make a chest-of-drawers with polished brass handles; all I have to do is open that top drawer and the documents are there for the reading. And yet I hesitate to hurry through the papers. I have months ahead of me, and I must ration my reading. Perhaps this evening I will dip into the first of the papers. Just a few.

Right now Lescalles is restless. Here we are, barely two days out of port, and already I know her as well as I know the freckles on my own nose. I shall put her out of her misery and suggest a turn about the deck . . .

CHAPTER I

NARRATOR : RUARTH

I DUG MY CLAWS INTO THE ROPE OF THE
rigging and tried to calm my chaotic breathing. I was
safe now, surely, no matter what happened. As long as
I held on.

I took a deep breath, aware I was shivering. Pure funk, of
course, not cold. When you're covered with feathers, you
don't feel the cold much, and even the stiff breeze that made
the shrouds strain against the mast of the *Amiable* could not
bring a chill to my skin.

The truth was that the terror I felt went so deep it could
have been part of my soul. I had just flown down from the
top of the stack that towered five hundred paces high above
the surface of the ocean. Five hundred *human* paces, that is.
And I hadn't followed the path, either. I had arrowed down
like a gannet towards the sea, driving myself lower with every
beat of my wings. All the while, I was thinking: if Kelwyn
Gilfeather kills Morthred right now, then I might end up with
my feathers splattered all over the ocean. No, not feathers.

Skin and flesh. I would be a very dead human, without ever knowing what it was like to *be* human.

To be quite honest, the closer Morthred's death came, the less I believed it would not affect the Dustel birds. The less I believed we were immune because we were born ensor- celled . . .

But apparently Kelwyn hesitated to kill the dunmaster, and I lived a little longer. As I sat there on the rigging I spared a moment to wonder what scared me the most: that Morthred would die—or that he wouldn't. I couldn't make up my mind. Both possibilities were entangled with horrors. I looked down from my perch and ruffled my feathers in an attempt to calm my panic. *Pull yourself together, Ruarth! Think.*

Four people stood on the deck directly below me. None had any idea I was there.

Flame was one of them. She was dressed as she had been while watching the race, in a green gown. The dangling ends of a heavily beaded sash kept the skirt from lifting in the wind. I might have thought it lovely had I not known it had been given to her by Morthred, a gift from among his plun- dered riches. Morthred, who had raped her. Who had con- taminated her, defiled her; tried to mold her to his image of evil.

She spoke to two sylv women, both subverted now to dunmagickers of course, and the *Amiable*'s captain, a one- armed Spatterman I knew only as Kayed. His forearm was missing, something he had in common with Flame, although his was gone from below the elbow, unlike Flame's, which had been amputated above the joint. I suspected he was a foul-mouthed bastard at the best of times; now that he was imprisoned with dunmagic he almost foamed with righteous rage, but powers that were not his kept his mouth from utter- ing the words he wanted to say.

I switched my attention back to the two sylv women. They were the lucky ones among Morthred's subverted acolytes; they had not taken part in the stack race because neither of them could swim. All those who had participated were probably dead by now, or at the very least doomed.

"I don't care what you think," Flame was saying to them. "We are leaving now." She turned to Kayed. "Cast off."

"We haven't paid the port fees—" the man began. I pitied him; the brown-red of dunmagic played over his shoulders and torso, imprisoning his will with its chains. He could not do much with his rage; every time he tried to resist, the dun-colored ropes of magic that were looped over his body well nigh strangled him. On our journey from Porth to Xolchas Stacks aboard his stolen vessel, his resistance had almost killed him several times.

"They won't see us go, and don't question my orders or I'll toss you overboard," Flame snapped. Dunmagic rippled outwards from her, foul with coercion. This time the man didn't hesitate. He turned to his crew and gave the order to sail. I dithered, trying to think of a miracle that would stop our departure from Xolchasport. I glanced upwards to the top of the stack. Cliffs loured over the harbour, a lethal rock-face that could sheer away at any time. Seabirds inhabited every ledge; large and brutal in their language, argumenta-tive by inclination, they were as foreign and incomprehensi-ble to me as fish in the sea.

"We can't leave without the Rampartlord," the older of the two dunmagickers, a middle-aged woman called Gaba-nia, protested. She'd worked for Syr-sylv Duthrick and the Keeper Council before her subversion to dunmagic.

Flame raised an eyebrow, even though she must have known Gabania was referring to Morthred. "Rampartlord?"

"The dunmaster. Rampartlord of the Dustel Islands. It—it's the title he prefers."

Flame snorted. Perhaps she recognized irony. There *were* no Dustel Isles, thanks to Morthred.

The second dunmagicker, Stracey, waved her hands in agitation. "He'll kill us," she whispered.

"He's not here, Stracey," Flame said and added nastily, "but I am. And I will kill you if we *don't* leave. Right now."

Stracey looked at Gabania for leadership and Gabania hesitated, obviously toying with the thought of resistance as she considered her own strengths matched to Flame's.

"Don't do it," Flame warned. Then she let the menace in

her tone slip away as she added, "Listen, this is our chance. Morthred won't call us back with the force of his will, I promise you. He is going to die any time now and we can go where we will, do what we will. And all the treasure on this ship will be ours . . ." I could hear no trace of the Flame Windrider I knew just then. "Think of the *power* we'll have, Gabania. Dunmagickers, with a ship, and these sailors as slaves, and all the money we'll ever want. Everything, in fact, that Morthred has amassed over the past few years since his powers returned."

A flash of hope sparked in the older woman's voice as the remnants of her independence asserted itself. "Morthred's going to die?"

"Yes. Those people who tried to rescue me back on Porth—I saw one of them here. I know those people. I know the way they think. They will kill him any minute now, while everyone else is still occupied with the stack race."

"Will we—will we be sylv again?" Stracey asked. She sounded puzzled, as if she didn't understand her own question.

Flame reached out to cup the girl's face in her hand. "No, sweetie. You won't. Because you won't let it happen, will you? You will use your own dunmagic to stay a dunmagicker. Now, go and make sure those fools of sailors obey my orders."

Obedience to Morthred had made Gabania and Stracey tractable, so they went without further argument. For a moment Flame watched them, then she leaned against the railing. I knew what she was doing; I'd seen it often enough. Tendrils of color floated outwards like a soft mist. Once it would have been silver-blue; now it was more a deep lilac color, and streaked with both silver and reddish-brown. She was going to cover our departure with illusion. It was a form of magic that no longer came so easily to her: it was a sylv-talent rather than a dun skill, and she was losing her sylv.

Above her, I felt ill, with an illness that was lodged more in my mind and heart than in my gut. I had tried to keep my Flame—the gentle, loving Flame—alive, but I really had no idea how to save her. I still didn't understand her present subversion, any more than Blaze and Kelwyn had last time I'd spoken to them. There was something odd about it. All I could do was hope that once Morthred was dead, it would make a difference. That her own integrity would allow her to fight, to give her a chance.

And above us, in the town of Xolchasbarbican, were the people who might be able to help. Kelwyn Gilfeather, the Sky Plains physician; perhaps there would be something he could do with his medications once Morthred was gone. And the others: Blaze Halfbreed, who had proved herself more than a friend; Tor Ryder, the Menod patriarch who would rid the world of magic if he could find a way; Dekan Grinpindillie, the Aware lad from Mekaté—they all wanted to help, but I had no idea how to stop her from sailing away from them and the hope they offered.

I'd assured Flame that there were those who would rescue her, who would ensure she never suffer again the tortures Morthred inflicted on her. She listened, I'll give her that. Then, on the last occasion we spoke at all intimately, she'd held me in the palm of her hand and closed her fingers around my body. Her thumb caressed my throat in a gesture that contained no love, no gentleness, no concern for the fragility of my bones. She raised me to the level of her eyes, only a hand span from her face. "I am a dunmagicker," she said. "I want nothing else."

"Flame—" I began.

"*Lyssal,*" she hissed, reverting to her real name. "Call me Lyssal." The thumb moved in a circle at my throat. "I can crush you, Ruarth, as easily as a thrush crushes a snail shell." She tightened her fingers until I found breathing an effort. "So simple. So very *simple* to do."

I kept absolutely still, feeling the extremity of my danger through the sweat of her fingers. This was not Flame. This was a stranger who wanted to snap my neck.

What held her back? Some remnant of the woman that still dwelled within—the Flame I had known since I was a fledgling living in the crannies of the walls of the palace of Cirkasecastle and she was the lonely, neglected Castlemaid, heir to a throne, who had fed the birds on her window sill?

We were in the Lord's House in Xolchasbarbican at the time and, perhaps luckily for me, a servant of the Barbican-lord had entered the room just then. Lyssal whispered in my ear, "If you ever come near me again I will kill you, Ruarth. Be warned." And she opened her fingers, allowing me my freedom.

I had not dared to test her promise. I'd not come near her again, choosing merely to watch from a distance. I continued to speak to her in gesture and whistle, but mostly she did not listen. That was easy enough; if she looked away, she missed all the visual clues and therefore most of what I said. And now, as I looked down from the rigging with my loneliness dragging at me like a yoke around my neck, I could not think of any way to persuade her to stay.

The crew were already hauling in the hawsers. Sailors manned the winches and sails shivered upwards. No one on the wharf as much as looked our way as illusion swirled about us, suffocating, unnatural.

Once, I'd gloried in the sylvpower Flame manifested. Once, I'd seen it as something of value. It had given her a chance to escape the unpleasantness of the fate her father and the Breth Bastionlord contrived for her, backed by the Keepers of The Hub: as a brood mare for a perverted tyrant. The Council of the Keeper Isles had wanted the Bastionlord to sell them his saltpetre and they'd put pressure on the Cirkase Castlelord to give the ruler of Breth what he wanted in return. Lyssal. It was an evil compact, with Flame no more than bait for the sharks. Her sylvtalents had *saved* her then.

But now, now it was her sylvpower that made her vulnerable to dunmagic subversion. Perhaps, I thought, Tor Ryder is right. The Isles would be better without any magic at all. Perhaps it is an evil thing. Not innately evil—not even Tor thought that—but evil because of the failings of mankind. There are too many people who use sylvmagic in ways that are either petty and trivial, or monstrous. *All power*, Tor said to me once, *should have checks and balances to keep it harnessed. Yet no one can bridle the sylvs of the Keeper Isles.*

He should have added: except a dunmaster. Morthred had done a fine job of bridling sylvpower.

A flock of birds flew across the wharf towards me, twittering as they came, each call distinct to my ears. They were saying their names, over and over—it meant nothing; it was just a way we Dustel birds had of keeping in touch as we flew in a flock. Of saying to others in the air about us, "I'm right here, by your wingtip." They were heading towards me, doubtless to give me news of what was happening in the upper town of Xolchasbarbican. I felt a flooding relief: I would be able to pass them a message for Blaze and Gilfeather.

And then the world lurched.

I have no other way to describe it. Everything around me dropped away, leaving my stomach somewhere above and my mind in limbo.

My last glimpse through avian eyes appalled me: I saw birds turn into people and fall out of the sky. And then Morthred's death swept over me, changing every particle of my body into something else.

For a moment I truly died.

There was darkness, a blackness so blanketing it contained only emptiness. Silence, an external muteness so intense I could hear the internal sounds of my body being ripped apart, particle by particle. Numbness, a lack of stimulation so pervading I felt I had no body. I thought: so this is what it is like to die.

I plunged into the darkness, into the silence, into the numbness, into that total deprivation. When I emerged, I was on the other side of death, in a life about which I understood nothing.

Everything had changed. Everything. All my senses had been altered so much I couldn't . . . well, I couldn't make *sense* of them.

I was Ruarth Windrider and I was *human*.

CHAPTER 2

WELL, I'VE READ THE NOTE YOU BROUGHT from Kelwyn Gilfeather. He says I should talk to you, and so I will, although I can't say I regard you Kellish foreigners with any particular kindness. You are all far too fond of pontificating on Glorian deficiencies for my liking. I hear tell there are some among you who want to bring in your priests to convert the Glory Isles to your religion; I even hear talk of a fleet of missionaries. What makes you think your beliefs are better than ours? Take my advice, and don't try it here on Tenkor. We are Menod on these six islands of the Hub Race. Always have been, always will be.

Doubtless you have heard that we of the Tideriders' Guild don't always see eye to eye with the Menod Patriarchy, and that is true enough. We are the temporal power on the islands of Tenkor and they are the spiritual power here. In fact, throughout much of the Glory Isles. We often have our differences, but don't make the mistake of thinking you can divide us; you can't. When threatened from outside we unite, just as we did back in 1742 at the beginning of the Change.

Guild and Patriarchy affairs have always been entangled so tight it would be hard to separate them anyway. Did you know Menod success in spreading the word of God stems from our Guild treasury? That's right, Menod wealth came from the longboatmen and tiderunner riders of the Hub Race. Still does. Without us, the Menod Patriarchy would be nothing. Of course, our support is freely given; we of the Guild are mostly Menod, after all.

Me? Oh . . . I've never been much of a one for religious observances myself. I attend the festival services, twice a year, and make my obeisance at the Blessing of the Whale-King, but no more than that. I was born full of sin, riddled through with evil, my father used to tell me, and then he'd beat me for my lack of piety. My reluctance to demonstrate religious devotion should not have puzzled him—for years he refused to allow me to enter the Worship House, saying that until I could control my wickedness I was not allowed the blessings of God. How he thought that would encourage piety instead of having the opposite effect, I have no idea. But then, my father always was a twisted soul.

However, I am still a Menod; do not doubt it. Just not a very good one.

Sorry, I'm rambling. You want me to start with the day the people fell out of the sky? Very well. I'll begin there. It's appropriate anyway, because to me that was the day the Change began. Blaze will tell you it started back on Gorthan Spit, but that's her story, not mine. To me, it began on the day of the Fall. We called it that, hoping an innocuous word would take away the horror; it didn't. It still doesn't.

The Fall was a watershed between the old world that went before and the world of the Change thereafter. On Tenkor, we always date events from then. "Oh, that happened two years before the Fall" or "Oh, he died about ten years after the Fall." Most of all, it was just a horror so intense no one who lived through it would ever forget.

I remember everything about it as if it happened yesterday, instead of fifty years ago.

I was down on the waterfront in Tenkorharbour, at the Guild Hall where we tideriders all had rooms. I was idling around, waiting for my turn of duty. I should have been using the time to study—I had a final astronomy examination the next week, followed by a string of papers on rider ethics, wave anomalies, tidal subtleties, and the new sand configurations of the Hub Race. If I didn't pass them all, I'd have to wait another year before retaking, and that would mean one more year before I had the Eagre Certification and full Guild membership, one more year before I earned myself the honorific "Syr-tiderider." I knew I needed to study. Instead, I was chatting to my best friend, Marten Lymik, in the Guild common room. He was a long and lanky fellow, Marten, a fine rider with good balance and endurance, but a bit slow in the brain department. The kind of man who saw the point to a joke ten minutes after the rest of us had stopped laughing. He wasn't stupid, you know, just slow and rather literal.

And me at that age? Well, I was only twenty that year, and about as callow and as irresponsible a young man as you could find anywhere in the Keeper Isles. There were only two things I took seriously: one was riding the waves, the other—well, the other was the same thing as preoccupies most young men of twenty. I imagine you know what *that* is even in Kells.

Marten and I were talking about the *Keeper Fair*, if I remember correctly. The ship had caused a bit of a stir when it sailed past Tenkor for its home port several months earlier, jury-rigged and with half of its poop deck scorched. *Keeper Pride* followed it in a day later with similar damage. Marten was curious to know if I'd discovered yet just what had happened.

I shrugged in reply. "Just because my father is Guildean doesn't mean I know anything of Keeper Council affairs. The Council loathes us Tenkormen and tells us as little as possible, you know that, Marten." And my father would never have dreamed of gratuitously passing on information to me either, but I didn't add that.

He thought for a moment, then ventured a hesitant opinion. "It's just the Menod Council and the Tenkor patriarchs they despise, not us *guildsmen*, surely. The Keeper Council needs tideriders and longboatmen."

"Maybe. Either way, Syr-sylv Councillor Duthrick is hardly likely to tell us anything he doesn't have to."

"They say in The Hub both ships took some damage when they were fighting the dunmagickers on Gorthan Spit, and they are having some refitting done at the far end of the harbour."

"Yeah, I did hear that. So what?"

It was his turn to shrug. "Dunno really. What I want to know is why no one is allowed near them, I suppose. Anyone would think those two ships carried the Keeperlord's treasure, the way they are guarded. And last week two more Keeper Council ships sailed up to The Hub as well. That's an awful lot of their fleet to have in port at any one time, isn't it?"

I had to admit he was right. "Hmm, odd, I agree. Wonder what they are up to?"

"Or what they fear," he said. He was like that, Marten. He'd make a remark without seeming to think about it, and come out with something succinctly to the point. I could never quite work out if the profundity was wisdom or accident.

Just then one of the tide boys came in to bring me a message. "There's a lady to see you, Rider Elarn," he said. By the way he smirked, I knew he used the term "lady" rather loosely.

"Cissy, I'll bet," one of the other riders in the common room said with a laugh. "That girl is never going to leave you alone, Elarn."

"I shouldn't think he wants to be left alone," Marten hazarded.

As usual, Marten was out of date. I had grown tired of Cissy, and was trying to extricate myself as best I could. I sighed and stood up. "What's the weather going to be like for the next run, Denny?" I asked the tide boy as I followed him out.

"The latest report was good," the lad replied. "Fine weather, water level at the Rocks is a fathom, downflow speed is twenty notches. With the moons as they are now, you should have a good run, all the way."

I nodded, pleased. It would be a fast trip, finishing up in the Basin of The Hub before nightfall. I considered which model of tiderunner was most suitable for the conditions and said, "I'll take the Flying Dragon and the bell-curve paddle, then. Check the waxing and the leash, will you?"

He grinned at me. "I already have."

I grinned back. He was a good lad, if cheeky, and he'd soon be promoted up to apprentice rider.

"Oh," he added, "Syr-tiderider Bennis came down the Race on the last ebb, and he said to watch the Serrated Spit. There's been an extra load of sand dumped there and it's extending farther towards the western shore. He reckons there'll be quite a break at that spot on the way up, and if you hit it when the sun is low in the sky, it'll be hard to see."

I nodded again. "I'll watch for it. Now where's the lady?"

We had arrived at the main entrance to the Hall, and he pointed to the porch pillars. A woman stood there, dressed in red skirts, her hair a little too tumbled and her bosom a little too visible to be quite proper. I repressed a sigh. "I'll go on up to Deliveries after this to collect the outgoing packets," I told Denny. I meant the Office of Tenkor Express Deliveries, but none of us bothered with that mouthful. Deliveries was an arm of the Guild and was, like all the main Guild buildings, up in Tenkorhaven, quite a climb from Tenkorharbour where the Tideriders' Hall was. It wasn't my job to collect the packets, but if I was going to escort Cissy home, I thought I may as well do something useful. "You make sure my gear is ready when I come back," I added.

I strolled over to Cissy. "Is there something wrong?" I asked. "You know you shouldn't really hang around here like this." I resisted the temptation to tell her to button up her bodice, and wondered at myself. The very thing that had attracted me to her in the first place was now an irritation.

She pouted. "You haven't been to see me all week."

"I've been busy."

"No, you haven't. You've been right here. You haven't been up to The Hub in three days. And Alva said she saw you go waverunner riding with Gerrick and his two sisters the other day, just for fun."

That was true enough. The weather had been fine, and the expected bore wave had promised to be perfect . . . it had all been just too good to resist. Besides, I loved tideriding upright, feeling the water beneath my feet. I loved the way the waverunner answered to a shift in weight, the way you could manipulate the runner even as the water manipulated you . . . To me, it was the ultimate experience between man and wave. When we were working, though, we didn't use a waverunner. It would have been too exhausting, with too many possibilities to lose the wave. And so a waverunner was just for fun.

In the end, I ignored Cissy's complaint, saying instead, "I'm on duty for the next tide, but I have some time still. Come, I'll walk you home."

She turned to walk with me, but she wasn't happy. "Why don't you come by any more, Elarn? What have I done?"

I kept a firm hold on my irritation. "You haven't done anything, Cissy. But I did warn you, you know, right at the beginning. I told you I just wanted us to have fun. No strings."

"Yes, you did," she agreed bitterly, "and that's great for you. Everyone thinks you're a fine lad, a gallant with the ladies. Everyone just thinks I'm a slut."

A pack of boys from the Menod school passed us on their way home for lunch, their collars twisted and dirty, their smell reminiscent of schoolboys everywhere. I waited till they had passed, then said, "You're not a slut, Cissy."

"They why do I feel like one?" she snapped. "That's the way you've made me feel, Elarn Jaydon!"

I didn't know what to say. Why did I always find seduction so easy and extricating myself so hard? "You're not a slut," I repeated. "There's nothing wrong with a bit of fun. We weren't hurting anyone. You don't believe all that blather from the patriarchs, do you, about chastity?"

"Oh, no, we weren't hurting anyone," she said, still bitter. "Just me."

"Nonsense. You enjoyed it just as much as I did."

"Enjoyed? Past tense? It *is* all over then?" The look she gave me was one of wide-eyed fear.

I was puzzled; indignation I might have expected, hurt even, but fear? "Cissy, you knew it wasn't going to last forever. I *told* you that, right at the beginning."

"And so you walk away, just like that? No ties, no regrets?"

"No regrets at all. We had so much fun and I loved your company. What is there to regret? And as for ties, we can be friends, always. Just not lovers."

"Friends? What have I got to be friendly about? I'm the one left with a reputation in shreds and a bun in the oven!"

I came to a standstill and stared at her.

She was silent.

I stuttered like a guttering candle, "B-b-but—that's—that's not possible!"

She tilted her head and stared back, a flat stare that was close to hate.

"We were so careful!" And I had been too, always using an apothecary's sheath. She'd been cautious as well, just to be certain, using whatever method was favoured by women then, or so she'd told me.

"Yes, we were, weren't we," she said, her tone thick with sarcasm. "Well, sometimes being careful is not enough, is it?"

She stood there, staring at me, wild-eyed and close to tears, and, God help me, I couldn't say a thing. I felt I'd been clobbered by my own tiderunner. I didn't want to marry Cissy. I didn't love her. I never had. She was a fisherman's daughter, of no consequence, and my family was second to none in Tenkor. My father was the Guildean—head of the Tideriders' Guild—and the Guild managed the whole of the Tenkor trade and delivery routes to The Hub. Mine was the richest family in Tenkor, and probably—or so I thought then in my naiveté—one of the wealthiest in all the Keeper Isles. There was no way I would ever wed someone like Cissy Lepanto. There was no way I would ever *want* to wed someone like her. Men like me bedded women like Cissy; we didn't marry them. And she should have known that.

A whole tidal-rip of thoughts rushed through my head: my father would kill me. Cissy's father would kill me. Cissy's four brothers would kill me. Father would have to buy them off. He'd *murder* me. Cissy would have to be sent away somewhere remote for a while. We'd have to persuade her to give up the child, to keep the whole thing quiet. It could be done, surely . . . but my father was going to be *furious*. It'd cost him money, and he hated to lose money. He'd cut my allowance, which was already miniscule, to nothing. I'd have to learn to live off my wages as a tiderider who had not yet passed his final Eagres. Damn it all, it wasn't fair. I'd been so *careful*.

For a moment Cissy continued to stand there looking at me, her face all of a sudden not so pretty. Her bottom lip trembled, then she turned, picked up her skirts and fled, leaving me standing there like a ninny. Several passers-by smirked at me. I was humiliated, and it was an effort to contain my anger at her. Why did girls have to be so blamed emotional about things?

Nearby a flock of birds moved along the gutter, mouse-like, picking up seeds that had dropped from a recent grain shipment bound for the Tenkorhaven granaries. I wanted to move, to continue on my way, but I felt rooted to the spot, in need of a miracle that could change time, transport me back to earlier that morning, when all had been right with the world.

And that was when it happened.

I'll never forget that sound, never. The wet, soggy blood-drenched splat of it.

A woman fell out of the air, screaming, and landed on the cobbles in front of me, not more than a few paces away. She was naked and old and wrinkled—and now also very dead. Her blood sprayed onto my shoes, rich and red and glistening. At the same moment, a dozen people flicked out of nowhere into the gutter next to me. Naked, living, pallid-skinned people. Men, women, children. For a moment they all stood erect, then every single one fell over as if they didn't know how to stand. One of the younger children started to wail, a terrible prolonged skirling of mindless terror, of fear

so great you felt there could never be an end to it. All the hair
stood up on the back of my neck. The sound was taken up by
others, and then echoed back from the streets around me,
even from the rooftops.

I was in such a state of shock, I couldn't move.

What had happened?

I had no idea. Nothing came to me. I just stood there and
stared at the woman who had died, noting the runnel of
blood that slithered its way to the gutter, hearing the wailing
that saturated the air from all directions. Forgetting, even, all
that Cissy had told me. Eventually I took a hesitant step towards one of the crying children, but she screamed all the
louder and shrank back against the nearest house wall until
her cries turned to gulps that shuddered her whole body.
One of the naked adults, a man, tried to catch hold of her. By
the similarity of their features, I guessed them to be father
and daughter, but she seemed just as terrified of him as she
was of me. He crawled towards her, and then raised himself
up until his face was close to hers. He tried to speak, but the
only sounds he made were incomprehensible grunts and
squawks. He moved his face nearer to hers, as if to kiss her,
and her renewed wailing took on a further note of extremity
that made him cower away. He huddled down into the gutter,
and tried to tuck his head under his arm as if he could stop
the sound from reaching his ears.

I backed away. I was shaking, and I couldn't stop. I turned
and began to run up the hill towards the Guild Chambers. I
wanted answers, something that would make sense of all this,
that would tell me I had not somehow awoken into a nightmare.

There was another man lying in the roadway a little further up. He, too, was naked, and he had what appeared to be
a broken leg. I slowed and skirted him, keeping my distance.
He did not ask for help as I passed, but looked at me dumbly
with eyes that were swirls of pain and confusion. I didn't
stop. I knew of no way to help him, and all I could think of
was that I must get to the Guild.

And then I saw Cissy.

Her skirt: the rampant redness of it draped across the

cobbles like a throw-rug, her feet poking out from under. One of her shoes had come off and lay forlornly in the gutter. Her upper torso was hidden under a naked body, another woman's this time. I froze. I don't think there was a single coherent thought in my head as I went forward and knelt there beside them both. I heaved the naked woman away—whoever she was, she was dead. I gathered Cissy up into my arms. There was blood everywhere, whose I couldn't tell. Cissy's head lolled on her shoulders, at all the wrong angles.

I stared, but couldn't believe it. I'd just been talking to her. Just a minute ago, she had been alive, angry with me.

And now—now, her neck was broken, her eyes permanently open. Blood already congealed on her lips. I don't know how long I held her like that; my mind seemed to have stopped functioning.

Someone gripped my shoulder. "Syr, bring her into my house."

I looked up. A man had come out of one of the artisan dwellings lining the road; by his clothes he was probably a carpenter. I didn't know him, but he probably knew me. It was hard to be anonymous when you were the Guildean's only child. "It's Cissandra Lepanto," I said, as if that explained everything.

"I know," he replied. "I know the lass, Syr. I'll send word to her father. Bring her inside."

Together we carried her past the other woman's body and into the man's parlour, where we laid her on the table. I made a gesture of incomprehension towards the street. "People fell out of nowhere," I said in a whisper. "They just—fell."

"I saw. Magic," he said. "Has to be the red magic."

I digested that. "Dun?"

"What else? Syr, you had better get along to your father now. There will be . . . things that need doing." We exchanged glances, each of us with thoughts we didn't want to utter. Dunmagic in Tenkor. It was unthinkable. "The bastards," he muttered. "The sodding bastards."

I gestured at Cissy as he flung the tablecloth over her body.

"I'll do what is necessary," he assured me.

I nodded and stumbled out into the street.

Dunmagic. I thought back over what we had recently heard about dun. Anything rather than think about Cissy.

Some sort of battle had taken place on the island of Gorthan Spit some months earlier, between dunmagickers led by a dunmaster, and the agents of the Keeper Council. The dunmaster, a man named Morthred, had escaped. Recent rumors rippled around about how he was ancient and had been the man responsible for sinking the Dustel Islands in 1652. Of course, most people thought it was much more likely the disappearance of the islands was the result of some kind of geological event, like an earthquake, rather than dunmagic.

Dunmagic . . . I'd grown up fearing a magic I'd never even seen until this day. I shuddered.

As I climbed the steep cobblestoned road towards Tenkorhaven, I tried not to think about Cissy, but I couldn't stop myself. A few moments before her death she had been desperately unhappy, in despair for her future. In trouble because of something we had both done. And I'd offered her nothing: not comfort, not understanding, not solutions, not even compassion. In fact, I hadn't thought of her at all. I'd been thinking only of myself. She must have died shattered by despair, while I'd been angry at her for shaking the foundations of my neat little world.

I had wanted a miracle to take me back to an earlier time when there was nothing to worry about. Well, it hadn't happened quite that way. I hadn't wanted her dead. That would never have occurred to me as a solution. And I wasn't glad she had died, exactly, but I *was* glad no one would ever have to know what a tangle we had woven for ourselves.

I wasn't glad she was dead, but I was . . . relieved the problem had suddenly vanished.

I swallowed. Poor Cissy, all nicely tidied away, along with our secret.

God, I thought, what sort of person am I, that I can look on her death as a solution? That I can't mourn a woman I was happy enough to bed? That I can feel relief knowing her pregnancy is not going to cause me trouble after all?

I suddenly didn't like myself very much. Elarn Jaydon, I thought, you've got to be the world's worst cad.

There was no comfort in the thought, and I still felt the relief.

MY FATHER'S CHAMBER IN THE TIDERID-ers' Guild was full of people when I arrived. Apparently the word of what had happened had spread with the speed of a darkmoon bore tide. Representatives from each of all the main administrative departments were there: the office of the High Patriarch, the Matriarchs' Bureau, the Menod University, the Chambers of Commerce, the Fishermen's Guild, the Menod Treasury, the Tenkor Guard. Most of them I knew; others I recognized only by their affiliation, indicated by the insignias sewn onto their clothes, or by their badges of office.

The room was silent when I stepped inside, a silence so drenched with emotion it was almost painful. My father did not acknowledge my entrance. When he did speak, it was in the low, measured tones he used when he was saying something of import: "So, we are agreed then. It is likely what happened today is a result of the death of Morthred the Mad, when his magic died with him. The naked people are the descendants of Dustel Islanders who had been transformed by his dunmagic into birds. When his magic ended, they fell out of the sky." He cleared his throat and frowned in the direction of the High Patriarch's emissary. "I find it distressing Lord Crannach never saw fit to tell this office of the existence of such ensorcelled birds prior to this moment." A painful silence followed while everyone, in their embarrassment, looked anywhere except at the emissary. It was almost unheard of for a Guildean to direct such a public rebuke to the office of the High Patriarch.

My father paused to give his displeasure time to sink in, then moved on to what was more important. He would not have forgiven, though, not my father. And he would never forget. "How many people are we talking about?"

The emissary, himself a patriarch, cleared his throat twice.

"Dustel birds? There must be hundreds here in the city . . ." His voice trailed away, then he started up again. "No one ever did a census of them. We had no reason to. They never were a bother. Not till now. Now . . . I counted two dead across the square on my way here, and another six injured. Perhaps fourteen more who seemed unhurt. Just in that short walk."

"All now people?"

"Yes."

"And there will be hundreds more?"

"I believe so."

My father nodded, and addressed the group as a whole again: "I want them all taken to the University, alive or dead. Put the students to work helping. And I want every healer and doctor and herbalist we have in the city to go there. Syrguildmasters, please mobilize your people to help—the survivors will need clothes, for a start. The Treasury must release some money to pay for food. I expect the Patriarchy to take the lead in ensuring the welfare of the uninjured." His eyes met mine across the room. "Rider Elarn, I want you to take a letter to The Hub on the next tide. How long do we have?"

"Just short of two hours before it's scheduled, Syrguildean," I said. When father was formal with me, which was almost always, so was I with him.

"Wait here, rider. The rest of you—start work." The room emptied in seconds. When the Guildean gave an order, you acted.

"Did anyone actually see birds change into people?" I asked. I was trying to remember exactly what I had seen. Birds pecking at grain in the gutter . . . and then . . . Dear God.

"Apparently, yes." A piece of parchment already drawn towards him, he opened the inkwell. "And it seems the Menod Synod have always known what they were." That still rankled obviously; he sounded more than irate.

"They don't seem able to speak," I said. "And the children are so frightened . . ."

I told him what I had seen—without, of course, going

into any details about Cissy—and he continued to write without making a comment. Only as he sealed the letter did he say, "This is not going to be pleasant for anyone, Elarn. A great many people died today, and not all of them were Dustels. I believe there's even a hole in the Worship House roof where a man fell through and landed on one of the High Patriarch's assistants." As with almost everything he ever said to me, his tone was larded with rebuke. You should have more restraint, the inflection said. You are the son of the Guildean, you should set an example with your courage and demeanour. There should be no quaver in your voice, no matter that you speak of death and horror.

And at times like that, I found it hard not to hate him. Hard not to blame him for driving my mother to suicide with his unjust accusations of infidelity. Hard not to hate him because he had rejected me for so long, refusing to accept even the possibility I could be his son. "You are an abomination in the eyes of God," he'd told me once. And he'd banished me from his household, to grow up on a remote mainland farm along the shores of the Hub Race.

My mother had killed herself from the shame.

When I was twelve I returned against his wishes, to confront him in this very room. We would both always remember that day, when we faced each other across that desk, meeting for the first time in seven years, and he saw the truth in my features. How could it be otherwise? I was a son who was a mirror image of his sire. Features not seen in the small boy were startlingly apparent in the youth. The same jaw line, the same creased dimple in the cheeks, the same way the eyebrows had of kicking up at the outer edge. If I wanted to know how I would age, I need only to look at his face.

I'd always known who I was, of course. My mother told me before she was forced to part with me. "Never doubt your parentage, Elarn," she whispered to me. "You are Korless Jaydon's son. It is not my lineage that makes you what you are, but his." I never saw her again. She died six months later. He took much from me, my father.

He sighed and handed me the letter. "This is for the Keeperlord. And I want you to bring a reply on the first ebb."

I looked up from the letter, startled, to meet his eyes. That would mean I would have only a bare couple of hours' rest in The Hub before I had to return, and I would be riding back in the dead of night. My father knew what he was asking of me, of course; he'd been a longboatman before he'd turned to Guild administration. It was the only way you could ever advance in the Guild.

"You want me to ride the ebb at *night*?" I asked carefully, just to make certain.

"Yes," he snapped. "When you arrive back, come straight to see me. Don't talk to anyone until you have done so. Don't let anyone see you. You can stay indoors at home until the effect wears off. If I have a freak for a son, then at least his deformity may as well be of value to us."

I froze. He hadn't used those words for years. *Freak. Deformity.* I had thought—I had hoped—that I had shown him I was neither of those things. I think I knew then that, no matter what I did, I would never be anything else in my father's eyes. I could look normal, act normal and hide my supposed wickedness from all the world, and still I would be nothing more to him than a deviant despised by God.

I tried to keep the hurt out of my eyes. "I'll see you tomorrow," I said.

"Hold to the wave," he said, giving the age-old farewell to the tiderider.

"As the King wills," I responded woodenly in return. There was no king, of course; the stock reply referred to the Whale-King, the bore itself when it was at its strongest in the darkmoon months. In the end, the success of any ride depended on the nature of each individual wave as much as on a rider's skill; and the bore—from the gentle quartermoon Minnow to darkmoon Whale-King—was notoriously fickle.

CHAPTER 3

NARRATOR: RUARTH

I KNOW YOU DON'T BELIEVE ANY OF THIS. Blaze has told me you don't think magic existed, that you don't believe that I—or any of the Dustel Islanders—was ever a bird. She says you Kellish people believe only in logic and science. You think we are myth-makers. Or liars, to put a more unpleasant slant to it.

Truthfully, I find that assertion strange, for I have spoken to the priests you have brought with you on your ships. They would have us believe that certain pious people among you *see* your God, see him in some insubstantial form that he chooses to take when he walks among you. They say he sometimes speaks in audible tones directly to those individuals, even though he has no body. But you don't deem *that* magic. What do you call it? Religious aetherials? A miracle of faith? Sounds like magic to me!

Oh, don't look so affronted, Syr-ethnographer. I do not scorn your god, or any god. In truth, I find it easy to believe in the reality of a deity, for I have known the reality of magic. I spent the first twenty-two years of my life ensor-celled by dun, remember. And every bone, every organ, every part of me was scarred when Morthred's magic ended. No, not with scars you can see. They are marks on my soul, on the essence of me.

I HUNG UPSIDE DOWN ON THE SHROUDS. My heels were caught in the squares of the webbing, saving me from the plunge to the deck. I was naked, of course. And featherless for the first time since I was a nestling in a niche of the palace wall in Cirkasecastle.

Not much time had passed. The *Amiable* drifted away from the dock and the sails still hung limply as the helmsman—Captain Kayed himself—stood staring at the naked bodies on the wharf. Some of them stirred, some groaned. Others did not move. One of the living, apparently unhurt, was a child. She sat among the dead and injured with an expression of utmost shock on her face.

By now, the whole ship was in a state of shock.

Below me, Flame stood like a statue, illusion forgotten and already unravelling around the edges. Her hands gripped the railing, the knuckles white. The set of her shoulders spoke of the intensity of her emotion, but I could not see her face. I wanted to call out to her, to tell her I was there. To say I lived still, to beg her to help me. But when I called there was no sound. When I flapped my wings, it was to find I had none. It was just as well my feet were trapped because, in that brief moment of confusion, I did try to fly.

The engulfing terror that followed the realization I could not take to the air hit me mid-chest with the impact of a fist. *I was hanging upside down far above the deck and I had no wings.* I tried to get a grip with my claws, and of course, there were none. I could not curl my feet around the rope . . .

At least I knew what had happened to me. At least I'd had some intimation it was going to happen. What about those poor fledglings? Children, Storm*hells* . . .

Hands, I thought, hands. I have hands now. I have to do something with my hands.

An easy thought, difficult to execute. I was unable to tell my arms what to do, let alone my hands or fingers. They flapped and flung themselves this way and that. The digits of a bird's forearm flex the flight feathers, they don't curl themselves up and hold things, such as the ropes of the rigging. I concentrated. Hands can hold things. I have hands. Grip the rope. Finally holding on—tight—I was able to haul myself upright, using my beak as well. Teeth. Yes, I was confused. Utterly confused. I still had the thoughts, the *learning* of a bird.

Down on the deck, Flame pulled herself together and reasserted her illusion. Captain Kayed, unable to resist the dunmagic, turned the wheel, the sails filled and we edged away from the dock towards the open sea. Several of the sailors had noticed me by this time, but they were wrapped so tight in dunmagic they ignored the sight of a naked man clinging to the shrouds. Their disinterest in anything, even their own misery, would have been heartrending if I'd had any concern for others right then.

The ketch was a small ship, and the helm was aft of the shrouds I clung to, so it wasn't long before Kayed also spotted me. Far from disinterest, his glance sharpened and his forehead furrowed. He looked at the two other dunmagicker women but, now that we were safely away from Xolchas Stacks, they were busy tormenting some poor wretch of a sailor, poking at him with a marlin spike and laughing at his antics as he tried to escape.

I'd watched Kayed closely on the voyage to Xolchas Stacks. I'd noticed that he seemed more alert than the other enslaved sailors. I'd even wondered for a time if he could have been one of the Aware, concealing his imperviousness to magic, but I'd felt no kinship to him, and eventually decided that he was as ensorcelled as the rest of the crew. It was just that he somehow managed to hold on to a core of independent thought. He tried not to let it show too much when he was around the dunmagickers. It never occurred to him, of course, to hide it from a nondescript bird that fluttered around the rigging and railings of the ship.

He was a large man, swarthy and broad, and he'd made the best of his missing limb by strapping a custom-made blade to his forearm. It projected out beyond the stump, serrated along one edge, hooked at the tip. He used it for everything from cutting his food to threatening his crew. He had a nasty habit of sharpening it with a whetstone while glancing from time to time at whomever had annoyed him last.

Now, once he was sure he was unobserved, he jerked his head at me, indicating I should get down to the deck. I didn't need to be told why. I was too conspicuous where I was. No sailors were needed up in the rigging of the ketch and I was hung out there like a piece of washing on a line. And naked, at that.

It took me a long while to climb down. I kept wanting to just let go and open my wings . . . I still couldn't control my fingers. A bird's claws automatically grip when relaxed, and have to be tensed to release hold; hands seemed to work differently. It was baffling. My toes wouldn't grip at all. My body felt enormous. My eyesight seemed dimmed, my hearing curtailed. But the sensuality of touch was astounding in its pervasiveness. Rope was prickly, rough, abrasive. The wind was cold. The salt of sea spray stung.

At last I reached the deck. My legs collapsed under my weight almost immediately, and I had to crawl. I wanted to go to Flame, to tell her . . .

I had hardly started when I was jerked back by the arm. Before I could protest or resist, I was flung forward and bundled down the hatchway into the forward area below decks. It was Kayed; he must have ordered someone else to the helm now that we had sailed beyond the harbour mouth. I wanted to tell him I needed to get to Flame, but when I opened my beak—mouth—all that would come out were unintelligible sounds. I had no control over my voice.

"Are you mad?" Kayed hissed at me. "You want that Windrider woman to see you?"

I managed to nod.

"That woman is a dunmagicker and she'll have you plucked and fried for breakfast if she knows what you are!"

I stared at him, trying to assimilate what he was saying.

He explained. "I noticed a bird sitting up there on the rigging. And then all those people fell down onto the wharf.

When I thought to look back at the shrouds, *you* were there, and you were naked. And I'll swear black and blue you weren't on this ship when we set sail. Unless you came on board as a bird . . . This is more dun sorcery, isn't it?" he asked.

I nodded again. At least I could control what my head did.

"There was a legend . . . I remember my granddad told me. About what happened to the Dustel Islanders when the islands disappeared . . ." He shook his head in disbelief. "That can't be *true*, can it?"

I couldn't blame him for his bewilderment. Many people had come to know about the original ensorcellment of Dustel Islanders, but few had any idea the birds had retained their sentience, let alone that later generations were sentient. No idea some of us were Aware, or sylv. No idea that the killing of a particular dunmagicker would revert us to human form.

"I'm a Spatterman," he continued, showing me his ear tattoo of a cockle shell inlaid with mother-of-pearl. "We grew up on the Dustel legends. Might never have believed it even now, though, except I overheard that Windrider woman talking to Gethelred, the supposed Rampartlord." He snorted. "Bloody dunmagicking bastard. He had the *gall* to pirate my ship, and turn me into a piss-hearted minion unable to refuse his orders!" He swelled at the memory and shook his knife-hand under my nose. "I'll kill the pox-hearted bastard if ever he gives me even *half* a chance!" At the thought of rebellion, the red of dunmagic swirled around his throat and tightened. His eyes bulged as he choked. Instead of resisting, he relaxed. Gradually the red eased away and he could breathe again. "The bastards," he said. "Their magic won't even let me *think* of harming any of them." He looked at me, considering. "*He*'s dead, though, isn't he? Gethelred so-called Rampartlord. Otherwise you wouldn't be here. I heard him tell Windrider he was the one who sank the Dustel Isles. Can that be true? It was *Gethelred* that did this to you? Ninety or more years ago?"

I nodded again. Not exactly true—it had been my great-grandparents, not me—but I had no way of explaining. I gestured, indicating I wanted to go back topside.

"Are you crazy?" he asked. "She'll kill you. Or one of those other mad bitches will."

I tried to speak, but the guttural sounds were, at best, animal-like.

"You can't talk?" he asked. "Not at all?"

I shook my head.

"Come, let's get you out of sight." He pulled me along into the crew quarters, and rummaged around in one of the lockers for some clothes, which he flung in my direction. "Put these on."

I tried, but fumbled miserably. Pulling on a pair of sailor's culottes was beyond me. I tripped over and sat down heavily on the floorboards. It *hurt*. Feathers 'n' tails, I thought, humans *hurt* themselves when they fall over.

The notion seemed absurd at first, then worrying. Things were happening too fast for me to absorb, too fast for me to see all the ramifications. I was trying not to think about the larger story, but somewhere inside my head I was aware a huge number of my people had died that day, and among them would be many members of my family, and countless friends. I wanted to grieve, but I didn't know whom to mourn. I wanted time to think, but I wasn't going to be granted that luxury.

I finally climbed into the culottes and pulled on the shirt. It was uncomfortably rough against my skin. I fumbled with the ties. My arms shot out in all directions and at one stage I managed to entangle myself in one of the hammocks strung across the room.

Kayed shook his head in exasperation, and did the ties up for me. "You're pathetic, you know that?" he growled. He looked me up and down. "You look like a tadpole. And you move like a pond skater, in fits and starts."

I didn't know what he meant then. I worked it out later, once I'd seen myself in a mirror. My body may have become that of a man, but it was influenced by the bird it had been. The muscles of my upper torso and buttocks were well developed, and without excess flesh. My neck was thick and short. My head was bald—I grew a good head of hair later on, but right then, my scalp was shiny and quite hairless. My skin had never been touched by the sun: it had the unattractive lividity of a fish's underbelly. The real problem, however, was with my legs and thighs. My legs were weak, underdeveloped things, painfully, pathetically thin and unable to carry my weight with any ease. He was right, I looked like a tadpole: all top end, trailing away to nothing. Worse, I was unbalanced. Birds are light-boned and almost weightless. When they fly, they are as buoyant as a cork on water. I was suddenly a heavy land-based monster. I could not move my limbs smoothly; I jerked and my arms and legs often seemed beyond my control. I misjudged how much *space* I needed. I banged into things. I found it hard to even move through a doorway without hitting myself on the jamb.

A pond skater shooting jerkily across the surface of the water.

Right then, I had no time to think about such things. I had to speak to this man somehow. I had to tell him that maybe, if Flame knew I was human, I could get through to her. Morthred was dead. It might make a difference . . . Part of me wasn't certain of that, but I had to try.

I made a gesture as if writing.

He looked at me doubtfully. "You can *write*?"

I nodded.

"Well, I don't have a quill or paper—they're in my quarters, and it's more than my life is worth to be found there. I'm just a slave on board my own vessel, no more, no less. It doesn't matter that Gethelred is dead; those three bitches have me ensorcelled now. The bottom-crawling mudworms! May they drown in their own middens," he added, spitting out the last words as if he could make them true. He grabbed a mug from a hook on the wall and filled it with water from the drinking barrel in the corner of the room. "Here, write on the boards with a wet finger," he said, pointing to the floor. "What's your name?"

I crouched down and dipped my forefinger into the water. I'd learned to write as a fledgling back in Cirkasecastle, using chalk held in my toes. It was harder now. My hand was not cooperative and I nearly spilled the water, but eventually I managed to spell out "Ruarth." Then, clumsily, "Aware." I pointed to my chest with what should have been a wingtip but was now a finger. This was going to take some getting used to.

His look was needle-sharp. "You're *Aware*?" The smile he gave me contained too much smug pleasure to be reassuring. "Ah, Tadpole my friend, that's the best news I've had since this nightmare began. Maybe we can get out of this intact after all."

I shook my head, frustrated. I wrote: "Go Lyssal. Friend."

He gave an exasperated grunt. "Forget it, Tadpole. She's no friend to you or anyone any more. She's a dunmaster, that one. The only thing that matters to her is herself. It's not Gethelred we obey now, you fool. It's *her.* Lyssal." He gave me a thoughtful look. "There was a bird on the ship between Rattéspie and Xolchas, a dark, purplish thing—was that you?"

I nodded.

"Ah. There's a great deal more to this story, then, isn't there . . . but there's no way you should risk your hide telling that dunmagicker who you are. She won't *recognise* you, will she?"

I shrugged. I didn't think it was likely.

He agreed. "Shouldn't think so. You look like a bloody halfwit. Why do you keep moving your head in that funny way?"

Even if I'd known the answer to that one, I didn't have a chance to reply. A sailor came clattering down the companionway, looking for Kayed. "Captain, Syr—the dunmaster wants to see you," he said listlessly. The dun-red of the foul coercion drifted over his skin. He smelled. At a guess he had not washed since he had been enslaved. I thought: they are calling her a dun*master* now. My Flame.

Kayed nodded, and turned back to me. "Stay here. Tadpole. Or you're dead, I swear. If one of those bitches comes below, you pretend to be enslaved. Trust me."

But I didn't trust him, not at all. Then again, I didn't trust my own instincts either. It was very hard to believe Flame would kill me, but sometimes it was even harder to believe she wouldn't.

CHAPTER 4

NARRATOR: KELWYN

WE HAD AN ARGUMENT OF SORTS, TOR
Ryder and I, that last day in Xolchas Stacks.

I remember looking at him and wondering if I disliked
him because we were both in love with the same woman,
who happened to prefer him, or whether I would have disliked him anyway. He was so self-assured, so darned *compe-
tent* at everything he did, that I felt inadequate around him. I
was clumsy, a Plainsman with two left feet, wild red hair and
freckles, a fact that had not bothered me overmuch before,
but which now—faced with this handsome, lithe Straggler-
man who exuded all the allure of male strength yet moved
with the grace of a woman—had become an issue. I was
quite old enough, of course, to be aware my reaction to him
was immature and adolescent, but it made no difference. The
truth was I was jealous of the man.

I was up on the roof of the Lord's House in Xolchasbarbican when Tor came and tackled me, again, about finding a
cure for magic. I had gone there just to feel the cleansing sea

winds through my hair, to rid myself of the horror in my mind. I had been to the hospice again. Of course, there was little I could do, little anyone could do. There were too many injured, too many dying, too many simply driven out of their minds, especially the children. Many of them were too young to cope with what had happened, and quite unable even to say who they were. I had been doing my best to match each child with his or her parents, using my skill at recognising residual scents left on the skin. I'd not always been successful. The grief, the terror, the pain of the legacy Morthred left behind with his death: it tore the very heart out of me. And it had been my hand that had wrought this change. It had been necessary, but knowing that didn't make it any easier to live with. It never has.

Blaze helped me while she waited for the arrival of the ship that would take her after Flame. Xetiana, the Barbican-lord, had sent word to Stabbing Stack asking for a suitable vessel to be dispatched from there—they used some kind of trained seabirds to carry messages between the stacks, I believe. Blaze had a tight clamp on her impatience, but I was aware of it nonetheless. She reeked with it. Rather than pace the palace in her agitation, she chose to help me with the Dustel children, which surprised me. I hadn't thought she would have much patience with the very young. I thought babies would leave her at a loss. It was odd, therefore, to see how moved she was at their plight, and how prepared she was to hold them, rock them, murmur the kind of things mothers whisper to a hurt child. Perhaps the sight of those dispossessed children had plucked her own distant memories into the present, reminding her of a time when she, too, had been an abandoned child, left in a cemetery at the mercy of strangers.

In the end it had been I who'd had to leave the hospice for a while, to gather my tattered emotions. It had been the sight of a child trying to smooth down the feathers she no longer had with a beak she no longer possessed that had finally snared me into a paralytic inability to cope any more. She'd looked up in such bewilderment, whimpering, and then she'd tucked her head under her arm. I had to go outside, to stand in the wind and smell the freshness of sea air. And that was when Ryder sought me out.

He took one look at me, and said, "Bad morning?"

"Aye," I said shortly, and wondered what he'd been doing. Flirting with Xetiana, perhaps.

He must have caught a whiff of my disenchantment with him, because he said, "I have been talking to the head of the Menod patriarchs here in Xolchasbarbican, getting something organized to help the Dustels."

"And catch Dustel souls for the Menod at the same time?" I asked cynically. I was immediately ashamed of myself; it was not a worthy remark.

He refused to take offence. "Well, there is that side of it, too, I suppose. But we are not a faith that thinks we offer the only way to the afterlife or to God. The best way, perhaps, but not the only way. We offer a guide for living—and dying—to those who want a good one, that's all." He smiled. "We have never actively tried to convert Xolchasfolk, you know. They have their Wind God, and he serves them well." As if in acknowledgment of his words, the wind swirled with renewed strength around us, and we both heard the plaintive notes that echoed from the Wind Temple on the Talon. "He must have heard me. Kelwyn, I have spoken to Captain Scurrey: the schooner is ready to leave."

"You're so sure I'll go with ye."

"There's no point in you going with Blaze. You said yourself that by the time she finds Flame, it will be too late to abort her babe without endangering her life."

I had to stifle the idea that he just wanted to keep me away from Blaze; he wasn't so petty. Instead, I acknowledged the truth of what he said. "Aye. The bairn must have quickened by now." A dunmaster's get, subverting her from within. Morthred's legacy.

"Then the only chance for Flame is that we find some way of destroying dunmagic."

"Why in all Creation d'ye think I can do anything about that?"

"You're a physician, and we now know magic is transmitted in similar ways to certain diseases . . . from mother to child. From child to mother. You might be able to find the key that explains it—and the medicine that cures it. You may be the one who finds the means to cure Flame."

"Don't be ridiculous, man."

"You *do* still believe it is an illness, don't you?"

I hesitated. I had thought so once, but at the time I hadn't seen all that magic could do. Since then, I'd watched people treat illusions as if they were reality, I'd seen dun kill people, I'd looked on while Tor himself was cured of an injury that should have killed him. Since then I'd seen birds turn into people. "I'm not sure. But that's only part of the problem anyway. Let's say it is a disease, what makes ye think I can do anything about it? If curing sickness was that easy, we Plains physicians would have rid the Isles of every illness that ever plagued it. What in all the islands makes ye think I will be able to find out anything about what dunmagic is— let alone concoct a cure?"

"If anyone can, it will be you."

"Ye want more than just to cure the subverted," I said. "Ye want to rid the world of *all* magic. So let's say I did find a cure. Can ye imagine us approaching the sylvs of the Keeper Isles, waving a herbal potion under their noses and saying 'Here, drink this—it'll rid ye of your sylvpower.'? I'm sure the sylvs of the Isles would love that! The truth of the matter, Ryder, is sylvs *like* being sylvs. And dunmasters revel in being dunmasters. No one *wants* to find a cure—except you."

He met my eyes and held the gaze, backed by the full force of his personality. "And you," he said softly. "And you, Kelwyn Gilfeather."

How did he read me so well? It was humiliating. The wind whipped around us, and I had to struggle with my tagaird to keep it from unwinding and disappearing in the direction of the cliff edge. I knew my hair must look as wild as a brush fire. Ryder stood watching me, his black patriarch's robe doing no more than ruffling slightly around the hem, his hair, swept back and tied at the nape, remaining neat. Damn the man. How did he know the demons that rode me? All those glimpses I'd had of hell . . . Ginna, the girl back in Amkabraig who had been raped by dunmagickers and contaminated by the child she bore as a result; Flame herself: beautiful, kind and rotting from the inside out; the Dustels falling from the sky. The bruised eyes of human children who had been born birds. ➛

My eyes dropped away from his. Aye, I wanted to rid the world of magic. I wanted it scoured from every islandom, cleansed from memory. And there was a terrible irony in that, of course, for any physician. Because sylvs did have the power to cure illness, to bring people back from the cusp of death. They could do what a Plains physician could only dream of . . .

"Come with me, Kelwyn," he said. "I have it all arranged with Captain Scurrey. We'll call in at Amkabraig to pick up the medicine chest your Uncle Garrowyn was to send there. And perhaps you could even send a letter to Garrowyn, asking if he would consider coming to Tenkor to help. With some of your Plains medical histories, perhaps. Then the task may be easier. Let's rid the world of even the *possibility* of another Morthred. You know you want it too."

"So what if I do?" I asked. "It's not going to happen. Not in my lifetime. Or yours."

"It will," he said with confidence.

I frowned. "Up until now, ye have no struck me as a gowk with butter for brains, Tor Ryder. But this is foolish."

"There is another element you have not taken into account," he said.

"And what is that?"

He paused, and then shook his head. "Trust me, there is something you don't know. I—I can't explain it right now, at least not in terms that would make sense to you. Let's just say there is a cure. I *know* it, as plain as I know it's you who will find it."

I stared at him, at a loss. I had no idea what was making him so certain. "Dinna tell me," I said, and there was an edge of annoyance to my voice, "ye have unearthed an ancient document that is actually a missing prophecy writ by our Kelvish ancestors . . ."

He laughed. Fantasy tales were more Dek Grinpindillie's speciality. "No," he said. "Nothing quite so Dek-inspired."

I was about to ask him why, in that case, he wasn't going
to tell me what he meant, when we were interrupted. It was
Blaze, who had seen us from the roofway between the hospice and the Lord's House. She came across to us, anticipation spilling from her, like the aroma of newly opened wine.
"I've just had a message from Xetiana," she said. "My ship
is arriving tonight and should be ready to sail tomorrow
morning."

"And I have just been telling Kelwyn we can leave any
time," Ryder said. "Now, in fact, if he could only make up
his mind."

Blaze looked at me, head tilted on one side. "Is this what
you want, Kel?"

I shrugged and sighed, wishing in my heart, I suppose,
that she would ask me to accompany her instead. "It's as
good a solution as any other. I canna ever go home, and I
have to find work. I assume the Menod are reliable paymas-
ters . . ."

Ryder gave a smile. We had not mentioned remuneration.
"Of course. Is that settled, then? We leave this evening?"

"Tomorrow morning is early enough." I was still oddly
reluctant to go. Perhaps it was just that I didn't like the idea
of parting from Blaze. I had no idea if we would ever meet
again, and that thought was shockingly painful. I glanced at
her, and wondered at myself: thirty years old and in love
again with such painful intensity.

Ryder shrugged. "As you wish. I will go and inform Captain Scurrey."

As he turned back towards the barbican and the path
down to the port, Blaze and I made our way to the roof entrance of the Lord's House. The guards sprang to attention
when we approached, and saluted smartly. I smelled the interest their training sought to conceal. Both of us had
achieved hero status in Xolchas; Blaze because of her
swordfight with a dunmagicker and her subsequent spectacular escape from the stack Morthred's power had tumbled
into the sea, and me because I had killed Morthred. I was at
a loss to explain why that murder was the source of admiration: his magic did not work on me and I had started by

smashing his head in from behind, and almost ended it by letting him escape. He'd finally died after I had partially slashed his throat and then kicked him in the wound. There wasn't much that was heroic or glorious in any of that.

We descended the stairs in silence. There was so much I wanted to say, and I didn't seem able to get any of it out. Finally I managed, "There really wouldna be much point in me sailing with you. By the time we caught up with her—"

"You don't think I can rescue her, do you." It was a statement, not a question, and it was heavily weighted: Blaze had once promised to kill Flame if a rescue and cure were impossible.

I shook my head. I had seen what dunmagic subversion had done to Ginna.

"She's strong," she said fiercely as we arrived outside her room. "Kel, there are things we need to discuss. Come on in." She drew me into her room, and sat me down in one of the chairs, then went to pour us both a drink. "I need some advice."

"Advice from *me*? Skies, Blaze, there's no much I can tell ye that ye dinna already know."

"Yes, there is. About being pregnant, about giving birth, about medications—abortifacients, sleeping drugs. Whatever happens, I do have to kill the baby, I know that. And I don't want to kill Flame if I can possibly help it. Yet I can't just go marching up to her and tell her to come to Tenkor with me and we might be able to cure her. She's not going to *want* to be cured. She's going to be a dunmagicker by the time I get to her. So I've been thinking, planning, wondering just how I can get close enough to her. How I could possibly bring her back across the Middling Isles to Tenkor without her consent. Don't look so damned surprised, you selverherding grass-eater. I don't always rampage around the place waving my sword and only stop to think later. I want to plan this carefully."

I managed a smile. "I've never underestimated your intelligence, Blaze."

"Liar."

I laughed. "All right, then: not often. And not lately. So what are ye planning?"

"Well, for a start I think I need to find a sylv to go with me."

"Who?"

"Someone who will come along for the money I can offer. Xetiana, fortunately, is quite generous."

"Will ye no find it difficult to find a sylv who is in need of money? Most of them are rich because they use their magic to gain the advantage in whatever their field of endeavour is. And it's my understanding that there aren't many sylvs in Xolchas anyway. Just as they dinna have Awarefolk."

"I wasn't thinking of someone from Xolchas. I know just where to go to find sylvs who are underappreciated, discriminated against, and just itching for revenge . . . and it's more or less on my way too." She sat down opposite me and told me what she had in mind.

When she had finished, my heart was beating uncomfortably fast. "And this," I remarked to no one in particular, "is what she calls rational planning! Selverspit, Blaze, ye're mist-mad."

"Probably."

"It presupposes you're right about Flame going to Breth, and that ye can find an obliging sylv who will no mind helping out at the risk of their own life."

"Yes," she agreed complacently. "So, can you give me any advice that will help?"

I sighed, aware she was not going to be talked out of her scheme. The best thing I could do for her—the only thing I could do for her—was to give her as much information as I could. "Right," I said. "Ye are going to have to listen, and listen well."

WE STAYED UP MOST OF THE NIGHT, AND all the while I was thinking that possibly nothing I was saying would make any difference. Blaze was probably going to her death, and even if she escaped, the chances Flame would ever be herself again were almost nonexistent. If there was any way I could have persuaded her not to go, I would have done it.

Sometime in the early hours of the morning, I stood up to go, and then hesitated. "I could change my mind and go with ye." I swallowed and then said what I really meant. "I want to do that."

"It's tempting," she admitted. "Your nose would be so useful . . ."

I snorted. "Ach, it's nice to be appreciated."

She refused to be diverted. ". . . but if I get Flame to Tenkor, and Tor hasn't found a way to help her, then everything I have done will be in vain. He needs you, too. More than I do."

The ache inside me was enormous, but I nodded, accepting her reasoning, accepting a burden I thought I probably wouldn't be able to discharge successfully.

She added, "One more thing: I shall need a sleeping draught and a poison. Just in case."

"I dinna normally poison my patients."

"I'm aware of that."

I swallowed my distaste and considered the request. "All right, I'll give ye something. It's a plant extract I use in diluted form to clean medical instruments. Undiluted and administered orally—it would be painless. And quick."

Her aroma of despair stopped the words in my throat. I couldn't have said anything more if I'd tried. I reached out and pulled her into my embrace, the smell of her pain flooding my senses.

"I'm sorry," I whispered finally. "I'm so sorry. I wish—I wish I'd been wiser. If I'd seen she was pregnant—"

"We . . . both made mistakes," she said. "It happens like that sometimes."

I felt my eyes filling. She'd told me once Flame was the only female friend she'd ever had. There had been something ineffably sad about that: the idea that a woman of her age could be so alone for so long. "Ye will take care, will ye no?" I asked. "I'm aware that's a silly question, of course. You've been looking after yourself all your life, but—well, this time ye are emotionally involved. That can affect your judgement. Keep your wits about you, lass."

The break in my voice gave me away. She pulled back

slightly to look at my face. Then she reached up and touched a tear on my cheek. "There aren't too many people have cried for me," she said softly. "Damned few, in fact. Ye are a fine laddie, Kelwyn Gilfeather. Dinna fret, ye great gawping lunk."

She had thickened my accent unmercifully, every nuance of it. I had to laugh, and that was the way we parted then, laughing.

I would have preferred to have been asked to her bed.

DEK WAS INSIDE THE ROOM WE SHARED. Xetiana had presented him with a sword as a way of thanking him for his aid in ridding Xolchas Stacks of the dunmagickers; he was cleaning it when I entered, although I was sure it was already spotless. He was as proud as a Plains boy who had just earned his first selver.

"Blaze says we are leaving tomorrow mornin'," he said, bubbling with excitement.

"Aye," I said. "She just told me. Ryder and I are leaving too, with Captain Scurrey."

He sighed. "Why can't you come with us? After all, you love her, don't you?"

"Flame?" I asked, surprised.

"No, course not. Blaze!"

I gaped at him. Was I *that* transparent? I closed my mouth into a thin line. The simpleton selver-herder, I thought, wearing his damn heart sewn to his tagaird for all to see. "Ye have no been prattling that sort of fiddle-faddle to Blaze, I hope," I growled.

"Nah, course not," he said. "I'm not daft." There was just a touch of emphasis on the "I'm." "Besides, she wouldn't be interested. She keeps on lookin' at Syr-aware Ryder." He sighed. "It's just like one of my ma's tales of heroes and unre—unrequitted love . . ."

"Ach, for all the wide blue skies, shut up, Dek. And it's 'unrequited.' " In more ways than one.

He subsided into a hurt silence as I went to throw things into my pack.

After a few minutes, I couldn't stand it any longer. I kept scenting his indignation as a pungently spicy aroma. "There's one thing I wanted to ask ye to do," I said finally. "A favour, an important one."

"Look after Blaze?" he suggested. His fervor at the idea was exactly what I feared.

"Er, no, not exactly. In fact, more the opposite. Blaze is quite capable of risking her safety on your behalf. She feels responsible."

"Oh. You mean, like a matter of honor?"

I stifled a sigh. "Aye, if ye like. For her, it's a matter of honor. Dek, I know your mother impressed upon you that men have to look after their womenfolk, and be honorable—"

His eyes went round. "How d'you know that?"

"Because I know the son she has raised," I said solemnly. "A young man of valor and honor. But *I* am telling you it is not your job to endanger Blaze because she has to think of your safety. D'ye understand me?"

He thought about that. "I think so. I have to do what she tells me, even if it means doin' nuttin'. If I try to fight or anythin', I'd just lose. The best way to be honorable is to make sure Blaze doesn't have to risk herself to rescue me."

"Exactly. Do what ye did on Porth, and fight only when ye have to, when there's no other way, and ye won't go wrong."

He nodded. "You can trust me, Syr. I swear."

I hoped he was right.

SAYING GOODBYE THE NEXT MORNING was just as hard as I thought it was going to be. Worse, perhaps, because it was Ryder's moment, not mine. He stepped up to Blaze on the wharf, and he was holding out his Calmenter sword in its scabbard. She had lost her blade and its harness when the stack she was standing on had fallen. "I'd like you to have this," he said.

She didn't move or speak for a moment. He had caught her off-guard, and the aroma I tasted from her was a mix of so many things: love, sorrow, wonder. She raised her eyes from the sword to his face. "It was a gift to you."

"I am a patriarch," he said. "I have no cause to wear a sword. My path—my path lies in other directions now. It would, er, please me if I knew it was in your hands, I need to know you are safe. As protected as possible. We both know a Calmenter sword gives its owner an added edge in a fight because of its length and lack of weight."

She nodded and took the weapon. She buckled it on and then stepped up to him to kiss him, lightly, on the lips. "Thank you," she said, then added, "Whatever we have done to you, Tor, you can overcome." She referred, of course, to our decision to ask the subverted dunmagickers to heal his wounds, and the subsequent dun contamination he had received as a consequence.

"With God's grace," he said. "I apologise for some of the things I said. To you, and to Kelwyn. What happened was not your fault. I have already come to terms with it."

For some reason she did not find his words reassuring. She nodded, stepped back, then turned on her heel and walked up the gangplank. On the deck she came to the railing where Dek already waited and looked down on us.

I stood at Ryder's shoulder, but she had not said goodbye to me.

I still didn't know much about ships, but even I could see that this one, a brig, was special. Xetiana had not broken protocol to come down to the port to say goodbye, but she had given her best: vessel and crew and supplies. She'd given Blaze a substantial purse as well. Payment, she said, for ensuring Xolchas Stacks was not threatened by dunmagicking neighbors in the future.

Ryder lifted his hand in farewell and walked away to our schooner, tied up at the next berth. It was only half the size of the brig.

I stayed where I was. I needed, for my own sake as much as hers, to attempt one more time to persuade her not to risk herself doing something beyond possibility. "Blaze," I said when Tor was out of earshot, "ye must give some more thought to what ye are going to do. Bringing Flame to Tenkor will no make any difference—we are unlikely to have anything to offer her. I dinna believe there will be any cure for magic." I knew I was telling her to commit a double murder and the smell of my shame almost choked me.

Her pain skittered along the docks on the wind in answer. "Tor seems so certain you will be successful. And so I *am* going to try to bring her to Tenkor for treatment."

The idea of her attempting to force a reluctant dunmagicker halfway across the Middling Isles was appalling. My mouth went dry. We'd already discussed this and there wasn't anything more to say, yet still I said it. "If she doesna want to come?"

"I've brought law breakers back to The Hub in the past. I was a bounty hunter for the Keepers, remember? It can be done. What I want to know is what makes Tor so certain he will have the cure?"

I didn't know. "He will no tell me. I think he believes I'd have no faith in his reason were I to hear it . . . Blaze, I know ye love her, but there are some things even you can't do."

She nodded, but I sensed she had not given up hope. I wanted to say: I love you. Don't do this. Instead, I just stood there like the gawkish Plainsman I was.

"Goodbye, Kel," she said.

I nodded, not trusting myself to speak. Then I smiled at Dek and walked away.

On the schooner, Ryder was already giving orders to leave. I wondered just how much money had left Menod coffers to pay for this journey, because Scurrey, the captain, was obsequiously determined to please.

Ryder gave me a thin smile as I came up the gangplank. "You are worrying unnecessarily, Gilfeather."

"Pardon?"

"You think Blaze will try to bring Flame to Tenkor."

I stared at him. Did he read minds or read lips, that man? Or was it just that as a patriarch he had known the thoughts of too many sinners to be unaware of how people's minds worked?

"She won't," he said. "Blaze doesn't break her word, Gilfeather. Not ever. And she promised Flame she would never leave her alive if she was subverted."

"She won't be able to do it," I said, with equal certainty. "She's going to try to bring Flame to us, expecting that we will have some miracle cure for her. Which is an unrealistic expectation: your doing, no mine."

"I have tried to persuade her to have enough faith to do just that, if she can," he said, "but I don't think she will. She is going to kill Flame and the baby." I smelled his regretful certainty; it had the rich smell of new leather.

"She won't," I said stubbornly. "Ye'll see."

We exchanged a look. It was a stupid game we played, both of us wanting to show we knew her best. And I think we both had the grace to be embarrassed by the silliness of our behavior.

As we sailed through the outer stacks, trailing skimming seabirds over the foam of our wake, I wryly contemplated the irony: me, the pacifist physician, hoping the woman I loved would murder her best friend; murder, in fact, a woman I had liked and admired.

I had come a long way since the day I met Blaze and Flame, since the day I killed my wife to save her from being stoned to death. Since the day I was exiled forever from my home and my people. It was a way that had wrought changes in all of us who had trodden the same path, and not all were changes of which we could be proud. And I wonder sometimes—would Elarn Jaydon's life have been different if our paths had not crossed the day we landed on Tenkor Island?

Anyara isi Teron: Journal entry
44/1st Double/1794

We go ashore for the first time tomorrow, at Port Mascerasia on Merinon Island, a colony of the Regal States. Already I can see the beaches from my porthole. And palm trees! My very first palms . . . how beautifully proportioned they are.

I have written so many letters to be sent on back to Postseaward, although how much can I have to say after three weeks on board a ship? So I told my family and friends that Sister Lescalles drives me to distraction with her prayers and her homilies. That it will be such a relief to walk on solid ground again tomorrow and even better to have fresh food. That I had no idea salted meat and pickles could be so tedious.

Oh dear, three weeks and I already complain. Shor would leap to say "I told you so" if he were to read what I have just written. We have completed but a tenth of our journey, and we have four more ports of call before striking out across the Unknown Sea to the Isles of Glory.

He and I continue to avoid one another. Sometimes I think he is being excessively childish. Today, however, he came to talk to me while I was on deck. I thought he was ready to "bury the antipathies," so to speak, but no—he wanted me to admit I was homesick and should therefore seek a passage back home from Merinon!

Fortunately, I have found a good friend in Nathan. He is teaching me the language of the Glory Isles so I can communicate to Glorians without the aid of a translator—putting him out of a job, he says with a laugh. He has shown me all his drawings from the Isles. He's not a good artist, but he has the knack of seeing detail, and it has been of great interest to me to *see his impressions of these people, their lands, their customs—so different from all I have known. If it weren't for his sketches of the tideriders, I don't think I could have imagined what it was Elarn Jaydon described. But now that I have seen Nathan's drawings, it all makes sense: the tidal bore wave moving up the estuary, the "runners" the tideriders use. Otherwise, I might have thought a tiderunner was some sort of canoe, but it isn't, not really, even though it has a paddle. It is too disproportionately long and narrow for a canoe, and not deep enough. He tells me they are made of exceptionally light and buoyant wood that is then varnished to keep it watertight. They are such elegant craft that I am eager to see the real thing. I wonder if I could actually ride one? Nathan assures me they still ride the bore from Tenkor to The Hub.*

Even if Shor is right and there is no magic in the Isles, it will all be magic to me.

Chapter 5

I SAT ON MY TIDERUNNER AND WAITED, feet dangling on either side for stability. Every now and then I dug down into the sluggish ebb flow with the paddle, just to stay in place. A hand's span of water under the keel of my runner separated it from the rippled sand beneath. Several onion-shaped skallions, as transparent as glass, buried themselves hurriedly in the sand when the shadow of the runner touched them. The clock on the tower of the Guild Hall told me I had about ten minutes to wait—if the bore arrived at the appointed hour. Plenty of time to mull over what had happened that day.

I glanced behind and to my left, towards the wharves of Tenkorharbour. At one end, in front of the Guild Hall, a single figure stood watching me. At the other end, where fishing vessels and inter-island packets jostled with coastal jobbers and tall-masted trade vessels, the place was a bustle of ships and longshoremen, as usual. It was here that fidgeting passengers and a plethora of goods were exchanged on a daily basis between larger ocean-going vessels and our shallow-draughted Tenkor longboats. It could be even more hectic than it was then, but the coming tidal bore was what we called a Minnow, too small for Guild longboats to ride. That day's longboat had already left, departing predawn on a more powerful Dolphin tide. Consequently, there was only me leaving for The Hub now, with the packets of letters to deliver. I not only had my father's letters, and the usual commercial mail. I also had a packet from the High Patriarch for the Keeperlord.

I raised my hand to the lone boy—it was Denny—outside the Guild Hall. Usually, there would be a scattering of young women and small boys loitering there every time I caught a bore. Like most tideriders, I had my own coterie of admirers, more than most, in fact. The women were selective, studying the riding schedule to see when their favorite riders were working so they could be there to wave them off, or welcome them back. Many would also signal their willingness to perform other services as well, free of charge. Their adulation mystified me, but I was as susceptible to their charms as any other lad, and had been known to avail myself of all they offered if I didn't have a particular girlfriend at the time. The small boys were less puzzling; they just wanted to be tideriders one day themselves and they took every opportunity to study their heroes. I had done exactly the same thing myself.

That day, however, no one waited on the docks except Denny. I'd wondered earlier if he would remember his duties after all that had happened that morning, but he hadn't failed me—or his Guild. He'd had my tiderunner waiting at the dock, with my lunch already stowed in the hollowed-out hull behind the seat and my waterskin in its holder. "Beef sandwiches," he told me when I came down to the docks.

"You know what happened?" I asked as I took my shoes off and dropped down onto the tiderunner, my weight on my hands on each side for balance, feet over either side. There's an art to that; a tiderunner is not a boat or a canoe—you do have a hollow to sit in and wells for your feet, but basically you sit on top of the craft. Step down into it the way you would a boat, and you tip it over.

Denny nodded. "Folk are saying those naked people were once all birds—is that true?"

"Apparently." I twisted around to stow the letters on top of my lunch, then jammed the hatch tight.

"Was it dunmagic?"

"So they are saying in the Guild." I didn't tell him anything more; he'd hear all the gossip soon enough, and there was bound to be plenty of that.

I had expected him to rush off as soon as I pushed away from the docks, but he'd stayed to watch me go. I would give him a commendation when I returned. It can't have been easy to ignore all that happened in the town that day, and quietly do his job instead.

I glanced up at the Guild Hall clock tower again. Another five minutes. I attached the strap to my ankle and made sure the other end was firmly tied to the tiderunner; the loop of the paddle was already slipped over my wrist. Anyone who had ever lost contact with a tiderunner, or a paddle, halfway up the Hub Race—and I had done both on occasion—took special care never to become detached from either ever again. They were not incidents I cared to remember.

Restless, I let my gaze wander from the harbour to Tenkorhaven, perched up on the hill. Ribbons of steep house-lined streets linked the town to the waterfront, but it was the public buildings that made the Haven the impressive city it was. The soaring Worship House with its wavelike roof and cresting spires; the Synod where the Patriarchy had its offices and quarters; the Matriarch's Bureau topped by onion domes; the University with a tower on every corner, no two alike; the Library with its spiralled pillars; the Menod Treasury with its colonnades; the Observatory with its flat roof, farscope, ornate wind-vane and anemometer; the Tiderider's Guild where my father's office was; the tree-lined winding streets between—we young tideriders pretended indifference, but as a Tenkorman, born and bred, I could not but feel the stirrings of pride in those elegant stone structures that capped the rise.

For the Menod Patriarchy such pride had an even more fundamental grounding. Many patriarchs were not

Tenkormen—in fact, they came from all over the Isles—but they were deeply proud of Tenkor. They were fond of saying that in Tenkorhaven lay the Menod's administrative heart, its spiritual soul, its political acumen, its learned mind, its material wealth. Legend had it that Tenkor had belonged to the Menod ever since there first was a Menod religion. Certainly, the islands had been the nurturing ground of our faith, the place where it had spent its infancy and our founding fathers had built the earliest shrines, where the holiest men and women had preached. On the islands of Tenkor, we Menod had always felt safe.

It was hard, therefore, to accept that so many people had died here that day. Hard to accept that somehow dunmagic had reached into the heart of Tenkor. It felt as if evil had touched our core and snatched away our security.

Were those Dustelfolk sentient when they were birds? I wondered. What had it been like for them, imprisoned in the spell of a foul magic? Did they know what had happened to them, those who survived?

My mind, against my will, drifted to Cissy. Alive one moment, and then . . . just gone. Those blank eyes looking at me, still suffused with hurt. I refused to think of the other life, irrelevant now, that she had carried. It wasn't my fault. None of it was my fault.

Then why did I feel so . . . guilty? Not so much guilty it had happened, as guilty because I didn't feel more sorrow. Let's be honest, Elarn: guilty I didn't feel *any* sorrow.

I glanced at the clock once more: two minutes, if the Minnow was on time, but bore times tended to be imprecise. There were so many factors that could affect the arrival of a tide. I glanced behind, to the south. There were six islands collectively called Tenkor Island, possibly because during the lowest tides they were all connected by causeways or shifting sand spits. The other five were strung out along the western shore of the Hub Race stretching back to the largest, Outer Tenkor, right at the ocean entrance, a good twenty-five miles away. The island called simply Tenkor High—where Tenkorhaven was—was the only one that was heavily settled.

The others had a few small fishing villages, numerous small farming hamlets—and a plethora of shrines.

As I looked to the south, I could see the standing wave as a long, low white line, far in the distance near the island called Tenkor Low, where the last of the outward flow battled to reach the ocean as the tide came in, ebb and flow in equilibrium for a moment in time. Not long now. I looked ahead of me, to the north, where I was going. The Hub Race stretched away, a long finger of water that pointed directly from the southern oceans to the center of the Keeper Isles, edged on either side by the reaches of land called the Ninth and Tenth Spokes. At the finger's base, the strategically placed Outer Tenkor Island, like the stone of the finger's invisible ring. At the fingertip, The Hub, the islandom's capital. I'd be there by nightfall.

It used to be said tideriders tamed the waves by the very act of riding them; that if there were no boats or tiderunners cresting the bore tides, the sweep of water into The Hub would be fierce enough to upend every ship in the anchorage, swamp every warehouse on the docks and submerge the gracious waterfront homes. They still argue about that, even now, after the event.

And I am one of the few people alive today who know the whole story about what happened the day the tideriders were afraid to ride the tide . . .

But I wander.

You will have to forgive me. I am an old man, and not as sharp as I used to be.

YOU HEAR THE TIDE BEFORE YOU SEE IT, always: a roar of water that fills the ears with an unimaginable volume of sound. Even a Minnow bursts with noise. Hear a Darkmoon tide in the distance, the one we call the Whale-King, and you'd think a mountain had been shaken from its foundations and was tumbling down to the sea.

It's the most exciting sound a man can ever hear. I tremble with the roar, even now; it still has the power to stir my

longing to feel a tiderunner beneath me once more; it stokes
in me a desire to take to the Hub Race one more time, to
sense the lift as the bore slips beneath the runner and I am
raised to the crest, to ride the wind . . .

I ARRIVED IN THE HUB BEFORE SUNSET.
I was tired, as always. My shoulders ached, my thighs ached,
in fact, just about everything ached. That was nothing new. It
was often necessary to use powerful strokes of the paddle to
avoid losing the wave when it suddenly started to die under
you, or to keep from being sidelined into a backwater, or to
avoid hitting a rock or some debris that had been dumped on
the sands by the ebb tide. You had to be continually alert,
ready to paddle like the wind, ready to scoot across the face
of a wave to better your position. You had to be poised, ready
for anything, for hours . . . It took a toll. Always.

I eased the tiderunner off the wave and into the Hub
Basin, which was protected from the worst of the tidal
surges by a breakwater wall. The Minnow churned on up
into the River Hub, where it would slip across the sunken
walls of the Hub Weir, to lose its force upriver. Sometime after the surge had passed the weir, the gates would be raised
behind it, trapping it upstream. When sufficient water had
collected to allow for the creation of a wave on the tide's
downward journey, the gates would be opened to free it.

I paddled into the pier that belonged to our Guild, and the
guildsman on duty came out. There was no one else around,
no admirers or idle bystanders. Even at the Keeper Council
Pier where the *Keeper Fair*, the *Keeper Pride* and several
other Keeper Council vessels were tied up, I could not detect
much activity.

"Hello, Maris," I said, wearily aware I would have to be
back in the water soon. "Am I to guess from the quiet around
here that you also had it raining people this morning?"

He nodded, his face somber as he took my paddle and
helped me lift the tiderunner out of the water. "It's not a joking matter," he said.

"I didn't find it funny, believe me. What happened here?"

"Some say birds turned into people and those that were flying at the time fell. There are all kinds of rumors. Everyone is edgy, looking over their shoulders, thinking there are dunmagickers about. The Council issued a proclamation, but who in the Guild ever believes the Council? What happened in Tenkor?"

"Much the same thing. Maris, I am going to snatch a quick wash and change of clothes, then I have to see the Keeperlord. I have two letters for him."

He turned to walk with me to the Guild Hall. "Ah. That's not going to be as easy as you'd think. Things are in a bit of an upheaval here. Emmerlynd Bartbarick died this morning."

I stared at him. The Keeperlord had been old but the timing seemed coincidental, to say the least. I blurted, "Don't tell me he was hit by a falling bird!"

"No. Close, though. He was out in his gardens at the time. There were some birds there hopping about, it seems. When they changed into naked people, Bartbarick had a heart attack. He died an hour or so later. That put the whole of the city into even more turmoil. His son Fotherly is trying to get himself voted in as the new Keeperlord, and Syr-sylv Councillor Duthrick has called a full Council meeting to settle the matter. It seems Fotherly didn't behave all that well during the time immediately after all those naked people appeared. Duthrick, on the other hand, gave an immediate explanation—something to do with a dunmagicker from the Dustel Isles. I haven't read the full proclamation, but it offered an explanation just when one was needed most. When it goes to a vote, I think Duthrick will win in spite of the fiasco over Gorthan Spit and that agent of his. What was her name?"

"Blaze Halfbreed." I knew her by sight: she'd been a passenger on our boats often enough. By all accounts she had recently made Duthrick look silly by hiding a missing islandheir from him, or some such thing.

"Things are going to be real messy here politically for a while," he said. "You know how the Menod Patriarchy privately thinks sylvmagic is unholy, and not far from the greater evil of dun—"

I stopped at the entrance desk and collected my room key. "Not always so privately, or so I've heard," I said as I signed in. "Some patriarchs on other islandoms publicly rail against it from the pulpits of their worship houses."

"Really? That wouldn't go down so well here. Not with so many sylvs worshipping at Menod altars." He was right. It might have been a paradox, but the Menod faith was stronger in the Keeper Isles than anywhere else and there were more worship houses in The Hub than any other city of any islandom. There was even a group calling themselves "Ethical Sylvs," who pressed for sylvpower with Menod morality. "Anyway," he continued, "since what happened this morning, there have been people saying that all magic should be banned. The patriarchs haven't said much—they've been too busy trying to help the injured—but I suspect many agree with the sentiment."

I grimaced as I went on alone to my room. Maris was right. Things could get messy. The ruling Keeper Council might have hated the power of the Menod Patriarchy, but it paid them to tread carefully. The Keeper Council, put in place by the will of the people, could be removed by that same will, after all. Now, however, it seemed possible that the Patriarchy and the Council may clash more openly.

I thought about the Keeperlord's death as I washed and changed. We Tenkormen and the Menod Patriarchy kept our eye on all that happened in the heartland of the Keeper Isles; in fact, it used to be said Tenkor knew what happened in The Hub before The Hub itself did. My father, I knew, favoured Duthrick, mostly because he loathed Fotherly, calling him a manipulative little snit, and my father was not normally given to open criticism of Keeper Councillors. I agreed with that assessment, but I wasn't so sure Duthrick was any better—just more sly, and probably more ruthless. I'd met the man on a number of social occasions; even been to his house several times. I had not liked him, or his snobbish wife, or his uppity daughter. The idea he could end up ruling the Keeper Isles was appalling.

And we had no control over that.

Tenkor Island was part of the Keeper Isles, of course, but

our Guild only ruled locally in Tenkor and had to follow policy laid down by the Keeper Council. All Keeper citizens
voted in the elections for the Council, but it was the Council
itself who elected their leader, who then became Keeperlord.

I dressed carefully for my intended meeting with Syr-
sylv Councillor Duthrick, putting on the finest suit of clothes
I had in my room at the Guild Hall. I then made my way up
to the Councillery, intending to be on my best behaviour as
well. I may have been heedless, reckless even, in my private
life, but I was still a guildsman, brought up to believe loyalty
to my Guild was what made a man a man.

Besides, a Tenkorman learned to step softly in the capital.

The relationship between the Keeper Council (who were
all sylvs), the Menod Synod that controlled Patriarchy affairs
(who were largely Awarefolk), and the Tideriders' Guild
(who were mostly talentless Menod) was complicated and
fraught with tensions. As far as the Keeper Council was
concerned, Menod loyalty to the Keeper Isles was suspect because so many patriarchs and matriarchs held other citizen-
ships. Sylvs had a natural antipathy to Awarefolk anyway,
because the Aware could see through sylv illusions, and no
one with a large nose liked to think his illusive surgery to
reduce its size was noticeable.

As if all that wasn't enough, people often hate most those
on whom they rely most, and Hubbian commerce depended
on tideriders. Without us, The Hub would have been no
more than a backward village, out of touch with the rest of
the Glory Isles. As a consequence, we tideriders were treated
with deference and courtesy in the streets of The Hub, but
none of us was unaware there was a thread of resentment beneath that polite behavior.

Surprisingly, Duthrick wasn't at the Councillery. It seemed
he had gone home to change for the Council meeting that
was to take place that evening. Rather than wait for him to
return, I decided to seek him out at home. It was no hardship
to walk the distance; as a Councillor, Duthrick lived in one
of the palatial residences on the waterfront near the foot of
Councillery Hill.

And so it was that only minutes later I was pulling the bell

at the main doors to the Duthrick mansion. A lamplighter
passed by while I was waiting, putting a taper to the street
lanterns, and the soft glow spread its way down the paved
streets. We lacked that luxury in Tenkor, where street lighting
depended on the generosity of the householders who may or
may not light lanterns on their doorways.

The butler, carefully trained to recognise the nuances of
dress and status, looked me over and asked for my calling
card. When I replied that I didn't have one, he inquired politely as to my name and whom I wished to see. My answer
was enough to gain an apology for not recognizing me immediately, and to have me shown into the library. A few
minutes later, Duthrick joined me. The Councillor was in his
early fifties at that time; a tall, handsome man, graying at the
temples—looks untouched by sylv, or so I had been told.
Distinguished and urbane would be the best way to describe
him, I suppose.

He smiled when he saw me and came forward to take my
hand. "Elarn, it has been too long since we've seen you in
this house. You are very welcome. And you have grown, I
see! Should I address you as Syr-tiderider now?"

I found myself smiling back at him. The man really could
be charming when he liked. "Not yet, Syr. I still have some
exams to pass."

"I am sure they will prove no problem to you. I am told
you have just come from Tenkor?"

"Yes, on the last tide."

"And am I right in assuming Tenkor was also hit by a
dunmagic phenomenon this morning? Unclothed, untat-
tooed people appearing out of nowhere?" Trust him to emphasize the lack of tattoo. Hubbian Keepers tended to be
paranoid about citizenship; they were all sure the rest of the
Glory Isles was desirous of living in Keeper paradise.

"Yes, Syr. Several hundred folk died, I believe. Um, I
have letters for the Keeperlord, but I understand Lord Bartbarick died this morning. I thought you would be the proper
person to take delivery of these." I handed across the letters.

"Indeed," he said, looking at them, and then inclining his
head with a slight smile. We both knew that with my action

the Tideriders' Guild was endorsing his candidature and giving him an edge over Fotherly the Fop. I may have been reluctant to see him become the Keeperlord, but I knew what my father would have wanted me to do.

I said, "Syr, I intend to take the next ebb back, if you wish to send replies."

He thought briefly about that, then nodded. "Yes, I probably will. Elarn, why don't you take a seat here and wait for me. I shall go to my desk upstairs and answer these. I will send my daughter to look after you while you wait."

The idea did not appeal, but I could hardly refuse. I murmured my thanks and sat down. I had not seen Duthrick's only daughter, Jesenda, since we were both fourteen or so. She had then been short, podgy and pimpled—hardly the kind of girl to attract a lad who could already pick and choose from a selection of admirers. Worse, her looks had not seemed to trouble her in the least. She had been far too sure of herself, too obviously amused by the quaint antics of the rustic from Tenkor. Or so it had appeared to me.

Determined not to be seen as someone in need of entertaining, I rose and wandered around the room. The view from this second-floor window was superb. The Duthrick mansion sat on the waterfront, remote from the dirt and noise of the portside, of course, and I could see clear across the Basin to the other side of the Hub Race and the Ninth Spoke. The sun had set, but the water still held a rippled memory of a sunset sky. The house gardens ended in a beach where there was a short pier and a boathouse, both now just black outlines in the gloom.

When the sky darkened and there was nothing more to see, I strolled over to the bookshelf and took down the first volume that interested me. It was a treatise on the tides of the Glory Isles and I had my nose in that when the door opened.

I took my time before I looked up, open book in hand, striking what I hoped was a casual, disinterested pose—and met the gaze of one of the loveliest women I'd ever seen. No, I take that back. She wasn't lovely. She was *sensual*, although not in the usual sense of pouting lip, voluptuous curves and a come-hither look, but rather because of an alluring combination of good looks and confidence. Just one glance at her told me I was going to have trouble putting two coherent words together in her presence. It would be an effort to drag my thoughts away from bedding her.

She was about my height, with rich auburn hair that tumbled to her shoulders and looked delightfully tousled as if she had hurriedly run a hand through it. Her eyes were that violet color common on the Keeper Isles—and they were shrewdly intelligent. Her complexion was flawless; her skin, paler than my sun-tanned one, was a golden color that spoke of warmth and an evening sun. She was dressed with the simplicity fashionable in The Hub of the day: a plain muslin with a scooped, sleeveless bodice and a skirt that fell in gathers from under the breasts. It was a fashion that managed to be both chaste and extraordinarily suggestive at one and the same time, especially on her. Her figure was that of an active woman, yet there were hints of interesting curves and softness in all the right places. The skirt clung to her legs as she walked. Her gaze challenged. She wasn't lovely, not really, but with her direct stare and her tumbled hair, with that figure and that skin, she was stunning. Even the way she looked me up and down, with open interest, intrigued.

She smiled, a broad smile on full lips and an overly large mouth, a smile that contained no artifice, no simper, nothing but genuine amusement, probably at my expense.

And in that moment, I was lost.

CHAPTER 6

I UNSTUCK MY TONGUE FROM THE ROOF of my mouth and came across to greet the vision. It wasn't until I was holding out my hand to take hers that I realized it actually was Jesenda, and I stepped out from under the wave of enchantment. Or tried to. One part of my brain was still hankering after the vision; the other was telling me she was sylv, for God's sake, and remember illusion, you stupid lunk. Without the illusion, she probably looked as attractive as the full-frontal view of a groper.

"Jesenda," I said and kissed her fingers in The Hub fashion. "How nice to see you again, after all these years. I would have known you anywhere."

As a spur-of-the-moment rally of my defenses, it wasn't bad, but she was equal to it. I had more than met my match. "Don't be ridiculous, Elarn. You didn't recognize me at all from across the room. And once you did realize who I must be, you decided I'm probably not much different from the pimply girl you ignored the last time we met. I am, you believe, hiding my ugliness behind a sylv illusion."

Which was absolutely correct. I struggled to gain ascendancy. "I would not be so ungallant as to assume your attractive, er, exterior is the result of anything but nature. And you weren't ever ugly. Just . . . at that awkward age. As was I."

She snorted. "They say you're a charmer. I can see why. And you've certainly grown gracefully past 'that awkward age.' " She looked me up and down in speculation. My lace-edged collar felt suddenly tight, and I had to resist pulling at it. She walked over to tug at the bell-ribbon even as she waved me towards the leather chairs. "Do sit down. I shall order tea. Would you prefer Spattish highland or Sathan lowland?"

Trust her to offer a choice. "Either is fine, thank you." Back home, we drank ordinary tea we bought in chests stamped simply "The Souther Isles." I put the book down on the low table and sat where she indicated. She took the seat opposite.

"I think there is something you should know about me. In fact, several things," she said.

"Oh?" It was the only thing I could think of to say. It had been a long time since I had been tongue-tied with a young woman. I didn't like being so ruffled, but I was at a loss.

"I don't use illusion to enhance my appearance. I do, however, admit to using illusion last time we met, although it was hardly enhancement I had in mind." She gave a wry smile, directed more towards a personal memory she had of herself than at me. "As you said, an awkward age. I thought people should like me for my mind and character, not for my looks."

I felt my eyes widen. Did she mean that at fourteen she had deliberately made herself look unattractive? The thought that a girl of that age had sufficient self-confidence and aplomb to make herself look plump and pimply was almost too much to swallow. And the idea that I had been predictable enough to ignore her was even more galling. I felt myself begin to flush. I tried to salvage what I could of my self-esteem. "That would have been a lot to expect of a fourteen-year-old youth. I fear I failed that test miserably."

"You did indeed," she agreed.

I was spared thinking up an answer as a footman entered and she turned to ask him to bring the tea. After he had left, she changed the subject, saying soberly, "Father just told me the Dustel birds changed to humans in Tenkor too."

I nodded. "I saw it happen." The images came flooding back, and in sudden revulsion, I knew I didn't want them there. I didn't want to recall any of it. Especially, I didn't want to remember Cissy. "Do you mind if we don't talk about it?" For the first time since she'd entered the room, I spoke without weighing my words, without wondering what effect they would have on her.

She looked at me curiously, but changed the subject. The perfect hostess. She indicated the book that lay between us. "You have an interest in the tides?"

"I'm a tiderider. The tides are more than interesting, they are our livelihood."

"I know the moons affect the tides, but I don't know how. Can you explain it to me?"

I wondered if she was just being polite, making conversation, but there was something intense about the way she leaned forward, something that said she had more than a passing interest.

"It's complicated," I said.

"I can cope."

Sarcastic bitch, I thought, but I couldn't stop myself trying to impress her. "For a start, no one really understands how it happens. All we know is that the moons pull the ocean's waters up into a bulge whenever they are overhead. Some of the Menod say it happens because it is God's will. That it is a divine force. Others say, divine or not, it is something measurable, an attraction cast by the moons. And to a lesser degree by the sun too. All we know for sure is that it happens, and when the Silver Moon slips behind the Blue Moon so that they are in alignment in a Darkmoon month, then we have very high tides." I turned to a diagram in the book that explained what I meant. "Imagine the sun is like a magnet that pulls at our world," I suggested. "And that the only thing free to answer that pull is the ocean. And so the water builds up on the side of the world that faces the sun . . . and when you have the two moons pulling in the same direction, like this, then the bulge is huge, a Whale-King tide. But that means there is very little water over here." I pointed at one of the diagrams.

She understood immediately. "So that's why the tide goes out so low immediately after the highest tides."

"That's right. And things become even more complicated in other months. The moons aren't the same distance from the world, and they move at different speeds around us, so one moon pulls against the other . . ." I forgot I'd wanted to impress her and launched into a more complex explanation of quarter moons, singlemoon tides and doublemoon tides simply because, like most people, I enjoyed talking about what interested me. I grabbed up a few ornaments from a sideboard and spread them out on the low table to represent the moons, the world and the sun. By the time the footman returned with the tea things and a tiffin carrier full of Hub delicacies, I had an improvised map of the Hub Race spread out there, and was talking of the variation in bore speeds. The man was forced to unload the tray onto the library table.

"So, when the incoming tide water is forced into the narrower channel at the beginning of the Hub Race," I explained as the footman left—unlike Jesenda, he left the door open to maintain propriety—"the water piles into a wave at the spot where it meets the outward flow of the river. It builds up into a wall of water, that's the standing wave, which becomes higher and higher until at last the bore overcomes the outward flow. It pours over and travels upstream as a wave . . ."

"And how big it is depends firstly on the phases of the moons—that is, on where they are in relation to the position of the sun—and secondly where the moons are in relation to each other?" Jesenda asked.

"Yes, exactly. Well, maybe not exactly because it's still a bit more complicated than that. The weather plays a part. And the narrowness or otherwise of the channel. The position of sandbars. The wind direction. The configurations of the sea bottom. How much water is coming downstream . . . Which is why we have a whole department in the Guild working on tide predictions. Our lives could depend on knowing what we will face during a particular tide. And then there's the alterations we have made, we guildsmen."

"You mean because you ride the waves?"

"Er, no. The theory that we decrease the intensity of a wave because we ride it is probably nonsense. Ask anyone who rides the wave and feels the power of the water! No, I mean because of the weir. You see, the size of the wave traveling up the Race is also determined by what comes down the Race, and the timing of it. Before the weir was built, the force of water coming downriver rarely made a wave. And that in turn made the incoming tide less predictable. Now we control that outgoing water. We call it an ebb tide, but in actual fact it's no such thing. It's water released by us to suit us, and it has little to do with the moon. It's carefully calculated to be of maximum benefit to our tideriders, and thus to Hubbian commerce."

We were both bending over the impromptu map I had created. Her hair hung over her shoulder and brushed my arm; the scent of her was fragrant with jasmine. Abruptly, as if she could smell the wave of my desire, she straightened. "Come," she said, "have your tea before my father returns with his letters and you have to go." She led me over to the library table where she poured the tea and loaded my plate with Hubbian delicacies. And changed the subject. "Tell me, why are there no women members of your Guild?"

"Women aren't strong enough," I said, and bit into a hot steamed bread-cake filled with spiced wader. Her sudden stillness warned me I had said the wrong thing. Poised to take a second bite, I looked up and then lowered the cake back to the plate.

"Explain that," she said pleasantly, but her eyes flashed.

I had been about to make a glib reply, the sort of facile answer I would have given Cissy. I changed my mind and gave her the truth. I suspected, though, that she wouldn't like it. "It's a five-hour journey up the Race. Every inch of the way there's a potential danger. A log floating just below the surface; a sand spit in an unexpected place; the bloated carcass of a cow drowned upriver. Every inch of the way there is something that could go wrong. A wave may suddenly die under you, even though it speeds by to the right or left. If you can't paddle like a whirlwind, you are lost behind. A rogue wave may try to slam you into a rock, or batter you against the bank. A broken wave face can get so large and churned up that it is like being caught at the base of a waterfall. The wave behind may suddenly run forward to join up with the wave you are riding, and without warning it feels as if there is a monster attacking you from behind. To deal with all these things, hour after hour, you need the strength of a man, the muscles of a man, the power of a man. Oh, a woman tiderider could deal with a good wave in kind conditions, I don't doubt that—but to ride those five hours, to do battle with the water—" I stood up, took my jacket off and rolled up my shirt sleeve. "What woman wants muscles like these?" Suddenly what I had done felt childish, the sort of thing I would do to show off to someone like Cissy. I flushed and hurriedly put the coat back on. "Sorry."

"What for?" she asked, and her eyes were full of mischief. She was laughing at me, enjoying my discomfort, mocking my adolescent bragging. "I don't mind looking at a well-muscled man."

My flush darkened and I hurried on. "There are Tenkorwomen who ride the bore when conditions are good, just for fun. Some of them ride the waverunners, in fact. But none of them would ever try to join the Guild. They know it is beyond their strength."

"I want to learn to ride a wave," she said. "The ebb is more manageable than the incoming tidal bore, isn't it? Could I learn to ride it?"

"Can you swim?" I countered. Most Tenkorwomen learned as children and many still swam as adults when the weather was warm, but in The Hub people were more conservative, I knew.

"Of course I can! I am not so silly that I would mention it if I couldn't swim!"

"Er, no. Of course not. Sorry." She made me feel like an idiot. I *was* an idiot.

"I swim all the time, right here in front of the house."

"Then there's no reason why you couldn't learn to tideride," I said. The idea of Jesenda in a swimming costume was definitely unsettling and I stirred uncomfortably in my seat. I said hurriedly, "And to start with the ebb wave is a good idea. It is more even, more controlled."

"I need a runner."

"Which would you prefer to learn to use? A waverunner?"

"Yes."

"I'll get you one custom-made in Tenkor . . ." I didn't need to think about her weight or height. I already had the idea of her firmly fixed in my head.

"Will you teach me to use it?" she asked.

I don't know why the question took me by surprise—she had obviously been building up to it—but it did. The idea of seeing her again, of spending time with her in the water, was overwhelming.

Before I could utter a breathless "yes, of course," she added, "There's one thing I want to make quite clear, though."

I held my breath. I had an idea I wouldn't like what was coming.

"I know all about you, Elarn Jaydon. You have girls here and girls in Tenkor. You take them to bed and then you dump them. Well, I'm not interested in being one of them—ever. I want to learn how to wave-ride. That's *all*. So, if you ever try anything with me, I'll make you wish you had never been born. Do I make myself clear?"

She was calm and appallingly self-assured, as if she had the means to carry out her threat right then and there. And I'd never before met a girl of my own age who was prepared, apparently, to talk about anything, no matter how embarrassing. I almost made a smart reply—something along the lines of: And just who said I was interested in you anyway?—but thought better of it in time. I laughed instead. "Absolutely clear," I said, and wondered if I was the world's biggest fool.

"Now," she said, "tell me just how you intend riding all the way back to Tenkor tonight, in the dark?"

I stared at her, wondering what to say without actually lying.

When I didn't answer immediately, she continued, "A longboat is twenty times larger than a tiderunner, twenty times stronger, and still night journeys are considered dangerous. I know enough to be aware longboatmen only do it with the aid of lanterns—and that those lamps are far too large for any tiderunner rider to carry." She was referring to skallion lanterns. The flame in one of these was amplified by the glass fashioned out of the many layers of polished bodies of transparent sea creatures called skallions. She continued, "My father might not understand the impossibility of what you are intending to do, but *I* do. So tell me, Elarn Jaydon, just how are you getting back to Tenkor tonight?"

"I'll go back with the longboat."

"They aren't going back till tomorrow morning." She put her head to one side, and those violet eyes of hers were sharp and hard. "I happened to speak to the weirkeeper this afternoon," she added by way of explanation.

I don't know what I would have replied right then, but we were interrupted. Duthrick entered the room, carrying several letters.

I think I paled. Jesenda was going to tell him she was suspicious of me. How the Trench was I going to explain a night trip without revealing the secret I'd worked years to conceal?

"I trust Jesenda has been looking after you well, Elarn," Duthrick said.

"Beautifully, thank you, Syr."

"I have letters for the High Patriarch and your father here. I hope you can get them back to Tenkor by morning."

I took the letters, refusing all the while to look at Jesenda. As her father and I spoke, exchanging our goodbyes, she came to stand at Duthrick's elbow. I kept on expecting her to say something, but she let the moment pass. I took my leave of them both, and the footman escorted me to the door.

AN HOUR LATER I WAS SEATED ON MY tiderunner at the Guild pier. Maris fussed like a hen wader settling on her clutch. "Elarn, I'd be failing in my duty if I didn't tell you this whole idea is mad. You can't ride a wave at night on a tiderunner. At the very best you'll fail to read the conditions and lose the wave. I don't need to tell you what can happen at the worst."

"And I've just told you, this is at my father's request. It's a full moon, Maris. I will manage."

"But only one moon! I can't believe your father would ask you to do this. He wouldn't want his only son to risk his life in such a foolhardy fashion . . ."

I didn't reply. The truth was my father did not care as much as a fish scale for my continued health. He would have been upset to lose Duthrick's letters, though, I suppose. "Here, hand me down the paddle." As I took it from him, several other people stepped onto the pier. I couldn't see them, but I could hear the boards rattle as they made their way towards us. Maris looked in that direction. "Better wait," he muttered. "That looks like someone wearing the Duthrick livery." A moment later he added, "Yes. A footman. And a woman."

Jesenda. What the Sea Devil was she doing down on the wharves at night, even with a footman in attendance?

She gave a single imperious gesture with her hand when she arrived, and her footman and Maris just melted away into the darkness behind. She sat down on the edge of the pier, her feet dangling over the front of my runner. My head was just below the level of her knees. "I know your secret," she said.

For a split second I didn't know what she meant. Then I didn't believe it. How could she know? "What secret is that?" I asked cautiously.

"I know what you will use to light your way home. I know why you, of all tideriders, are the only person who can ride the Hub Race in the dark on a tiderunner." She smiled at me, and the smile was more friendly than mocking. "You're sylv."

I stared at her, heart beating wildly. And then I calmed. It didn't matter if she knew, not really. Memories swamped me. "Oh," I said. "I remember. And so do you, evidently."

She nodded.

We had both been about three or four years old. Duthrick wasn't yet a Councillor, and my mother was still alive. We came to The Hub to visit my mother's aunt, who was ailing, and Duthrick also happened to be visiting her with his family, because she was his father's cousin. The adults left Jesenda and me to play together.

In each other's company we were as prickly as two sea-urchins. Jesenda made an illusory kitten, ill-formed and rough as children's illusions are, and I—although I was strictly forbidden ever to use my sylv—squashed it with an illusory dog. Jesenda, of course, retaliated with another illusion, and taunted me, saying I was a mannerless Tenkor brat, echoing some remark she must have heard from Hub adults at one time or another. Our battle took on epic proportions, with poorly controlled illusions escaping our influence all over the place. Of course, it attracted the attention of the adults, who put an end to it. Rather unjustly, Jesenda received all the blame, her parents assuming she'd been the source of all the sylv. Korlass Jaydon's son was not supposed to have sylvpower. Jesenda, predictably, proclaimed her partial innocence at the top of her lungs, but no one believed her.

Except my parents, who knew exactly what I was, and they kept their silence.

Jesenda, the adult Jesenda, said, "You owe me an apology. Half that sylv was yours."

I grinned at her. "Better late than never? Syr-sylv Jesenda, please allow me to apologise for my boorish behaviour when aged four." I took one of her feet and daringly kissed the curve of it, where it emerged from her slipper. "I didn't think you'd remember."

She choked back a laugh. "Oh, I remembered because of

the injustice of it, that no one would believe me. Although to be quite honest, I've only just woken up to who that boy was. I still don't understand, though. Why didn't your parents just acknowledge you were sylv?"

I paused briefly before replying. Why did she have to ask such awkward questions? Finally I offered her the truth once more. "My father is a traditionalist Menod. One of those who believe magic is akin to sin. He thinks sylv is only one step away from dun, that illusion is just deception, no different from cheating."

I half expected her to hotly defend sylvmagic, but she said merely, "What about sylv healing?"

"Thwarting God's will. Although why that should be so, but taking a herbal remedy is not, I have never been able to fathom."

"And what do you think, Elarn Jaydon?"

I hesitated. "I don't think it's necessarily sinful. But I *am* a Menod. I don't like illusion, and sometimes I believe we'd be better off without magic of any kind."

"And yet you're going to use a sylv light to get home."

I nodded. I didn't tell her it was the first time I had used magic since I was twelve. "Yes. And I'd probably submit to sylv healing if I was hurt too. Without a qualm."

"Hypocritical, aren't you?"

"Horribly."

"You are a very strong sylv, you know. I know a fair bit about children and their abilities now, and from my limited memory of what we were up to that day as toddlers, you were very talented."

"Sylv has brought me nothing but trouble. I'd be obliged if you didn't mention it."

"You conceal it?"

"What do you think? In the end, my father wouldn't even allow me to be raised in Tenkorhaven until I had learned to hide my sylv and he could be sure I would." He'd had another reason as well, of course: his erroneous belief that I was illegitimate. But I wasn't going to mention that. "Jesenda, I have to go or I shall miss the release of the ebb. I'll be in touch when your runner is ready."

"Do you need money for it? I brought my purse—"

I shook my head and pushed the tiderunner away from the pier. "A gift," I said. "To pay for squashing your sylv kitten." It was a stupid gesture; I would be short of money for months while I paid it off.

She laughed and stood up. "Here," she said, "catch!" But it wasn't money she threw to me, it was a sylv light, sent by the power of her mind. It was beautiful: a silver glow, as if she had captured moonlight and rolled it up into a ball. Without even thinking about it, I caught it with the power of my mind. Gently, I pushed it into place so that it stayed a few paces in front, lighting my way as the runner drifted.

I looked back at her on the pier, and the implications of what she had just done cascaded in on me. *Impossible*. She had done the impossible. She had made someone else—one of the non-Aware—see her magic, not the illusion of it, but the magic itself. No one could do that.

And then I caught the whisper of her words over the water. "I knew it. I *knew* you'd see it." A sudden wind whipped her hair out of its ties and tugged at her dress, outlining her thighs. The gust—or was it desire?—shivered my skin with its touch. In the lamplight she was both beautiful and appealing, and I think that was the moment I first started to fall in love, rather than just to lust after her.

I knew it was stupid.

She had just shown me she must be one of the greatest sylvs ever born. And I had always known she was the daughter of Duthrick. Together, that made her the powerful heir of a man who had unlimited ambition and no conscience.

She had to be dangerous.

CHAPTER 7

I STARED AT CAPTAIN KAYED IN HORROR.

I had thought I had reached the nadir of misery, but what he had just told me was more than salt in the wound, it was another wound, one that was heartbreaking.

"What's the matter?" he asked, puzzled. "You look awful. But we were always going to Breth, to Brethbastion—you knew that, surely. Why do you look so shocked now just because I told you that's where we are bound?"

But I couldn't explain it to him; I didn't have the words. Yes, when we had left Porth our ultimate destination had been Breth—at Morthred's command. I knew that. I'd been there when the dunmaster had first told Flame he intended her to marry the Bastionlord, Rolass Trigaan. I'd been there on the *Amiable* sailing out of Porth when the bastard had spelled out his plan in all its diabolical detail: after bearing the Islandlord an heir, she was to kill her husband and establish herself as regent. In the end she would marry him, Morthred. "We shall rule the Middling Isles one day," the dunmaster told her. "You and I, commanding the cannon-guns, squeezing the Keeper Isles between Breth and Cirkase like a shrimp caught in a crab's pincers . . ."

Flame had loathed the idea. She had shuddered every time Morthred had mentioned the name of the Bastionlord. He had coerced her into submission, but she had not wanted it, not then. Feathers 'n' tails, she ran away from Cirkase to escape that very same marriage!

And yet now Kayed was telling me she was going to Breth *of her own volition.*

Subversion. Every day that passed, the subversion gained a further foothold in her personality, twisting it, perverting her. And there was nothing I could do. Nothing. I bowed my head and stared at my feet as if I had been broken in two. Foot-staring: that's a bad habit birds have, you know, when they don't know what else to do.

Sometimes I remember that journey to Breth as a continuous blur of pain, and I try to keep it that way. It's worse when I remember the details, when scenes emerge, etched deep by the heartfelt agony of a moment in time. I loved Flame so. All my conscious life she had been there, my window to a human world, to human emotion, to the kind of life I hungered to attain. She was the human side of me. And now it was hard even to *find* the person I'd once loved. The body was there, but the woman was not.

I found myself thinking of this dun-saturated creature as Lyssal, as if by using her birth name when I thought of her, I could somehow divide that person from Flame. As if I could keep my Flame, the one I knew, pure—simply by playing semantics in my mind.

Sometimes I wondered if I was quite sane.

For the first few days on board the *Amiable*, I was ill much of the time, whether from seasickness, or as a result of my change to a man's body, I couldn't say. Ironically, Lyssal—who had been so sick on the trip between Lekenbraig and Amkabraig—did not appear to be ill at all. Dun, it seemed, provided an unexpected cure for seasickness.

Kayed's idea was to keep me secreted in the crew quarters until I was strong enough to overpower and kill the dunmagickers—Lyssal included. A simple plan, to his mind, and one that only I could perform because I was the only person on the ship who was impervious to dunmagic.

"It'll be easy," he murmured one day as we ate in the wardroom. "Windrider's no swordswoman. And Gabania's old. You can pick them off one by one . . ." The dun around him thickened, and he quickly changed the subject. "But you have to get stronger. Walk up and down . . . exercise those muscles. Trench below, will you *stop* doing that?"

I looked puzzled. I was just drinking from a mug, and I thought I managed quite well. I hadn't dropped the mug, nor spilled any water.

"Look at you! Taking a sip and then sticking your nose up in the air so the water runs down into your throat. You're not a flipping bird any more, you feather-brained dolt!" He made a sound of deep disgust. "You *must* learn how to talk, Tadpole. You are driving me to drink, I swear, and I don't mean water."

Outwardly I went along with his plan. If Gabania and Stracey died first, then I would be in less danger when I approached Flame. And I had every intention of telling her who I was. I needed to be strong, I wanted to learn how to speak. If I couldn't talk to Flame, how could I help her to turn her back on the contaminating dun?

Every available moment I worked at being human. I tried to learn how to use my human senses, to accustom myself to human hearing, human sight, human touch, human taste. To learn how to walk without blundering into the doorways. To eat using utensils, to drink without slurping. To learn how to move my eyes instead of my whole head when I wanted to look at something. To learn how to wash without using a beak. To learn how to use the ship's head. To use my hands instead of my feet to manipulate things in the world around me.

There were problems that plagued both my intention and Kayed's desires, though, and none of them was minor. Firstly, I wasn't sure I could cold-bloodedly kill two women who were, after all, not to blame for what had happened to them. The closest I'd ever come to harming anyone was

when I'd pecked Kelwyn Gilfeather's hand hard enough to
make it bleed back on Mekaté, hardly a life-threatening injury. It wasn't easy to think of planning murder, let alone to
act on it. I suddenly had a rush of sympathy for Gilfeather.
Once, I had been irritated by his reservations about killing
Morthred on Xolchasbarbican. Now I discovered it was one
thing to go along with a murder when someone else did it,
and quite another when you had to hold the weapon yourself.
It was a salutary lesson, and one I deserved.

My efforts to speak did not progress as fast as I'd hoped.
My first attempts were abortive—nothing emerged that resembled the sounds I was trying to make. In the end, I decided I would have to learn to talk the same way a baby
does. I started by making random noises and then I concentrated on replicating the sound at will. It was weird, at first.
A bird's sounds come from deep down in the chest and have
little to do with movements of the tongue and beak. Now I
had to learn to manipulate my tongue, move my lips and
make the sounds in my throat.

Oddly enough, I found it was easier to whistle than it was
to speak. I could imitate the sounds of Dustel Island birds
by whistling much more successfully than I could form recognizable words. In despair, I wondered if I would truly
ever be human . . .

I was still learning the rudiments of speech, still building
up my lower body strength, when Stracey upset all our plans
anyway.

ON THE WAY TO XOLCHAS STACKS FROM
Porth, the *Amiable* had been a hellish ship. Morthred and his
two true dunmagickers had revelled in the torture and mental
anguish of the crew, and they'd had a boatload of subverted
sylvs to back them up. There had been nothing too base, too
horrendous, too perverted, for them to contemplate. The
only thing that had kept the worst excesses under control
was the need to have enough healthy sailors to man the ship.
What they had done to Flame, what they had made her do to

others, would haunt me for the rest of my life. But they were dead now, all but Stracey and Gabania, and those two were amateurs by comparison. Lyssal held herself aloof from their games, although Kayed swore he was more scared of her than the other two. "She may not hanker after torturing us," he muttered, "but she's both smart and without heart, that bitch. If she thinks anyone is going to be a danger to her, she'll just have them jettisoned. Without a second's thought. And she doesn't even have to do it herself. All she has to do is order one of my crew to drop them over the railing, and they'll obey like it was the most natural crudding thing on all the high seas." He spat and ran a finger over the blade of the knife extending from his arm.

On my worst days, I wondered if he was right.

In the end, though, it was Stracey who uncovered my presence. A timid woman, Stracey, but with a sly and nasty streak. I suspected the Stracey who had once worked for the Keeper Council had not been much different, just less vicious and possibly more righteous in her games. This Stracey was pure sneaking evil. She liked being pleasured, and she was working her way through the more presentable members of the crew. Her tortures were petty, yet cruel.

She had enhanced her appearance as a sylv, and was continuing to do the same now that she was dun, but my Aware sight seemed to have been affected by my transition to my human body. When I glimpsed her around the crew quarters, the dun was thicker and more tangible than it had been when I was a bird. It was true of Gabania and Lyssal as well: when I saw them, I glimpsed them only through a dun-colored fog. That wasn't the way it was supposed to be. Awareness was not supposed to obscure vision, but enhance it. I, however, had lost my sharp avian eyesight, with its ability to see a range of colors and distant details in ways humans never do, and what I had been granted in return was flawed.

On the fourth day out from Xolchasbarbican, Stracey wandered down into the crew quarters looking for some poor sod to torment, and found me instead. I was in my hammock, alone, babbling away like a baby in its cradle. "Ba-ba-ba-ba. Ma-ma-ma-ma. Ta-ta-ta-ta . . ."

"Well now, what have we here?" she drawled, interested. "I don't remember seeing you before."

I tumbled out of the hammock, and stood mute, eyes downcast.

"*Why* haven't I seen you before?"

I shrugged and made a few strangled noises. Terror was remembering I could not lift my wings and fly away . . .

She smiled, apparently thinking I was too scared to talk. She took a step forward and cupped my chin, digging the nails in. "Well, pretty face, you don't need to be scared of me. Perhaps we can have some fun, eh?" Then her eyes scanned downwards, and she added in amusement, "Well, perhaps not. A little wasted away in the nether regions, aren't you! Do you have anything at all under those culottes, mister skinny thighs? Why don't you just pull them down and let me have a look, eh?"

I smelled the coercion. I could almost smell her lust, her curiosity, her appetite. And I knew I had to do what she said, or she'd know I was not affected by her magic. I untied the waist of the culottes and lowered them. And experienced an indignity that was more than just embarrassment; it was deeply humiliating.

"Syr-lady, he's a simpleton."

I had never been so glad to hear the captain's voice. I risked a glance, to see him outlined in the doorway. I guessed he had seen Stracey head off down the forward hatchway and had followed her. "Not much use for anything, I fear," he added, trying to sound casual. "Underdeveloped in more ways than one."

Her glance flickered downwards at my non-responsive body. "So I see."

"I hired the useless piece of shit as a cabin boy, but in truth he has never been much crudding use. His skin burns too easily and he never seems to tan, so we put him to work below decks, or polishing the brass at night. He doesn't seem able to talk, though he understands well enough. We call him Tadpole."

She laughed at that, a tinkle of malice. "I can see why." She thought for a moment, then said, "The Lady Lyssal is in need of a personal servant. She has been complaining." She laughed, and clapped her hands. "This one . . . why not? Tadpole, you are about to become the, er, *handmaiden* to the Castlemaid of Cirkase. Come with me." I grabbed up my culottes and she hauled me out the door. A moment later we were in what had once been the captain's cabin, and was now Lyssal's, and my human form was face to face with her for the first time.

"Look," Stracey said, "I have someone for you! Isn't he funny? He will make the perfect servant for you!"

Lyssal had been facing the mullioned windows at the stern of the ship, and she turned to look only slowly. Her glance at me was perfunctory. I couldn't see her face under the obscuring mist of dun. "More like the perfect buffoon. He doesn't look very bright," she remarked. "But never mind, he will do. Leave us, Stracey."

Stracey seemed disappointed at her lack of enthusiasm. She pouted. "He's mute," she said on her way out of the cabin. "But not deaf."

"Good." Lyssal came across to me.

I lifted a foot and tried to scratch my neck—once a nervous habit of mine. Immediately off balance, I thought better of it and lowered my leg. I felt her stare, but my gaze could not penetrate the dunmagic to meet her eyes. She will know me, I thought. Of course she will know me. How can she not? We have loved each other!

But her tone did not change. "You will do all I ask of you, without question," she said. I smelled the coercion.

That hurt more than I would have thought possible. Flame did not know me . . . Lyssal was enslaving me. Making me into another stringed marionette to dance at her whim. Or so she thought.

She continued, "You will not harm me in any way, and will always think of my comfort first. Is that understood?"

I nodded. I remained frozen in place, in an agony of indecision. Morthred was dead. Maybe Flame was already beginning to struggle back from underneath what he had done to her. Maybe I could tell her now and we could fight it together . . . I could snatch up a piece of parchment and write it all down . . . tell her who I was.

And yet, I could discern nothing that told me she was throwing off the coercion. Her expression—what I could see of it—was remote, her voice indifferent. You fool, I thought, grinding down the hurt to something I could understand. This is not Flame, this is a dunmagicker. Forget it, and you die . . . Be patient, Ruarth. Patient.

She gave me the verbal outline of what I needed to do, most of which I already knew anyway. I knew how she liked her tea in the morning, and how she liked her bath water. I knew what she liked to eat. Once upon a time, there had been very little I did not know about Flame Windrider.

And so I started work as Lyssal's slave.

I knew there was something I wasn't understanding, right from the beginning. As the days passed and we were further away from the moment of Morthred's death, the more confused Gabania and Stracey became. They didn't cease to be dunmagickers, but they did seem less dangerous and more unfocused. I would have expected the same to happen with Lyssal, but it didn't. She should have been *less* affected by subversion than Gabania and Stracey. She had not been subverted as long as they had, surely. However, the dun in her seemed to grow stronger, not weaker. The blue-silver of sylv faded; she glowed with dun-red. I was forced to acknowledge Morthred's death didn't seem to have had the effect we had hoped it would. The only thing giving me some reassurance was that she did not seem as mindlessly cruel as other subverted sylvs. She never physically hurt anyone on the ship. She kept them coerced into submission and obedience, but that was all. When she gave orders to me, it was without threat; when I did as she asked, it was without praise. If the end result was not up to her standard, she was scathing in her criticism, brutal in her spite, but she never went further than that.

But when I looked for signs of my Flame, of the gentle loving woman I had known, I could not find them; this creature was hard and cold and remote.

* * *

STRACEY WAS THE FIRST TO DIE.

It sounds simple when I say the words. And in a way, it was.

Kayed came down to wake me one night. "Stracey's up on deck, Tadpole," he hissed in my ear. "Alone. Leaning on the railing." He did not dare say more than that, but the look he gave me was clear.

It was just as he said: she was leaning over the railing near the stern, watching the wake. I came up behind her bare-footed, and toppled her over before she even had time to react to my presence. She fell soundlessly, hit the water and disappeared. She couldn't swim, I already knew that. In her terror, she didn't have the time or the thought to blast the ship out of the water.

Kayed came up, grinned at me and clapped me on the shoulder. He had been engaging the helmsman's attention so the sailor would not notice what was happening behind him. "One overboard, two more to go," he whispered.

I shrugged off his hand and went below, back to my hammock in the crew quarters. I didn't sleep.

I'd just killed a woman. The ease of the death was in itself an insult; no one should have their life ended in such a facile manner. Useless to tell myself she was better off dead, that her real self would have preferred death to what she had become. I'd done something that would have been unthinkable just a few short days before, when I was still a Dustel bird. I had murdered a human being.

Something inside changes when you do that. You have a secret place inside your soul where you dare not go. It lingers there for a lifetime, and something tells you that when you die you will have to face the accounting for that death. You hide it away, don't think about it if you can help it, and rationalize it when you can't. Not that I found it easy to excuse: how could I, when I was planning to save Flame from the same fate, and *not* kill her? To make my reasons for Stracey's death genuine, I had to intend Flame's death as well. And I didn't.

But do you know what the true horror is? The second death is made easier by the first, because you have already lost your innocence.

GABANIA DIED TWO WEEKS LATER. SHE was cautious after Stracey went missing. She never went near the railing. She coerced one of the sailors to follow her about when she was up on deck; he had instructions to protect her, no matter what.

But still, my chance came and when it did, I took it. A storm arose as we beat around the south-west of Breth Island, an area famous for the wrath of its oceans. Gabania and her guard were up on deck when they were both swept off their feet and into the scuppers by a wave. Under the pretext of wanting to help Gabania, I scrambled over to her side. Terrified, she clung to me as another wave came sweeping across the deck. I gripped the railing with both hands and kneed her in the stomach just as the water hit us. She gasped and slithered under the rail into the ocean. I still remember the look of disbelief on her face. Everyone else was too busy trying to save themselves to notice—in fact, it was a close call for me too. Only the strength in my arms as I hugged the railing prevented me from following her over. And I had no idea whether I could swim or not.

That particular storm was the only time Lyssal was seasick on the voyage. The next day she was on her feet again, apparently unaffected, even though it was still rough enough to make me queasy. The deaths of the two dunmagickers seemed not to bother her at all. Even more odd, she did not show any particular interest in *how* they had died. It didn't seem to occur to her to wonder if she would be next.

I didn't know what to think. Nothing about her subversion was predictable.

After the two women vanished, she maintained the coercion of the sailors herself. Part of every day she spent discussing our route and our position with Kayed. She didn't coerce him to carry out specific orders with regard to the sailing of the ship, though, but merely urged him to speed the journey by whatever safe means possible.

She had her reasons for wanting to arrive soon, of course, of which I knew nothing. I had not been privy to Blaze and Gilfeather's conclusions about who was subverting her, and I did not realize she had a valid reason to want to climb into the Breth Bastionlord's bed at the earliest possible moment. Nothing about her made sense to me; the only thing I was sure of was I didn't want her killed to save her from dun. Blaze had rescued her last time; there had to be some way for us to do it this time. Gilfeather would find a cure. Or we would force the Keepers to sylv heal her. Something. I would never give up, never.

THREE DAYS BEFORE WE WERE DUE TO arrive in Brethbastion, Captain Kayed sought me out in the crew quarters, late at night. "Meet me in the wardroom," he whispered in my ear, waking me up. "Now."

I rolled out of my hammock, and followed him.

"She's planning something," he told me bluntly as I seated myself opposite him at the mess table. "She doesn't intend for us to sail into Brethbastion with the harbour pilot at the helm. Here, you want some rum?"

I refused the drink and thought about what he'd said. He slapped some chalk into my hand and rapped the wooden boards of the table. "Tell me what's going on," he barked.

"Ship drenched with dun," I wrote. "Glows with it." It swirled around me until I was endlessly caught in its entrails, my sight blurred by its pervasiveness, but I didn't tell him that.

He understood what I was getting at right away. "You mean Awarefolk would spot it a mile off and have the town guard alerted. And in Brethbastion, there's bound to be officials who are Awarefolk."

I nodded.

"I thought it might be something like that. She's been using coercion on us so long we're all red to you, aren't we?"

"Yeth. Yesss."

He gave a derogatory sneer at my lisp, and then said, "She has been asking me about ways in which she can disembark somewhere quiet. I am afraid she's going to leave the ship and then blow us all to smithereens with dunmagic before we can sail away. So none of us can say what happened to us . . ."

I shook my head. "No. Won't."

"How can you be so sure?"

I wrote: "I know her. She's not like others. You can see that."

"She's a *dunmagicker*," he said in disgust. "That's all I see. Tadpole, you're not coming under her spell, are you? She *can't* just walk away and leave us all alive. The dun coercion will wear off, and there's not one of us who wouldn't tell the first Keeper ship or Breth guard what we have endured aboard this vessel." He leaned over the table and hooked the end of his forearm knife into my collar. He pulled me until I was almost nose to nose with him. "You have to kill her. Tomorrow. Or we're all dead." Dun curled from his torso to his throat, squeezing. He choked and grabbed at it, but there was nothing tangible there to touch. With enormous effort, he calmed and gradually the dun wisped away.

I shook my head. "No."

He laid the edge of the knife along my neck. "Are you daft, man? She could tell me to sail to the ends of the world, and by the time I had broken free of her spell, that's where we'd be. Without food or water. In the middle of the ocean. And you are the only Trenchdamned frogspawn of a man who can stop her from killing us whatever way she chooses. *Do you understand me?*"

I jerked my head away. "Yess."

"Then do it."

I took up the pen once more: "I promise I won't let you or your ship or your crew be hurt."

"Blue barnacles, you *are* crazy! How can a runt like you make any such promise? The only way you can stop her is to—" He thought better of what he had been about to say as dun teased around his face, and said instead, "What are you going to try to do? Reason with a dunmagicker? Chat to her, friendly like, and suggest she lets us go? Crabdamn it, Tadpole, she may not be able to kill you direct, but she can coerce one of us to kill you, and we would do it as easy as swabbing a deck! And that's exactly what she will do once she realizes she's been harboring one of the Aware on this ship." He ached to kill me himself, I could tell. He wanted to rage at me, slice me into submission with that knife of his. But I was the only hope he had. If he was right about the depth of Lyssal's inhumanity, then I was the only hope any of them had.

I returned his stare, and in the end it was his eyes that dropped. "Please," he said. He was not a man accustomed to begging, but he swallowed his pride to do it, which made his words all the more powerful. "Please, Ruarth. I don't know what your history is, although I can see enough to know you cared for what this bitch once was. But she's not that any more, and if you think she is, then we are all going to die."

I picked up the chalk again, and started to write: "I must know something first. How do you hold on to your freedom to think, how can you urge me to kill her, when others of your crew cannot?"

"I am Kayed," he barked at me. "No one gets the better of me. No one!"

I stared at him, unmoving.

He took a deep breath. "It's about having a piece of yourself no one can touch. You keep it here." He tapped his chest.

I waited for more of an explanation than that, and finally he gave it to me. "When I was an able seaman, a long time ago, I sailed with a bastard of a captain who had a passion for flogging. I did something to make him as wild as a whirlstorm and earned myself thirty lashes. An old salt on that ship—he gave me some advice. 'Make yourself a place no one can touch,' he said. 'Inside. Where the lash can't get to. Where no one but you can go.' I've had that place ever since. No one can touch it, not even a bitch of a dunmagicker."

I thought: that's how she does it. She keeps part of herself in a place the dun cannot go. But for how long?

"Ruarth, I'll beg you, if that's what it takes. This is my

ship and these are my men. How can I let them go to their
deaths as meek as squid drawn to the night lights of the
squid boats?"

I wrote some more: "You have no choice but to trust
me, and to trust my knowledge of her. I am going to go
ashore with her when the time comes, and you and your crew
are going to sail away from Breth. None of you will be able
to speak of this, to anyone, ever. That will be the price for
your freedom."

"How will she know we will hold to such a condition?
And how do *I* know *she* will hold to such a bargain?" he
asked.

"You don't," I wrote. "You will, however, be coerced to
keep silent. Like most coercion, it will last for a week or so.
After that you will be able to speak of it—she won't be able
to stop you—but she will weave a curse on you all. Anyone
who speaks of it to someone who is not on this ship will
shortly die."

He looked at me, frowning. "She can do that?"

I nodded. "And more. She is a dunmaster." It was all a lie,
of course. When coercion wore off, it was gone forever and
there was no such thing as a curse.

He sat there for a while, his shoulders slumped as
he whittled a few notches in the table edge with the knife
strapped to his forearm. When he looked up again, it was to
glare his frustration.

"You have no choice," I wrote.

"No," he agreed heavily. "None."

A moth flew by. I snapped it out of the air and ate it.

Another tedious day, listening to Sister Lescalles praying—and telling me I should spend more time on my knees.

Does she never stop?

All right, I admit it, sea travel is horrendously boring. I know everyone on this vessel. I know their names, their histories, their ailments, their stories told and retold in their tedious voices. I know I am an ungracious wretch to be complaining when this is what I wanted . . . !

Thank goodness I can slip away to the Glory Isles whenever I want. I can listen to those far off voices of people who lived the bulk of their lives a long time ago in another land. I can whisper to them and wish them well, and tell them I am coming.

At the moment it is the Castlemaid who captures my imagination. Flame Windrider: there is romance in the very name, and in the way the others speak of her, for she only has voice through the others. Does that mean she died?

I could ask Shor, of course, but I won't. I suppose Nathan would tell me if I asked, but no, I shall read on and find out for myself.

Dear God, I feel for her! The horror of her situation. I tremble just to think of it, and sometimes I wonder why I was so mad to leave the safety of Kells for a land as barbaric and as mysterious as these Isles . . . Poor Flame. I shall pray for her tonight, and Lescalles will think me pious.

CHAPTER 8

NARRATOR : RUARTH

I TOOK A KNIFE FROM THE GALLEY, JUST in case, and went to Lyssal's cabin.

I didn't knock; I just opened the door and entered. That she had not barred the door from the inside was a mark of how safe she felt.

It was already well into the midnight watch, yet she had not gone to her bunk. She was standing looking out the stern window at the white splash of the wake in the darkness of the sea. There was a lantern lit, and the slight smell of burning oil permeated the cabin. She had her back to me, but she heard the door open, and turned. She had evidently not used magic for a while; the wisps of dun around her were thin, enabling me to see her face. The nightgown she wore, something taken from Morthred's pilfered goods, was a beautiful thing, falling from the tiny straps to the floor in a pleated bell of satin and lace. Standing there in the softness of the lamplight, she was almost beyond beauty.

For the first time in my life I felt the stirrings of human

male desire. I wanted to let my mind explore the feeling further, I wanted my body to experience the sensation. I made a movement, wanting to enfold her somehow in my wings, to touch her breasts. It was an effort to change direction, to focus on what was more important.

She must have been surprised to see me—Tadpole would never ordinarily have entered without permission—but there was no sign of it in the smoothness of her expression. "Yes?" she asked. I don't think she quite believed I had done something as bold as this.

I closed the door behind me, and stood there—mute—for a little too long.

A faint frown wrinkled her forehead. "Is there something wrong?"

I knew I must speak. I knew I would have only one chance. I formed the word, and forced it out. I was almost taken aback when it fell into the silence with the resonance of a man's voice, deep and full. "Flame . . ."

In that moment everything changed. The coldness of the gaze, the composure of her stance, the cruelty of her indifference—it all melted away as if it had never been. She was just Flame, my Flame. And she recognized me.

"*Ruarth?*" No more than an incredulous whisper. "You are *Ruarth?*"

I nodded.

What I saw next was more than I could bear. The momentary spark of pristine joy. The dun struggling to reassert itself, to dominate. The Flame she had once been fighting back, and triumphing. But behind the despair and love in her gaze, I could see the cruelty of her future crouched, poised to reclaim her.

I wanted to speak, but I didn't have the words as yet. So I whistled. It seemed to come more naturally, more easily to that tangled mouth of mine. I whistled the words in the Dustel tongue, and gestured the sign language of my people with my body. I didn't care that I must have looked ridiculous, a figure of fun. Nothing mattered, but that I speak to her.

You can fight this. Morthred has no control over you

*any more—it is just you, now. Flame, the bastard's dead.
You can win.*

She seemed to understand. I took a step closer, wanting
so much to touch her, to preen her hair and skin. To nibble at
her cheek with my beak . . .

She stammered, "I thought you were dead. I saw the Dustels fall, on the wharf. I thought you were one of them . . ."
Tears were trickling down her cheeks. I stepped still closer,
wanting to put my arms around her in a human gesture, but
she held up her hand to stay me. "No. This cannot be."

I saw her battle. She panted with the exertion of keeping
the dun at bay, of holding back the overwhelming avalanche
of it. She whispered, as if that way she could keep the dun
from hearing. "Ruarth—you have to kill me. God knows, I
have tried to do it myself but he won't let me . . ."

He's dead, Flame. He can't do anything to you any more!

She shook her head in a sorrow so searing that it stilled
me. I knew then there was more, something even more terrible that I would have to know. And have to learn to live with.
I thought for a moment I was going to suffocate on horror,
even before she said the words. "Not Morthred," she said.
"Not this time. His son. Ruarth, you *must* kill me. I had
given up hope that there was anyone to help. He won't let me
do it myself . . . I have tried. So many times I have tried. But
you can do it. In the name of the love you bear me, you
must."

I didn't understand. I took another step towards her, but
she hurriedly retreated. "Don't! It's all I can do to keep him
at bay. If you were to touch me . . . Charnels, Ruarth, you
must end this! If ever you have loved me, even a little,
you must end this now! How can you bear to see me as a
dunmagicker?" Even then I thought I heard the taint of
Lyssal's hatred under her agony.

*They are all working to save you, Flame. Blaze, Tor, Gil-
feather . . . you mustn't give up hope.*

She whispered a reply, so softly I could barely hear it
over the sound of wind and waves and the creaking timber.
"I cannot survive that long . . . he grows stronger, day by
day."

I didn't stop to think about what she was saying. I was so frightened I would lose her again, lose the Flame I knew to the dun, and I had to focus on the reason I'd come to speak to her. *Listen—I will stay with you when you go ashore. You can trust me, the sodding dun can trust me not to harm you. In return you will allow Kayed and his ship to sail away.* I was stumbling over the words, unable to gesture with my tail, my hands awkward, the whistled notes pitched so differently from a bird's they seemed a foreign language to my ears. I had no idea if I was making sense to her. *Tell him a dunmagicker's curse will kill them all if they speak of you again after the coercion wears off. It will keep them silent. Sailors are a superstitious lot.*

"Ruarth, please—"

And then, weakened, under siege, she was gone, as if someone had shuttered the lamp within. The person who stared back at me now was Lyssal, dunmagicker. She pursed her lips in thought. I could see her considering if deception was possible or worthwhile, wondering how to turn such a bargain to her benefit.

"All right, you have an agreement," she said finally. "I don't care what happens to them, as long as they don't interfere with my plans. But you . . . it will be exquisite to watch your pain. Ruarth. Tadpole. Who would have thought it?" She laughed and came forward to touch me. To run mocking fingers down the side of my face in parody of a lover's touch. "Yes, stay with me, be my protector. Have you any idea of how ridiculous you look? Skinny-shanks! Fish-underbelly! Whatever made you think a woman like me could possibly love a man like you?" The sneer was scathing. It seized on all my fears and gave them voice. "I look forward to the day I take a real man to my bed once more," she added. "How will it feel next time, Ruarth? Will you be riddled with jealousy next time, knowing at last it *could* be you—but never will be?" I felt my confidence shrivel, my self-esteem shrink. Tadpole. Skinny-shanks. Dustel nobody. And she was the Castlemaid.

I blocked off the thoughts. It was the dun speaking. It had to be.

"Get out of here," she said.

I went, and her mockery followed me in her laughter.

I TRIED TO SLEEP, AND FAILED. I ROSE, wrote another message for Captain Kayed on a piece of parchment I had stolen from Lyssal's cabin, and went up onto the deck. He'd been unable to sleep too, and had come topside to take over the helm. I handed him the message. His knife-hand still on the wheel, he read the words by the light of the lantern hanging over the compass. "It's done," I had written in my poorly penned script. "You all sail away co-erced never to speak of her again, under pain of a dun death if you do."

He looked up at me, then deliberately opened his hand. The parchment whipped away into the wind and disappeared over the stern. "And you *trust* her?"

I didn't reply.

I went to the stern and leaned against the taffrail. Beneath me was Lyssal's cabin. The *Amiable*'s wake left a path on the ocean lit by the glow of a stern lamp. Perhaps she watched it too, from her cabin's mullioned windows.

I needed to think about what she'd said, but my mind kept skittering away from it. *Not Morthred.* His son. Morthred's *son* had subverted her? It didn't make sense. There had hardly been a moment when I had not been with Flame, from the time we had left Cirkase, to the moment we had landed on Xolchas Stacks. If there had been another attempt by someone else to subvert her, I would have known. I would have seen. If Morthred had a son who'd somehow ap-proached her, then I would have met him.

I forced my mind to concentrate. I went through our journey, step by step. I reviewed in my mind all that had happened, all the people we had met, and nothing came to me that made sense. There had been no one Morthred had acknowledged as his son. There had been no man who . . .

But a son didn't have to be an adult. A child, perhaps. I tried to think of children who had crossed our path . . . Dek.

No, he'd known who his father was, and Dek was Aware. Then who?

And then it hit me.

Oh no, mercy, no, not that.

But the thought had come and I was stilled. My heart stopped beating, my life momentarily paused as I contemplated the unthinkable.

She could prevent conception. All sylvs could.

But Morthred had been more powerful than she was . . .

Trench take all the Gods of Glory. We had been so stupid. So damned arrogantly sure of ourselves.

She was pregnant with the dunmaster's child. What was it he had told Blaze? *My legacy will span the archipelago.* Flame was bearing his legacy, she was contaminated from within. Tainted. And every passing day was going to increase her defilement as the child grew.

I collapsed onto the deck, kneeling, suddenly with no strength in my legs to hold me up. I cowered, rested my face against the railing and cried. It was a new experience. For a moment I didn't even know why my sight blurred, why my cheeks were wet.

Oh, Flame, I am so sorry. So very, very sorry.

She was right. I would have to kill her. There was no hope. The dun would grow in strength as the child grew; it would make her into a monster capable of conceiving any evil and carrying it out with relish. Sooner or later she would kill me, I knew that now. Perhaps not just yet—there was enough of my Flame in there somewhere to prevent it at the moment—but one day.

To save my life, I should abandon her. To save her sanity, I should kill her. To save the world, I should kill her child.

I wept as the ship sailed on.

THREE WEEKS AFTER WE LEFT XOLCHAS Stacks, Kayed dropped Lyssal and me at a beach down the coast from Brethbastion, together with Morthred's looted treasures—ten huge sea chests of the stuff. Lyssal left the ship with one last burst of coercion and a curse for everyone on board. They were to collect what supplies and water they needed from a nearby fishing village, and then sail away and not stop until they were back in Porth.

To be quite honest, until the *Amiable* sailed away, I had not been sure she would keep her side of the bargain; the actions of a dunmagicker were never governed by compassion, after all. I had banked on there being enough of the old Flame there, leashing as best she could the worst viciousness of the magic within her. An unborn child could hardly be specific about what she was to do; it just supplied the subverting magic. Or so I supposed.

And she was indeed still thwarting the dun to a degree, something I doubted any of the subverted sylvs had managed to do before her. Perhaps it was because her source of contamination was still an embryo, but I chose to believe it was because she was a kind and gentle human being with a compassionate heart. The dun could try to overwhelm that, but she held on to a core that was true. I was proud of her. I loved her still. I was as foolish as ever, believing something that possibly had no more grounding than salt on a sea wind.

We stayed on that beach for over a week, sheltering in a fisherman's hut built of driftwood, a place used only in the mussel-collecting season, if the shucked shells stacked behind the shack were any indication. Every day I went out and bought food from a nearby farmhouse. I paid in cash—one thing we had plenty of was money. In fact, setu coins, jewellery, ornaments, gold bars, silver ingots: we had it all.

Most of the rest of my time was spent digging a pit to bury the bulk of this treasure. Lyssal made me move all the shells from behind the hut first, then dig a hole deep enough for all but one of the trunks. Once I had buried them, the mussel shells were placed back on top to cover the evidence of my excavation.

Even when I had finished this task, we didn't set out immediately for Brethbastion. Lyssal was still alive with color because of all the magic she had expended. It played over her skin, lingered at the back of her eyes, clung to the tips of her fingers and intertwined with her hair. And the color was dun-red. Any of the Awarefolk would be able to identify her as a dunmagicker at a glance, and Lyssal knew if she wanted the Bastionlord to marry her, she could not risk arriving openly tainted with dun.

It was a strange interlude. She taunted me all the time, in different ways. She delighted in calling me names rooted in my appearance, of which Tadpole and Skinny-shanks were among the most innocuous. She mocked me for my devotion to her, calling me lapdog, bootlicker, leech and other even less flattering terms. She taunted me with her body, undressed in front of me, ran her hand up and down her thighs, bathed naked in the shallows of the ocean, brushed close to me in passing.

"Don't you want me, Tadpole?" she would ask, and lick her bottom lip with the tip of her tongue.

My response was always the same. I would smile and look away.

"Why don't you come here and kiss me?" she asked one day. She had just emerged from the sea, naked as usual, and still dripping.

I stepped away and handed her a towel.

"I could kill you so easily, you know. One night while you sleep . . ."

I nodded.

Her eyes flashed fire. "How can you be so sure I won't, spindle-thighs?" She stepped in closer and cupped my face.

I removed her hand firmly, holding her away from me.

"How will you like it when I bed the Bastionlord, Ruarth? How will you like it when he sl—"

I released her and walked away.

It was a dangerous game I played; I knew that, but it was the only way I knew how to play.

The next morning when I awoke, she spoke to me again. This time her voice was more uncertain, betraying a doubt in her mind, and the question she asked was unexpected, coming then as it did, and not much earlier. I can see that scene still: the sunlight streaming into the hut through the numerous chinks between the driftwood boards, Lyssal lying on the bedding she'd made the sailors leave behind from the captain's cabin, me curled up on the floor on some sacking.

That did not worry me too much; I'd never slept in a bed, after all. I was more bothered by the pain of my sunburn, and all the sand fly bites that made both days and nights a misery. I envied the fact that the remnants of her dun kept insects away from her.

I had been awake a while, just lying there and trying to see a solution to a situation that seemed to have no possible resolution, when I heard her stir. She rolled over in her bedding and looked at me. "Did you kill Gabania and Stracey?" she asked.

It was the first time she had ever shown any interest in their disappearance. That she had asked now might mean she was more rational—but it could well be the rationality of an evil mind, not one returning to sanity.

I tried to reply, to lie. And couldn't. Not to her. Anyway, if she thought about it, it was obvious. I had been the one person on board the *Amiable* not coerced into a total inability to hurt the dunmagickers, and they certainly would not have been likely to jump overboard by themselves.

So I just lay there, looking at her.

"Ruarth, Ruarth, what am I to do about you?" she asked softly. "If you can kill them, then you can kill me."

I shook my head and gestured my negation with my hands to make it doubly clear.

"Perhaps not," she agreed. "But you *could* talk to people in Brethbastion. You could spoil all my plans by telling them I'm subverted."

I can't talk, I signed to her. That was no longer actually true. I had been practicing diligently every day when I found a private moment, both on board ship and since we had arrived on the beach. I spoke to the farmers where I bought the food, and they understood most of what I said now. I just didn't want her to know. I signed, *If I tell anyone in Brethbastion, they'll kill you. I won't do that.*

"You can write," she said. "You could send a letter to the Menod in Breth or in Tenkor. You could write to the Keepers. To Blaze. How can I take you with me? You will betray me. And I can't coerce you because you are Aware . . ."

I was silent. She was right, of course. It would be insane of her to let me accompany her to Breth, to allow me to live. The only reason I had survived so far was because the real Flame still lurked there within her somewhere, preventing her from taking the logical course, preventing Lyssal from killing me one night while I slept, or coercing someone else to kill me. It was just a matter of time . . .

We stared at each other, united by our past, our love and our regrets, divided by the dun that inhabited her.

You can't do it, I gestured.

"It's only a matter of time," she told me softly, echoing my thought, and I heard the lingering sorrow there, mixed with a gleeful anticipation that was all poison. "He grows in strength. He drips more dun into my body every day."

He's an embryo, I replied. *He can't think. He can't know. Not yet. Only you can do that, and you can resist.*

"And when he is born, you will kill him . . . because only if he is dead will your puling Flame have a chance. Or so you believe. How can I let you do that?"

It was true, everything she said was true, and I was silent.

"Ah, Ruarth, sometime before he is born, you have to die. What I am becoming will soon overcome what I was . . . and you will be the first to know." A warning. I heard the unspoken words Flame could not say: run, Ruarth, run now while you still can. Keep yourself safe.

My presence was a dilemma neither of us knew how to resolve. I could betray her in any of the ways she mentioned, but I didn't want her harmed. If the Keepers took her away, I couldn't be sure they would be able to heal her. Perhaps they would simply kill her, just as they had killed their own subverted sylvs. They may be a little less eager to do so, seeing that Lyssal was the Castlemaid, heir to a throne, and the potential consort of the Lord of Breth, but they'd do it if necessary.

And if I told the Menod, what good would that do? I knew Ryder dreamed of a cure for magic, but it was still just a dream. In the meantime it was more likely the Menod would think her better dead; better to free her soul, than have her soul contaminated against her will.

I stood up so that I could make myself understood better: *I will never betray you to the Menod. Or to the Keepers. Or to anyone who would harm you.*

She frowned and sat up. "There is something I am not understanding. What is it?"

It was difficult to find words easily expressed with human gestures, by human whistling, but I had to try. My life could depend on it. *We Dustels, we had so little protection against the dangers of the world while we were birds. Even a sodding magpie could spell our death. The only thing we had was our loyalty. To our families, to our friends, to our flock, to our people. Nothing else. To us, loyalty was honor. With loyalty to one another we could survive. And you, you Flame, you stayed with me, even though I was just a Dustel bird. You never wavered, although there was no guarantee I would ever be human. How can I walk away from you, though you may never be sylv again? I am here till one of us dies. And I will neither harm you, nor give you to another to be harmed.* I shrugged. *If you kill me, so be it.*

"And what of my child, Ruarth? I see you make no mention of him." She stood and came across to me, her hair still tousled, her eyes heavy with sleep. "I believe you. But I also believe your silences, what you have *not* said. You will kill my son, the first opportunity you get."

I shook my head, but she went to stand in the doorway for a moment, looking out at the ocean, a faraway look in her eyes. The red of dun, occasionally sprinkled through with silver like distant stars in the sky, still played over her skin. It was dulled now, and it no longer blocked the details of her expression, or hid subtleties from me.

"The day my child is born will be the day you die, Ruarth. I promise it. Until then, I shall revel in your misery."

I could not think of anything to say.

Still looking out at the sea, she said softly, "You think Blaze will come, don't you?"

I didn't reply.

"She won't, you know. She doesn't know where we went. She would never believe I would voluntarily marry the Bastionlord. Oh, she will hear eventually, of course, but by that time it will be too late." She looked back me, and smiled. "You see, Morthred told me how to subvert sylvs. By the time Blaze gets here, by the time the Keepers know what has happened on Breth, it will be far too late. I will have a power that will make Morthred's efforts on Creed look puny."

What makes you think you can do better than him? I signed.

Her smile broadened. "Because I will be taking over a power that is already there, Ruarth. The *temporal* power of the Bastionlord. Oh, it will take a little longer than I originally planned, thanks to your interference. With Gabania and Stracey and myself, and a shipload of coerced slaves, it would have been easier. We could have been more, um, frontal in our dun attack. But you had to kill those two bitches, and I find it hard to control so many people on my own. So now the plans are changed . . . but it's a minor point. Perhaps a little finesse will produce better results anyway." And she began to outline her plans to gain control of the Breth ruling house and its administration.

It was all I could do to listen in silence. I didn't know whether to be appalled she might succeed—or worried that when she failed she would bring so many innocent people down with her.

CHAPTER 9

NARRATOR : ELARN

A LITTLE WAY UP THE RIVER HUB, THE weirkeeper started the mechanism that allowed the barrier to sink under the water. The downflow spilled forth in a wall that sped on its way out of the river and into the Hub Race. I heard it coming a long time before I saw it churning up out of the darkness behind me. A Tenkor engineer, a man named Gormas Jaydon and, according to my father, a direct ancestor of ours, conceived the idea of a weir that could be winched from the bottom of the river to allow water to collect behind it. Then, when the ebb was at its height, the barrier could be quickly dropped to create an outgoing bore. After that, the prosperity of both The Hub and Tenkor was assured. There's a statue of Gormas in the main square in The Hub: a portly man, wearing the frilled, unflattering clothes in fashion some two hundred years ago. The plaque underneath doesn't mention Tenkor origins—But I digress.

Waiting there, hearing the whisper of rushing water become a hiss, hearing the hiss become a roar, feeling the excitement build . . . I lived for this. It was a drug, as potent as the starfish extract the Kitalfolk of Breth smoked to produce visions, or the anemone toxin some Southerfolk put under their tongues to give them hallucinations. This was living, this was *life*.

I kept Jesenda's sylv light in place in front of my runner, and conjured another to illuminate the wave behind. I was surprised at how easy it was to work the sylv again after all the years of resisting the temptation. It responded so easily to my thought, it came into being, vibrant and healthy, as if I had spent my days nurturing it, not resisting its call. It felt *right*.

The wave swung around the bend of the river and the sound doubled. It never failed to frighten: the crescendo that spoke of cataclysmic disaster rather than a tide. The view of white water—now stained silver-blue with magic—seemed to bear down on me like impending death. For a moment my heart stood still, as always, but then the instinct of a trained tiderider took over and I dug the paddle in. And finally, that magical moment when the water slid underneath the runner and lifted its burden as easily as a ripple under a floating leaf . . .

It never failed to cast its spell on me, a natural magic that had nothing to do with sylv or dun. The intense power of the wave made me feel I rode a living creature, an animal that could devour me if I made one careless move. The way in which the fearful sound died, as if the knowledge of its menace vanished now I was part of it; the way the tiderunner became part of me, an extension of me, the rider—I was a centaur of the ebb tide, a man-beast who rode the Hub Race home.

I knew all that, had known it before. This time, however, was different. I had never done it by night before. Never with sylv light casting its soft sheen on the water and sands of the Race. Never by moonlight. I had never been so attuned to the world about me. I had never been so alive before. What was it that made it that way? The unaccustomed working of magic? The glory of the sylv light pooling around me in the dimness of a one-moon night? The fact that earlier that day I had escaped death when others around me had died? That I had looked on Jesenda Duthrick and lost the arrogance of an intact heart?

Perhaps it was all that.

At one point in that journey I thought I had company. Something made me look to my right. Another person was in the wave, their face and shoulders exposed, riding the bore without the benefit of a runner. I was so startled I lost concentration and almost lost the wave. For a brief moment in time we gazed at each other, and shared the magic of the night. After the initial shock, I wasn't frightened. There was nothing threatening about my companion rider. I wondered if it was one of the mystical creatures sailors spoke about with awe and reverence. Sea-nymphs, they said, who sometimes rescued the shipwrecked and carried them to shore. Longboatmen and tiderunner riders spoke of them too. Wave sprites, they said, mischievous spirits who would upset your runner or your boat and toss you into the Hub Race.

After five minutes or so, the creature disappeared as mysteriously as it had come, sinking into the wave and out of sight, another memory of that journey down-Race, another part of the whole I can still recall. It is as clear to me as if it were yesterday: every nuance of it, every shadow, every dancing splinter of sylv light on shallows over the sands of the Race.

Although the night was imprinted on my soul as a joyful ride, it had a darkness at its heart. The knowledge that I felt no shame when I should have been consumed with it. The knowledge that I should have felt remorse. My cast-off lover had died, along with my child, and all I could feel was relief. Worse, I apparently felt so little for them that I'd found it easy to hanker after another.

Jesenda. Her name whispered on the breeze that whipped by me. Jesenda. Jesenda.

On the straighter stretches of the run, where the wave was well behaved and the depth even, I spared a thought for the things that troubled me about that day: Jesenda had made me see her sylv light. Duthrick was manoeuvring to be Keeper-lord. My father had been so intent on finding out what had happened in The Hub, that he had asked me to return in the dark, even knowing what that meant. And how could a man win the heart of a woman if she despised his past behaviour before he even began his courtship? Jesenda, I thought. I will win you. I will have you. I must.

I DID AS MY FATHER HAD ASKED. I WENT home from Tenkorharbour by the back routes so none of the Awarefolk, in the unlikely event they were on the streets at that hour, would be reminded—if they had ever known—that the son of the Guildean was a sylv. I delivered the letters to his bedroom in the hour before dawn, together with the news of the Keeperlord's death. I was exhausted. I felt like a mast bent before the gale, close to snapping with the tension of too much stress in too short a time.

I received no sympathy or words of concern from my father. If he was pleased I had taken the initiative to go to Duthrick rather than leave the letters with some nameless flunky, he made no comment. Instead, he ordered me to stay at home until the sylv aura had faded from around my body.

I should have left it there, but perhaps I was just too tired. Perhaps I'd just reached a point where I could no longer do all he asked of me without question, not when I received no thanks and no praise and no respect for doing so.

"And how am I to tell when the sylv color has dissipated and it is safe to go out, without asking one of the Aware?" I asked.

"Don't you go near one of the Aware!" he barked in alarm.

"I can hardly be blamed for the way I was born," I snapped back. "Why should I be ashamed to proclaim my sylv heritage?" We'd had this conversation before, of course, and I was a fool to start it again.

"It's an abomination!"

"Why not just God's will? I was *born* this way, after all."

"It's a filthy way of cheating your fellow men. Of blinding others to truth."

"I've never used it that way." I'd hardly used it at all.

"You would if I allowed you the use of it. How can you even *think* God would encourage the birth of such deformities as the magic-tainted?" Unspoken words hung between us. Even he could not quite bring himself to call me Sea Devil spawn, but I knew he thought it.

I stared at him and tried not to feel the hurt. "Ever since I returned to Tenkor to live, it has been *my* choice not to use my magic, not yours," I told him evenly. A year or two earlier and I would have shouted at him, but I was a little wiser now. "It is hardly against the law to use sylv in the Keeper Isles, not even here in Tenkorhaven. And you're a fine one to talk. It was you who asked me to return tonight with news. You had to know the only way I could do that was use a sylv light. If that was a sin, then it is on your shoulders."

I turned and left the room, and what I felt was not anger, but grief. Grief that I had never known a father's love.

For a brief moment I thought yet again of Cissy. It would have been good to fall asleep in her arms as the sun came up. But Cissy was dead, and I wasn't sure that running to a woman's arms was going to be the answer any more. There were some things I had to learn to deal with on my own. And anyway, the only woman I could think of now was Jesenda.

I STAYED AT HOME FOR A WEEK. AND I told myself I was doing it for *me*. I didn't want the added complication of everyone knowing that Elarn Jaydon, the Guildean's only son, was sylv. Not just then. It would have been hot news, arousing an old debate in Tenkor circles. Were Menod sylvs sinners simply because they were sylv? Or were they sinners only if they *practised* sylv? Or was there no sin unless they used their power to cheat and deceive? And by extrapolation, was Elarn a sinner or not? It was the last thing I needed just then.

So I stayed at home and sent a message to the Guild that I had a touch of influenza. I asked one of my father's manservants to visit the runner-maker to order a new waverunner, and to deliver a condolence letter to Cissy's family on his way back. I studied for my exams. And I delved into the Guildean's library, which was extensive, to find out all I could about the less well-known aspects of sylvmagic.

At first, all I could discover was what I already knew: magic could only be seen by the person who created it, and the Awarefolk. The effects of magic—such as illusions, sylv healing, dun sores, the solidity of warding and so on—were obvious to all, of course, but not the magic itself. And a sylv light was a ball of elementary pure magic, nothing more. It did nothing. It just was. As such, Jesenda's sylv light—and the light it cast—should only have been visible to herself or to someone who was Aware. I should not have been able to see it, control it, and certainly not—as I'd done in the end— dissipate it.

After five days of extensive research, I finally came up with information that touched on something similar: an account of a pair of sylv twins who could see each other's magic. At the end of the week, all I'd proved to myself was that there might occasionally be aberrations of magic. It was intriguing that Jesenda, based on a childhood memory, assumed I could see and use her sylv light. Intriguing, but not earth-shattering.

In fact, what was happening in Keeper politics that week was more interesting. The Keeper Council met, but neither Fotherly nor Duthrick emerged as a clear winner of the election for a new Keeperlord. It so happened another death among the Councillors resulted in an even number of members sitting on Council, and the vote was divided right down the middle. Much lobbying took place, and another vote was taken, in which several people were persuaded to change sides by the two factions. As a result, the vote was again a tie. When this happened a third time in as many days, the Keeper constitution was invoked and the solution proposed there was instituted. The oldest of the candidates, in this case Duthrick, was decreed to be Interim Keeperlord for the next six months, after which another vote would be taken. In other words, Duthrick had exactly six months in which to prove himself.

I turned up again at the Guild on the day of the first examination, and had to endure much ribbing about how I'd faked a bout of influenza so that I could study.

WHEN THE NEW WAVERUNNER WAS ready, I sent it to Jesenda on the next longboat. After that, every time I made a trip to The Hub, I met her for a lesson. I had thought it would be a wonderful opportunity to get to know her; I was only partially right.

I would ring the bell at the garden gate of the Duthrick mansion—the same house, as the family had not moved to the Keeperlord's residence—and a footman would conduct me to the boathouse. There I would wait until Jesenda appeared. She was always on time; it was pointless to be anything else when tides were involved. She was always alone and apparently impeccably dressed, carrying her parasol as if for a stroll through their gardens. Her dress, I quickly discovered, was only an illusion. She was already wearing her swimming costume—and only that. Of course, Hubbian swimming costumes were conservative outfits that covered from neck to ankle, but hers was a snug fit, outlining her attributes in a way that delighted me. Being a healthy young male, I could have spent the whole day sneaking surreptitious glances at that outline . . .

The trouble was that for each rest period I spent in The Hub, there was often only one daytime ebb tide. One wave, and sometimes Jesenda was not available then anyway. And then there was the difficulty of catching that wave—if she paddled too slow, for example, and missed it, then the lesson was over. Once she had dropped off the wave, the lesson was over anyway. Jesenda would thank me, we'd return to the family boatshed, and she'd disappear. It was frustrating. The only time we had together was when I towed her into position or back again afterwards (I used my tiderunner and paddle), or while we were waiting on our runners for the water to be released.

She never invited me into the house. I had to change in her boatshed, and by the time I was clothed, she would have already vanished into the house. When we did talk, she wanted to discuss the finer points of tideriding and how to improve her technique. She was one of the most intensely focused people I'd ever met.

Fortunately, she also took the time to teach me how to use my sylv more effectively. Until then, my sylv education had been desultory, at best. When I was a toddler, my father had been forced to employ a sylv to give me basic lessons, aimed, of course, at encouraging me to hide my skill. When I was banished from Tenkor to the mainland, I had befriended a sylv family nearby. The children there had helped me to develop my power rather than just control it, until, at twelve, I finally decided to deny my sylv heritage altogether and return to my father's household in Tenkor. Now Jesenda was only too happy to take my education in hand. "It's criminal how little you know," she growled. "That someone so powerful should have been left to train themselves . . . !"

I didn't know why she said I was powerful. After all, she was the one who possessed unusual magical strengths, not me. I struggled to learn from her, but was also reluctant to return to Tenkor reeking of sylvmagic. Someone would be bound to tell my father. My ambivalence annoyed her, of course.

"Oh, goodness gracious, Elarn," she said in exasperation one day, "you have to make up your mind whether you want to be sylv or not! You can't keep shilly-shallying around like a rudderless boat."

At the time, we were on our way back to the Duthrick boatshed, and I would have been much happier if we had been chatting about meeting up for a cup of chocolate afterwards, or something equally enticing, and less unsettling. Instead, there we were talking about my irresolute character. She was right, of course. I had to make a decision. When I was with her, I did not doubt my desire to be a sylv; back in Tenkor, things seemed less clear cut.

One thing I was sure of, I was hopelessly in love for the first time in my life. Now, so many decades later, I can say that—while it may well have been love—I was also consumed with a lust all the more attractive because the object of it seemed unattainable.

I was very young.

THE RESULTS OF THE FINAL EXAMINA-tions were put up on the board at the Guild. I passed every-thing, admittedly without any kind of distinction, but with sufficient scores to make me a Syr-tiderider, and a full Guild member. I don't remember much about that night. My friends whisked me away into the inns up in Tenkorhaven, and from there into some of the less salubrious bars down in the port, where I believe we ended up in a brothel towards morning. I truly don't remember much about the evening af-ter the first hour or so, and I'm fairly sure whatever hap-pened in the brothel didn't involve any action on my part, because I wasn't capable of anything by that time.

I woke the next morning in my bed at the Guild, with no clear idea of how I had got there, and the worst headache I've ever had in my life. Apart from that indiscretion, life went on much as usual. I avoided my father as much as pos-sible, and volunteered for as many extra trips to The Hub as I was allowed. Several weeks went by pleasantly enough— and then the schooner arrived. It flew a Mekatéen flag and had colorful woven sails of a type I had never seen before. I happened to be down on the wharves and, as I was off duty, I decided to take a closer look. I wasn't the only interested spectator; the ship had attracted a crowd. It was odd to see a vessel like that in the Keeper Isles; it was more a short-haul jobber, and there was a peculiar lingering stink about it, as if it carried manure. And yet it was riding so high in the water it must have had no more than ballast in its holds, and not even much of that.

When the pilot brought the ship into the docks, I saw that one of the passengers leaning on the railing was a man wear-ing Menod robes and the sigil of our religion, made of black coral, around his neck. I knew him by sight: he had been pointed out to me once by my father. "Name of Ryder," my father had muttered, "from the Stragglers. Watch him, Elarn, he has an odd history, and I don't trust a man who comes and goes the way he does. Rumour has it he's a swordfighter and an archer. Some say the High Patriarch is grooming him to be his successor." He'd snorted. "Why in God's name the Menod would need an armsman to lead them, I have no idea."

More recently, I'd heard Ryder was now a fully fledged Menod Councillor in spite of opposition from the more conservative on the Synod. He was apparently an unorthodox priest, one who did not bother to hang around the corridors of power or be sycophantic to the powerful. I admired that.

He was a handsome man of over thirty, a tall, broad fellow, but I barely glanced at him as the ship bumped against the dock and the hawsers were run out to the bollards. The man next to him was far more interesting. I'd never seen anything like him. He may have been about the same age, but he wasn't as tall or as broad. He was red-headed, with a gingery streaked beard to match. His clothing was striking: a beautiful silken shirt without a collar, buttoned at the wrists, a snug pair of dark green trews beneath. Both items of clothing were half concealed under an extraordinary wrap of rough-woven woollen material in dark green and red. Wild was the word that came to mind. His hair and beard grew every which way, or maybe he had just forgotten to comb either that morning, and the wrap was one of the untidiest items of clothing I'd ever seen—it appeared to have been roughly pleated then thrown on, rather than worn. I couldn't imagine where he was from.

While I was still gazing at him, and trying to look as if I wasn't, someone tugged at my jacket from behind. I turned to find one of the Dustels clutching at me. My heart sank. Just to see any of them always reminded me of the Fall, of things I didn't want to think about. He wore clothing, and so did the two children who were clinging to his legs, but none of them looked as if they were comfortable with being clad. Their shirts were untied, their culottes were on inside out and unbelted, their feet were bare. Few Dustels who had been birds wore shoes, not in those days.

"What do you want?" I asked, politely enough.

He made a series of silent gestures that meant nothing to me, pointed to the ship and then out to sea. He had not yet accustomed himself to being able to move his eyeballs in their sockets and so he shifted his whole head when he wanted to look at something. It was eerie, but common enough among the Dustels.

He said something incomprehensible, and indicated his children while waving his hands, fluttering his fingers and bobbing his head. I had no idea what he meant. Just looking at him, I felt pity. He was—like many newly human Dustels—short, broad-shouldered and skinny-legged. His skin had burned and peeled, until he resembled a lizard shedding. A fuzz of black had sprouted on his once bald pate, but he was still an unattractive sight.

And then the man on board the ship, the bearded fellow, called out to him. "Hey, friend," he said. "I understand ye, I think. But this ship sails for Mekaté in a day or two, not the Dustels."

The Dustel looked up at him, gestured some more, then whistled, a pretty, undulating tune.

The redhead nodded. "I'll see what I can do. Where are ye staying?"

Some more gestures and another bit of a whistle.

The redhead seemed to understand. "I'll come and see ye in a few days. What's your name?"

Another whistle. This time he had to repeat the sound several times before the man on the ship understood. I just gaped, disbelieving there was someone who could make sense of the gibberish.

The Dustel nodded his thanks and turned to go. I dug in my pocket and fished out a couple of wrapped candies, which I shoved into the hands of the children. The man grinned at me and shuffled away, a pathetic figure with his two silent offspring, a sight that made me somehow feel guilty for being whole.

I turned my attention back to the ship and the weird red-headed fellow. I tried not to look as if I was fascinated, but I caught the attention of the patriarch anyway. "Hey, Syr-tiderider," he called to me, identifying my Guild from the journeyman's uniform I now wore. "We have baggage to take on up to the Synod. Do you think you could round up a few strong lads and a pushcart for the heavy stuff?"

Had it been anyone else, I might have been indignant—I was a guildsman, not a wharf lugboy. But Ryder was a Menod Councillor, and that counted for a lot on Tenkor. I did as he asked. By the time I returned with three lugboys and a handcart, the harbourmaster had checked the identity and citizenship of the arrivals, and the baggage had been unloaded onto the wharf by the longshoremen. The largest item belonging to the two men was a huge wooden chest, cumbersome and heavy. We all had to lend a hand to load it onto the handcart, but no one seemed to have a rope large enough to fit around it so that it could be properly tied on. It was obviously about as much weight as the handcart could take, so the three lugboys started up the hill with their burden, two pulling and the third pushing from behind. I offered to help carry the remaining pieces of luggage, mainly because I was curious to know just who the red-headed man was. They accepted the offer and we started trailing up the hill behind the handcart. The redhead told me his name—Kelwyn Gilfeather—and said he was from Mekaté, but that seemed odd to me. I'd seen Mekatémen before, and they had been dark, clean-shaven Southerfolk. They hadn't dressed themselves in pleated blankets either. I wanted to ask him about the Dustels, and was still trying to think how to word the question, when he started the conversation himself.

"That Dustel fellow talking to ye," he said as we left the wharf, "he was just asking if the ship was bound for the Dustel Islands. He wants to go home. He wants to take his bairns home."

"Bairns?"

"Children."

"How can you understand what he said?"

"Well, let's say I understood their language when they were birds, a little. It sounds—and looks—rather different now. Wee bit of guesswork involved, but I think he was just trying to find a way to get to his ancestral home." He had the most extraordinary accent, full of rolling r's and with a musical lilt.

I thought about what he'd said. "Who *are* you?" I asked.

"Just a man who once called a Dustel bird a friend. He was probably killed on the day they . . . on the day they changed."

"Oh. I guess that means they were sentient, even when they weren't human?"

"Ach, aye, indeed."

"Where were you that day, may I ask?"

"Xolchas Stacks. What did ye say your name was, Syrtiderider?"

"Elarn. My father's Korless Jaydon, the Guildean of Tenkor." As we climbed the hill, now some distance behind the cart, I added, "They say here the Fall happened because a dunmaster died, a man called Morthred. Is that what you believe too?"

It was the patriarch who replied. "Yes. Yes, that's true. That's exactly what happened. The man who had ensorcelled the Dustels ninety years or so ago was killed."

Something about the way he answered alerted me. "On Xolchas?"

He nodded.

"You were *there*?"

He nodded again.

I wanted to go on asking questions, but something stilled me. There was a hardness about the patriarch that was almost frightening; he had a way of holding himself that told me to keep my distance. He was polite, there was no hint of patronisation towards someone of lesser rank, no contempt for a lad with too many questions—and yet I wanted to step away from him.

And then the whole world seemed to break loose.

We were climbing a steep narrow section of the route up to the Synod, where the lane squeezed between the rows of terraced houses. On one side a line of water butts positioned to collect rain from the roof guttering made the roadway even narrower. Twenty or more paces ahead of us, the lugboys were having trouble easing the handcart over some of the rough cobbles. To make things more awkward, a group of people, mostly women burdened with laden baskets, were descending the street on their way back from the market, and wanted to pass.

One of the lads tried to wrench the cart to the side, but the shaft he held broke with a sharp cracking sound. He fell, still holding the broken pole. The cart slewed and swung the other boy at the front into a house wall. He yelped and let go of the unbroken shaft on that side. The women with the baskets screamed and jumped out of the way. The lad who had been pushing from behind fell headlong onto the cobbles and the cart rolled back over him to hit the house wall on the other side of the street. It bounced off, straightened up and started to careen down the roadway, pitching over the cobbles and gathering speed. The huge chest jolted and jounced but somehow stayed where it was, still on the cart.

My mouth went dry. If we flattened ourselves against the house walls to the side we might be lucky and escape unscathed—or we might be crushed flat by either the cart or the chest. We could try to outrun it, but it was fairly flying now. Unless there was an open doorway, we might have to run all the way to the bottom of the hill—and I was sure we would not make it.

The cart hit a loose cobblestone and left the ground, only to slam down again. We had a split second to make a decision that could save our lives—or kill us.

Ryder and Gilfeather leaped for opposite sides of the lane, and unfortunately both of them grabbed me by an arm as they did so. For a moment I was pulled in two, anchored in the center of the street and the perfect target for a runaway load.

I didn't think, although if I'd had time to do so I probably still wouldn't have done it any differently. I called on my sylvtalent.

I shot two undulating ward poles of light upwards on either side of the street not far in front of me, and instantaneously melded them together with silver filigree, the sylv net of warding. I'd never worked sylvmagic so fast in all my life. The cart struck some more unevenness, jerked abruptly to a halt and hurled the chest straight at me like a stone from a catapult.

The crowd of people from the market screamed as one.

My concentration almost slipped in shock—even knowing the ward was there, it was still frightening to see that thing hurtling towards me. Ryder let go of my arm and Gilfeather jerked me to his side of the narrow street, trying to cradle me from the impact he thought was coming. He couldn't see the ward. The chest hit the filigree at the same moment, full force. The warding gave a little, bulging to cushion the box and then hold it in mid-air, rather like tangled prey caught in a cobweb. The cart tumbled onto its side and then rasped on downwards until it too reached the ward and was halted by the strands of magic.

I swallowed, licked my lips and blessed Jesenda for teaching me how to make a ward strong enough to stop something like that. Gently, I released the anchoring poles and allowed the sylv net to collapse inwards so that the chest was lowered carefully to the ground. Even to non-Aware watchers, it could not have appeared as anything other than magic: they might not have seen the sylv color, but they would have seen a chest halt miraculously in mid-flight and then sink down to the roadway.

I let out my breath, miserably aware there was no way I was ever going to be able to hide this use of sylv. Everyone in the street seemed to be looking at me: the women and their children, the lugboys, Ryder and Kelwyn Gilfeather.

I was just beginning to wonder if there was some way I could persuade everyone that Gilfeather had been the originator of the sylv, when he turned to me, grinning. "Skies above, Syr-sylv," he said, loud enough for everyone to hear, "that was quick thinking! Ye have undoubtedly saved my medicine chest from becoming little more than potpourri and kindling. How can I ever thank ye?"

"Don't mention it," I said, from behind gritted teeth.

Chapter 10

IT WAS THE PATRIARCH, TOR RYDER, WHO
took charge.

An efficient man, I'll give him that. He sent two of the
lugboys off to find another cart, and set the third, who was
bruised but otherwise unhurt, to guard the chest until they
were able to deliver it to the Synod. He directed the gathering crowd to clear the laneway of debris, and they obeyed
him too without question. His demeanour commanded respect. By way of contrast, one of the women—who had
bowed to him—spat in the gutter as I walked past. "Dustel
murderer," she muttered at me.

The accusation was so unjust, I could do no more than
stare at her in astonishment. Ryder came back, took my elbow and ushered me past her.

"Let's go on up to the Synod," he said.

I attempted to excuse myself. I did not want to appear at
the Synod building glowing like a silver beacon, thereby
proclaiming my sylvtalent to the whole Aware Patriarchy,

but Ryder overrode my objections. "I want to talk to you," he said.

I felt sick. The man was doubtless an anti-sylv fanatic. God knows what sort of a sermon I would receive over this. I did think of refusing to accompany him, but that might have made matters worse, so I trailed miserably up the hill with the two men.

Gilfeather was worried about the contents of his chest. "Medicines," he told me. "Herbs and potions and curatives and supplies. They are well packed, but still, things could have been broken. Some of it is irreplaceable." He sighed. "My uncle will have my beard hairs for toothpicks if I dinna give it all back in good order. I cannot thank you enough, laddie."

I looked at him doubtfully. "If you are thinking to set up business here, you might be disappointed in the number of patients. Everyone *says* they don't like sylvmagic, that it's ungodly, a sin and all the rest of it, but if they have the money, when they fall sick the first person they run to is a sylv healer."

He raised an eyebrow. "Really? That's a tad hypocritical, isn't it?"

He sounded genuinely surprised, which surprised me in return. Was the man so naive? But from what he said next, I realized that the hypocrisy was not what had surprised him, but the idea of sylv healing being evil.

"I would have thought," he continued, "that healing powers would be considered God-given. It seems such a, um, *bonnie* thing to have."

I didn't want to even comment on that and glanced instead at Ryder, striding along beside us, his expression grim. "It's not the healing power that the Patriarchy has a problem with," he said. "It's the other manifestations of magic. If I was ill, I'd be happy to be sylv healed if it was possible. But given the choice between no magic at all, and the magic we have now, I would still prefer the absence of it. Of *all* of it." He gave me a glance. "That woman back there—what did she mean about Dustel murderer?"

I sighed. "There's been a sort of—backlash against magic since the day the Dustels fell." It occurred to me that these two men had probably spent most of the time since the Fall on board ship. They might not be aware of the general public revulsion, even though—from what we heard—it was a widespread reaction, not just something found on Tenkor.

"Explain," he said.

"Well, it was so—so *visual*. It happened in front of all of us. People killed. Crippled so badly. Children spattered on the ground. Body parts tumbling from roofs. People impaled or disembowelled or just—broken. Blood—screams . . . Most people had never seen death like that before. It was horrible, and so . . . so *real*. It happened just when children were on their way home from school for lunch, which didn't help. Some of them died as well. Now so many others can't sleep, or they have nightmares, and wake up screaming. Not just children either." I struggled for words. "It was searing. If you saw it, you know what I mean, surely. People won't get over it so easily. They can't."

Ryder nodded. "And they need someone to blame."

"I suppose so. We all knew it had to be a result of dunmagicking, of course. And then people heard the whole story, of the ensorcellment of the Dustel Islanders, how they had been condemned to live as birds for generations. Everyone rallied around to help." I shook my head. "Maybe if that had been possible . . . to help, I mean, but it wasn't, not really. So many dead. So many maimed. And even the uninjured ones, so many just went mad, unable to cope with being human. Some killed themselves. Some still try to fly. Some won't eat anything but bird food. Some refuse to wear clothes and then they die of pneumonia. And many had things wrong with them, as if . . . as if the change between bird and human didn't quite go the way it ought to have gone. Some are blind, or partially so. Others are deaf. Some lost parts of themselves when they changed to humans. Genitals, the tongue, ears, fingers, toes . . . not really the sort of thing sylv healing can mend. The Menod tried to take them all in, of course. They were fed and treated and clothed . . . and some did just fine. They are learning to speak, to walk properly and so on. But others . . . " I shook my head. "Tenkorfolk are upset. Who wouldn't be? And it didn't happen out of sight, but right under our noses. Under everyone's nose, because everyone pitched in to help. And some were so enraged that they blamed magic, all magic. There's a Ban Magic Society now."

Gilfeather looked at me blankly. "They blame *sylvs*?"

"Sylv, dun . . . They don't make a distinction. Funny thing is, from what I hear, the Ban Magic Society is doing even better in The Hub than it is here. It seems the more sylvs you have in the neighborhood, the greater the resentment from nonsylvs."

Ryder gave a faint smile as if he found all I said encouraging. Gilfeather just looked unsettled.

By then we'd arrived at the Synod. A junior patriarch on duty at the gate bowed his head the moment he saw the Patriarch Councillor, and we were granted entry. Ryder took us straight up to his suite of rooms. To my surprise, I found he was lodged immediately next to the High Patriarch. A mark of esteem, I assumed, although the rooms themselves proved to be spartan.

Once there, he waved me into a chair, while he summoned servants—one to arrange a room for Gilfeather, another to inform the High Patriarch that Councillor Ryder was back, yet others to collect their laundry, unpack their bags, run their baths. I began to feel even more ill at ease and out of place.

Gilfeather seemed to sense my state of mind, because he said to Ryder, "What do ye want with the young man, Ryder? He's been assuming all the way here that ye have something uncomfortable in mind for him, but now ye seem more interested in your bath. Put the poor laddie out of his misery, for pity's sake."

Ryder turned to face me. "You said you are Jaydon the Guildean's son?"

I nodded.

"Does he know you're sylv?"

"Of course."

"But it's a fact he doesn't want bruited about."

I shrugged, embarrassed. "He has never approved of me using it. And in fact, I normally don't, or not much. It just seemed that—well, the situation warranted it just then."

"Indeed it did," Gilfeather agreed. "And I am truly grateful for it. He's telling ye the truth, Ryder," he added casually, as if he knew that for a fact. He then wandered over to the windows and looked down on the town and harbor, apparently indifferent to the conversation. You could see all the way to the entrance of the Race from there—but I doubted he was entirely riveted by the spectacular view. He listened to every word we said.

"Your father is bound to hear about this incident," Ryder said.

I nodded. The thought of the forthcoming interview with my sirc was daunting, to say the least. "He won't be pleased," I said. "There has always been the odd rumour about me, but mostly it was dismissed as gossip aimed to discredit my father. The truth will be all over Tenkor within the next hour."

"Yes," Ryder agreed. "I've heard him rail against magic, and urge the Patriarchy to take a stronger stand against its practice. However, it is hardly your fault that you were born sylv."

"Tell that to Korless Jaydon."

"He blames you?"

Part of me wanted to spring to my father's defence, but suddenly I was tired of the lies. "As much as he can. Either me or my late mother."

"I will write a note for you to take back to him, explaining what happened."

I doubted that would help, but I thanked him anyway. Gilfeather gave a tiny smile as though he knew exactly what I was thinking.

"How old are you?" Ryder asked as he seated himself at his desk and opened the inkwell.

"Twenty."

"And you work for the Guild, obviously. A tiderunner or a longboatman?" He made an exasperated sound when he found the inkwell was empty, and rang again for the servant.

"I've done both, but I prefer using a tiderunner."

"And you hate being sylv."

I paused to think about that, not knowing where this line

of questioning was going. "I hate being blamed for something I can hold no responsibility for: being *born* sylv," I corrected.

The servant came in and was wordlessly handed the empty inkwell. Ryder waited till the man had left before he asked, "If you could rid yourself of magic, would you do it?"

I thought about that. A few weeks earlier I would have said yes, without question. But since then, I had fallen in love with a sylv, and I'd just used sylv to save myself from serious injury—or death. Now I wasn't so sure.

Once again Gilfeather intervened. "Beware of how ye answer, laddie. He means to use you, this devious priest."

His eyes were twinkling as he said it, but it annoyed Ryder anyway, I could tell. He said, "Gilfeather, we need a sylv. You said so yourself. And who better than one who doesn't want to be sylv? The man has dropped into our laps; does that not tell you something?"

"Ye're not going to say this accident was divinely inspired, are ye?"

"And why not? God works in wondrous ways. There is little point in prayer, Gilfeather, unless one accepts the necessary corollary that prayers are answered."

I shifted uneasily. I wasn't sure I liked where all this was taking me. "I never said I didn't want to be sylv."

Ryder began to sharpen one of the quills on the desk. "No, that's right, you didn't. And while we're giving out warnings, let me give you one about Gilfeather here. To him, lies have a stench. Never try to stretch the truth in his presence, or you will make a fool of yourself."

I was really annoyed now. They were using me to gain points in a stupid game that was played between the two of them, as if I was some sort of idiot. "If you don't mind, I'll go now." I stood up, but before I could bow and take my leave, the servant returned with the ink.

"Just a moment longer," Ryder promised. He started to scribble the note for my father.

Gilfeather grinned at me. "Sorry, laddie. We've been forgetting our manners. Too long cooped up in a ship that's smaller than my house back home, with nowhere to go . . .

Seeps the good humour out of a man, that does. And Ryder is right. We do need a sylv to work with us. But now is not the time to consider it, I think."

"What work?" I asked.

"Research," he said. "Into sylvmagic. What makes it different to dunmagic. And why the Aware are not affected by magic at all. Is sylv something in a person's personality? Or something in his blood? Fascinating questions, are they no?"

I stared at him, wondering if he was serious, and decided he was. Next I wondered why I had never asked those questions of myself. Because, I thought, you, Elarn, were always too busy asking, "Why me?" instead. Bring it all down to the personal, that's Elarn Jaydon. Not: *Poor Cissy,* but, *Thank goodness she's dead, and I don't have to explain about the baby.*

Ryder interrupted my thoughts. "Here's the note," he said, handing it to me. "I hope it makes him a little less irate with you. And you can expect to hear from us, with a proposition. Whether you accept it or not, will of course be entirely up to you."

"Thank you," I said and took the note. I hesitated, then asked, "May I ask you something?"

"Of course."

"Do *you* think being sylv and being one of the Menod are incompatible?"

"Not at all. Not any more than, say, being physically strong is. I do, however, think that using one's muscles to intimidate another is a sin. Similarly, using illusion to deceive is a sin. Elarn, there have been many fine men—and women—who have been both sylv and Menod. You have heard of the Ethical Sylvs, haven't you? There have even been sylv patriarchs and matriarchs. What counts is what a man does and does not do, not what he is."

With that priestly homily, he ushered me out. He shut the door behind me, but it didn't close properly. As I stood in the passageway, trying to collect my thoughts, I heard him say, "Well?"

Gilfeather gave a low laugh. "What d'ye expect me to say? The laddie's in a turmoil. He just had a narrow escape

from being squashed flat by my runaway medicine chest—
now there's an irony for ye! Add in a young man's normal
fears of failure, his unresolved conflict with his father,
and a strong dose of unsatisfied sexual desires; throw in a
smidgeon of mystery; give the whole brew a stir—and nine
times out of ten ye'll produce exactly that kind of scent. Not
much different than you or me ten short years back. He may
not want to work with us."

"Do you never believe in the mysterious ways of God,
Gilfeather? We need a sylv, and lo and behold one just drops
into our laps the moment we set foot in Tenkor."

Gilfeather made a noise that sounded suspiciously like a
snort. Then, "That's stretching the reality of what happened.
I told you while we were still aboard ship that the laddie had
a skerrick of sylv aroma about him. So ye stared at him
down on the docks, saw some sylvmagic sticking to him and
decided he was just what we needed. Where's the divine intervention in that? Secondly, ye told me yourself that sylvs
are common here in the Keeper Isles. So it was not unlikely
we'd bump into one fairly soon. There were at least another
two I was aware of as we came up the hill. Where's your
logic, man?"

The door swung to and latched this time, leaving me
wondering what in all the Isles they were talking about. And
just what was going on between those two men. The tension
had almost been strung tight enough to pluck a tune on.

I READ THE NOTE BEFORE I GAVE IT TO
my father. It started with a politely worded greeting from a
Menod Councillor to someone of higher rank who was already known to him. He then went on to say that he deeply
appreciated the aid that I—Elarn—gave him and his companion that morning with my sylvtalent, thereby preventing
a disaster that could have resulted in death or injury to one or
both of them. He concluded by remarking that the Guildean
had every reason to be proud of having raised such an able,
well-spoken young man, capable of making quick decisions
even at the risk of being scorned by those who do not approve

of sylvmagic. His signature was followed by his rank and the official seal of a Menod Councillor.

Guiltily, I did my best to reseal the letter, and went to find my father.

He was in his office in the Guild building, and of course some town busybodies had already ensured that he knew of my perfidy before I arrived. He was furious, which meant that I was met with a coldness that manifested itself in a stare of flat contempt. He bade me enter and told me to close the door behind me, but I knew better than to sit down. Before he could start in on his tirade, I handed him the note.

"What's this?" he asked.

"It's from Syr-aware Councillor Ryder."

He read it and laid it down on the desk. "And I suppose you think that this will ensure that the incident will be forgotten."

"On the contrary, I am quite sure it won't. And I do not doubt that you would be far happier to be organizing my funeral right now—so tragic, a fine young man squashed flat by a runaway piece of luggage."

There was no way he could actually answer that, so he leant back, elbows on the padded chair-arms and steepled his fingertips. "I think it's better you go away for a while."

No word of relief that I had not been hurt. No word of sympathy for my predicament. Nothing.

"To The Hub," he added. "You can stay with your great-aunt." He was speaking of his own aunt, Bertilda, a pious Menod lady who lived the quiet life of a childless widow. Just the company for a young man with a passion for tideriding.

"And my work—?"

"You are relieved of tideriding duties until further notice."

"Just like that?"

"I think it's best." And he was the Guild's Guildean. His word was final. The only thing he couldn't do, without a full meeting of the Guild and a vote, was have my Guild membership revoked.

I tried to blanket my emotion. There was no point in

showing him my vulnerability. "And what do I do for money if I don't work?"

He reached forward to open a drawer and extract a small coin bag from his desk. "This will be enough to go on with. I shall arrange for you to draw from my account at the Guild Treasury in The Hub, an equivalent amount to your present wages."

I would have liked to fling the money and the offer back in his face, but I wasn't quite that foolishly proud. I took the bag and nodded. "I'll leave on tomorrow morning's tide," I told him. "Unless, of course, you want me to catch tonight's bore." And use a sylv light again.

"Indeed I do," he said, calmly. "You can go on tonight's longboat."

I stared at him, the full extent of my punishment beginning to become apparent. He meant me to go without my tiderunner. And of course, he was quite within his rights. Technically, I didn't own a tiderunner. It was the property of the Guild. In practice, each Guild tiderider had three runners for their personal use—each designed for different bore conditions—and no one ever used someone else's runner. I supposed mine would now languish, unused, on the boatshed rack.

He waited for me to lose my temper, so that he could then step in with his cool cruelty and rip me to pieces with his sarcasm. I took a deep breath and inclined my head. "I will get out of practice," I pointed out. My rage churned, but I was damned if I would give him the pleasure of chiding me for a childish lack of control.

He just looked at me, expressionless. And I knew then that he never had any intention of seeing me return to the Guild's employ. Not in his lifetime, anyway. He held my stare, and there was nothing there that spoke of a fatherly concern.

I inclined my head again. "As you wish. I shall be on tonight's longboat, if they have room for one more passenger."

"I have already checked. You are booked a place, together with one trunk. The rest of your things can be sent later."

It took a moment for me to conquer my rage. He had

made up his mind to send me away even before he had heard my side of the event. With an effort, I said calmly, "In that case, if you will excuse me, I shall go home and pack my belongings." I didn't actually have all that much in my room at his house. Most of my personal belongings had long since been transferred to the Guild Hall down on the waterfront, where I preferred to live. Even though the room was small and I shared the facilities with everyone else, it was still an improvement on the cold luxury of the Guildean's house. Nonetheless, I had always made a point of dining with my father once a week, and I slept under his roof on that evening.

"There will be no need for that," my father said. "I shall ensure everything is packed up and sent on."

I shrugged. "As you wish. In that case, I will take my leave." I stood, turned on my heel and left his office without looking back at him, or offering a word of farewell. Right then, I did not care if I never saw him again.

I didn't go straight to the Guild Hall. I went on into the town first, to pick up a new suit of clothes I'd ordered and to buy a couple of other items that would be hard to find in The Hub. When I did arrive in the Hall, I was waylaid half a dozen times between the main entrance and my room by people wanting to know whether what they had just heard was true: was I leaving the Guild? I dodged most of the questions, but when the guildsman in charge of longboats called me into his office, I obeyed without a second thought. He was an elderly man called Wendro, and he'd been more than fair to me over the years, turning a blind eye to all but the most audacious of youthful indiscretions.

"I've just had a private note from your father," he said. "He says you are leaving by longboat this evening." He walked over to his desk and picked up a sheet of parchment.

I nodded.

"He says that you are to take only one trunk with you, that the rest will follow later." He cleared his throat rather noisily, and I realized that he was deeply embarrassed and didn't quite know what to say next.

"And—?" I asked.

"Well, he says something odd . . ."

I waited.

He fumbled for his eye-glasses, perched them on the bridge of his nose and glanced at the letter. "He says he feels that, from now on, waverunners are not to be carried by longboats. That they are too long and cumbersome, take up too much room, and delay the handling of other more important cargo." He removed the eye-glasses. "An odd request, seeing as we don't transport many waverunners. I thought you should know."

I nodded dumbly. The petty meanness of that letter was staggering. I did own a waverunner and I had intended to take it. I took a deep breath and finally managed to say, "Thank you, Syr, for telling me."

Outside his office once more, I had to take a minute or two to compose myself. Of all the things that my father had ever done—including his initial rejection of me as his flesh and blood—I think that letter was the most hurtful, simply because of the depth of its meanness.

I straightened with an effort and went to find Denny. I sent him with a message to Marten, then began to pack a trunk with the essentials. I had almost finished by the time Marten came strolling in, smelling strongly of beer. Denny was on his heels, so I told the lad to scout around for some of my things. "Beckin has my best waistcoat, and Tollick borrowed that special board wax of mine. Timwit has my designs for a new double bent-shaft paddle. See if you can get them all back, will you? Tell them I'm leaving Tenkor and I need 'em." They both stared at me in shock. "Go on," I urged Denny and he scurried out, his eyes still wide with surprise and unspoken questions.

Marten frowned. "They say you're sylv," he said flatly. "And I've been telling everyone that's blathering nonsense, cos I would know if it's true. And you're about to tell me it *is* true, aren't you?"

" 'Fraid so."

"Bastard. You crab-picking utter *bastard*."

"Yeah, I know."

He turned on his heel and made for the door.

"Marten—please. Don't go."

He stopped to look at me. "Why the Trenching charnels didn't you tell me? I'm supposed to be your best crudding *friend*, and you didn't trust me enough to mention that you're a frigheaded sylv? Did you think I'd bleeding *care*?"

"No, I didn't."

"Then why the Trench didn't you tell me?"

"It didn't seem to matter all that much." Not quite true, but it would have to suffice. "I never used it. I never wanted to use it."

"And now you have, apparently. In a rather spectacular fashion if even half of what I've heard is true."

"Yeah. It was use it or risk being splattered all over the laneway. Marten—my father is banishing me to The Hub, and I don't know that he'll ever let me work for the Guild again. And he's not letting me take a tiderunner with me. Or even my own waverunner, it seems."

Marten's anger vaporized as quickly as it had manifested itself. He stared at me, appalled. As a tiderider, he knew what it meant to me. He forgot about leaving and sank down on my bed instead. "Charnels. What are you going to do? You'll never be able to afford a tiderunner of your own. Even a good paddle costs a scabbing heap of coin."

"I'll have to make do with my waverunner. At least that is my own. But he has forbidden the longboats from loading waverunners as cargo. And to send it by road would cost more than I have."

Marten was speechless. Finally he managed to ask, "He did that just so that you don't have the pleasure of riding the waves?"

I nodded.

"Trenchdamn, Elarn, what in all the Isles did you do to him?"

"Got myself born with sylv. That was enough. Marten, I want you to help me."

"Anything," he promised, then hesitated and added, "As long as it doesn't get me thrown out of the Guild."

I told him what I wanted him to do.

He gaped. "Sodding barnacles, Elarn, you're bleeding mad!"

We have just left Port Zmamag in our colony on the coast of Western Sazan. I have never before seen such poverty—and the flies! Dear God, it was impossible to breathe without inhaling them. I was grateful to Nathan, who warned me to take a veil for my hat, and I'll admit to pulling it down and viewing the town through a haze of gauze. (Shor never warned me, even though we spoke of the trip ashore several times beforehand. I wonder if that was deliberate: is he perhaps still hoping that I will find traveling so appalling that I will turn back? Oh dear, there I am being uncharitable again.)

The worst was to see the faces of the children just covered with a crawling mat of black flies. Many of them have eye infections, and there seems to be an abnormal number of blind adults in the streets. I wonder if there can be a correlation? I did ask Dr. Hensson afterwards, but he looked at me as if I was joking, and told me not to bother my pretty head with such matters. I suppose I must have given one of my ferocious frowns (Mama says they make her think of a cat just before it scratches), because he took a step backwards and hastily changed the subject.

Something has been puzzling me.

I have been listening to Captain Jorten and the scientists on board and I've heard all they say about their travels to other lands, to our overseas colonies. Now I have my memories of Merinon Island, the Regal States colony where we revictualled, and Zmamag. And so I wonder why our Kellish Protectorate has not colonised the Isles of Glory.

When I asked Shor whether it is because the Isles have cannon-guns and can defend themselves, he was dismissive, saying that the Menod, of all people,

*control what guns there are. And, he concluded—his
voice heavy with scorn—we Kells are not afraid of
Glorians anyway.*

*That didn't seem to make much sense, seeing as up
until now, in the papers I have read, it is the Keeper
sylvs who have the guns, but I dared not say so for fear
that he would guess I have been reading more of the
Glorian files.*

*So I asked the question about colonization at the
dining table. The replies were both enlightening and
puzzling. The consensus seemed to be that the unity of
the Isles is so cohesive that it would be pointless to
confront them—if you tried to conquer one islandom,
the others would rush to its aid. And why bother
anyway, when they are an easy people to trade with,
obliging, astute and helpful? True, it is perhaps not
quite so lucrative to trade as it is to exploit a colony
(Nathan's word—and much disputed by the others who
seemed to think that colonies benefited from our
benevolent rule far more than they were exploited),
but at least trade is not as much trouble. The Isles of
Glory is a long way to send troops, and to keep a grip
on scattered islands would be a nightmare of . . . what
is the word the navy uses? Logistics?*

*The ideas seemed reasonable, except for one thing.
How could they talk so easily of the unity of the Isles,
when everything I have been reading seems to speak of
islands that are as diverse as a bucketful of seashells
randomly collected on a beach, and as solidly independent of one another as their citizenship laws can
make them?*

*There is a mystery here, and I resolve to solve all
mysteries before the end of my sojourn in the Glory
Isles.*

CHAPTER 11

NARRATOR : ELARN

SO MUCH HAPPENED THAT DAY TO CHANGE me. The Elarn Jaydon I was when I awoke in the morning was not the same person who boarded the longboat that evening, and never would be the same. Bitterness and anger warred with pain and—resolution, I suppose. The way my father had behaved had infuriated me into being a stronger person, not a weaker one. Unhappily, it also added another coating to the skin I was growing between myself and the world.

The boat—there was only one that night—pulled away from the docks in darkness; the singlemoon was hidden behind cloud. Besides myself and one other passenger, there was also the sweepman, the lantern-sweeper and the six rowers on board, plus the usual amount of cargo. The sweepman was the key to the success of any trip. He steered the vessel with the long oar, or sweep, and shouted the coded instructions to the rowers in words that meant nothing to a non-guildsman, but which meant everything to us: *Baste . . . Dig left! Tickle . . . Crest!* It was a tough, challenging job.

To be an oarsman, on the other hand, required only that you be strong, muscular and capable of quick reactions. And, I suppose, patient. On an uneventful trip you spent most of your time in your place with your oar resting across your knees, always at the ready, but rarely called. On a good run, the wave—not the rowers—moved the boat, which was guided by the skills and power of the sweepman. As a sweepman needed both hands for the steering oar, at night it was up to the lantern-sweeper to direct the beam from the skallion lamp to illuminate the way. A good sweeper never took his eyes from the water ahead. The boat, its cargo and the safety of everyone on board depended on him just as much as it depended on the skills of the sweepman.

Every oarsman dreamed of being the sweepman, but it meant enduring a full five years or more of rowing and then several years as lantern-sweeper before you were even considered for the job. Which was one reason why I had wanted to ride a tiderunner instead. It was far more exciting, and just as challenging. Many never made the grade.

I glanced up at the wharf again. I had the feeling that my father had sent someone to make sure I departed and that I left without my waverunner, but I couldn't see anyone in the darkness behind the small group of well-wishers who had come to see us off. I was about to stop looking when I had another thought: You're sylv, and now that everyone knows it, why bother to hide it? If there's any of the Aware about, too bad.

I conjured up a sylv light and sent it back to the wharves as the oarsmen stroked away. There were two people there in the shadows, one at either end of the docks. One was wearing a cloak that shaded his face, but from his build—tall and narrow-shouldered—I guessed him to be my father's secretary, Villios. The other was Syr-aware Tor Ryder. He could see my light of course. He smiled slightly as it hovered over him, and raised a hand. I couldn't tell whether the gesture was intended as a benediction, or just an acknowledgment that he knew I had seen him.

I shivered. There was something dark and tragic about that man.

Out in the middle of the Race, the rowers rested on their oars. The lantern-sweeper lit the oil lamp and adjusted the angle of the beam of light that shot forth over the water. I glanced behind at the illuminated clock in the Guild Hall tower. Still twenty minutes before the bore was expected. It was a Moray tide that night, a sixth-level tide named for the expected power of its break. Not an easy wave to ride under the best of conditions, and a night tide was always difficult.

I took off my jacket and slipped out of my shoes. "Syr," I said quietly to Lamas, the sweepman, "I fear I must leave you now. Hold to the wave." And before he could protest I stepped out of the boat. The water was waist-deep and cold.

"Elarn! You young fool—what do you think you are doing?"

"You'll see," I told him. With that cryptic remark, I swam away from the boat and into the darkness.

Only it wasn't dark to me. I had the sylv light high above and it lit up the area like a beacon. God, I thought, to think that all these years I've had this ability and never used it. How can anything so harmless be against God's will?

I could easily see what I was looking for. Over at the edge of a sandbar that separated two of the main channels of this part of the Race, Marten was sitting on his tiderunner. He'd anchored himself against the flow by beaching his board on the sand. And next to him was my waverunner, complete with its ankle strap.

He couldn't see me coming, and when I stood up on the sandbar next to him he jumped so high that he almost tipped himself off his runner. "Sod it, Elarn," he said. "You made me just about bite my heart in two."

"Sorry. Thanks for coming—I appreciate it."

"Well, I've done what you asked, but believe me, this is the craziest thing you've ever thought of, let alone undertaken." He dug into the hatch behind him and took out a couple of items. "Your waterskin and your gear."

As I stripped off my wet clothes and put on the oiled top and culottes of a rider, he continued to scold me. "Are you aware, you daft idiot, that no one—absolutely no one—has ever ridden a waverunner all the way to The Hub? That the record for a ride is a measly five miles along? That no one has ever even ridden a *tiderunner* all the way at night, let alone a waverunner? That—"

"Yes, they have," I interrupted. I took the waterskin from him and slipped my arm through the carrying strap. "I have, just a few weeks back. Using a sylv light, just as I intend to do tonight. Marten, quit worrying. If I lose the wave, I'll have to wait for the next one tomorrow. If it takes me days to get up the Race, so be it."

"And what if you run into a log or something?" he asked darkly. "It would be hard enough during the day. To do it at night is suicide."

"Stop worrying." I handed him my wet clothes and knelt on the waverunner. "You had better get back to the docks quick smart, or you'll be paddling against the bore. Off you go."

He hesitated a moment longer. "I'll come and see you when I'm in The Hub."

I smiled at him, although I doubted he would see. "Of course! Thanks, Marten. For everything."

"Hold to the wave, you scadding sylvhead!"

I watched for a moment as he paddled away towards the lights of the wharves. Denny would be there to help pull him out of the water and get his tiderunner stored safely away, without anyone seeing, or so I hoped. I headed out to where I had a better chance of catching a good break on the bore wave. I didn't have long to wait: it came a few minutes early that night. It sounded like the wrath of a sea-dragon, even though it wasn't nearly as ferocious here as it would be where the channel narrowed farther inland.

When it loomed up out of the darkness and roiled towards me, it devoured the shallows of low tide like the monster it was: a Moray. I knelt on my board and dug my hands into the water to drive myself forward as if I wanted to flee the danger, gathering up speed to match the behemoth. And then it was there, forcing itself under my moving board, strong enough to throw me upwards and forwards as I stood, crouched, ready to fly across the shallows ahead: a swift on the darkwind, a tiderider on his waverunner. To harness the power in a wave: there can be no better feeling on all the earth.

For the first part of the journey, I gloried in the loneliness of my ride. I kept to the west channel, which usually produced a better wave for a runner. I could see the searching light of the longboat about a mile to the east in one of the central channels, where there would be more water under their keel, but our paths would not converge for the next two hours or more. For the time being, I rode the wave on my own and it felt good—as if I'd left not just Tenkor Island behind me, but my troubles with my father as well. As if hope lay ahead, and not an uncertain, aimless future.

When I risked a glance back, it was to see a series of rough waves following mine, like a pack of orca pursuing prey: an unruly bunch, all rough edges and gnarled white water. It was more comfortable to look to the front than behind, more comforting to see my pathway ahead lit with silver light.

I enjoyed the first hour. It was the longest tideride I'd ever taken on a waverunner. An hour's successful ride would normally have translated into a long and arduous return paddle, against the flow, back to Tenkor, so we didn't try it too often. When we did, well, on a waverunner it was just too easy to lose a wave. The moment your attention faltered, the moment you misjudged a shift of weight, the moment the wave threw up something utterly unexpected—that was all it took to have the rider swallowed by the very creature he rode. There would be a churned-up instant of panic when the world seemed upside down, then he'd be spat out behind as unworthy, and the wave would be gone.

But this time I had nothing to prove. I didn't have to stand all the time. I could lie prone or kneel when conditions allowed it, with no one to call me a ninny. And I could use sylv, and that made all the difference. Illusion would make no difference to anything, of course—but wards were real. I'd given it a great deal of thought and worked out a way to comb the water just ahead of the runner to deflect flotsam using ward filigree. And best of all, if I felt my balance become unstable and realized I was about to be flung off,

I could use a ward like a sweep and dig it into the water to nudge the waverunner into a better position. It took split-second timing, but I could do it.

The second hour was painful. Muscles ached. The stress of being continually alert was draining. And I wasn't even halfway yet. When the channel narrowed at a place called Benderby and forced the wave higher and faster, I was glad because it also brought me close to the longboat. They still couldn't see me—their light was cast in front, not to the side—so I swung my waverunner closer still, until I was running alongside. One of the rowers spotted me first and almost dropped his oar in amazement.

"God, are you out of your mind?" Lamas yelled at me when he saw what had attracted the attention of the others. "Elarn, you'll never make it!"

"I've come this far!" I shouted back. But the journey had begun to tell on me. My back ached, my arms ached, my shoulders ached, my feet were freezing and I worried they would soon be too numb to feel the subtleties of the movement of the runner.

In the end, it was my fellow guildsmen in the longboat who made the rest of the ride possible. They might have been Menod to a man, but I was a guildsman, and that was of more importance to them than whether I had contravened religious precepts by being a sylv. The idea that a guildsman might be able to ride a Moray all the way to The Hub on a waverunner—at night, what's more—fired their imagination, and their initial shock turned to encouragement. Without them, I would never have made it.

They talked me through the next three hours or so, raising my spirits when the cramps came, offering advice, warning me of impending wave changes when my concentration faltered, telling me jokes when all I wanted to do was give up. And when we all slipped off the main wave into the Basin of The Hub, they sent up a cheer wild enough to wake people in their beds along the waterfront buildings.

I believe they still speak of that ride even now in Tenkor. It has never been successfully repeated, probably because there has never been another sylv tiderider. What they don't tell you nowadays is that I had cramp so bad I had to be lifted from the runner and carried to the Guild Hall afterwards.

I STAYED OVERNIGHT IN THE HALL BUT left the next day. The Guildean had made it quite clear that I was no longer welcome to stay on Guild property, even though I was still a guildsman. However, I was now a hero, not just the recalcitrant sylv son of a Menod father. There was no shortage of people to help me, I found. Before I even woke, a message had been sent to my great-aunt to expect me. The moment I stirred, I was plied with an enormous meal and several beers at Guild expense, followed by a session with the Guild masseur. Still later, after several more beers, a cabriolet was hired to take both me and my trunk to my great-aunt's house—also at Guild expense. When I left the Hall, I was applauded by the guildsmen. It was heady stuff to a man as young and as untried as I was.

To this day, I appreciate the risk those men took. They knew their actions might anger my father, but still they showed their appreciation of what I had done. I think I knew then that, no matter what, my future had to lie with the Guild—and that I would fight anyone to regain that future.

Aunt Bertilda did not exactly welcome me, and I can't say I blamed her. What woman of sixty wants a twenty-year-old man foisted on her, especially one so obviously at odds with his father? Still, she took me in, and gave me the spare bedroom, which was furnished with heavy pink brocade and yards of knotty crocheted cloth that seemed inexplicably to multiply every time I left the room. She cooked her own meals, but made it clear that she had no intention of cooking mine. The only other inhabitant of the house was a maid, Aggeline, who was even older than my aunt and who did all the other work of the household. She did not appreciate having an extra body to care for, and made her feelings quite clear. To me, she was merely a servant, paid to do a job, and I was unconcerned by her complaints. It never occurred to me to behave any differently than I had done at my father's house, or even at the Guild Hall in Tenkor: I left my dirty clothes on the floor and expected them to be collected and returned laundered, I left my bed unmade and expected to return to find the room neat and spotless. My presence in the house was probably like a splinter driven in the foot, an irritation that both women would have loved to have done without but didn't quite know how to extract. I was aware of the tension, of course, but it never occurred to me that there was anything that I could do to alleviate it. I was polite, even deferential to my aunt, and sublimely arrogant in a way that perhaps only a talented young coxcomb can be. It was not a happy household.

My main worry was financial. The money my father had bestowed on me did not last long. All very well for him to give me an allowance equal to my Guild wages, but in The Hub, I was not granted any of the Guild's benefits. I could not get free meals and beer in the Guild dining hall, and the cost of a meal was twice as high in The Hub as in Tenkor. I suddenly found I had to pay for many items I'd once received free, from boot blacking and haircuts to candles for my room and wax for my waverunner. In Tenkor we went everywhere on foot: The Hub was a city, not a town, and it sprawled across six miles of harbour and riverside. Most people hailed a two-pony cabriolet to get about. These were small, two-wheeled hooded vehicles that took two passengers and were driven by coachmen who all seemed to be midgets. They were pulled by Keeper ponies, shaggy short-legged animals about half the size of your Kellish horses (which, of course, we had yet to meet). The whole thing cost money to hire. Prepared at first to walk everywhere, I soon discovered that wasn't always feasible. It rained a lot in The Hub, and a three-mile walk in the rain was not the best way to start an evening out. And the same three-mile walk home in the dark was a good way to be waylaid and robbed.

My financial shortfall became apparent to me on my second day in The Hub, when I met Jesenda again. I received a message from her, inviting me to call on her that afternoon, between the hours of four and six. Fortunately, I had suitable clothes packed in my trunk, and although they were a little

crumpled and Aggeline conveniently disappeared when I
suggested she try to make them presentable, I arrived at the
Duthrick house appropriately dressed. Or so I thought. I
wasn't so sure after I was introduced to some of the other
young bloods present. What was considered a gentleman's
raiment back in Tenkor would hardly have been fine enough
for the servants in the Duthrick household. Still, the young
ladies, of which there were several, did not seem to be worried by my simple apparel. Apparently, word of my exploit
had reached Hubbian society, and I was the talk of the town.
Everyone wanted to meet me. The men wanted to take my
measure and diminish my stature in the eyes of the women,
if they could; the women simply wanted to flirt.

A few months earlier I would have enjoyed myself
hugely. Now I only had eyes for Jesenda. She welcomed me,
and saw that I was properly introduced to her duenna—a
plump lady of forty or so, who eyed me suspiciously—and
then to her friends. After that, she hardly seemed to notice
my presence. I found it irritating, especially as I could not
decide whether she ignored me simply to tease, or whether
she really was indifferent. She looked so poised, so confident . . . One of the young men seemed to be the focal point
of most of her attentions, a handsome fellow with a boyishly
attractive smile (or was that just sylv illusion?), called Syr-
sylv Wendon Locksby. Another young man made a point of
telling me that Locksby and Jesenda were the closest of
friends. Locksby himself made a point of talking to me
pleasantly, apparently to make me feel welcome. He also
turned a puzzled glance in my direction when I described
my journey from Tenkor, then asked me, "But what is so
special about riding a piece of wood all that way? Surely it
would have been wiser and more sensible to ride in the longboat?" I couldn't decide whether he was stupid or diaboli-
cally clever.

I forced a laugh. "At last, a sensible man who is willing to
reduce the feat to its proper place, among the annals of stupid things young men do. Locksby, I salute you!" I raised my
glass in his direction, and everyone laughed.

A little later, I managed a few private words with Jesenda, my first of the afternoon, when she pressed me to try the speciality of the house: an iced cake sprinkled with a fine blue powder. I stared at it, puzzled. "What is this?" I asked, and poked at the blue dusting with a fork.

"Exactly what it looks like," she said with a laugh. "Powdered sapphires."

"*Sapphires?* I should *eat* it?"

She nodded.

"This is an illusion, right?"

She looked affronted. "Elarn, the Duthrick household would never trick its guests in that way! That would be . . . so . . . so *vulgar.*"

It struck me that eating an expensive powdered gemstone—which could not possibly enhance the taste of the dish—was probably the ultimate in vulgarity, but I didn't give voice to the thought. Instead, I asked, "Why? I mean, why serve it?"

"It shows that we think enough of our guests to spend a lot of money on them, that's all. It is a compliment to you."

I dug the fork in and ate some. The powder was so fine I was almost unaware of it, but I didn't do much chewing anyway. I have rarely eaten anything I appreciated less. I changed the subject. "Are you still wanting tideriding lessons?" I asked. "I have more time for that now."

"Yes, I heard," she said. "Everyone knows you are sylv, so your father threw you out."

"News travels fast."

"My father is the Interim Keeperlord now, remember. There is nothing that does not come to his ears."

"And yours, evidently? My father is not so confiding with his offspring."

She laughed and tapped my arm with her fan. "Don't jump to conclusions, Elarn. I'll meet you at the boathouse tomorrow, in time for the morning ebb release. Which will be at ten."

She flicked her fan and smiled at me over the top of it. She could be utterly charming when she put her mind to it, but something warned me, even then, that I had better be on my guard. Jesenda was no superficial society miss hunting a husband.

IT WAS A STRANGE MONTH I SPENT IN The Hub. Sometimes it had a dreamlike quality; it seemed a hiatus between two facets of my life. Yet it was also a period that took on a life all of its own, where I was suspended between the two realities that were past and future.

On Tenkor I was the Guildean's son and a Guild member, both of which meant that I was accorded a modicum of respect, but mostly I was just a tiderider who never had much money to spend, just like all the others undergoing training. In The Hub, however, I was addressed as Syr-sylv, and was accorded status as a result. I was welcomed in the Duthrick household, and therefore in other houses of The Hub's elite families. I was included in their outings, their picnics, their card evenings. Society matrons studied me to see if I was an acceptable sylv match for their marriageable daughters. Women I had no interest in courted me—yet their brothers often despised me as a poverty-stricken interloper. Locksby and his friends sought to make me uncomfortable in subtle, clever ways, or by illusive practical jokes. They thought it fun to fool the Tenkor bumpkin and offered me nonexistent chairs to sit on, or invited me into a cabriolet that was already full, so that I ended up sitting on the lap of a girl who had blurred herself into invisibility.

When Jesenda and a group of her friends included me in a country excursion, I accepted. I found to my dismay that it started with the hiring of a number of cabriolets to the edge of the city, followed by the rental of Keeper ponies and the buying of lunch in a roadside inn—all of which the young men paid for, blithely refusing my contribution. They knew I couldn't afford to make more than a token offering anyway, and they aimed to shame me. They succeeded, and when the next such outing was proposed, I refused.

I had more invitations than I could handle anyway and—as was soon obvious to me—an inadequate wardrobe, even after the arrival of the rest of my belongings. Most of the invitations I turned down for that reason, with the result that I apparently garnered a reputation for exclusivity, which made me more sought after, not less. It was crazy, but I became the prize catch for a society matron's musical soirée or an intimate dinner; if I accepted an invitation, then the evening was considered a guaranteed success, at least by the ladies.

"This is absurd!" I protested to Jesenda one day. "It's as if I am some sort of prize animal in the menagerie, the star attraction!"

She grinned at me. "Elarn, the only gen-u-ine long-necked ten-toed tenkorfalump, on display tonight! Roll up, folks . . ."

That night the Duthrick family invited me to join them in their theater box to see that week's illusive drama. It was the first time I had seen a sylv-enhanced performance. For a few hours I was swept into another world, watching the unfolding of a story where the players and the setting were almost too real. My mind might have told me that the starving child in act two was not really starving at all, no matter how thin and ill he looked, and that the fiery climax in act three did not involve real flames—but my senses told me a different story, and by the end of the evening my involvement had been so intense that I felt emotionally tattered. It was the start of an addiction for the theater that has lasted all my life, even into the years when there were few sylv actors, and if there is one regret I have about the Change, it is that we do not see such performances any more. It is our loss.

AS THE WEEKS WENT BY, JESENDA AND I developed a relationship that was both pleasant and extraordinarily frustrating. We attended many of the same functions, and I was a constant dinner guest in the Duthrick house. At these times I was on my best behaviour, treating her a little distantly and with unimpeachable manners. But, thank God, there was also the time we spent together on the three or four days a week when we went tideriding. Then, when we were alone, out on the water, I could relax, lower my guard, be myself. In some ways, it was rather as I imagined it might be to have a sister. We experimented with sylv illusions, teased each other and sometimes confided in each other. I told her about my father, about how my mother had died; she dropped hints that implied she found her mother's pride in her lineage irritating, and her father's pride in her unsettling. I looked forward to those moments, yet found our shared intimacies frustrating, because it was the intimacy of siblings, not of lovers. I valued the friendship, but the sight of her—as demure as her swimming costume was—had my body tied up in knots and my emotions entangled.

I could have eased my physical frustrations by visiting some of my old friends down in the portside district; plenty of girls there were willing enough to oblige a tiderider in exchange for an evening of fun and a few drinks, but somehow I couldn't. I hadn't slept with a woman since Cissy. I hadn't wanted to. My abstinence was born partly of a need to prove Jesenda wrong when she had chided me with having a bevy of girls to satisfy my lusts in both Tenkor and The Hub, but also partly because I knew that such a liaison would leave me unsatisfied. It wasn't another Cissy that I wanted. It was Jesenda.

A month passed. I grew more and more unsettled. To some degree it was nothing to do with me: there was an atmosphere in The Hub itself, a feeling of excitement, of changes in the wind. The area behind the wharves, where most of the manufacturing industries were to be found, bustled with new business. The iron and brass foundries, the shipbuilding yards and all the associated craft guilds had garnered as much work as they could handle, and the flow of business spilled over to touch the lives of all Hub citizens with added prosperity. The capital was booming—but this ebullient bustle only served to make me more discontented.

By the end of that month, I knew that I could not stand the life I was leading, not indefinitely. It was too aimless, and not even Jesenda's company was enough. I wanted to be working towards a future that had a place for me. I wanted to be independent of my father's charity. I would have liked to be back working for the Guild again, but failing that, I still wanted something better than what I had.

And that was how the situation stood when two things happened on the very same day, and they both changed my life. The first was a conversation I had with Jesenda. The second was when Aggeline knocked on my door to tell me that I had a visitor downstairs, and I entered the morning room a moment later to find Tor Ryder leaning elegantly against the mantelpiece, his clear gaze holding those dark secrets I knew nothing about.

CHAPTER 12

NARRATOR: RUARTH

I WON'T BORE YOU WITH DETAILS OF how Lyssal and I finally arrived in the Breth Bastionlord's audience room; to tell you the truth, I'm not sure I remember all the details now anyway. As I recall, we paid a farmer to give us a ride, along with one of the sea chests, in his ox-cart to Brethbastion. We stayed for a while in a comfortable guesthouse "for genteel travellers", or so the sign over the entry stairs said. Lyssal then wrote to the Bastionlord, and eventually that letter reached the right person at court, and she was invited to an audience. I think we'd been in the city about two weeks before the invitation arrived. You haven't been to Brethbastion yet, have you? Then I suppose I should tell you about the place . . .

Towering granite cliffs line that part of the Brethian coast, great walls of stone as solid and strong as an anvil cast in iron. The sea approach, a narrow opening through these cliffs, is a stark and forbidding gateway to the round, steep-sided harbor that is Hell's Vat. On the far side, there is another way in and out where the Scour River carved a canyon to empty itself into the harbour. Otherwise the Vat is encircled by sheer, black cliffs—a grim location. And yet it is also a fine, safe harbour, and sailors irreverently call it the Washerwoman's Tub, as if changing the name would wipe clean its dire history. It was once home to the Sea Wolves of Breth, you know, the Bastionlord's murderous forebears who preyed on the shipping of the Isles, before they settled into becoming more respectable Islandlords.

The city itself? Well, that is carved into that black cliff wall, opposite the sea entrance. Rising up out of the water, it imposes its presence, Brethbastion: oppressive, dramatic, still seeped through with the tragedy of past sufferings.

Hordes of slaves carved the granite in levels, inch by wretched inch. Twelve levels, or lodes, as I recall, each named after those who live there, or used to live there. At the top is the Lord's Lode, where the palace sprawls, with its spacious windows and balconies. Underneath is the Buccaneers' Lode, where the palace Securia and his guards have their barracks and their interrogation cells, and the palace servants have their quarters. Then the Nobles' Lode, the Merchants' Lode and so on progressively down, through the various artisan levels, each a degree less elegant than the lode above, to the very bottom, which is Scum's Row. A line of holes strung along the back of the wharves are the hovels of the city's poorest.

Streets are slotted between each lode, with the outer side open to the light and weather, while the roof, the pavement and the other side of the street are all solid granite. Every so often, a spiral staircase leads up or down to the houses or shops on the levels above and below. At rarer intervals there is a framework projection out over the bay, rather like a floorless balcony, half hidden in a forest of ropes, winches and pulleys. These are the calling stations for basket-like platforms called trugs. Goods—or passengers—are hauled up and down between levels in a trug. Of course, you have to pay for this service, and in those days it was run by guardsmen and the money went straight to the Bastionlord's coffers.

When we first arrived in Brethbastion, we were winched down from the top of the cliff to the level of our guesthouse, and I decided I hated trugs. In fact, I was finding that without wings I had a horror of heights, and the trug was hardly my idea of a safe way to scale a cliff. From the first day we arrived in Brethbastion, I used the stairs as much as possible, especially as it seemed a good way to further increase the strength in my legs. I hated being called Tadpole.

Fortunately, my skin had darkened in the sun at the beach, and I no longer had the appearance of a fish underbelly, but Lyssal had insisted that I dye my hair—which was growing well—to yellow-blond. She wanted me to look Cirkasian.

I thought she would dress with particular care for the audience with the Bastionlord, in order to appear regal, a beautiful woman who was heir to a throne. Instead her choice of dress and jewelry and hairstyle seemed to emphasize her youth rather than her maturity. She looked painfully young and boyish. I was mystified at first and wondered if she was just anxious to hide her pregnancy, which, I guessed—remembering her behavior on Porth—must have begun on Gortham Spit. That meant she was now about five months along. She didn't look pregnant, although her abdomen had lost its flatness. Then, with a sinking heart, I knew what she was trying to do: appeal to the Bastionlord's perverted tastes. Lord Rolass Trigaan preferred boys in his bed. Children, in fact. She was trying to decrease both her femininity and her maturity. She taunted me with her laughter when she saw me look away, upset.

I turned back. "Flame," I said, "don't."

And for a moment, the briefest of moments, I saw her there in Lyssal's eyes again: painfully aware of what was going to happen to her, and grief-laden—but the grief was for me, not herself. She pitied me with all her heart, when she should have been mired in misery for herself. And in that moment I loved her more than I had ever done. And then the compassion was gone and only Lyssal was there, mocking me.

Look at me, now, an old man—and still my eyes fill with tears when I think about it. Yes . . . well. There are moments of poignancy that score the surface of your memory so deep you can still feel the roughness of it half a lifetime further on.

Just before we left for the palace, she sat down at the table in her room and, with deliberate precision, rewove the illusion of her Cirkase coming-of-age tattoos onto the back of her remaining hand. She could still use sylv to do it, and she took care to use only the smallest quantities of magic. To me, it seemed that she was reweaving the prison of her heritage, the very heritage she had tried so hard to escape.

"What if the court Awarefolk see that it is illusory?" I asked. By then, I was confident enough to use my human voice to speak to her, even though the words were still raw in their enunciation, the vowel sounds corrugated, the consonants grater-rough. But she seemed to understand.

"The ones in Cirkase never noticed."

"You hardly ever saw the court Awarefolk in Cirkase."

She held up her hand for me to see. "Well? Can you notice the sylv?"

I nodded. And remembered another place, another time, when she had done just that—shown me her faked tattoos. She had been eighteen. And we'd had such plans, she and I. "Yes, I can," I said. It was true. Even a minor working of sylv seemed to blare into my consciousness now.

"Well, I just have to hope not every one of the Aware is as observant as you. And if they are—" She shrugged. "I will explain it away somehow. Just as I will explain how I lost my arm in some sort of tragic accident."

"You lost your arm for nothing," I said bitterly. We'd thought the amputation would save her from dun subversion, and it probably had—until Morthred raped her again . . .

For a sliver of a second, she hesitated. Then Lyssal was back, changing the subject. "I want to give you a citizenship tattoo. I don't want anyone questioning my legitimacy, and if I have a Cirkasian servant with me, it will appear more proper." She took hold of my ear and began to work her magic. "This is just in case. Stay away from anyone who is Aware. And you will keep your hair dyed that color. Every few days, if need be." She stepped back to look at the results of her illusion. "At least your eyes are the right color, and your skin has turned golden. And now that you have a few muscles in your legs you are not quite so much of a freak—Stop that, Ruarth!"

She glared at me. I had been poised to snap up a beetle that was walking along the table edge. Some habits were hard to break.

She dressed me as her equerry, in clothes that were heavy with embroidery and scratchy to wear. At the best of times I didn't like clothing; that suit was purgatory. It was something she'd found among Morthred's plunder. A Brethian tailor had altered it to fit me, in anticipation of our court debut. The footwear was even worse. Shoes made me feel unbalanced and uncertain, and they always pinched; these had heels that seemed high to me, and smart silver buckles that dug into the top of my foot. The smile that Lyssal gave at my discomfort was spiteful.

Guardsmen escorted us to the Islandlord's palace. We ascended a stone staircase to the street level above the guesthouse, then walked to the trug station that went to the Lord's Lode. The guardsmen marched on either side and I felt we were trapped animals on our way to slaughter, rather than honored guests. Lyssal walked several paces in front of me, strolling along, smiling to bystanders as if she did not have a care in the world. Heads turned, of course; she was still astonishingly beautiful.

Once we were in the trug and being winched upwards, she conversed pleasantly with the young officer who had been sent to accompany her, while he stuttered and stammered in his nervousness. I just looked over the edge and prayed the ropes would hold. Skies, how I longed for wings. For the freedom of flying once more . . . When I looked straight down from the trug, I was gazing at the tops of ships anchored along the wharves at the foot of the cliff, and I felt a wave of nostalgia. This was a bird's eye view.

We were a long way up; these cliffs had to be as high as the stacks of Xolchas. Xolchasfolk, though, had no choice where they lived. Brethmen did, and just why they had chosen to remain in this place was a mystery to me. True, the Vat was still a superb anchorage, but the disadvantages were legend. For every residence, only the single outer wall could have windows, so most places were only one or two rooms deep. The cliff seemed solid enough, without the constant rock falls of Xolchas, but the trug system was cumbersome and dangerous: people did die from time to time when ropes frayed or pulleys stuck and trugs unexpectedly tilted. The worst disadvantage for Brethbastion, though, must surely have been its position on the island. The sheltered shores along Breth's southeastern province were rich with the things that made the islandom prosperous: the fertile grain-growing plains, the copper and silver mines, the tall stands of Nepetha trees that made fine ship masts, the herds of long-haired sheep. Yet the capital, the heart of their commerce and culture, was this stone-made city, distant from the regions of the islandom's greatest wealth, looking out on an eternal ocean no one ever crossed. That may have been an advantage in its piracy days, when a secret hideaway was essential, but no longer.

"Quite a sight, isn't it?" one of the guardsmen remarked to me, while the officer was busy talking to Lyssal. "Gives me the shivers, though, it does, being up so high. I was born in the Scums."

"Does the sea ever get rough down there?"

"In the Vat? Nah. But sometimes ships can't get themselves through the entrance when the weather's filthy. Takes a good sailor to bring a ship in safe and sound then. And when the wind comes from the northwest, the whole sodding Vat down there fills up with weed. Trenchdamn stink then, I can tell you. Nothing like rotting seaweed to make you wanna puke. Doesn't pay to live down near the sea's edge."

"I can smell something now, even from up here."

He grinned at me, displaying a mouth largely devoid of teeth. "That's your Cirkasian shit, little man."

"Pardon?"

"Where d'you suppose it all goes? Down there into the Vat. Every time you visit the privy. Along with everyone else's. Plus whatever they sling outta their windows: eggshells 'n' cabbage stalks 'n' dead cats—whatever. That there bay down there is our middenheap, lad. Which is fine when the tides and the river's flow sweep the place clean, but once in a while, when the wind blows a certain way, and the tide doesn't do its job properly . . ." He pulled at his nose. "You can get a stink that will curl your hair. And then, believe me, it doesn't pay to be a lugboy or a road-sweeper or a stone-breaker living at the back of the wharves. It's why I joined the palace guard—we live in barracks on the Buccaneer's Lode right up there under the palace. Nice and windy and all you can smell is the salt in the air."

The trug jerked to a halt and the attendants slipped in the bolts that anchored it to the trug station. Lyssal stepped out and the officer pointed to the guarded double doors in front of us. "Through there, lady," he said. "It leads straight to the waiting room. The Bastionlord will be told you have arrived, and when he is ready you will be admitted." Lyssal nodded and sauntered across to the doors. Guards sprang to open them and I followed on her heels. She did not speak to me while we waited, except to tell me to walk one step behind her when she was called.

We didn't have long to wait. A few minutes later we were in the audience room, walking down the long purple carpet towards the throne at the other end. Perhaps for normal audiences the room was filled with people, but that day it was empty, except for the Islandlord and a handful of courtiers and advisors gathered around him. Bastionlord Rolass Trigaan was approaching sixty, a grossly fat beast of a man given to cruelty and debauchery, despised by the people he ruled as well as by his fellow Islandlords. I had seen him before, of course, just over six months before in fact, when he had been in Cirkasecastle on a state visit to the Cirkase court to see Flame's father. He didn't look any different. Just as fat, with rolling jowls that melted into sagging chins, his knees spread wide to support his belly.

He waited until Flame had reached the halfway point down the hall, then rose to his feet. Unaided, which surprised me. I had thought he would require help to rise, but I did him an injustice. He levered himself upright, and gazed at Lyssal in obvious astonishment. I realized then that he had not expected that the person who had requested this audience would really be Lyssal, Castlemaid of Cirkase. He'd expected some kind of impostor, or at best a servant with a message from the Cirkase Islands, but he had once glimpsed her unveiled face and he knew her now.

He came forward to greet her, honoring her by so doing, and bent to kiss her hand. "Syr-lady Lyssal. This is an unexpected pleasure."

She smiled at him, then lowered her head with a demure simper. I wanted to be sick. "You told me once that you wanted a royal wife," she said, as if that explained everything.

He stared at her, in shock at her bald statement. At her boldness. He lowered his voice to such a soft whisper I was probably the only one present who heard his next remark. "And you told me you would only wed Rolass Trigaan when your age matched his poundage."

She replied just as softly. "I was hasty. I have since found that I would rather be a royal wife than a royal daughter."

He paused, probably to give himself time to think. He must have wondered what in all the Isles she was up to, ignoring all protocol with her unannounced visit, with her outspoken forthrightness. Usually, a first meeting like this would have involved nothing more than polite inquiries as to the other's health, or similar inanities. He continued to hold her hand as he murmured, "And what makes you think that the Bastionlord would still wed you? He heard rumors that you ran away from Cirkase some months back. Breth's bride should be above reproach." His tone carried an edge even sharper than the words.

Neither seemed to faze Lyssal. She murmured, "Breth needs an heir, and it is this lady's understanding that it may be a, er, difficult undertaking. She, however, has the willingness to do whatever is necessary . . ." She raised her chin and looked him full in the face. "I have an understanding of the problem and I am willing to accommodate it."

"Indeed."

I could almost hear him thinking, wondering what he was

missing. She looked so young and innocent, but her words ran counter to her looks. He may not have been renowned for his wisdom or learning, but he was no fool either. "What is it you want in return, my lady?" he asked. His flat stare made it clear he expected to hear an answer he could believe.

"Freedom. You know my father's court, where women go veiled and live a walled life, separate from their menfolk. I want more than that. I want to be a valued consort. Who my husband beds is of no consequence, as long as he accords me the respect that is due to his consort." She gave him a moment to consider that, then added, "But such details can be discussed later, can they not?"

"Indeed," he said again. He inclined his head, and turned to introduce her to those of his inner court.

IT WAS THE SCANDAL OF A GENERATION, of course. The female heir to an islandom arriving mysteriously, and in the company of a stunted male equerry who could barely articulate a sentence. There was no retinue, no duenna, no ship bearing gifts, no previous letters of intent or invitation.

Apparently Lyssal's disappearance from Cirkase had not become common knowledge, or it would have been even more of a scandal. The Bastionlord knew only because he had pursued the Keepers for news of the progress of his suit and they had finally told him that they did not know where she was. His pride did not allow him to spread that titbit further.

Fortunately, no one realized that I was a Dustel or that would have added to Lyssal's aura of mystery. My hair and my tattoo pinpointed me as Cirkasian, and although people were already aware of what had happened elsewhere in Breth, there never had been Dustels in this city. Dustel birds had a passion for grass seeds, and there simply were none on those barren cliffs. Because of that, most of the city's inhabitants remained unaware that newly human Dustels looked and sounded a lot like me.

We were granted apartments in the palace. I suppose some poor soul was ejected from them first because they contained evidence of a hasty departure. These chambers had once been hacked out of the stone of the cliffs, but that was not immediately apparent because they were lavishly panelled and carpeted. Apart from the decorations of gold leaf, the glitter of which attracted my acquisitive bird's eye, I could see nothing attractive. With its overt ornamentation and lack of space, it oppressed; the palace, it seemed, was as overstuffed and obese as its Islandlord ruler. Our things were fetched from the guesthouse and Lyssal was accorded every courtesy due to a royal heir. A duenna was installed in the room next to hers, a maid was sent to attend to her needs. I had a room on the other side of her personal reception room.

No sooner had Lyssal settled in, than she started to receive a string of courtiers and nobles, all vying for her approval, all intensely curious. The ambassadors from other islandoms came to pay their respects, including the Cirkasian one. He was almost beside himself with outrage: he knew nothing of Lyssal's disappearance, but he did know that she could not possibly have had her father's permission to come all the way across the Middling Isles unveiled and without a proper escort. He could not bring himself to look her in the face, and ended his first visit by begging her, for the sake of decorum, to veil her features. She laughed at him.

No one paid much attention to me, not even Lyssal. When I spoke, I kept my words to a minimum, perpetuating the idea that I was either a mute or stupid, or both.

AS THE DAYS WENT BY, THERE WAS NO talk of a wedding.

"Well, what did you expect?" I asked her a day or two after our arrival at the palace, when we were alone. "He would have to be daft not to be suspicious of your motives."

She gave me a sharp, annoyed look. "You are speaking more now, aren't you?"

"I've been practicing."

She gave a sarcastic laugh. "Not enough, I would say. You sound like a strangled frog."

I shrugged. "True. Most people don't understand me."

She changed the subject. "Soon there will be other ships in from Xolchas with tales of the Castlemaid being in the company of someone there who turned out to be a dunmaster. Soon it will be obvious I am pregnant. I have to be able to coerce Rolass Trigaan." She added, exasperated, "And I can't do that until I find out who the Awarefolk are at court."

"So you can kill them," I finished for her.

"You Awarefolk sense one another, don't you? You can tell me. You can identify every single one."

"I could." I was uncertain about the truth of that. My Aware senses were still so muddled that they confused me as much as they helped.

"Well?"

"I could—but I won't. How could I live with myself if I were to do that? They'd all be dead within a day once I told you, and I would have to live with the fact that I had betrayed them. I will not betray you, it's true, but I won't help you either."

"Don't be ridiculous. What difference does it make?"

She had a point. By not warning them, I would be just as complicit in their deaths. "You forget, I was a Dustel bird," I said. "We have generations of experience in non-interference in the affairs of men. We have observed from our window sills and rooftops. We have listened and heard and watched. And never interfered. You cannot change what I am overnight. I will not betray anyone. You must find your own Awarefolk."

"Damn you, Ruarth. Why do I keep you alive?"

"Because you'd be lonely without me." A flippant answer; the real truth was in my following thought: because Flame is still there inside you somewhere.

She stared at me, then added softly, her voice full of menace, "Time is running out for you, Spider-shanks." •

She was right, but it didn't change anything.

I had already pinpointed her main danger: the Bastion-lord's Chief Advisor, an Awareman who was called simply

Ikaan of Sedin. He was another predator of small boys, which I—as a fellow Awareman—found obscurely shaming. It was humbling to find that I could recognize a kinship to someone so vile; somehow, I had always thought the Aware to be finer folk than most. Silly, I know. In my heart, I hoped he would be the first to fall to Lyssal's attack.

I found another one of the Awarefolk just hours after my conversation with Lyssal: a matriarch who had come from Tenkor as the Menod Ambassador. She also doubled as the spiritual advisor to the court, mostly because the other Menod clergy who had once fulfilled that role had long since been dismissed. She was a gray-headed woman, born a Breth Islander, whose gaze expressed her intense sorrow with the world. She attended a dinner that night, in honor of Lyssal's presence. Her name was Issuntare.

Rolass Trigaan enjoyed baiting her. He taunted her with remarks loaded with innuendo, and openly fondled his boys in front of her, hugging them or kissing their cheeks in ways which might have been considered innocuous if not for his reputation—and the fact that most of the children were terrified. They did their best to hide their terror, which made it all worse, if that was possible.

Flame was present as well, of course, and perhaps part of what the Bastionlord did was aimed at her, but she never flinched. She leaned back in the padded chair at the head of the long table, a look of unforced amusement on her face, and watched all that went on. From my post standing behind her chair, I tried to emulate her composure, but it was hard. Whenever Trigaan addressed her, she would smile slightly and say something neutral, such as, "As my lord says," or, "I am sure you are right."

Sometime after the main course, Ikaan took one of his selected boys onto his lap, and began to feed the child sweet-meats. The boy was nervous, but as yet untouched—a fact that the Chief Advisor was careful to point out in his conversation to those around him. "He will be my dessert tonight," he said, smiling at the matriarch. "Would you like me to describe the nature of my bedtime supper?" He was playing on his Aware connection to Issuntare: the kinship, the closeness, the sense of companionship that was hard to deny. It made his taunting all the more vile. The tension between them was something everyone felt, me more than most. To me, it was personal, for I, too, shared that connection. True, it was no longer as sharply defined as it had been when I was a bird, but it did still exist.

Issuntare stood up abruptly. "God will punish you," she said to Ikaan, her voice husky with loathing. "There can be no greater crime than that against a child." Her eyes swept over the seated courtiers and lingered on the Bastionlord. "Are there none among you man or woman enough to take a stand against this pervert and his corrupted soul?"

The boy on Ikaan's lap looked up at her with fear-filled eyes.

The Bastionlord raised an eyebrow. "You sail close to the wind. Beware, matriarch." If I had not feared him before, I would have then. His voice held all the menacing certainty of a man who had no problem fulfilling his threats.

They exchanged stares, then she lowered her eyes and bowed slightly. The center of Menod Patriarchy power was a long way from Breth. "I am indisposed, my lord," she said quietly. "I seek your permission to retire."

He smiled, and for a moment I thought he would insist she stay. Then he waved her away. "Begone, take your sour face elsewhere. We want none such here. Tonight is for celebration." He raised his glass to Lyssal.

Issuntare inclined her head and walked out of the room. I took advantage of the movement of the servants in and out of the servery kitchen behind me to leave as well, and followed her. She did not, however, go to her apartments. She descended to the street below. At that hour of the night, there were not many people around. She walked without the briskness of someone with a destination, although she was agitated. In fact, after following the street for five minutes or so, she simply stopped and leaned against the granite balustrade that overlooked the bay. I came up to lean next to her.

She did not move, or even look at me. She did not need

to; she had probably sensed my Aware presence ever since we had left the banquet hall.

"You will find it a hard court to live in, Syr-aware," she said at last.

"Yes," I agreed in my guttural, clumsy speech. "I think I will. I already do."

Only then did she turn to face me. "Aha," she said. "You *are* Aware. I wasn't sure. I thought I could sense something . . . but then I wouldn't. There is something very strange about your Awareness, young man."

I didn't reply.

She continued. "Your mistress is not the Castlemaid. And you talk after all, although I was informed you did not. Who are you? Who are you both?"

I looked out over the Vat and breathed in the fresh salt air, tinged only with the smell of oil burning in the small lamps that sat in wall niches down the street. It was pleasant after the stink of the spiritual corruption of Rolass Trigaan's court that evening.

Beside me, Issuntare persisted. "So, what's the story, Syr-aware? And don't try to tell me any lies. I've heard enough untruths in this sinkhole of rottenness to recognize one coming the day before yesterday. That woman's hand tattoos are sylv illusions. And so is your ear tattoo."

"Lyssal is the Castlemaid," I said. "I've known her since I was a fledgling. She just didn't want to have coming-of-age tattoos. So she faked them. It was clever of you to spot that; she went to great lengths to try to hide her use of sylv. I hope Ikaan hasn't come to the same conclusion."

She snorted. "Him? All he thinks about are his boys." She paused, then added, politely neutral, "You were a, um, flagellant?"

I sighed. My speech was still obviously a mess of sounds. "*Fledgling!* Sorry. I know what to say, I just have trouble saying it correctly. Until a few weeks ago, I had a beak. I was a Dustel bird."

"Ah."

"You don't believe me."

"Well, let's just say that in this place it is unwise to take anything anyone says as necessarily true."

"Anyone? Don't you have other Awarefolk you can trust? Other Menod?"

In the combination of moonlight and lamplight, her face seemed heavily lined. She looked weary. And puzzled as she strained to understand me. "Awarefolk I can dust? Oh, trust! Well, most of them have long since left. Decent folk don't want to belong to the Breth court. There're only the three of us—Ikaan, Yebenk and myself."

"Yebenk?"

"The Securia. His tastes run more to women, but he's just as nasty as Ikaan and Trigaan. And as for the Menod—there are but a handful of the faithful, down in the Scums. The last to be found in all Brethbastion. Up until now I've managed to hang on simply because Trigaan likes to have me around so he can bait me. But as you saw tonight, that's not likely to be for much longer." I thought I saw a tear glisten on her lashes, and wondered why she found leaving the Breth court a matter for grief.

"Surely the Menod sends patriarchs here to tend to their congregation," I said.

"There's no point any more, now there are not enough of the Menod faith here for them to minister to. It's not a place that nurtures a respectable religion. The evil of the court trickles down from lode to lode like the spillage of some vile poisoner's brew." She sighed. "And when a man or woman of integrity does open their mouth in criticism . . ." She hesitated. "They either shut up or they disappear." She gestured towards the Vat. "It's a long way down. In other words, my Aware friend, you would be wise to keep your mouth shut." She made a gesture with her hand towards my ear. "You don't even have the protection of a genuine citizenship tattoo. The only thing that will keep you safe is the protection of your mistress. Don't put a foot wrong, or you may find even that is not enough."

I nodded. "Well, in that case, I shall maintain the pretence of being a mute."

"A—? Oh, mute. Yes, of course. Well, I'll keep your secret,

if that helps." She was silent for a while, then added, "If you have known Lyssal of Cirkase most of your life, you must have quite a story to tell, master equerry. I hope that one day you'll tell it to me."

"Perhaps. Right now—Syr Issuntare, you must leave the court. If you don't, you will be dead within a week. Murdered."

She took a step closer so that she could see my face better in the poor light. "Did I hear you aright? Did you say dead?"

I nodded. "Yes."

"Was that a threat?" She sounded more mystified than afraid.

"No, of course not. At least, not from me. It was a warning, and one that I *know* to be justified. I would advise that you leave tonight. I would advise that you leave the city."

"You know this for a fact?"

I nodded again.

"And you have been here barely a day or two?"

"Truth sometimes lands in the lap of the lucky."

"Just like that?" She managed to sound both sceptical and resigned. "Do you know why I stay in the first place, Syr?"

"You mean, apart from it being your Menod duty to be at hand to minister to any of the faithful who still remain in this God-forsaken hole?"

"God never forsakes any hole," she said in rebuke. "But yes, apart from that."

I shook my head.

"Because of the boys. I am their only comfort. The only adult in this . . . hole . . . who offers them compassion."

"Dead, you will offer them nothing."

She continued to stare at me. "Just because you are Aware does not make me trust you. I've learned that much in this rabbit warren."

"I hope you've also learned to be wise. Issuntare, for twenty-two years of my life I was a bird, with no real power to do anything. In danger every day of my life from just about everything you care to name: kittens, hawks, snakes, humans, a strong wind. Believe me, it has made me wise beyond my years. You could do much good with the time remaining to you. Stay here, and that time may only be one more day. Flee now, and perhaps you can measure that time in years, and the people you help may number in the thousands."

She didn't answer that. "What is your name?" she asked.

"Ruarth."

"Wrath. I hope, Wrath, that your nature does not match your name."

It was my turn to sigh. I obviously still had a lot to learn about pronunciation.

THE NEXT DAY THE DISAPPEARANCE OF the matriarch was the talk of the palace, not so much because she had gone, but because she had taken six of the palace catamites with her. The oldest of them was only ten. The Bastionlord was furious and a search was organized. At least half the city guard was dispatched to search the landward side of the city; the rest were sent to search the port and every ship that had tied up or anchored anywhere in the Vat or the river.

Lyssal sent for me. "Your doing?" she hissed at me.

I shrugged. "You should be grateful. One less of the Aware for you to bother about."

"Oh. And are you going to tell me who the other Awarefolk are?"

I returned her stare. At least, now that she used so little magic, I could see her face.

Unfortunately, I knew it wouldn't take her long to be certain about the number of Awarefolk in Brethbastion, and so it was. That night, Ikaan and the head of the Bastionlord's guards, Securia Yebenk, both disappeared from the palace. Later the next day, their bodies were found floating in the Vat. Neither of them had any injury except those that could be expected if the men had jumped from the Lord's Lode into the water.

"Your doing?" I asked cynically of Lyssal.

I knew the answer, of course. I had woken that morning to the stench of dunmagic and the color of it drifting into every corner of the building. My first thought had been: Feathers 'n' pox. Lyssal, what have you done . . .

I found out once I was up. Quite apart from the news of two Awarefolk who appeared to have jumped to their deaths, Lord Rolass Trigaan and his remaining advisors were all crisscrossed with lines of red magic, and Trigaan himself stared at Lyssal as if he was besotted. Before nightfall he asked his Chamberlain to arrange the wedding for the end of the week.

BEFORE THE MARRIAGE TOOK PLACE, Lyssal had one last humiliation in store for me.

"My sylvpower has almost entirely vanished," she announced one evening just before I was to escort her into dinner. "I can use dun to maintain the illusion of my own tattoos, but it is hard for me to maintain illusion at a distance. It is not a dun skill."

I fingered my earlobe.

"Yes, exactly. When I am not around, that tattoo of yours fades. I want you to go down to the local ghemph and get a genuine Cirkasian ear tattoo."

I stared at her. "Genuine? No ghemph will do that—you know that!"

"Genuine," she repeated. And she waved a bundle of papers at me. "Birth certificate, citizenship certificate, all authenticated by the Cirkasian Ambassador to the court of Breth."

"You coerced the Ambassador?"

"No, not at all. I merely explained, with a request for secrecy that he was only too happy to comply with, that you were a Dustel bird. He was hardly likely to question the word of the heir to the Cirkase throne. Under Glorian international law for the dispossessed islanders, you are entitled to the citizenship of the land you were born in. The Ambassador provided the papers and signed them; the palace Registrar endorsed them as belonging to you, my equerry."

I took the papers from her and flipped through them. And there was her final indignity, my name: Tadpole Spindleshanks. I flung them back at her. "You want to take both my heritage and my name from me at one stroke of the pen? Well, you can't! I won't do it!"

"Oh, but I can," she said.

"What's the point anyway? It doesn't matter any more! The Bastionlord has accepted you as the Castlemaid and me as your equerry—"

She shrugged. "Perhaps just because this is proof of my dominance over Ruarth Windrider. And that gives me such a perverse pleasure."

I shook my head. In my anger, I found it hard to speak. I kept on trying to ruffle feathers I no longer had. All I managed to do was make all the hair on my head stand straight up, much to her amusement, I forced myself to calm. "No," I said. "This dun version of you has not won yet, Lyssal. You only win when you can bring yourself to kill me. Then I will know that there is nothing left of the Flame I knew. Until then, you have not won."

She stared at me, but it was she who looked away in the end. She gave a shrug as if it didn't matter. "Go to the city's ghemphs tomorrow, Tadpole. If you don't, I will order my maid to jump into the Vat from my window. Do I make myself clear?" She gathered the papers together and gave them back to me.

And this time I took them.

CHAPTER 13

NARRATOR : ELARN

THE DAY THAT CHANGED EVERYTHING for me? Ah, yes, it began with Jesenda. When I woke that morning I could think of nothing but being able to spend a whole day with her . . . Jesenda's waveriding had improved so much that I had suggested a more ambitious outing. I'd proposed we catch the ebb wave for a couple of miles or so, come ashore, and wait for the afternoon incoming bore, which we could then catch to return. I'd planned it carefully. I chose a Whiting tide, which I always think is the easiest of all to ride, easier even than the smaller Minnow, and arranged for us to wait for it in a private parlour at an inn overlooking the Hub Race. Jesenda sent her personal cabman ahead to the inn with a change of clothes for us.

I worried that she might lose the wave on our way downstream from The Hub, as she had never ridden so far before, but I need not have worried. She only stood for a small part of the journey, a big grin on her face, and she used sylv warding for added stability, but still her sense of accomplishment shone from her. To my eyes, she was more desirable than ever.

We stashed our runners on the riverbank, relieved to find the cabman—a morose man twice my age called Hatherby—waiting for us there with our cloaks and shoes. With a bit of illusion as well, we looked quite respectable when we strolled into the inn a couple of minutes later. I waited in the empty taproom with Hatherby while Jesenda went to the upstairs parlour to change. I ordered Hatherby a beer, but it didn't seem to improve his mood. "Syr-sylv," he said, shaking his head at me, "you had better watch your step."

"You mean, if Syr-councillor Duthrick gets wind of what we have done today? He has given his blessing to Syr-sylv Jesenda's tideriding." True, I had not actually spoken to him personally about it, but I knew there could be no way that he was not informed of all we did. Besides, Jesenda assured me that she told him everything beforehand. I might have wondered at his lenient attitude, but I did not fear his ire.

Hatherby looked at me in pity, as though he couldn't believe anyone was so stupid.

I moved uneasily on my bar stool. "I would not act against the Interim Keeperlord's wishes, I assure you."

"There are cat's paws, and there are cat's claws," he said obscurely. "I know which one I would rather be."

"I don't know what you mean."

"You ever seen decoy finches, Syr?" he asked.

I nodded. "They live in stinger vines but never get stung themselves." The vines were predatory, and absorbed the carcasses of the birds that were lured to it by the decoy finches, then stung to death.

I did not have the slightest clue what he was getting at, except that it was clear he was trying to warn me against his own employers. I frowned, annoyed at his presumption. "You know where you owe your loyalty, Hatherby," I said. "I think you overstep the bounds of appropriate behaviour."

He stared at me. "Oh, yes. And you could doubtless see to my dismissal. But nonetheless, I'll say it because you remind me of a young man who once came to The Hub, and sold his good name for brass. Watch your step, young Syr."

"Don't overstep yourself," I snapped. I was both shocked at his forwardness and alarmed at what he was saying. The fact that he risked so much to speak to me only lent weight to his words.

His demeanour changed. He pulled his forelock and said, "No, Syr. Begging your pardon, Syr." With that, he picked up his beer and went to sit elsewhere. I had enough wit to know that he was mocking me, for all his dour exterior.

When I was sure that Jesenda had had enough time to change, I went upstairs. She was seated at the table by the room's bay window. "It's a beautiful view," she said. "Thank you for bringing me here. And for thinking I could do it. I just hope I can manage the bore as well."

I flung off my cloak. "You'll be fine," I said. "You have a natural skill and great balance." I paused but she didn't move. "Are you going to wait downstairs while I change?"

"It is not appropriate for me to wait alone in a public tap-room," she said demurely, but with her head cocked to one side and a grin on her face. "I'm a lady, not one of your bold jades, and I do *not* display my charms in bar rooms."

"Then you can go for a walk outside. Hatherby can ac-company you if it is not, er, appropriate for you to be alone."

"Or I can stay right here and look."

I stared at her. She was serious. "Somehow I don't think that is particularly appropriate behaviour either," I re-marked. "In fact, it sounds more like the action of a rather bold jade."

"But who's to know?"

Something inside of me flipped over, but I pretended nonchalance. "As you wish." I turned my back and took off my wet things, towelled myself and dressed. I could have concealed myself with an illusion, but I was damned if I would. If she wanted to see me naked, then let her. "Do your parents know you are here?" I asked as I dressed.

"Certainly!" She sounded offhand, as if that was a matter of course.

I thought I could feel her eyes on me the whole time as I

changed, but when I turned to face her afterwards she was looking out of the window again, apparently indifferent to me as she watched a Keeper Council vessel negotiating the channel on its way up-Race. I didn't know whether to be annoyed or just admiring of her cheek. She was like that, Jesenda; I never knew quite what to expect. She kept me continually off balance, unable to know how I felt. And I was suddenly troubled by the idea that Duthrick was content for his daughter to be so much in my company, often alone. I didn't know much about Hubbian society, but I was learning, and his leniency was beginning to seem more and more unusual.

"Why does your father allow you so much freedom?" I asked as I sat down opposite her.

She shrugged complacently. "My father knows better than to restrict my behaviour unreasonably. Besides, he is— preoccupied of late."

"That's to be expected, I suppose, now that he is Interim Keeperlord."

"Yes. And Fotherly is working hard to bring him down. In fact, there is nothing that Bart the Barbaric, alias Foth the Fop, will *not* do to ruin my father's chances in the next election. That man has the morals of a mudskipper. Or worse. And this latest piece of news with regard to Blaze Halfbreed hasn't helped Father either."

"What news was that?" I asked, interested. Blaze Halfbreed was a woman that intrigued: bold and somehow larger than life. If half what I had heard about her over the years was true, she truly was a formidable woman.

"Charnels, Elarn, don't you read the scandal broadsheets? It seems that she was the one who killed Morthred and saved Xolchas Stacks from total annihilation! And poor Father has just spent the last five or six months—ever since he came back from Gorthan Spit—telling everyone that Blaze is no longer in his employ and he utterly disowns her and everything she has done! He's even put out orders that she is to be brought back to the Keeper Isles in chains for her attack on him. And now she's the hero of the Isles. Thanks to her, the Dustels have been returned to human form, the most

monstrous of all sorcerers has been killed, the Xolchas
Stacks has been saved from dun slavery, or worse. And my
father looks like a fool."

"But all those Dustels *died*—"

"That was hardly her fault. People here blame Morthred
for that, not Blaze. Believe me, the Glory Isles will end up
singing her name as the news gets around. Father is furious.
She had better not cross his path again, or he'll rip her heart
out." I wasn't sure she was joking.

"Is it true? Did she really kill Morthred?" I asked. "Or is
that just rumour?"

"Who knows? There must be some truth in it, although
one of Father's spies did say it was a friend of hers who
committed the actual deed, a Mekatéen. Father has spies
everywhere, you know; on just about every ship that sets sail
from every port, for a start. He pays them well. And this
news came from his own sources. But that's not the worst of
it, apparently—"

Just then there was a knock at the door and the innkeeper
came in with several servants carrying our lunch: roast meat
and vegetables, which was standard Keeper fare, cordial for
Jesenda, a beer for me, fresh baked bread and several other
side dishes. It was far more than we could eat, and my heart
sank at the thought of the hole it was going to create in my
month's allowance.

"So, what *is* the worst of it?" I asked her, once we had
taken the edge off our hunger.

"It's something that Father just heard yesterday. From
Breth. It seems that the Castlemaid of Cirkase arrived there
about a month ago, to marry the Bastionlord."

"But—wasn't that what the Keeper Council wanted? I
thought I heard something to that effect, oh, ages ago."

"Yes, it was. But we expected to promote it, indeed to
make it possible, and thereby reap the benefits from a grateful Breth Bastionlord. Instead, we earned the animosity of the
Castlemaid, thanks to my father's bungling of the whole mission. And now the Breth Bastionlord owes us nothing, because we did not produce the Castlemaid for him. She turned
up on her own." My eyes widened as I took in the bitter anger

behind her words. "Now they will marry without our aid, in fact probably have already done so, and they will owe us nothing but enmity or indifference. And we will never be able to buy what we want from Breth at a reasonable price."

"Then perhaps we should shop elsewhere," I said lightly. "What can Breth have that we either do not produce ourselves or cannot obtain from our other trading partners?"

"Believe me, there is one commodity that we desperately need from Breth. The Keeper Council is *furious* with Father. They blame him for jeopardizing our chances. If there was another vote tomorrow, Fotherly would win it by a landslide." She pushed her plate away, and started tapping her fingers on the table top. I had never seen her so wound up.

When my surprised expression registered with her, she stopped her drumming and said in exasperation, "You really don't understand anything, do you? You are just like the rest of them—Locksby and the others. So impressed with your own sexual prowess you can't see what really matters!"

"Jesenda, you're not being fair. I know all about Tenkor politics, but I have only lived in The Hub for a month, and my aunt's household is hardly at the center of Hubbian political life. Give me time. And I suspect you know I have not been entertaining any light-skirts lately."

She stared at me, made a gesture with her hand that could have been an apology, and said, "Get me a beer, will you? I'm sick of drinking cordial. I need something stronger."

Now that was something I did know: unmarried women of Hubbian society were not supposed to drink anything stronger than ratafia cordial, although married women were allowed the occasional sherry.

I must have hesitated, because she said, "You're not going to tell me I can't have a beer, are you?"

"No, of course not. I'm from Tenkor, remember? We don't have a genteel society with its own set of silly rules." I went to the door and asked the footman waiting outside to bring me two more beers. "Calm down," I told her as I shut the door again, "and explain everything. Then maybe I can sound a bit more intelligent."

"I'm sorry to be so snappish, Elarn." She smiled apologetically as I seated myself. "I really am a beast sometimes. It's just that there is no one I can talk to. All Mother cares about is her—her status. What people *think*. And Father believes that because I am female, then I have no place being interested in politics. And my friends—" She made a dismissive gesture. "Why don't people see what is really important?"

"So tell me." To be honest, I was fascinated. For the first time I felt I was beginning to see the truth that was Jesenda, and the idea that she would reveal this side of herself to me—only to me—was intoxicating.

"Father made a mess of things, and that's the truth of it," she declared. "And unless he can redeem himself within the next few months, Fotherly will win the election. And we will have a Keeperlord who will lead us to one disaster after another; we will be living in a place where it is more important to look good, than it is to rule well."

I refrained from remarking that sometimes that already seemed to be the case, at least to the nonsylvs of Tenkor. The waiter came back in with the beers—both of which he placed in front of me—and cleared the table.

When he had gone once more, Jesenda took one of the mugs and resumed her tirade. "Elarn, many islandoms are jealous of us here in the Keeper Isles. We are richer than they are, stronger than they are, more stable than they are. We don't have dynastic struggles between sons like they've had in Calment or Quiller or the Dustels. They don't understand our generosity to our own people, they don't understand that we believe everyone can vote for leaders. To maintain our way of life, we need to be strong, otherwise they will pounce on us like hungry sharks."

"But we are strong," I said. "We have more sylvpower than the rest of the Isles put together—"

"Sylvpower is vulnerable. It can be subverted by dun, for a start. We need more than that to be sure we are safe. And there is something that will supply that safety. I am sure you've heard rumors about what happened on Gorthan Spit?"

"About the battle between the sylvs and the dunmag-ickers?"

"Well, it wasn't sylvpower we were using. Sylv is not a destructive magic, you know that. It was our cannon-guns."

And that was when she explained about the cannon-guns, and the need to buy high-grade saltpetre from Breth and sul-phur from Cirkase to make black powder. About the experi-ments Hubbian alchemists were conducting to make better black powder, and better cannon-guns. About the foundries they were building, about the complicated way they had to refine the ingredients for the powder. I just sat there and gaped at her.

"How do you know all this?" I asked as she leaned back and sipped her beer. I couldn't believe that her father had made her privy to Council secrets.

She grinned, her eyes danced with mischief. My heart melted when she looked like that. "Well, it's partly rumors. You can't keep a secret like that, no matter how you try, es-pecially when the two ships that had the cannon-guns mounted are right here in port being repaired after the battle, and others are having the guns installed." Her eyes were still twinkling as she added, "I haven't been spending all my pin money on fripperies." I looked blank, so she explained some more. "If my father can pay informants, I decided I could too. Being well informed is half the battle."

I wanted to ask just how much information pin money could buy, but decided that would be rude, and kept my mouth shut. The other questions I should have asked right then didn't even occur to me: What battle was she fighting anyway? Who was the foe?

She drank some more of her beer and continued. "But most of my information I garner myself. I am a very good il-lusionist, as you know."

"I've noticed. But what do you mean—information you garner yourself?" I asked. Something about her confidence made me uneasy.

"Well, I can't sneak into the Keeper Council meetings, unfortunately, or anything like that," she said, "because they employ Awarefolk to guard against that sort of thing, but I can come and go into my father's study in the house. Or any-where they don't have Awarefolk about. It's been less risky since that bitch of a halfbreed hasn't been around."

I swallowed. "You mean, you spy on your own father?"

"No, silly! It's not spying. I am just keeping myself in-formed so that I can help him. So that I can help the Keeper Isles."

I looked at her dubiously. I was feeling more and more uncomfortable.

"Elarn, we can't risk having Fotherly as Keeperlord. It's got nothing to do with me wanting to be the Keeperlord's daughter—you don't think that, do you? I don't care about things like that! In fact, that's the sort of thing I despise about my mother. What matters is Keeper integrity. And Keeper strength. Fotherly wants power for *himself*, not for the Keeper Isles, and he'll go after it any way he can, includ-ing bribery. In his hands, the Keeper Isles will lose influ-ence, because he will use power to enhance his *own* wealth, not that of the islandom. Believe me, I *know* this. I've heard what he had to say to that weaselly friend of his, Gellian Mestro, when they thought no one was listening. I've spent hours listening to the repulsive man, watching his sleazy payments and hearing his filthy plans." She slapped her hand down on the table in frustration. "Why can no one see what I see? Why has no one else got the guts to act, to pre-empt the situation? Not even my father!"

"You've been spying on Fotherly? Listening to his con-versations?" One part of me was horrified, the other part ad-miring. She believed in something and she was willing to take appalling risks to achieve it. I went cold just thinking about it. I leaned forward, and put my hands over hers. "Je-senda, if ever you get caught at this, it will mean disgrace for you. The end of you in Hubbian society. Using your powers to blur yourself into invisibility, and then spying on others—that's an enormous breach of sylv rules. They could im-prison you for that!"

She looked at me scornfully. "I won't get caught. I really can blur myself into invisibility, unlike most. And no one knows, except you. No one." She smiled. "You are the only person I trust. You're the *only* person I've ever trusted. I'm not wrong about you, about being able to trust you, am I?"

"No, of course not! I'd never betray you." I meant it, too. But I was still appalled.

She smiled, and in that moment she seemed to me to be heartbreakingly alone and heroic. "Gradually the whole Keeper fleet is coming in to be refitted with cannon-guns. My father is sending the *Keeper Fair* out as soon as all the repairs are completed," she said softly, "and maybe some of the other ships too, if they are ready. He wants to regain his credibility. He would like to go himself, of course, but Fotherly would seize the opportunity to do enormous damage while he is away. He can't risk it. So he has to send someone else. Unfortunately, there are so few people he can trust . . . They will sail with orders to come home with a contract to buy saltpetre in their pocket, and Blaze Halfbreed in chains." She drank the last of her beer. "Do you think I could have another one?"

I laughed and shook my head. "I think you had better not. You won't be able to stand up on the waverunner." I was only half listening to myself; I was more interested in what she'd said. I asked, puzzled, "Is Blaze Halfbreed also in Breth? I thought you said she was in Xolchas Stacks?"

"She was. But apparently there are two people she cares about. One is a Menod patriarch called Ryder. And the other is the Castlemaid Lyssal. Well, Ryder recently turned up in Tenkor, and we know she is not with him. So, she will be in Breth with Lyssal. My father is sure of it."

"*Ryder?*" I could scarcely believe it. He was all Menod priest—and the halfbreed was, well, a paid assassin and bounty hunter. "Why is your father so keen on capturing her?"

"She betrayed the Keeper Isles. He doesn't like people who make a fool of him. She had the audacity to pluck the Castlemaid from under his nose, from his own ship. She made him look like an incompetent dolt. She held a sword to his throat and threatened his life. Perhaps he can use her capture as a lever to control the Castlemaid's cooperation, or even Ryder's. There is talk that the High Patriarch is ill and Ryder may step into his shoes."

"Sometimes I think your father is not particularly . . ." I let that thought trail away, for fear of offending her, but she only laughed.

"No, Elarn, he's not particularly nice. He can't afford to be. But he is a *leader.* A man of vision. He has made mistakes, it's true, but he strives to make the Keeper Isles the strongest islandom in all of Glory, a center of culture and peace, where all can come to contribute to the greatest civilization the world has ever seen. He sees beyond himself to a future we can only dream of right now." Her face was shining with the same glow it had held out in the Hub Race. God, she was beautiful! Hers was a beauty that no illusion could emulate. I think it was in that moment that I went from just thinking myself in love, to completely losing my heart.

It's the only explanation I have for my foolishness. For the unquestioning way I accepted all she said, without seeing its flaws. For not wondering more about the strangeness of her life.

CHAPTER 14

THE JOURNEY BACK WAS UNEVENTFUL. The bore was superb; just the sort of ride I had hoped it would be, and Jesenda caught the wave like a true professional tiderider. We passed the Keeper ship we had seen from the inn, and I read its name on the prow: *Keeper Courage*. Yet another vessel to be fitted with cannon-guns?

By the time we paddled into the Duthrick boatshed, Jesenda was close to exhaustion. I could hardly blame her; the length of the ride would have challenged many much more experienced riders—and I told her so. She was gratified, of course, but she deserved the praise.

Normally, she would have left me to change then, while she went on up to the house, but that day she asked me to lend her my arm for the walk up through the garden. "My legs feel wobbly," she said with a groan. "Do you mind?"

I took her arm, revelling in the feel of her body close to mine.

"Elarn," she asked as we left the boathouse, "what do you intend doing?"

"About what?" I asked.

"About yourself. Are you just going to wait here, living on a measly allowance from your father, waiting for mercy knows what, for the rest of your life?"

"No, of course not. I don't think my father will ever allow me to return to the Guild of his own volition. So I am planning to challenge his decision at the annual guildsmen's meeting. If the majority of guildsmen vote for my reinstatement as a working guildsman, there will be nothing my father can do to stop it. Unfortunately, I have to wait nine months for the next meeting."

"And in the meantime?"

"In the meantime, I have been approached by the fellow who makes tiderunners and waverunners back in Tenkor. He wants to open a shop here in The Hub. He wants me to run it, and to make tideriding popular in The Hub—" I didn't get any further before she interrupted.

"You are from the leading family of Tenkor! You can't be a *tradesman*!"

"I can't live off my father's largesse either," I said, heavily sarcastic. "I don't even have any guarantee he will continue the allowance anyway. Earning my own salary is surely better than that." As I spoke, I felt glad I didn't possess the Hubbian snobbery that had prompted her remark.

She said, "Have you no pride? Elarn, you are *sylv*!"

"So? Lots of sylvs run their own businesses!"

"Exactly. They don't do it for someone else. They pay people to work for *them*!"

"And where do you suggest I obtain the money to start my own business?"

She looked at me as though I didn't have a brain in my head. "Elarn," she repeated, "you are *sylv*. Sylvs have countless ways of getting money. And you have an added advantage because not many ordinary people realize you *are* sylv. They don't expect it of a Tenkor tiderider."

"What in all the Isles are you suggesting?"

"I don't know—go to one of the dockside brothels you men frequent and use illusion to steal the night's takings. Cheat at dice using wards in some sleazy inn somewhere—"

"For God's sake, Jesenda! Are you serious?"

"Of course I am serious! Oh, I'm not saying you should steal from an honest person, but there are countless other *dishonest* people and places, surely. And by blurring yourself—" She shrugged. "Elarn, to get anywhere in this life, you've got to be prepared to make opportunities for yourself. There can be nothing wrong with stealing from a thief, surely. And to find a thief is easy when you can make yourself pretty much invisible."

My blood ran cold. I remembered what she had said about paying her informants. Did she really have that much pin money? Or had she stolen it? I didn't want to even consider what she might have done . . . but she had a point. There must be countless ways a sylv—especially one who wasn't generally known to be sylv—could steal. I considered the irony of her suggestion: she thought being a tradesman beneath me, but recommended that I steal to set up my own business! God, I thought, there is something very wrong with the way she has been raised. Someone as lovely as she is ought not to think that way.

I shivered and drew my cloak more firmly around my body.

"Think about it," she said, and clung to me tightly as we went up a few steps.

And I did, although I wasn't sure that they were thoughts I wanted.

"Come into the house with me," she said as we reached a side door. "You must be tired too. Come and rest for a bit."

I thought she was joking. "I'm hardly dressed for visiting." We were both wearing illusions of clothing and our real cloaks, which Hatherby had delivered to the boatshed, but underneath, all we had on were our tideriding costumes. The rest of my clothes were still back in the boatshed.

She laughed and grabbed my hand. "Come on," she said, "we'll blur ourselves." And she vanished from sight. Her ability was uncanny; I could feel her hand tucked into mine, but she was gone. If I stared really hard. I could see a shimmer of her, a slight distortion in the air—but that was all. I gave a quick glance around, but there was no one about. I felt sure I didn't do it as skilfully as she did, and that anyone who was looking for something unusual might have been able to find it, but she was already pulling me to the door.

"Try and be quiet, you whale-footed Tenkorman!" she hissed at me as we crept across the entrance hall.

To tell the truth, I was petrified. I was sneaking into the house of the Keeperlord. I was about to compromise the chastity of the Keeperlord's daughter, if she really was dragging me up to her room. Or suite of rooms, as I soon discovered. The opulence of her apartments took my breath away. She had an entire *room* for nothing but her clothes; her shoes covered rack upon rack. She had her own schoolroom where she had once been tutored by a succession of learned men and women. She had her own sitting room. And every inch of it was decorated with gold leaf or wood inlay or porcelain fixtures or woven tapestries. I think it was only then that I understood the real power of sylvmagic. It was only then that I began to have a true inkling of the economics of the islandom I called my own. Sylvmagic wasn't about wards and illusions and healing, not really; it was about the distribution of wealth and wealth's attendant power.

Right then, of course, I didn't have too much time to think. No sooner had we entered the bedroom than Jesenda went around locking all the doors. Then she dropped her cloak, and her illusions, and came across the room towards me, untying the strings on her swimming costume.

"Jes," I said, "I'm not sure this is wise—"

She laughed, a low and husky laugh that sent shivers through me. "Of course it isn't. I don't believe in being *wise*, Elarn."

And then she was standing naked in front of me, as beautiful in body as I had ever imagined, and without a hint of shyness.

Remembering Cissy, I managed a hoarse remark about not having an apothecary's sheath with me, a statement which had her laughing again. "I'm sylv!" she said. "I don't get pregnant unless I want to, and believe me, that's not on my list of things I want to accomplish just yet."

I LAY ON MY BACK IN A TANGLE OF sheets, awed by my luck.

I had started bedding women when I was a scant fourteen years old. I remembered the wonder of the first time, but the others—all the others—disintegrated into a blur against what I had just felt with someone I loved. For a moment in time nothing mattered, just Jesenda and me, and I would have risked anything not to lose that moment.

"Oh God," I said. "That was—"

She rolled onto her side to look at me. She had a contented, satiated look that meant more to me than anything she could have said just then. "Yes?"

"I don't think I have the words."

She gave that low laugh of hers that had the power to do things to me. "There will be more such times. But remember, my Tenkorman, no more of your dockside women."

"I promise." And I meant it too. I didn't have the slightest desire to have anyone in my bed but Jesenda, and if she had wanted it that way for the rest of my life, I would have sworn to it there and then.

"It may be hard," she warned. "This won't happen very often, you know."

"Too risky," I agreed. I started sweating just at the thought of getting out of there undetected.

"Not just that. Elarn—I want us to have a future. A real future." She sounded serious.

"Do you mean that?" I felt my excitement pounding in my veins.

"Oh charnels, yes. Have you any idea of how much I despaired when I looked around at the young men of The Hub? I found them so—so puerile. So shallow. So greedy. And half of them are only attractive because they make themselves so. You are real! Real in character and real in body. Real in sylvpower. So like me. Elarn, we are two of a kind.

Together we will go far. We will take the Keeper Isles to places beyond even my father's vision!"

That was going too fast for me. I didn't want to think about the distant future right then. I just wanted to think about us. But while I was still hunting for the words, she was off again, dragging me along with her into her dream of the future.

She propped herself up on one elbow. "Elarn, you have to go back to the Guild. You have to be reinstated. And you have to make a name for yourself. And then we can marry."

"Wh—? How can I return? My father will never—" My heart was thumping.

"Yes, he will. He will have to, if the Keeperlord insists on it. And he will."

Hope and scepticism warred. "You can do that for me?"

"Yes. I will tell Father that I have found the man I am going to marry. He will object, because you aren't wealthy enough, or powerful enough. So I will tell him to insist that you are reinstated. Your father will have to oblige. And then my father will show an interest in your career . . . and we will still see one another because you will still be tideriding to The Hub. Elarn, one day it will be you who are elected Guildean. And such a Guildean! One who works hand in hand with the Keeper Council . . ."

"It—it sounds wonderful."

"My father will do anything for me." Then she frowned slightly. "But you will have to prove yourself, of course. Do well, I mean."

"That—that will take time," I said, worried about just how rich was rich in Jesenda's book.

"Well, there are ways we can hurry things along." She must have seen misgivings on my face, because she laughed and said, "Don't look so anxious, Elarn! I am not asking you to do anything terrible, like murder your sire. No, I think information is the key. Knowledge brings success, it really does. You tell me what is going on in Tenkor, or what you see on the docks, for example, and I will use it to make Father think highly of you."

"You mean—be a spy?"

"No, of course not, silly! Just keep me informed, that's all. So that I know things first. That's the sort of thing that gives one an edge. In fact, most of what you'll tell me will be for me, not Father."

"For you?" I echoed, sounding stupid.

"Yes. Elarn, I want to be somebody all by myself. Not just Duthrick's daughter. One day I want to be a Councillor of the Keeper Isles. That's not an unworthy ambition, is it? There are hardly ever any women Councillors and there should be more. Perhaps one day I can even aspire to be Keeperlord. Will you help me?" She nuzzled at my cheek and placed my hand on her breast.

"Of course," I said, and forgot every misgiving I had.

LEAVING THE DUTHRICK HOUSE WAS even more nerve-racking than entering it, because I did it on my own. But there was a spring in my step that hadn't been there before. I felt I'd just had the tideride of my life—which, I suppose, in a way, I had.

And the day was still not over.

I went back to my aunt's to bathe and change. I was about to go out, intending to search for somewhere cheap to have dinner, when Aggeline came to tell me there was a visitor for me in the morning room. Then she stalked away before I could ask who it was.

When I entered the room a few moments later, I found Tor Ryder leaning against the mantelpiece, very much at home. My eyes widened. "Syr-patriarch?"

"Syr-tiderider," he said. "I have come to ask you to dine with me."

I opened my mouth, and closed it again. "I would be honored," I said finally. "Puzzled" would have been a more honest remark, but I didn't say it. True, he had said that I would hear from him, but a man as highly placed as he was would normally have sent an underling, not asked me out to dine.

He hailed a cabriolet and took me to an inn I had never visited, on the far side of town. "Best food I know of in The Hub," he said by way of explanation.

On the cab journey, we spoke of the Fall and its effects: how the Dustels in Tenkor were clamouring to go home now that they had heard that their island chain had truly emerged from the ocean; what he had heard of Dustel deaths from other islandoms (the carnage in the Spatts and the Stragglers had been devastating); how the movement to ban magic was spreading throughout the Isles of Glory. "It's odd," he told me, "how spontaneous that seems to have been. There has not been time for the idea to spread from Tenkor to other places, for example. It's just that everyone seems to be angry about what happened."

I just stopped a shudder. "I don't blame them. I'll never forget what I saw, never."

"Do you remember my question: if you could rid yourself of magic, would you do it? Now I ask you this: if it was your choice, would you see an end to magic—all magic—just to make sure such a thing as the Fall could never happen again?"

I felt cold creep along my spine, and remembered the family of Dustels pecking at seeds in the gutter. Remembered the way one of the children had shrunk away from her own father, not recognizing him in his human form, her mind shredded with a fear too great for anyone to comprehend.

I thought of the opulence of the Duthrick house, of being served cake with powdered sapphires on the icing, of what being a sylv could mean. "I'm not sure," I faltered. "Perhaps." And I wondered at myself, even as I said the words. I could almost see Jesenda frown in disbelief. "But it can't be done, surely."

"It can be attempted," he said.

I was curious, of course, profoundly. Had he come all the way to The Hub just to ask me to help him with this strange work he and Gilfeather were doing on sylvmagic? But I didn't ask, not then. I was young enough and hungry enough to want to have dinner first. So when we sat at the table in the inn, I let him do most of the talking. To my surprise, I found him both charming and possessed of a dry humour that was an undercurrent to many of his tales. He spoke of his first years as a scribe, when he was seventeen or eighteen, both naive and adventurous—a dangerous combination. I laughed at his numerous stories of things that went wrong, but I also felt vaguely uneasy. It felt as though some of what he said was hitting a little too close to home, but I could not put my finger on why. My father had hinted at this man's violent past and Jesenda had spoken of his attachment to the swordswoman, Blaze. And I could not rid my mind of the idea that there was something at the back of his eyes, a sort of stark tragedy that spoke of darkness within.

You are being ridiculous, Elarn, I thought. The man is a patriarch, for God's sake.

We were enjoying a beer when he finally turned the conversation to why he'd come looking for me. "I want you to work for me," he said. "For the Patriarchy, in fact."

"On your sylvmagic studies."

He nodded.

"What would I have to do?"

"Sylvmagic. Illusions, healing, that sort of thing. In controlled conditions."

"I've never used it much, you know."

"I know."

"My father might not appreciate this."

"I know that too. If you agree to come back, I shall have the High Patriarch speak to him."

"Why do you want to study sylv?"

"Because we want to rid the world of dun. And there aren't too many dunmagickers who would consider helping us. We are hoping that if we study sylvmagic, we will also understand dunmagic."

"They are opposites, surely?"

"Are they? And even if they are, understanding sylv will tell us what dun is not."

There was more to it than that, of course. There had to be. If the Patriarchy understood sylvmagic, then they understood the Keeper Council who ruled them . . . Perhaps that was part of it. Perhaps there was even more.

Jesenda would be interested in this, I thought. But I would prefer to be a tiderider . . . would she be able to do that for me or not? Or was it better to take this offer and at least get myself back to Tenkor? Finally I decided to be honest. "I'd rather be a tiderider. If you can put pressure on my father to have me back working for the Guild, at least part of the time, then I will come and work for you the rest of the time."

He smiled, that rare smile of his that made you forget a lot of other things about him. "All right," he said, "it's a deal."

CHAPTER 15

NARRATOR: RUARTH

I DID AS LYSSAL HAD ORDERED: I WENT to the ghemphs.

In fact, I wondered why I hadn't thought of it earlier. Ghemphs might provide a way to get in touch with Blaze. I'd overlooked them, as we all were in the habit of doing, even though I should have known better after what happened on the Floating Mere. It was ironical in a way. Lyssal, who now sent me to them, had no idea of the opportunity that might exist. She'd left the Mere before the ghemphs put in an appearance, and no one ever told her they came to our aid, or how much we owed to their intervention. They had gone against their normal gentle natures in order to save Blaze, Tor and Kelwyn. And they had done it because Blaze had once befriended a ghemphic female called Eylsa.

I didn't wait till the next morning. I went to find the ghemphic enclave that night. One of the guards on duty at the lowest trug gave me directions, then sent me down to Scum's Row. A walk of several miles around the bay to the very end of the lode brought me to where the River Scour flowed into the Vat. The ghemphs' carved-out dwellings, a group of five households, were just rough holes in the canyon wall, set back a few paces from the water's edge. As usual, I thought, they like to separate themselves as much as possible from the rest of us.

By the time I arrived, several of the house-holes were in darkness. I knocked at one where lamplight still gleamed through window shutters. A moment or two later the door opened and a pair of watchful gray eyes regarded me. I guessed from the wrinkles on the face that it was old, and therefore a male. "Syr," I said, "I have come for a tattoo."

There was a long silence. *"Syr?"* he said at last, as though he did not quite believe that I had addressed him with an honorific.

"Syr," I agreed. "I have a deep respect for your kind. I was one of those present at the Floating Mere." I hoped he would know what I was talking about, and indeed he seemed to, because he opened the door wider and gestured me inside. "I have need of a citizenship tattoo," I said. "And for a citizen of Cirkase, not Breth."

I won't say that he raised an eyebrow, because he didn't have any—like all ghemphs he was hairless—but he did manage to convey an expression of intense surprise.

"I was a Dustel bird," I explained.

"Ah."

"My papers," I said and gave him all that Lyssal had given me.

He took them and flipped through them. Then he looked at me again with another questioning look. "Tadpole Spindleshanks?"

"Er, no," I said. "But you will find the description given there fits me. These papers are mine, right enough, but my name is Ruarth Windrider. That's a long story."

He gestured for me to sit down at a table. "Ghemphs," he said softly, "have a love of good stories and a reluctance to grant tattoos that may not be legitimate."

We stared at each other by candlelight, and I wondered if

I measured up to some unknown criteria of ghemphic peoples. "Then I shall tell the whole tale."

He held up his hand, as if to stop me beginning. "Wait," he said, and disappeared into a connecting room. I heard a murmur of voices, and took the opportunity to look around.

There was little to see. There had been no attempt to cover the rough rock of the walls and floor; the table and chairs and some shelving were all the furniture there was. The shelves held the paraphernalia associated with tattooing: a small brazier and a crucible, china bottles containing dyes and glass ones containing shells and pearls and semi-precious stones, a small mirror, a bowl of gold and silver nuggets.

A few minutes later the ghemph returned—at least I thought it was the same one—but not alone. "Wrath, everyone would like to hear your story," he said. "Do you mind?"

I shook my head. It seemed, though, that my pronunciation needed still more work.

He made no attempt to introduce anybody, not even himself. He sat down at the table, and so did several of the more elderly. The others, some of whom were children, simply sat on the floor. None of them spoke, although there was constant movement among them. It was language: as a Dustel I recognized that. I had long understood that the ghemphs communicated with body movement and gesture and touch, which they used in preference even to their own spoken tongue, let alone ours.

The first ghemph gestured for me to begin. And so I told them everything that had happened to us—to Blaze, Flame, Tor, Gilfeather, Dek and I—since we had left the Floating Mere. From the way they listened, sometimes nodding, sometimes exchanging glances, I guessed that they had actually already heard much of it before, presumably from tales spread by their own kind.

When I finished, there was silence for at least a minute, although it was accompanied by a flurry of unobtrusive gestures, each so minimal I doubt that most people would have even noticed. Eventually the first ghemph said: "We will, of course, give you a citizenship tattoo. You are entitled to one from Cirkase, it's true. You could also have a Dustel one, and we would be willing to give that to you."

I looked down at my hands and didn't speak. I knew what I *wanted*, but it seemed a petty desire. Some things were more important than a few marks on an ear . . . I was a Dustel, no matter what the ear tattoo said.

"We have a policy of non-interference in human affairs; you know that," he added.

"And yet you did, in fact, save my friends on the Mere."

"Those of Eylsa's pod had an obligation to Blaze."

I said, "You know that the spread of dunmagic would be disastrous to ghemphs. Dunmagickers do not care for ghemphs."

A long silence. Then: "What would you have of us?"

"Tell me where Blaze is. Or Tor Ryder. Or Kelwyn Gilfeather. Send a message to Blaze, to tell her what is happening here. No more than that."

There was another prolonged silence and more gestures. I felt a bitter argument was in progress, although I couldn't have quite said why I had that impression.

Then, finally, "We will not do this. Nor do we know where your friends are. But we will tell Eylsa's pod."

The unspoken implication was that Eylsa's pod would deliver the message. I gave an inward sour smile. Humans weren't the only ones who knew how to pass on a hot coal. I said, "Thank you."

"And that tattoo?"

I took a deep breath. The words were surprisingly hard to say, as if I was rejecting part of my own self. "Of Cirkasian citizenship."

THREE DAYS LATER, I STOOD IN MY ROOM in the palace, absently fingering that mark of citizenship in my earlobe—an aquamarine set in a tattooed eye—and looked down on Hell's Vat and the wharves below. Some of the ships had edged away from the docks and anchored out in the bay; it was that kind of night. Free kegs of beer and bottles of cheap spirits, distributed to the lower lodes so the residents could celebrate the Bastionlord's wedding, meant three-quarters of Breth was now riotously drunk. Wise citizens simply went home and locked their doors. Ships' captains decided their vessels were safer anchored in the bay. Already a fire raged on one of the wharves, and I could see people silhouetted against the flames as they passed buckets of seawater to put it out.

In the palace, things weren't much better. Many of the invited guests, the elite of Breth from the higher levels, had disappeared as the day's revelry disintegrated into nighttime debauchery. The Bastionlord's most intimate cronies seemed to have designed the festivities around their own excesses, and from what I'd witnessed, there was no way that the Bastionlord would be able to bed his new wife that night. He'd eaten and drunk enough for twelve men, and sometime during the afternoon I had even wondered if he would live through the experience.

I had to accept that this was the day that Lyssal married the man she'd once despised so much she'd given up her status and her rights to the throne of Cirkase in order to escape him. Once, she had also loved me . . . perhaps somewhere deep inside, she still did, but all I could do was watch. My loneliness cowled every waking moment with its darkness. And I had no one I could talk to about it, no one.

The worst moment had perhaps been at the beginning of the banquet, when Rolass Trigaan—still sober at that point—rose to his feet to toast his bride, and let it slip to all that she was pregnant. "That's right, my friends," he'd said in a roar that extinguished all other conversation, "your royal lord was a bit of a dog while at the court of Cirkase. He stole a march on this marriage, and bedded the lovely Castlemaid in her own home before the knot was tied . . . and the sweet maiden, maiden no more, sought me out to rectify the omission. And so it has been done here today. Ladies and gentlemen, a toast to the next heir to Breth!"

I gaped at that. There was no way that Trigaan had ever bedded Flame in Cirkase. Even if she'd wanted it, which she most certainly had not, he could never have come anywhere near her privately. Not at the Cirkase court, where the royal women were kept apart. It had never happened, and yet he seemed to believe it had. After his speech he'd beamed slyly at Lyssal, and wisps of dunmagic curled from him. Somehow she had used the tricks of dun coercion to give him a false memory. He believed it. He believed the child she carried was his.

I think I felt terror then. Lyssal was proving herself capable of using dun in subtle ways that had never occurred to Morthred. Instead of turning men into walking marionettes with no initiative, she could craft their minds with memories they could never have had, keeping them both whole and yet enthralled.

The cleverness of persuading Trigaan he had bedded the Castlemaid in Cirkase was inspired. Now, instead of everyone having to be coerced to believe in an heir born barely three months after conception on the wedding night, they had only to believe that their lord had been a little premature with his passion. The illegitimacy of the conception wouldn't matter; what counted was that the lord had publicly accepted the child as his, and it would be born after the marriage. If it arrived a little late, well, few would even remember when exactly the Bastionlord had been in Cirkase, and fewer still—if any—would bother to do the calculations.

Oh, Flame, I thought, sometimes you—no, not you. Sometimes this dun-laced creature you have become is just too clever.

I spent that night standing there, looking down on the Vat, wondering what Flame was doing. What she was thinking. How she suffered. My grief was scarifying.

IN THE DAYS LEADING UP TO THE WEDding, she'd largely ignored me, except for the odd moments when we were alone. Then she would ridicule me in every cruel way she could devise: laughing at my physique, mocking my stupidity, denigrating my motives, poking fun at my timidity. I hoped she did it because she wanted me to flee, to leave before the dun that was devouring her forced her to kill me. That was my hope, but sometimes it was hard to believe.

She knew me so well, and it was so easy for her to mine my vulnerabilities and then stack the slag heap of them before me for us both to see.

I suppose I should have been grateful that most of the rest of the court left me alone, thinking me under the protection of the Castlemaid, because there was hardly one among them who could be thought to be anything but debauched or cruel—or both. The only Brethians I saw there whom I could have felt any kind of friendliness towards were a handful of civil administrators who clung on to their books of regulations and attempted to keep the islandom running smoothly. I didn't approach them. I tried to make myself unobtrusive. I didn't speak, I faded away into the background whenever I could. It had always been easy enough to do as a Dustel; it was not much harder now. Amazing how many people didn't notice servants, and the Castlemaid's equerry was, after all, only a glorified servant; a largely mute one, what's more.

And so I was ignored—and lonely.

Yet I didn't lose heart, not at first. I kept on thinking Blaze and Gilfeather and Tor would arrive any moment. Tor would have chartered Scurrey's schooner. I would soon have help and somehow we would save Flame.

But the days went by and there was no sign of them. The passenger packets from Xolchas came and went any number of times. I began to think of all the things that could have gone wrong, shipwrecks being high on the list. I remembered the storm we had encountered. I remembered all the thousands of sea stories there were about the ocean around the Glory Isles; there was not an islandom that could not tell of lives lost and countless tragedies every year.

After the wedding, the slide down into despair was unending.

LYSSAL DISMISSED HER DUENNA AND moved into rooms adjoining the Bastionlord's apartments. Once again she took malicious delight in lodging me in a room with direct access to her reception room, where she spent part of each day receiving her guests. Gradually she tightened her dunmagic hold on Trigaan and the court. Everyone came under her dunspell, obeying her whims with an alacrity that sickened. The Bastionlord's eyes would follow her around like a dog wanting to attract his master's attention, although I doubt that he ever did manage to bed his wife. The courtiers fawned and flattered, butterflies to an over-scented flower. And all of them wore the dun-red of her magic like the flutter of wind-tattered banners.

She began attending the meetings between the Bastionlord and his officials: Chancellor, Registrar, Steward, his new Securia. When the Chief Advisor's post was filled, it was Lyssal who occupied it. At first she did not say much, but that did not last long. Soon she was asking searching questions, then offering advice. Finally decisions were made at meetings where the Islandlord may have in theory presided, but where in practice orders came from Lyssal. Eventually administrators began bringing their papers to her first, for approval, before asking the Bastionlord to sign them. Rolass Trigaan, once a tyrant in his own islandom, was reduced to a mere cipher, who put his signature where he was told. Given his previous history, I was not sure that what Lyssal did was entirely bad.

As the weeks passed, debauchery at the Brethian court seemed to fade away. Children and servants remained unmolested, the screams I had once heard night after night were heard no more. Courtiers seemed listless and uninterested in anything except drinking themselves into a quiet stupor. The color of dun crept into even the remotest corners of the building, fogging my vision, making everything smell and taste foul until I found myself gagging on my food. It seemed unbelievable to me that I was apparently the only person who could see it. That none of those who were coerced seemed to think anything was wrong, that those from other lodes who dealt with them could sense nothing amiss.

And so the lonely days rolled by into weeks of morose solitude. Each day was marred by my inaction, yet I did nothing to change that. I watched, waiting for something; I was no longer sure what.

ONE OF THE FIRST EDICTS MADE UNDER this new reign of the Bastionlord's was to increase the military forces. A law was passed ordering all young men of Brethbastion to give two years of their life to the guard units of Breth. Training was hard, even brutal. To pay for it, taxes were raised and rigorously collected. All this might have led to unrest, except that the extra taxes were also used in ways which benefited many of the people who might have objected the most. The house-hole dwellers of the lower lodes were told that they were to receive piped water and drainage—neither of which they had ever had before—and the work was begun. Security was tightened around the lower levels and wharves. Dark areas, once the domain of prostitutes, pimps and criminals, were now lit and patrolled. Young men who had no prospects suddenly found themselves being offered guardsmen's jobs, with regular pay and food and accommodation. Tailors found there was work making uniforms; blacksmiths and armorers found there was regular business to be had; shoemakers were offered contracts for guardsmen's boots. Ship owners and captains paid the extra customs tariffs gladly in exchange for a safer, better regulated port. The rich paid the extra taxes because they could now walk the streets in safety at night, and the pilfering of their imported goods ceased.

None of this happened overnight, of course, but some of the improvements were quickly noticeable and much of the initial unease about the new Brethlady at court faded away as people whispered that she was responsible for the improvements.

"See how easy it is, Tadpole?" Lyssal said to me several weeks after the wedding, basking in her own success. "By the time I have finished with Breth, the whole islandom will be as helpless before me as a hermit crab without its shell." She smiled, a predatory smile. "They give up their freedoms for dubious reward and without a fight, singing the praises of the lady who secretly gnaws away their viscera."

"You are expending too much power," I told her. Her belly may have been increasing, but she herself was thinner. She looked gaunt, and I suspected she did not sleep well. In order to keep a hold on those she controlled, she had to constantly renew the coercion. Every officer of the guards, every head of every administrative department, every port official, every lode's provost—they all had to see her at least once a week, ostensibly to report, but in reality to have their coercion renewed, their unquestioning obedience to her laws and rules reinforced.

"I will have help soon," she told me complacently. "Sylvs to subvert. Then things will be easier. Soon no Brethman will dare to breathe without asking my permission . . ."

One of her biggest disappointments had been to find that there were no sylvs in Brethbastion. She'd expected to find a pool of talent just ready for subverting; instead she found a city where sylvs, long unwelcome, were no longer resident. "Where are you going to find sylvs?" I asked. "This is not the Trenchdamned Keeper Isles. Are you going to kidnap every sylv merchant who arrives by ship? You'll have to be careful too. If the Keepers get wind of sylv disappearances, there'll be a whole blasted fleet in here with their damn cannon-guns pointed right at you."

She stared at me, that flat hard stare I hated so. "Charnels, Tadpole, I sure as the Trench is deep don't know why I let you live."

I taunted her. "What's the matter? Don't you like to hear the truth?"

"I don't need you, Tadpole, or your sodding Awareness. I have already had Trigaan pass a law that aims to regulate the use of magic. Or so everyone thinks. So that there are no more disasters like the dunmagicking of the Dustels. People are eager to condemn even sylvs at the moment."

I cocked my head, birdlike, and tried to focus on her face. "What the scabbing hells have you done?"

"All sylvs anywhere in Breth now have to be registered; only then can they use magic legally. Even if they want to sylv heal. I have sent a detachment of guards out to start the registration process—they have gone to Kysis on the Scour.

Some of those who register will be told they have to come to Brethbastion for their registration to be finalized. I expect the first sylvs to be turning up on my doorstep, oh, in another week or so. There will be no stopping me then, my spindly friend."

I felt sick. "How the charnels can you do that?" I asked. "You *know* the hell of subversion. You know how much you suffered." I pointed to her missing limb. "You gave up your arm rather than be subverted . . ."

She laughed. "Ah, my dear, I was a different person then. Now I am the Lady of Breth, and she delights in the thought of subversion!" She chucked me under the chin. "Your poor featherless hide. You really just can't get used to what I have become, can you?"

"I don't doubt I will get bleeding used to it," I said with pretended carelessness. "I'll just never accept it. Not ever. Not so long as Flame looks at me out of your eyes. And she does still, for all that you try to hide her."

I lied. In truth, so much dun-red swirled around her I found it hard to see anything at all in her eyes. I cursed my oversensitivity. Around Lyssal or those she had magicked, my vision was dimmed; everything was blurred and indistinct. It was as if by transforming to a human, I'd developed an allergy to magic, and my Awareness overreacted.

I felt sometimes that I was living in a choking, blinding soup of dun.

Anyara isi Teron: Journal entry
6/1st Single/1794

Our last port of call before we reach the Isles of Glory is behind us. Fort Venthwar—a Kellish name for a very un-Kellish place—is a wretched outpost of our civilization, a bedraggled settlement squatting along the banks of a wide, languorous river of brown water. The fort itself is little more than an armed garrison, manned by soldiers of the Eastern Colonial Regiment with a mandate to keep hostile natives under control in South Tromannaland. Our troops are needed to protect our shipping trade along the coast; the area is famous for the ferocity of its native pirates, it seems. Oddly enough, in this miserable, rat-riddled settlement, we found the best of Kellish colonialism, as well as the worst.

The menfolk—Nathan, Shor and the other scientists—were granted a guided tour of the town by the fort Commandant, Ethword iso Lagmin. I met him briefly and must admit I found him an arrogant, unpleasant fellow. I had to agree with Shor's assessment of him: the kind of low-class man who, educated to a higher station in life, then turns on those less fortunate. Put simply, he was a bully.

Lescalles and I were not invited to join the gentlemen on their tour; it was deemed insufficiently salubrious for gently bred ladies. Instead, we were taken on a short boatride upstream to the mission, where we were welcomed by a group of aetherial nuns and a small number of converts. Some of these remarkable nuns have lived there for two decades, battling everything from cases of the plague to native riots—all with unfailing faith and dedication. (They made me feel quite guilty of my petty complaints about shipboard life: I must endeavour to be more stoical in future.) I was impressed with all they have achieved at the mission in a humanitarian sense. Their spiritual successes, on the other hand, are insignificant. Few natives have been converted to our notions of a Kellish God—but the nuns do not let that deter them from their selfless work.

What shocked me, though, were the stories they had to tell—stories of atrocities involving appalling brutality inflicted by the native pirates on any Kells they manage to lay their hands on, and it doesn't matter whether they are men, women or children. Commandant Ethword's solution to this violence is to pursue a course that is equally without conscience. I saw some of the results in the hospital, and I must admit, they turned my stomach. Apparently, Ethword's men retaliate every time there is an attack on traders or soldiers or any of the settlements, and they don't care whom they retaliate against. They go upriver and seize the first people they see, bring them back to the fort and imprison them. Some are executed, others are maimed, some are beaten. A boy I saw in the hospital can have been no more than twelve. Our Kellish policy, in effect, is little better than that of the pirates.

Lescalles and I rejoined the men, quite subdued.

Back on the ship this evening, over dinner, I recounted all we had seen and heard, which led to a lively discussion. Opinions were divided, from Captain Jorten who agreed with the Commandant's methods of retaliation, to Nathan and Dr. Hensson who are both adamant that Ethword should be made to answer for crimes against the people under his protection. Shor, while he deplores the retaliatory violence, just thinks it is none of our business.

I couldn't sleep after that, and so here I am, writing in my journal instead. Somehow I feel ashamed to be Kellish. We are supposed to be better than those we colonize, and I have suddenly realized we are often not. We are supposed to be God-guided, but I wonder about that too. We are supposed to set an example to those *more primitive, but I have come to the conclusion that I no longer know who is primitive and who is not.*

Nothing seems to be black and white now. How is it possible to be pious when I can't see the world in anything but shades of gray? How is it possible to believe when I can think?

I think of Flame Windrider and dun and a baby yet unborn. And nothing seems clear any more.

CHAPTER 16

NARRATOR : RUARTH

I DON'T KNOW WHAT CRITERIA WERE used to select them, but the first sylvs arrived in Breth by boat along the Scour within two weeks: two middle-aged women escorted by a small squad of guardsmen; and, on the same day, a man and his daughter, accompanied by his non-sylv wife, who came by themselves because they'd heard of the registration requirement.

The first I heard about any of them was when a message from Lyssal sent me to the guard quarters down on the Buc-caneer's Lode without explaining why. That was the next residential level below, separated from us only by the street between. I took the stairs down, made myself known to the guards, and was taken through into the prison cells. "Lady Lyssal told me I was to show you the prisoners," the guard in charge said, "and that I was to answer any questions you may have."

He showed me to two windowless cells at the end of a row. The door—a grille of iron bars—admitted light from the lantern in the passageway outside. Still, the place was dark and it took a moment for my eyes to adjust. Each cell held a middle-aged woman, both well-dressed Brethian sylvs. And both fluffed up with anger. No sooner did they see me than I was assailed with their rage: how dare they be locked up, they had done nothing wrong, they just came to be registered as ordered, that was all, they were respectable cloth traders from Kysis and . . .

I let most of it flow over me. I nodded to the guard and retreated back down the passage. I'd seen enough. Each of the women had a dun mark on her right hand. The physical aspects of the contamination weren't obvious yet, so the women weren't even aware it had been done to them, but I could already smell its foulness and see its color. I was shaking as I returned to the palace level and sought out Lyssal.

She was in the Registrar's office, overseeing some paperwork, and when she saw me she waved the Registrar out. The poor man, cowed and conditioned by the bonds of coercion she had slithered around him, bowed and obeyed.

"Well?" she asked. "I assume you have seen my catch?"

"*Catch?*" I spat at her. "They are *people*, Lyssal."

"Sylvs." She sounded smug.

"You have subverted them."

"Yes."

"They will use illusion to escape."

She held up a set of keys for me to see. "No amount of illusion will get them out of there. I have the only keys. And the guards have been informed that they are sylv and they are to ignore anything they see. Or don't see. Anyway, it wouldn't matter much if they did escape. Once the subversion takes root they would return to me, subservient and grovelling. That is the nature of subversion."

"As you will one day be subservient to your son?" I reminded her tartly. I took a deep breath and calmed myself. "Why did you want me to see them?"

"I want you to see exactly what your silence, your inaction, is complicit with."

I felt as if she had kicked my legs from under me. She

was right. If I did nothing to stop her, then I was part of all she did—and her crimes became mine. No matter what my motives were, I could not wash my hands clean. I turned a misery-filled gaze to meet hers, to plead I don't know what—and she smiled and said, "I enjoy your horror."

I stood there, looking at her, helpless, useless, hating myself. Hating her—the person she had become.

"In a week or two, when they are properly subverted, I will release them. Then I will have some of the help I need. Eventually I will have enough dunmagickers to have them spread all over Breth . . ." She rang the bell on the desk and the footman outside entered. "Bring the sylv man and his family in," she said.

I felt sick. "More of them?"

She nodded. "And not a word out of you, Tadpole, or so help me, I will kill one of them while you watch."

I started towards the door, as if to leave. I didn't think I could bear to see this.

"No," she said softly. "You will stay."

I felt myself pale, and turned back to face her. "Flame—no."

"Yes, Tadpole. You will stay."

Then she turned to greet the people who were ushered in.

The moment they entered, I knew someone had been using sylvpower recently, a lot of it too. The silver-blue, with its strong, perfumed smell, was just as potent in its own way as Flame's dun. I felt a moment's hope: perhaps these people could thwart Lyssal. True, dun was destructive and sylv wasn't, but it was not easy for an ordinary dunmagicker to overwhelm a sylv of power.

The two women who entered first were, I guessed, mother and daughter. The Brethman who followed dwarfed us all. He was tall, dressed plainly, and he glowed with sylv light. I put his age at about forty, but it was hard to tell. He was using illusion to mask his true features, possibly to make himself look younger and more handsome. I found it hard to tell what was real and what was illusion, as it was all blurred to me, half concealed under the mist of sylv. He wore his auburn hair long, tied at the nape of the neck with a ribbon, and he walked with an easy assurance. His glance slid past me to focus on Lyssal, and then he swept off his hat and executed an elegantly deep bow. She stood and came around the desk to offer her hand, which he took, to brush the back of her hand with his lips. He was a graceful man.

I remembered the mark on the hands of the women in the cells, but there did not seem to be any dun in Lyssal's touch this time.

"Your name?" she asked.

"Syr-sylv Keren Kyros, a traveling healer of Yebeth," he said, naming one of Breth's outer islands. "May I present my wife, Trysis, and my daughter, Syr-sylv Devenys."

His daughter was, at a guess, about thirteen or so. She had a sour expression on her face as if she had no wish to be where she was. Her clothes were fussy, with a great many bows and frills in a style that had long gone out of fashion, and I suspect she knew it. She wore them as though she hated every stitch, and picked bad-temperedly at the bows.

His wife, Trysis, was a small woman, ridiculously so considering the size of her husband. She too wore a mask of illusion, presumably the work of either her husband or her daughter, as Keren had introduced her without a Syr-sylv prefix. Once again I had trouble seeing through the sylv to what lay under the illusion, but I thought I glimpsed wrinkles and graying hair. She was older than the mask suggested then. Oddly enough, the illusion did not make her beautiful, just younger and very ordinary. Perhaps Trysis was unaware of that—the illusion might have been her daughter's doing, its plainness a petty revenge for the outmoded dress.

"Please forgive us if we are inappropriately dressed for an audience with the Lady of the Breth Bastionlord," the man continued. "We were told we needed to register if I was to continue my work as a midwife and healer; I had no idea we would be ushered into the presence of you, Syr-lady." His voice was husky, and softer than I expected.

"Procedures," Lyssal said dismissively. "They can wait."

I found myself stirring uneasily, as if something had struck a note within me that resonated. It was an odd feeling, similar to the sort of thing I felt with Awarefolk. Feathers 'n' pox, I thought, could one of them be Aware? It would have to be Trysis, because the other two were sylv. My stomach lurched in panic, but when I directed my senses towards the woman, I found no trace of Awareness. I breathed again. Nothing about my senses—not touch, nor smell, nor sight, nor hearing, nor taste, nor Awareness—was the same as it had been when I was a bird. I could no longer trust anything I sensed, and I would do well to remember that.

Almost as if she had read my thoughts, Lyssal turned to Trysis. "You are not sylv? Or Aware?"

"No, Lady, neither. I assist my husband merely. There are many ladies who will not let a male healer attend to them without another woman present. And my husband is a specialist in women's troubles and lying in. You understand how it is."

Lyssal inclined her head.

I wanted to scream at them all, tell them to run, anything but stay. I kept on waiting for Lyssal to make her move, to pour dun into them, but she continued to chat pleasantly. "Where are you bound?" she asked the man.

"We are itinerant healers," he said. "We go where the fancy takes us. I have a belief that sylv healing should be available to all, not just the wealthy. And I have a desire to see new places. And so I travel. A few months here, a few months there."

"The palace lacks a healer at the moment," said Lyssal. "That is an oversight I am anxious to remedy."

The man was no fool. There was a moment's silence—a little too long to be anything but deliberate—then he said, "Forgive me, Syr-lady; we would not have come here at all, except that we were told we had to register. It has been our understanding that sylvs were not welcome at the court of Brethbastion. Correct me if this perception is a mistaken one."

He's a brave man, I thought. Not easily intimidated. Or is he just foolhardy? At least Lyssal didn't seem intent on subverting him, or his daughter. Yet.

"No, that *was* the situation," Lyssal replied smoothly.

"But the two men who were at the heart of the problem are no longer at court—the Lord's Chief Advisor, Ikaan, and the Securia, Yebenk. Both were Awarefolk, with their own antipathies. It is not commonly known, you understand, but I am a sylv, and I have every intention of welcoming sylvs at the court of the Bastionlord."

The man and his wife both smiled. Some of the tension in the room should have dissipated; it didn't. Someone was as taut as a spider's web in a breeze, and I had no idea why.

"That is wonderful news," Keren said. "In that case, may I offer my services to the court as sylv healer?"

Lyssal smiled in return. "Nothing would please me more." A trail of dun wisped out of her and twined around the three of them, a gentle nudge rather than coercion, and there was no way any of them would have noticed it. "Do you swear to serve me to the best of your abilities, and do no harm to me with that service?"

"Of course," Keren replied.

Trysis and Devenys murmured their assent as well, and the smile Lyssal bestowed on them was benevolent. It sent shivers through me. She turned to me, saying, "Go find the House Steward, Tadpole. Ask him to arrange an agreement of remuneration for Syr-sylv Keren. And then go find a suitable set of rooms for our sylv healer and his family. The last Securia's apartments would be suitable, I think, since the new man has moved into Ikaan's." She ignored my astonishment, then looked back at Keren and placed a hand over her growing abdomen. "As you can see, I am expecting the heir to Breth. I will need a good healer for the delivery."

I let out the breath I had been holding. Of course; I should have realized. She wanted a sylv healer for herself and she was prepared to offer one of the palace's best apartments to obtain one. Keren and his family were safe enough—for the time being.

The man bowed low. "It will be an honor. May I also have your permission to serve the ordinary people of Brethbastion?"

"But of course! As the Lady of Breth, how could I refuse such a request? However, be reminded that your first service is to me. And the Bastionlord, of course. And now my equerry, Tadpole Spindleshanks here, will attend to you. He only speaks one or two words, but he can understand you. He's a little simple-minded, I'm afraid."

I ignored the slight, and ushered the family out.

I indicated wordlessly that they were to follow me, and headed for the Steward's office. Along the way Keren asked politely, "May I ask, Syr-equerry, are you perhaps one of the Aware?"

I shook my head. "No." I said it calmly enough, but my heart started pounding. "What makes you think I might be?"

He hesitated, then shrugged. "Rulers—or their consorts— often have one of the Aware as their closest advisor."

"There are none of the Aware in Brethbastion."

"Ah. My wife will be delighted to hear that. She, er, asks us to enhance her appearance, you know. But we love her the way she is, so all we do is remove a few gray hairs and a few wrinkles. Even so, she hates meeting any of the Aware because they can see straight through the magic."

Except me, I thought sourly. All I see is the magic. I can't really see what is beneath it.

His remark seemed innocuous enough, but still I wondered. Did he somehow sense something about me that indicated I was Aware? Was his wife Aware? But if she was, then why were they calmly preparing to live at court instead of denouncing Lyssal? Or maybe that's what they were going to do, the moment they had a chance.

I thought about that, and decided I was being paranoid. There was nothing in their demeanour which hinted at fear. Nothing that told me they had been shocked when they had met Lyssal. So why was I worrying? It was Keren that bothered me, I decided. Everything about the way the man moved was purposeful, and uncompromising. When he spoke to me, I wanted to lower my head to protect my throat. When he came close, I felt as if the feathers on my neck rose up. Not a man to cross with impunity, I decided.

We arrived at the Steward's office, and I left them there while I went to solve the problem of their accommodation.

Apartments were always at a premium, and someone else had moved into the Securia's rooms the moment it was clear the man was dead. I had to move the new occupants out, and they weren't pleased. It was some time before I was able to return to the Steward's office.

The family was waiting for me in the anteroom, their business with the Steward completed. The daughter, sulky and bored, had taken off her footwear and was wriggling her toes. When I smiled at her, she glared at me and hurriedly stuffed her feet back into the shoes. What I had glimpsed of the outlines of her face under the sylv illusion suggested that she was an unattractive girl and her scowl seemed permanent.

"I notice from your tattoo that you are from Cirkase," Keren said as I took him to their new quarters. "Have you been here long?"

I shook my head.

He gave me a puzzled look, as if something about me troubled him. For a moment I thought he would give voice to whatever it was, or ask me to explain something, but he changed his mind. Edgier than ever, I wondered what it was that I had done to make him suspicious.

We reached the Securia's apartments, and I opened the door for them. Trysis gave a gasp as we entered. The interior decorations were extraordinary, even to someone like me who had been brought up in a palace in Cirkase. The last Securia had been a hunter, and the floor inlay, of different colored woods, depicted a hunting scene of men, dogs, speared animals and arrow-stuck pheasants. Obviously not something that appealed to me particularly. The walls of the reception room were lined with molded bas-relief porcelain panels that portrayed naked women in various provocative poses.

"Ah," Keren remarked to Trysis, "that *will* be useful if we need help with female anatomy."

Devenys smothered a laugh. Trysis snorted. "And who was responsible for all this?" she asked me, waving her hand at the walls. It was easy to see she did not approve. "The Bastionlord?"

I shrugged, but I guessed this was not the case. From Lyssal's apartments, I had seen parts of Trigaan's adjoining rooms and they had been full of marble statues of naked men and cherubic boys.

"Hey, y'should take a gander at this in here," Devenys called from the main bedroom. "The ceiling has—"

"I don't think we need go into the details, my dear," Trysis said hurriedly. "I can guess."

I gave them the information they would need about palace routines. When I had finished, Trysis said, "Have you thought about having a healer attend to your speech problem, Syr? If it is physical in origin, we may be able to heal you. Would you like us to help?"

Her kindness stung. My silence could kill these people, I thought. They had no idea they were dealing with dunmagic. Keren and Devenys could be subverted any time Lyssal felt like it.

And yet I said nothing. My head drooped.

"If you do need us any time," Keren said, "just ask."

I nodded, feeling about as low as a caterpillar.

WHEN I COULD NOT SLEEP AT NIGHT, I roamed the palace. The guards—and there were guards outside every apartment—knew me, of course, and I was never stopped. My freedom stemmed from a rash statement of Lyssal's that I could go where I liked, a demand with its origins in a silly incident one day when I could not carry out one of her requests because I was stopped by a guard. Since then, I could go anywhere that I had the keys to, and I had access to Lyssal's keys.

I used the freedom to keep an eye on what she was doing. By the end of the first month I was worried; by the end of the second I was scared. More and more young men were being recruited into guard detachments, not just in Brethbastion, but all over Breth. She planned to put these detachments under the orders of subverted sylvs. She was encouraging the mining of saltpetre, and arranged for its storage in a port town called Kovo, where alchemists experimented with its refinement. She had written to her father in Cirkase, indicating Breth's willingness to buy sulphur. She sent woodcutters in to devastate the forests of Theron Reach, to the north of Brethbastion, to make charcoal, and to cut timber for more ships. She ordered miners to scour Ayin Island for more lodes of zinc and copper and lead. She enticed bronze and iron workers, carpenters and ship builders from all over the Isles by offering them higher wages. Worse, she'd sent people to The Hub to offer outrageous amounts of money to the men who outfitted Keeper ships with cannon-guns and to the foundry workers who built the weapons, in exchange for their designs—and she didn't seem to care what the Keeper Council would think of that if someone told them.

Appalled, I sifted through her papers and realized the true extent of her ambition and the reach of her arm. She envisaged a military islandom run by a hierarchy of subverted sylvs, ultimately responsible to her.

Fortunately, though, things were not so simple. From some of the correspondence I read, it was clear that the making of black powder and cannon-guns was not as straightforward a process as Lyssal had imagined. Saltpetre had to be refined by processes no one on Breth yet understood. Black powder—when mishandled—was unstable, often with fatal results. Cannon-guns sometimes exploded when fired. It was no wonder that Lyssal had turned to bribery of Keeper workers as an easier way to achieve her ends. From what I could discover, though, not even this was as simple as Lyssal imagined: Keeperfolk tended to be loyal to their islandom. The scope of the Brethlady's vision was frightening, but the progress she had made did not keep pace with her dunmagicker's dream.

In the Breth Registrar's office, I saw the foundations she had laid to pay for her schemes. She'd started by having the national treasury seize the assets of Chief Advisor Ikaan and his whole extended family, which included property scattered through the Breth Isles from Yebaan to the Attis Coast, plus a fleet of ships. Then she systematically began to target other rich families—but not Brethian ones. She selected foreigners living in Breth, knowing that there would be less

protest when their property was confiscated in the name of
the Bastionlord on some trumped up charge or another. And
Brethian merchant houses were fast learners; they now knew
that all they had to do was to denounce a foreign-born competitor, and he was a competitor no longer. Once the merchants and traders were happy, she began edging their taxes
higher.

As I uncovered more and more of what was happening in
Breth, and when I remembered that Lyssal had only been in
the islandom for a matter of weeks, I felt all hope shrivel.
She wasn't Morthred, she didn't bother with torture or rape
or even gratuitous deaths, but nonetheless what she was doing was without conscience. And if ever we did manage to
save her, to return her to what she had been, it seemed unlikely that she would ever be able to forgive herself.

ONE NIGHT, ABOUT FOUR WEEKS AFTER
the first of the sylvs had arrived, I let myself into the offices
of the new Securia, wanting to check on just how many sylvs
were now down in the cells. I had a candle lantern with me,
which I placed on the table while I took a look around. I was
still searching for what I wanted when I heard a clicking
sound. My head jerked up. Someone was trying to enter the
room by picking the lock.

I opened up my arms, tried to take to the air in panicked
flight but failed to leave the floor. I blundered into the table,
then had to sort myself out. I finally managed to do something sensible: I snuffed out the candle and headed for the
only place offering me a chance to escape detection. As with
all palace rooms, there were full-length wood-louvred doors
leading out onto a balcony. I stepped out, closed the doors
behind me and flattened myself against the wall. I would be
invisible to anyone inside, but in full view if anyone decided
to step outside. I stood there and wished for my wings. I was
sweating, another thing I had not yet learned to accept as
normal.

A moment or two later I heard the murmur of voices—at
least two people—but I couldn't work out what they were

saying. A dull bluish light escaped between the louvres of the doors. *A sylv light.*

I stayed where I was.

When no one showed the slightest interest in venturing onto the balcony, I risked edging closer to the door to peek through the louvres. It didn't help. I could see the outlines of two cloaked people poring over a stack of scrolls on the table, but they kept their single sylv light focused downwards onto the parchment they read. All I could be certain of was that one was tall, the other short, and that they had no business being where they were. Everything about them spoke of stealth; the whispers, the subdued light, the all-covering cloaks.

The fact that they were using sylv pointed to Keren and Devenys, of course, but I had no idea of the significance of what they were doing. I suppose I could have marched into the room and demanded to know what was going on, but I didn't. At heart, I was still just a Dustel bird who had spent most of his life nervous of human size, human aggression, human weaponry.

Unfortunately, the real significance of that sylv light escaped me entirely.

When they finally packed up and left, I waited a while, then followed them out. There was no way I could tell what they had been looking for, and I never did check to see how many sylvs were now imprisoned.

I never said I was brave.

AS THE DAYS PASSED AND MORE AND more sylvtalents were added to the cells down on the next level, my guilt grew. The only good thing was that they didn't seem to be emerging from their imprisonment as fully fledged dunmagickers. In fact, they did not seem to be emerging at all. I began to wonder if Lyssal was quite as strong as she had thought.

I visited the ghemphs again, but the only news they had for me was that not even members of Eylsa's pod knew where Blaze was.

CHAPTER 17

NARRATOR : ELARN

I STARTED WORK AS A TIDERIDER AGAIN,
making six journeys to The Hub a month. I never did discover whether it was Duthrick's intervention, or the High
Patriarch's through Ryder, that had ensured my reinstatement in the Guild, but at least it happened. When I bumped
into my father in the hallways of the Synod on the morning
after my return, he deliberately turned on his heel and
walked away. I tried not to care. After all, I was back on my
tiderunner, living at the Hall among friends and, thanks to
Ryder, earning more money than I ever had before. I saw
Jesenda every week. I even managed to slink into her bedroom in their riverside mansion on a regular basis, the excitement of doing something illicit almost as powerful as
the act itself.

In addition, she continued to teach me how to control and
work my sylv, until I realized, with growing bemusement,
that I was a talent of considerable skill. My illusions were
almost as good as hers, and soon we were sneaking into

places around The Hub together, listening at doors and spying on meetings. We even flitted in and out of the Keeperlord's office, unseen, and read his correspondence. I loved the excitement and the danger of what we did, the idea that if we made one wrong move, we could be caught. It was thrilling, and I discovered that I enjoyed the thrill. The stakes were high; the punishment for using sylvmagic to spy on one's fellow sylvs was total ostracism, for a start. The numerous ways in which sylvs cheated nonsylv citizens were tolerated, even condoned with amusement—but pity help the person who used magic against another sylvtalent. Jesenda looked at me as if I was saltwater mad when I pointed out the double standards of sylv ethics. "Charnels, Elarn, what's more important? Being loyal to other Keeper sylvs, or ignoring your talent in order to please everybody?"

"We are hardly being loyal," I hissed back at her. It was late at night, and we were sneaking into the offices of the Keeperlord's chief administrator at the time.

"Yes, we are," she said loftily. "How can we work for the prosperity of the Keeper Isles if we don't understand what is going on in its leadership? How will I ever be a responsible Council member in the future if I don't understand the way our islands are ruled? How will you be a great Guildean if you don't know what drives politics?" She lit a sylv light. "Come, let's look at the papers on his desk. I want to know what they are doing about the Castlemaid and that damn halfbreed woman. And tell me if you find anything about the readiness of the Council's ships and the black powder for the cannon-guns . . ."

At worst, what Jesenda and I did might have been close to treason. Although most of what we learned seemed to be mundane and we never passed any of it along to anyone else, our spying was surely against the law. The puzzle was that I didn't care. I was addicted to the exhilaration of it, and we added to the euphoria by making love in the very rooms we had no right to enter in the first place. If it was madness, then I was drunk on it; if it was Jesenda who initiated events, then I was the one who was intoxicated by what we did. That particular night we made love on the chief administrator's desk in the glow of our sylv lights.

When I caught the ebb ride back to Tenkor in the morning, I was happier than I'd ever been.

I passed another two ships on their way up-Race. Both were Keeper Council vessels. I had lost track of just how many Council ships were now undergoing refitting at The Hub shipyards. The sight of them should have made me uneasy about the growing military potential of the Keeper Isles; instead I felt pride. This was our country, our strength, our might.

Somewhere along the line, I had stopped thinking.

JESENDA WAS FASCINATED BY WHAT I was doing with Ryder and Gilfeather, of course. She wanted to know exactly what they were trying to find out and how they were going about it. Difficult, seeing as I was as much in the dark as she was.

The first day I made my way up to the Synod rooms where I was to meet Ryder, I found Gilfeather rushing out the door with a medical bag in his hand. "Oh, sorry, laddie," he said over his shoulder, "bairn on the way." With that cryptic remark he was gone, his peculiar garment billowing out behind him.

"Come on in," Ryder said. "He's gone to deliver an Awarewoman's baby."

"Oh." I stared after Gilfeather as he whirled down the stairs. "Does he always wear that strange piece of cloth?"

Ryder laughed. "Yes, he seems to prefer it. It's called a tagaird. Anyway, take a seat and I'll tell you what we want to do."

I sat down, and took a good look around the room. Along the shelving and benches, rows of bottles and flasks in strange shapes and all sizes jostled for space with charcoal braziers, tongs, knives, measuring weights and scales, filters, scissors, magnifying lenses in brass tubes and things I could not identify. One machine looked like a sort of butter churn operated by a foot treadle. I couldn't identify the contents of the bottles either. They contained liquids, powders, crystals, pickled specimens of things I could not name.

"That's a separator," Ryder told me when he saw my gaze linger on the butter churn. "Work the treadle and the bowl inside spins as fast as a top." What it was supposed to separate, he didn't say.

I think that was when I had my first inkling of how important this project was. The amount of money it must have taken to assemble all this was surely an indication that the Menod Treasury had thrown its backing behind everything that Gilfeather and Ryder hoped to achieve. I let my gaze come back to Ryder.

"We want you to use your sylvpower, and while you are magicking, we want to try to catch it." The look I gave him must have shouted my scepticism, because he added, "I know it sounds . . . bizarre."

"It does. *Catch* the sylv?"

"We have a different view of magic to yours. You can will it to happen and you know what it does, but the Aware can *see* it. And smell it. Gilfeather—well, Gilfeather smells it too. We therefore both know it has dimension. Measurable reality."

"So you want to measure it?"

"Yes. We want to . . . collect it."

I was instantly suspicious. "So you can use it too?"

The revulsion on his face was so sudden and intense I knew I had not hit anywhere near the truth. "No. We want to understand it. What it is."

"Why, if not to use it?"

He smiled slightly. "Well, we'd prefer to work with dun, but we can't find a dunmagicker anywhere near as obliging as Elarn Jaydon. So we have to make do. We think if we can understand dunmagic, we can also defeat it. Or cure it. A noble objective, I am sure you will agree."

I thought in surprise: he's a cynic. He doesn't think he's being noble at all. That was odd; I had thought a strong faith was not normally nurtured inside a cynical nature. Deeper inside myself, I was still sure there was something he wasn't telling me. And I felt a prickle of reluctance. If this research enabled him to understand sylv, then maybe he could turn his knowledge against sylvs too. I remembered the question he had asked me: if you could rid yourself of sylv, would you do it?

He must have seen my doubt, because he added by way of explanation, "We have a friend in common, Gilfeather and I. She is a sylv contaminated by dun, subverted to dunmagic by a dunmaster. We want to find a cure for her."

It explained it all so neatly. Why, then, didn't I believe a word of it? I determined there and then that I would dig up the whole story eventually. I asked, "So what do you want me to do?"

"For a start, create a few simple illusions. And while you are doing that, we want to collect samples—of your sweat, your breath, your saliva, your urine. That's all for the time being. Maybe later Gilfeather will want a few drops of your blood as well."

It seemed simple enough, and we set to work.

THEY WORKED HARD, THE TWO OF THEM, I will give them that. For a start, Ryder also had Menod duties to attend to, and Gilfeather was always off talking to pregnant women and delivering their babies. I thought at first that the latter activities had nothing to do with the magic, but I was soon disabused of that idea. Gilfeather was delivering the children of Aware mothers, and collecting samples from what he called the afterbirth, for his research. I wasn't even sure what an afterbirth was, till he brought one back and explained. He pored over something that—as far as I was concerned—was as attractive as raw liver, while giving me a lecture in fetal nutrition. With Gilfeather, I discovered, all you had to do to get him talking was to look interested and ask a few intelligent questions. Apparently he was investigating if Awareness was passed from mother to child, along with the nutrients. It all seemed weird to me.

I told Jesenda what he was doing, of course. I told her everything, but she couldn't understand what they were up to either. We discussed it, and she encouraged me to find out more, to gain their trust. I was willing enough to do that, but they weren't exactly forthcoming.

Both men had secrets, I was convinced of it. Ryder seemed to spend an inordinate amount of time praying, even for a patriarch. He sometimes reminded me of someone who'd suffered a devastating loss and was unable to put it behind him. I would see him sometimes gazing off into the distance with an expression of bitter distress on his face. He was an odd mixture of a man. He had a dry wit, although he rarely gave more than a wry smile himself. I knew from the work he did with the Dustels that he was compassionate, yet at other times he seemed intolerant, especially when he had to deal with the stupidity of underlings or his fellow patriarchs. And then there was that darkness in him, prompting an unease in me, as if I had an itch I couldn't scratch.

Gilfeather was even less easy to read. On the surface he seemed to be a naive country boy on his first visit to a city. He would exclaim over things that to me were so mundane I hardly noticed them, anything from hot chocolate shops or daily rubbish collection, to the city's drainage system. And yet at other times he appeared to be as astute and streetwise as a town whore patrolling the alleyways of the port. He instinctively understood things about people. I expected him to be easily gulled by the tricksters who were always on the lookout for unwary newcomers, but he never was. Sometimes I felt he read my mind, even that he sensed my intention to betray all they were doing. He certainly seemed reluctant to explain how they intended to use their knowledge.

Nonetheless, because he was so alone in a strange place, I tried to be friendly. I took him with me to meet my friends. He didn't fit in. He was uninterested in drinking or women, which, outside of tideriding, was the predominate passion among tideriders, so although he came with me several times down to the inns on the portside, he obviously did not enjoy himself. The odd thing was that he made me look at myself with new eyes, and I began to wonder if an evening out with Marten and the others was nearly as much fun as I had once thought. Getting riotously drunk and pinching the bottoms of a few barmaids suddenly seemed . . . childish, or it did when Gilfeather was around. Of course, the way I felt about Jesenda might have had something to do with my reformed behavior too.

One day, when I had been out on my waverunner with friends, I found him at the beach when we brought our runners back in. I thought he was waiting for me, but he was doing no more than looking out at the sea, with a faraway expression on his face. "You like the ocean?" I asked, propping my runner up on the sand to drain it.

"Not particularly. I was raised a long way from the coast. Nay, lad, it's just the wide open spaces that I love, and the sea is that. I enjoy the aroma of the wind when it comes up from the south like this. I find cities . . . too closed in. Too smelly."

I picked up my towel and began to dry myself. "Ryder told me you are from the Roof of Mekaté. He said that's a place of grassy plains and not too many people."

"Aye, that's true. He obviously neglected to say it is also the bonniest place in all the Isles of Glory." He grinned at me. "He's not been there, y'understand."

"If it is so wonderful, why did you leave?"

His smile vanished. "I was exiled."

"Why?"

"For killing my wife."

I was speechless. If I was sure of anything, it was that Kelwyn Gilfeather was a nonviolent, gentle man. If anything, he was overly concerned with the feelings of others, hardly the sort of husband who would raise a hand to his spouse. I finally gathered my wits together and said, "And that statement, given without the explanation that it must surely have, is—I suppose—your way of continuing to punish yourself for whatever *really* happened?"

He gave a half smile. "Self-excoriation as a purgative for guilt? Ye're probably right. I just wish it worked. Take a piece of advice from an old hand at this, Elarn. Try to avoid doing anything that'll give ye a lifetime's burden of guilt. Ye can learn to live with almost anything else, but the lacerations of guilt leave their mark on your path through life."

His sincerity made me shiver. "Is—is that what bothers Ryder as well?" I asked.

He shook his head. "His battle is not with guilt, but with dun. And that's a battle he may well win one day. Especially if we can find a cure." He shaded his eyes with his hand, looking out over the ocean, and changed the subject. "What's the ship out there?"

I followed his gaze. "Another Keeper Council vessel." I squinted against the light. "That looks like one of their merchantmen."

"These ships of theirs dinna seem to ever sail out again," he remarked. "Ryder says they are fitting every ship they own with cannon-guns. That they have to strengthen the decks and build gun-ports. And train their sailors in their use, of course."

I shuddered and wasn't sure why. "There are rumors," I admitted. I didn't like the topic, I realized. It made me think of death.

"Now I wonder," he asked softly, "just who does Duthrick think is the enemy?"

I HAD BEEN BACK IN TENKOR ABOUT two weeks when something happened which gave me a further clue to Gilfeather. I had just surrendered some more blood to him and he was examining it under the apparatus they called a magniscope—it magnified very small objects—when he suddenly stood straight. The expression on his face was odd.

"What is it?" Ryder asked, looking up from his reading. He had been delving into a pile of files and scrolls that belonged to the Synod library.

"Uncle Garrow is here," Gilfeather said. His tone was a curious mix of relief, exasperation and pain.

"Good," Ryder said. "I'm glad he decided to come. Why don't you go and meet him, Kel? Take Elarn with you; he's beginning to look bored."

I trailed after Gilfeather, glad enough to get out of the room for a while. I assumed that Gilfeather had made some arrangement to meet his uncle at the main gate to the Synod, but when we arrived there we just kept on going. "Where is he, this uncle of yours?" I asked.

"Down in the port," he replied, sounding unusually abrupt.

"Is he really your uncle?"

"Aye, for my sins. Garrowyn Gilfeather, Sky Plains physician, a doctor who does not like blood. If ye thought me odd, laddie, wait till ye meet Garrow!"

He walked unerringly downwards until we reached the wharves, and then went to stand at the edge of one of the docks, to look out to sea.

"Where is he?" I asked, glancing around. A group of merchants waited in the shade of one of the chandlers' awnings, idly talking among themselves. On the Hub Race a ship was riding out beyond the standing wave, several miles off, close to the open ocean. I guessed that the merchants were waiting for the tide that would allow the vessel in to dock.

Gilfeather continued to gaze out to sea. "On board that ship," he said. "How long will it take to come in?"

"They won't try to cross the standing wave. They'll wait for the next bore." I looked at the tide times on the board outside the harbormaster's office. "Due any time now. Then it will be a while before it docks. More than an hour. But how do you know he's on board, anyway? Or that it's the right ship? I can't even see the flag from here."

"I dinna need to see the flag. Come, let's go and find a place that sells hot chocolate while we wait. I love that stuff. We dinna get it up on the Sky Plains."

We headed back the way we had come, to the row of eateries behind the wharves. As we passed the harbormaster's office, I paused to ask one of the men there what the name of the waiting ship was. "That's the *Castleman*," he said. "The packet from Mekaté."

I ran after Gilfeather. "How did you know?" I persisted. "How did you know the packet boat had arrived? How do you know he's on board?"

"Lad, there are some secrets that are no mine to tell. I

wrote a letter asking him to come, because he is a fine man for herbals and medicines, none better. We thought he might be able to help."

I wanted to protest, to say that there was no way he could have known the ship had arrived at the entrance to the Race, and there was still no way he could be sure his uncle was on it, but he held up his hand, forestalling my question. "Nay, lad, dinna ask. Because then I'd be forced to say something daft, like the fact that my uncle smells as strong as a selver wet with rain."

I felt hurt. He didn't trust me, and that rankled—perhaps because deep down I recognized the wisdom of the distrust. I was not trustworthy. Whatever he told me, I would have passed on to Jesenda. I knew it, but wouldn't recognize any perfidy in it. I was good at rationalizing: it was all for the benefit of the Keeper Isles. To help sylvs. Anyway, Ryder and Gilfeather hadn't been honest with me, so why should I be honest with them?

I was only twenty, remember, streetwise in many ways, but lacking in wisdom nonetheless.

KELWYN GILFEATHER WAS RIGHT. HIS uncle made him look normal.

Garrowyn's grizzled hair and his beard were wilder, his tagaird enveloped him like a blanket wrapped around a ship-wrecked sailor, his accent was so thick I could barely under-stand him, and there was something distinctly uncanny about much of what he said. He looked me up and down when Kelwyn introduced us on the wharf, and said, "Hmph. Addiction to risk is a dangerous way to live one's life, lad-die." A wave of fear shivered through me, which brought his head around to gaze at me again. "Hit a raw spot, did I?"

I blushed red, and it was shame, not embarrassment that brought the color. How did he know? How *could* he know?

His focus, though, was on Kelwyn, not me. "Your fam-ily's in bonnie health, laddie," he said, "at least as bonnie as ye have a right to expect. Jaim and Tess already have a wean on the way, and that keeps your mam looking forward, not back. Your da's just, well . . . resigned, ye ken. Your gran, well, maybe she took it best of all. She's a grand one, my ma. She sent her love and said to tell ye that 'them that say ye needs must tread in the footprints of them that went afore, wear another man's clogs.' Ye'll need a while to understand that, no doubt."

Kelwyn laughed. "Ach," he said, "seeing you is good for the soul, uncle."

"Aye, that may be, but now it's your turn. What happened to those two lassies? And how did you end up here when I told ye to go to Breth?"

Kelwyn gave me a glance, and said, "A long tale, uncle. Let's just say for now that Flame is pregnant, carrying Morthred's bairn. And we think she is contaminated by the bairn. The patriarch Tor Ryder I wrote you about—he and I seek a cure."

"Ah." Garrowyn ran fingers through the wildness of his hair. "Not an easy task ye have set for yourselves."

"Aye, I ken. We need your help, uncle. Luckily, I've just had some good news. Two Menod ladies who are both sylvs have agreed to allow me to deliver their bairns. They dinna hold with sylvmagic."

They started to discuss the finer points of human anatomy and the transmission of disease, losing me in the first minute or two. I trudged back up the hill behind them, wondering just who Flame was.

ONCE HE WAS SETTLED INTO A ROOM AT the Synod, Garrowyn Gilfeather joined us in the laboratory, where he proceeded to turn all their research upside down. He asked penetrating questions about what they had been doing, and tore most of it to shreds. He thought nothing of calling Ryder "laddie" and growled that it was time the patriarch forgot the dun in his belly and remembered the brains in his head that his God had seen fit to bestow on him. He chastized his nephew for not considering that if sylv color was a vapor visible to the Aware, it didn't necessarily mean that basic sylv*power* was a vapor too. Why couldn't it just be a component of the blood that tainted the air because of its magic properties when it was activated by its possessor? Arguments flowed to and fro, much of which I couldn't understand.

I was beginning, though, to pick up a few facts concerning what had happened in the past. It seemed that Ryder had at one time received some sort of dun contamination; it still tainted him, but was apparently not life-threatening. Kelwyn Gilfeather had once been told that sylvpower flowed through an afterbirth into a baby, and based on this observation, he now believed mothers infected their children at or before birth. They also knew that dun fathers had dun children, and that the nondun mothers were infected along the way, if not by the father, then by the baby. So what they wanted to do was find out exactly what it was that passed from mother to child and from child to mother. They wanted to isolate magic . . .

Awareness was harder to fit into the picture because no one could see it. Or smell it. All they knew was that it tended to run in families. Apparently Kelwyn's theory was that sylvmagic was a mild infection of a disease and dun was the more virulent form, while Awareness was the immunity. "Think of it like this," he said to me when I looked blank, "children only get measles or mumps once. After that, they are protected. They have immunity. Awareness is the immunity to magic. Simple. Maybe if we can isolate enough Awareness, we can use it to kill dunmagic, or at the very least, give it to people to make sure they cannot be subverted."

I thought: or kill sylvmagic. Did the Menod dislike sylvmagic enough that they were prepared to destroy it? Ryder did, I was sure of that.

When I spoke of my misgivings to Jesenda a night or two later as we lay curled up together in the luxury of her four-poster bed, she seemed just as worried. "Father always distrusted the Menod," she murmured. "It looks as if he was right. Elarn, they intend to render us impotent. All of us, dun

and sylv alike. And once that happens, it will be the sancti-
monious bastards of the Menod Patriarchy who rule in The
Hub. They must be stopped!" She propped herself up on
one elbow. "And you're the one who has to stop them. You
have to sabotage their efforts. Make sure they don't ever find
what it is they are looking for. It's going to be entirely up to
you . . ."

I felt my heart skid somewhere to the region of my stomach.

"You aren't having second thoughts, are you?" she asked,
running a finger over my lips, chin and chest.

"No, of course not."

The finger wandered lower and any misgivings I had
truly did vanish.

Sometime later, she added, "You are going to have to do
without me for a bit."

"Why?" I asked, alarmed. Do without her? I was no
longer sure I could.

"I'm leaving The Hub for a few weeks. Father is sending
out the three ships that have cannon-guns and sufficient
black powder to use them. *Keeper Fair, Keeper Pride* and
Keeper Just. And I'm going with them. I have a command."

I was stupefied. "A command?"

She nodded. "As I've told you before, he has to send
someone he trusts, and he can't be sure about anyone, except
me."

"But—you are not even a Council member! He's not putting you in *charge*, surely!"

"Well, not in command of the ships, no, of course not.
But I carry his orders. And what orders I give to others about
where they have to go and what they have to do when they
get there . . . those orders have to be obeyed, because they
are the Council's will. So in some ways, I am in charge."

"Where are you going?"

"To Breth. Father received some disturbing new dispatches from his spy at the Brethian court. There are whispers that sylvs are being called into Brethbastion, and we
have long known that the Bastionlord—while he has never
been stupid enough to hurt sylvs—does not encourage them

at his court or in his city. We even had to send a nonsylv
Keeper ambassador, would you believe! So there's something strange going on. And then there's this whole business
of the Castlemaid marrying the Bastionlord. And what we
heard earlier about the Castlemaid being on Xolchas Stacks
in the company of this dunmaster Gethelred. Father thinks
Gethelred may have been the same person as Morthred. Father also believes I may be able to coax the Bastionlord into
selling us the black powder. And he wants me to check that
the Castlemaid is not subverted. Not that it's likely, mind.
But it is odd that soon after the Castlemaid arrived at the
Brethian court, the Awarefolk there either died or disap
peared."

This was too much information to digest all at once, so I
seized on the first thing that set my mind racing. "What's her
name?" I asked.

"The Castlemaid? Lyssal."

"She's never been called Flame, has she?"

"Not that I know of. She couldn't be this person that the
Gilfeathers and Ryder spoke of, surely!" She stared at me in
shock. "*Carrying Morthred's child?* The Castlemaid?"

"No, no, of course not. Silly idea. The Castlemaid would
hardly be sylv, would she?"

"But that's just it. Elarn. She is! My father found that out
when he was on Gorthan Spit . . . I'll ask him if he knows
the name Flame."

My throat tightened. "Jesenda, be careful. You *are* taking
Awarefolk with you?"

"Yes, of course. But only one. Some fellow called
Satrick Matergon. I don't know him. Charnels, I wish we
had more of the Aware in our service! But they seem to prefer to be Menod patriarchs, or to serve the trading families
instead. Anyway, really, Elarn, there's no way that the Bastionlord would ever have married a dunmagicker. The
Awarefolk were alive when the Castlemaid arrived and they
would have warned the Islandlord."

I thought: not if she hadn't been using magic for a
while . . . But the whole idea seemed so absurd, I didn't say
the words. "Yes, I suppose so. Jesenda, I'll miss you," I added,

and I meant it. I was so overwhelmed by the thought that she would not be around—for weeks, even months—that I gave no thought to any of the other things I should have been thinking about.

I was struck by the irony of Duthrick's trust in her. It never occurred to me to think that I had it the wrong way around. I should have been questioning mine.

CHAPTER 18

NARRATOR: ELARN

THE LAST GLIMPSE I HAD OF JESENDA was on the *Keeper Fair*, the very next day. I took the ebb tide out from The Hub, and so did the Keeper Council's fleet of three. For the first reach, from the breakwater to Brenton's Curve, several miles down-Race, we matched pace. I was seated on my tiderunner with my paddle, riding the wave as easily as thistledown on the breeze. The ships, on the other hand, were as clumsy as flotsam caught up in the foam, but they did manage to ride the ebb, strung out across the Race, by virtue of being wind-assisted. Jesenda, and the Council women who escorted her, stood on the deck of the *Keeper Fair* dressed in traveling garb. I thought that was the way I liked her best; dimity or muslin or cambric were all very well, but Jesenda was not the demure, dainty woman such clothes suited. I preferred her dressed the way that matched her character: in trousers, tunic, boots and tricorned hat. She waved to me, and blew me a kiss.

At the turn of the river, the *Keeper Fair* lost the wave

when she scraped the sandbar, and I was swept on my way. A few minutes later the other two vessels, slow to turn, dropped away as well.

LATER THAT EVENING, WHEN I WALKED into the workroom in the Synod, it was to find Kelwyn jubilant because the first of his two sylv patients had just given birth, and he had managed to extract blood from the afterbirth. While Ryder stood with folded arms, quietly watching them, Kelwyn and Garrowyn argued about how best to proceed.

"We know now the sylv is in the blood of the cord and placenta," Garrowyn was saying, "just by smelling it . . ."

"But where does that get us? We know we can't put one person's blood into another," Kelwyn reminded him. "It has been tried a great many times in the past. Remember the experiments by Howel of Ran—and that woman from Mon? What was her name? Veramon, that's right. She tried to save folk who had blood loss. They usually died."

"So we have to try to extract just the sylv. And we already understand how to separate out the red part of blood; we do that when we separate ichor from selver blood. Let's try the same methods, and see just where the sylv is, then—in the red blood, or in the ichor."

"We'll have to watch for contamination."

"Fashin' difficult—"

Before the argument became too technical, I said, "Three of the Keeper vessels are on their way down the Hub Race." There was no harm in telling them that; tideriders would spread the news soon enough. I just wanted to see their reaction.

Ryder looked at me sharply. "Which ones?"

"*Fair*, *Pride* and *Just*."

"All armed with their damned cannon-guns, I'll wager. Do you know where they are going?"

"I did hear Breth mentioned."

"To persuade the Bastionlord to cough up more black powder," Ryder said with certainty.

"More than that," I said. I couldn't see any reason for secrecy, so I added, "They are worried that the Castlemaid

may have been subverted on Xolchas. Oh, and Duthrick is
after a traitor, one of his Council agents, who is thought to
have headed to Breth."

Kelwyn and Ryder both spoke together. "Blaze!"

I wasn't the only one who was surprised by the way the
two men exchanged glances. Garrowyn's eyes narrowed as
he looked from one to the other. "So that's the way the wind
keens, is it?" he murmured.

I doubt they heard. Neither of them looked happy.

"How in all the wide blue skies could Duthrick have
found that out?" Kelwyn added.

"Bastard has his spies everywhere," Ryder replied.
"Blaze used a Xolchas ship—there would have been countless sailors and port officials who knew exactly where it was
bound." He looked back at me. "It is Blaze you mean, isn't
it?"

I nodded.

"Is Duthrick on board one of the Keeper vessels?" he
asked.

"No," I said. "He dare not leave The Hub now, because of
the political situation. He has sent his daughter."

Ryder looked astounded. "His daughter? She's only a
child, surely?"

I bristled, then tried to cover it up with studied indifference. "She's the same age as I am."

Garrowyn gave a bark of laughter. "Blaze will crunch her
up for supper if the lassie tries to bring her in."

"She's clever," I said, "and she's sylv, and she has an
Awareman with her. She also has three ships and cannon-
guns and numerous sylv guards, Keeper Academy graduates. I would say she's a match for anyone, wouldn't you?"

They were all silent for a moment.

"I wouldna bet on it," Kelwyn said finally. "I really
wouldn't."

"And they will have a dunmagicker to contend with," Ryder added. "Who may even be a dunmaster."

"You mean this Flame woman? Or the Castlemaid?" I
asked.

There was another silence.

"God, you make me sick, the lot of you!" I exploded. "You want me to help you, you take my sylv and you use it for God knows what purpose—and then you keep me in the dark like a grouper in a hole."

"We dinna trust ye," Kelwyn said bluntly.

"Well, thank you very much! I don't trust you either. You want to do away with sylvmagic as well as dun, don't you? And you've been using me to do it. You haven't been honest."

"And neither have ye, laddie," Garrowyn said calmly. "Ye've been taking all that ye hear in this room and—what? Peddling it to Duthrick?"

It was close enough to the truth to make me even angrier. How could he know that I had betrayed their secrets? I cried, indignant to the last, "I haven't *sold* anything to anyone! And may I remind you that Tenkor and The Hub are part of the same country? I am a Keeper. And the Keeper Council governs me. The Keeperlord is our elected ruler. They have a right to hear any truths that would help them—instead Jesenda is going to Breth not knowing things she ought to be aware of. It's not me who's the traitor! It is men who accept the protection of the Keeper Isles and then serve different masters." I glowered at the three of them.

Ryder pushed himself away from the wall and took several steps towards me. All of a sudden he appeared much larger than life, and the darkness in him seemed very real indeed. "They go to buy hellish ammunition for their hellish weapons," he said. "Weapons that blast the innocent to pieces in the street and leave them bloodied and dying. And don't tell me I should support such a horror simply because the country I live in is the one that wreaks it! I have *seen* what cannon-guns do, Elàrn Jaydon. I have cradled the dying in my arms, and Keepers should be ashamed to see the flag that flew at the masts of the ships that slaughtered those people. If there is a difference between the horror of cannon-guns and the horror of dun, it is not one of degree, only of method."

He took a deep breath and calmed himself. "Yes, you are right. I would see an end to sylvmagic, if I could. No one should have such power over others, power to cheat and lie and hide the truth. Did you know that Keeper elections are a mockery of deceit, Elarn? Did you know that Keeper merchants control trade in many islandoms with their illusions? They keep whole communities poor, and then say the Menod should solve the problem of poverty with their charitable endeavours. They create the problem, then ask us of the Patriarchy to bleed ourselves dry to cure it! Did you know that Keepers impose international laws on other islandoms—laws that they exempt their own sylvs from having to obey? Trading laws, shipping laws, laws about money transactions, citizenship, magic . . . I'm not talking about the odd rotten squid in the basket of fish, Elarn. I'm talking about a conspiracy of Keeper sylvs, to rule the world to benefit Keeper sylvs."

"You exaggerate," I said, confident I was right. "And cannon-guns will be a deterrent to war and battle. If we are stronger by far than anyone else, who will ever endanger us? Cannon-guns mean peace, not death."

"Dunmasters endangered us, even though we appeared to be stronger. And so it will be with cannon-guns. Others will learn to use the weapons. Or they will learn to use the black powder in other ways. We will pay a high price for Keeper Council folly."

I only half listened. I needed to talk to Jesenda. All I'd have to do was paddle out to meet the Keeper ships when they reached Tenkor . . . but I had to know more first. I said, "If you want me to help you, then you have to be honest with me. Otherwise I'll be damned if I will aid you any more."

"The laddie has a wee point," Garrowyn said.

Ryder calmed and shrugged. "I don't suppose he can do much more harm. The Keeper fleet is already on its way, after all. Gilfeather, you tell him all you think he needs to know. I have an appointment with the High Patriarch." With that he turned on his heel and left the room.

Garrowyn and Kelwyn looked at one another. "Do ye think he meant me?" Kelwyn asked.

"Ye're the one he calls Gilfeather, laddie." Garrowyn moved his gaze to me, his sharp eyes seeming to miss nothing.

I tried to meet the look without flinching, but I had a horrible feeling that there was nothing he did not know about me. "I doubt that the lad is comfortable in my presence, Kel. Be off with the two of ye, while I work on this new specimen ye've brought in today. I'm going to separate out the ichor . . ."

"Come, Elarn," Kelwyn said. "Let's go to my quarters. It'll be private there."

A FEW MINUTES LATER, AS I GAZED around Kelwyn's room, I wondered about the kind of life he was leading. He had made no impact on his surroundings: none. There were no ornaments, no personal belongings anywhere that I could see, other than his hair comb and a pair of scissors on his night stand. I assumed he must be keeping his clothes under the bed, and there can't have been many items anyway, for I never saw him wear anything other than his white shirts, trews and tagaird. He had no weapon except the dirk he sometimes shoved into the waistband of his trews. The only other personal belonging I saw him carry was his waterskin.

"You travel light," I remarked. "Apart from your medi-cine chest, of course."

"Aye. 'Tis the way of the Plainsfolk. We believe that we have no rights to plunder the land we live in. We take what we need, no more, and my needs are few. And the medicine chest is Garrow's, not mine. Would ye like a cup of tea? I can ring for the servant."

"No, thank you. Don't you believe in—" I made a gesture with my hand to encompass the room "—I dunno, beauty, perhaps? A painting on the wall, or a carved bowl on the table. Something for the—spirit. Or the soul." I wondered at myself, even as I spoke. Marten would have laughed at me for even thinking of such things.

He smiled. "Ah. On the contrary, I have a great need of beauty. For the peace and renewal that beauty brings. And when I have such a need, I walk down to the sea and watch the waves, or slip out into the High Patriarch's garden when he is busy at his prayers, and listen to the birds or smell the flowers."

He was serious too. I felt uncomfortable, as if he had chided me for my extravagance. "So," I asked, "is Castle-maid Lyssal your friend Flame, by any chance?"

"Aye. Flame Windrider. Her choice of name."

I had suspected it, but his confirmation shocked me nonetheless. "And she is now a dunmagicker. The heir to the Cirkase throne uses dun."

"Aye."

"And she has married the Breth Bastionlord."

"So we have heard."

"And she is pregnant with what is probably being presumed to be the Brethheir—but is actually a dunmaster's get?"

"So we believe."

"And neither you nor Ryder thought that this information should be told to the Keeperlord or the Keeper Council? That it might be important enough for them to know?"

He shrugged. "I have no doubt that Ryder told the Menod High Patriarch. Whether Crannach passed it on, I never asked."

"He didn't."

"Ah."

"Is that all you can say?" I asked hotly. I was getting madder by the minute. "Don't you understand the—the gravity of what has happened? An Islandlord is married to a dunmagicker who will herself be an Islandlord one day. And she is doubtless surrounding herself with a coterie of subverted dunmagickers—"

He interrupted. "We have no evidence to confirm that she can do what Morthred could do, and subvert sylvs. The source of her contamination is a bairn not yet birthed; that alone may alter many factors."

"All right. We don't know that she can subvert others," I conceded. "But you can't be sure that she hasn't either."

"Aye, there is that."

"The damage she may do is incalculable! How many

people may die because of what she has become? And you just sit here in Tenkor and not tell anyone. What were you going to do, wait till she came to you, asking to be cured? Wait till she coerced an army consisting of every young man in Breth, all itching to march under her banner because they cannot resist her coercion?" My rage entwined with the fear I had for Jesenda into a naked wretchedness.

He said, with infuriating calm, "First of all, we did do something. We tried to stop her getting to Breth in the first place. And we killed Morthred. True, we failed to rescue Flame, Lyssal. However, two folk went after her. Awarefolk."

"You mean this Blaze Halfbreed."

"Aye. Blaze and a lad called Dek."

"Just two people. To stop a dunmagicker."

"Nay, lad. Not 'just' two people. Two *Awarefolk*. Elarn, it doesn't matter how many sylvs ye send against a dunmagicker, they can still lose. Only Awarefolk have a chance, and Blaze is the best."

"She's a traitor to her islandom."

"*What* islandom? She has no country, thanks to the likes of Duthrick and his ilk." It was the first time I had ever heard him sound angry, and the change was startling. I had thought him just a harmless scholar-physician with odd ideas. Now I wondered. He was a large man, after all, and he carried a dirk. He continued, ignoring my involuntary step backwards, "Duthrick would never recommend her for citizenship, though she served him and the Council loyally for more than fifteen years. And aye, in the end she turned on him because he wanted to sell the Castlemaid to a man she despised, all to ensure a military gain for the Keeper Isles. Did ye know Duthrick kidnapped the Castlemaid, and held her against her will on his ship? Blaze saved her. Dinna speak to me of traitors, Elarn."

I stared at him, wondering if he was lying, or just misinformed. I couldn't believe that what he said was true. Duthrick was hardly going to kidnap the heir to an islandom . . . the idea was ridiculous. "And you think that this Blaze can save her now—and bring her to you for a cure that you don't even *have* yet?"

My scorn was obvious, and to my astonishment he went as red as a cooked crab. "Aye," he said. "Exactly."

"You're saltwater crazy." I felt bitter towards him, and Ryder. They had kept this secret and as a result Jesenda and the Keeper ships were up against an Islandlord under the influence of a dunmagicker. The possibilities were horrendous, and endless. And *Jesenda didn't know.* Not for sure.

"What else did you just *happen* to neglect to tell the Keeper Council? What about this dun-sylv cure stuff?"

"We all want to stop dun, Elarn. And we want some way to cure subverted sylvs. Do ye know what the Keeper Council did to their own folk on Gorthan Spit, the ones who had been subverted weeks before? They killed them. Every single one. We want to find a cure so that does not have to happen again. Or better still, a way to make it so that folk cannot be infected in the first place, just as the Awarefolk cannot be."

"You think it can be done?"

"Well, I admit that I thought it unlikely at the beginning. But now . . . with Garrowyn's ideas and knowledge and the information in the papers he brought with him, with both sylv and Awarewomen's afterbirths to take extracts from . . . aye, we may just do it."

"Do you think that the Keeper Council will allow you to go on experimenting if they realize that Ryder, at least, and possibly the whole of the Menod Patriarchy, want to put an end to sylvmagic?"

He considered that, but only briefly. "Ach, aye. Because they want an answer to dun, just as we do. And we cannot 'cure' a sylv without their permission, can we? So why should they fret?"

"No, that's true," I agreed. "Even if you found out how to rid the world of sylv, it wouldn't make much difference except to a few Menod sylvs who would be delighted to be nonsylvs. All right, then, I will continue to help with your studies. But I think someone ought to tell the Bastionlord what he is married to, and just whose baby it is that his wife carries."

Kelwyn shrugged. "Oh, I don't doubt that Blaze will do

that eventually. If she hasna already. In fact, it's possible that she may be on her way here with Flame right now. We had a good reason for not telling Duthrick, ye ken. His hatred of Blaze is irrational. Had he been certain where she was, he probably would have sent someone after her before this." He ran a hand through his hair in an embarrassed fashion and his face went pink again. "Ryder and I are, er, both fond of Blaze. We have no wish to see her cut down by a mob of sylvs Creation-bent on revenge. Besides, we feel that she has more of a chance at getting Flame back here than anyone else." He took a step closer to me. Once again he suddenly seemed intimidating. And yet his tone was still friendly enough as he said, "I do realize three Keeper ships are still on their way down the Race, and all ye would have to do is paddle out and ye could still tell Duthrick's daughter all ye have learned here. I do not think that would be in our best interests."

I tried to sound calm. "No, I understand. All right, as you wish. I won't tell her."

"Or anyone."

"Or anyone." I lied, of course. I had every intention of telling Jesenda.

He sighed, and retreated a little to lean against the wall, where he tugged at the bell pull. "I canna get used to this sort of thing," he said. "Having servants around, I mean. They dinna exist where I come from. Everyone shares the chores. We are all selver-herders, up on the Sky Plains."

He was changing the subject, and I wasn't sure why. I felt uneasy. Something was wrong.

The servant knocked at the door and Kelwyn opened it. "Could you tell Syr-patriarch Ryder that he is needed here, please? And ask him to bring a couple of Aware guards with him." The servant bowed and disappeared.

He closed the door. "I don't understand—" I began.

He raised a hand. "Please. Dinna say anything more. I hate it when people lie."

"But—"

He interrupted again. "Ryder and I are both in love with Blaze Halfbreed. We both also have considerable affection for Flame. Both of us would do a great deal to protect either of them . . . which includes preventing you from meeting up with this Jesenda woman and giving her information that might endanger them. I'm sorry, Elarn, but I am going to ask Ryder to have ye locked up for a couple of days till the ships have left the Race."

"You can't do that!"

"No, but I think your father could. And he will listen to High Patriarch Crannach. And Crannach will listen to Ryder."

"How dare you!" I made for the door, intending to push past him, and found myself with my back flat to the wall, and one of the man's forearms pressing my chest hard so that I stayed that way. His other hand held his dirk, and the point of it pressed into the top of my neck where it met my jawline. I was stunned. So much for thinking him clumsy and placid. He certainly knew how to handle a knife.

He said calmly, "It will be a while before Ryder gets here. We can be sensible about this, and ye can sit down and wait calmly, while I tell ye an entertaining tale of our adventures with Morthred. Or we can stay uncomfortable, like this. Now, which is it to be?"

I gave a wry shrug. "All right, all right. I'll wait quietly."

He stared at me, and sighed. But he did let go.

I used my sylv to vanish. I stepped noisily to the left, wanting to entice him away from the door, but he didn't move. He looked in my direction, but that might have been because the floor creaked.

I moved back—silently—towards the other wall and, uncannily, his eyes followed me. I crouched down, and his eyes dropped. All the hair on the back of my neck rose up. Either my illusion was not as good as I thought it was, or he was seeing me.

I concentrated and made another illusion to distract him. His bedding burst into flames. He didn't react except for the end of his nose, which twitched. His eyes never left me for a moment. Oh God, I thought, he must be Aware. And yet I was sure he wasn't . . . Muddled. I lost my hold on my invisibility.

"I have an unfair advantage," he said. "And it will enable me to make ye look daft. Which is not my intention. We have a saying up on the Sky Plains: if ye get stung by a hornet, dinna poke at the nest. In other words, don't make things worse." Then, unexpectedly, he stood away from the door, and made a sweeping gesture with his hand, as if to say: go ahead, try it.

I didn't move. We stayed like that for several minutes: him looking at me, me wondering if I could escape, if I could get out of there and hide, and eventually make it to the *Keeper Fair*. In the end, I broke the silence. "Just as you want to protect Blaze, so I want to protect Jesenda. She is twenty years old, sent to do something dangerous without knowing a quarter of what she should know. Let me go, Kelwyn. She needs to be warned."

"I'm sorry," he began, "but I canna do that—"

As he started to speak, I snapped back into invisibility and leapt—as silently as I was able—for the door. And he tripped me up. I fell sprawling at his feet and blurred back into sight.

He crouched down beside me. "Don't, Elarn, please."

"What *are* you?" I asked. I sat up. "You really do know when I lie, don't you? You and your uncle, both."

He nodded.

I rubbed a bruised elbow. "I love her, Kelwyn. And what you are doing could mean her death."

"She has three ships laden with weapons and sylvs," he said bitterly. "All I'm doing is evening up the battlefield. Slightly."

"We are supposed to be on the same side! It's not supposed to be a battlefield . . ."

"Exactly. But that is what the Keeper ships will turn it into, given the choice."

He helped me to my feet, and that was when Ryder entered, with two guardsmen in tow, saying, "This had better be good, Gilfeather—"

The Plainsman straightened his tagaird. "Elarn and I had a conversation. Unfortunately, he still feels the need to catch the Council ships on their way down the Race. He wishes to speak to Duthrick's daughter."

"Ah." Ryder turned to me. "Is this true?"

"It really doesn't matter what I say, does it?" I asked.

"No. I'm sorry, Elarn, it doesn't," he said. "We know Gilfeather here is never wrong when it comes to ferreting out lies. You may remember, I did warn you."

He had too. I just hadn't listened.

CHAPTER 19

NARRATOR : RUARTH

WHEN I WOKE IN THE MORNINGS I often felt helpless. Paralyzed. Like a spectator to history, I wrote my notes somewhere in my head, but never actually did anything to change what happened. Of course, that had been my fate too, pretty much, when I was a Dustel bird. A bird no bigger than the palm of a man's hand cannot do much to change the world.

Now, however, I was a man. Not a very large one, and certainly not a handsome one, but a human nonetheless. And I knew things no one else at the Breth court knew, except Lyssal. I had power; the power of knowledge. I had the body to do something about it, the language to speak of it. Yet still I did nothing. I watched while sylvs came and were subverted and imprisoned. I waited while the guards and courtiers, while the Bastionlord himself, were coerced into instant obedience or listless indifference. I kept my mouth shut, and my opinions to myself.

Trench knows what I waited for. To be killed when Lyssal

so decreed? It was only a matter of time, after all. For the baby to be born and the chance Flame could break free from his spell? Hardly—I was unlikely to live long enough to see the delivery! For Blaze to arrive? I didn't have that excuse any more either; it was obvious by now she was not coming. Something had prevented her. Perhaps she had not survived what had happened on Xolchas. Maybe it had not occurred to her that Flame would come to Breth. Perhaps she was searching elsewhere.

When my guilt over my inaction became too much to bear, I thought of confiding in the sylv healer, Keren. Outwardly, he seemed a compassionate, thoughtful man. I saw him and his wife go down to the lower levels to treat the sick there. He was pleasant to everyone. Among the courtiers he soon became popular, with people swearing it was good to have a sylv healer at court again—their gout was much better now, or their arthritis did not bother them any more, or their dyspepsia was much improved. The guardsmen liked the couple too; Keren and Trysis were frequent visitors to the level below, insisting that free treatment for Breth's soldiers was all part of what Lady Lyssal ordered. I doubted that, but it cast an interesting light on the character of the healer and his wife. It intrigued me further when I found they treated the prisoners as well. Keren apparently loftily informed the palace guard that "illnesses starting in the cells can spread to courtiers," and proceeded to cure the hacking coughs of a number of incarcerated lawbreakers.

When I heard that, I descended to the cells myself, and spoke to the guardsman in charge. "The Lady Lyssal would like to know if you have allowed the healer to see the imprisoned sylvs," I told him.

He looked at me as if I were daft. "Of course not. Lady Lyssal would have my head. Her instructions were quite explicit: no visitors unless specified by her." Thoughtfully, I returned up-level. Something was making me unsettled, and I could not quite put my finger on it. I felt a bit like sailors feel when they see an impending storm: watching the buildup, preparing for it—but in the long run, aware that their fate is not really theirs to decide.

Perhaps if I'd not seen those intruders in the Securia's office, and suspected them to be Keren and his sylv daughter, I
would have approached him. After that incident, however, I
believed Keren was some sort of spy, probably a Keeper
Council agent. And if he reported back to The Hub, then he
could also be a potential assassin of Lyssal. If the Keepers
knew she was dun-subverted, if they felt she had been too
long subverted for their healing powers to be effective, she
had no chance. There was another reason I was reluctant to
speak to Keren: I didn't like the way he studied me every
chance he had. I couldn't see his expression through the
mists of sylv illusion, but I felt his suspicion and distrust.

I remained as ineffectual as ever. The days wore on, and a
canker of shame blighted my soul, rotting my self-worth
from within.

LATE ONE NIGHT, THE BELL RANG IN MY
room. As it was connected only to the bell pull in Lyssal's
bedroom, I knew who must have rung it. I flung on a dressing gown, and answered the summons. She stood in the middle of her bedroom, in darkness. Darkness, that is, except for
the glow of dun which was, as usual, everywhere. The door
to the Bastionlord's adjoining bedroom was shut.

"Ruarth?" she whispered.

The use of my name alerted me. Hope flared, stupidly jubilant. *"Flame?"*

"Yes." Madder-red swirled in the air. I could scarcely see
her.

I approached and she seized my right hand. She pressed
something into it and guided it upwards. Only then did I realize I was holding a dagger to her chest, aimed to slip between her ribs into her heart. Her hand was clasped over
mine.

"This is all that is left to me," she whispered. "My last
strength, the very last. But he won't let me thrust it in . . .
lend me your strength, Ruarth. This one last time. End it.
Please, I beg of you."

I wanted to see her face, but the dun wouldn't allow it. I

hunched up, birdlike. My answering whisper—words uttered at last in a human voice, as I had ever wanted to say them—was a dream made real, yet rendered tragic by the circumstances: "I love you."

"I know. And I have wronged you so badly."

I shook my head. "No. It was never you."

"Now, Ruarth. This will be your greatest act of love."

And—I swear—my hand tightened over hers.

Then the door to the Bastionlord's bedroom opened, lamplight streamed in and the Islandlord entered. He looked at the two of us, but did not appear to really *see* either of us. Did not appear to notice that we stood so close together, that there were tears in my eyes, that we clutched a dagger— none of it seemed to register. "Lyssal," he said, tremulous, "tell me again why that sweet little boy doesn't come to my bed any more?"

And the moment vanished. Lyssal pushed me away. "Come back to bed, Rolass," she said, and went to take his arm.

He looked puzzled, but he obeyed.

As she pulled the door shut behind them both, she gave me one last look. "Too late, Tadpole," she said, "and that was the only chance you'll get."

By then, she was over eight months pregnant.

I had run out of time.

I WENT BACK TO BED, BUT OF COURSE I couldn't sleep. I lay there and—as usual—wondered what in all the wide blue skies I should do. Turn my back and walk away? Kill her, as I had just been prepared to do?

Half an hour later, with nothing solved, I rose and dressed. Then I collected Lyssal's keys to the Securia's office, took up a lantern, and stepped out into the main passageway. Not one of the guards on sentry duty gave me a second glance. They were used to my nocturnal wanderings.

In the relative safety of the Securia's office, I lit the candle in the lantern and took out all the orders and letters dated the day before. It was just a hunch, I suppose, but it was a hunch based on my knowledge of Flame. Something had jerked her back to reality during the night. Something too terrible for her to bear . . .

Methodically I went through the papers, one by one. And then I found it. Signed by the Bastionlord, it was a command to the guards to eliminate all ghemphs from the city by whatever means necessary, with all their property to be forfeited to the Bastionlord's coffers.

I stared at it, unable at first to comprehend why she demanded such a thing. My heart started pounding painfully. She wanted ghemphs dead? After all they had done for us? I had no idea if the order had already been executed, but it occurred to me that soldiers had a preference for carrying out instructions like these at dawn, when their targets were drowsy with sleep. Maybe, then, they had not yet done anything about this. I skimmed the other scrolls to make sure there was nothing else, then just left them all over the table. I didn't care any more.

I ran from the room, already trying to think of the quickest way down to Scum's Row. The guardhouse in the palace manned their trug all night long for use in the event of emergencies but I had no idea what constituted an emergency. The Lady Lyssal's equerry demanding he needed to get down to the port an hour or two before dawn?

Feathers 'n' tails, why couldn't I *fly* any more?

I skidded around a corner straight into someone coming the opposite way, and we clashed with enough force to leave me gasping. My lantern went flying and hit the wall with a crash. Glass splintered, and the person I'd slammed into dropped a tray full of brass lamps. The sound was like thunder in the silence of the predawn hours, and it brought several guards running up.

An oil lamp burned in a nearby wall niche of the passage, and by its light I saw I had collided with a servant on his rounds to replace empty lamps with full ones. Because the palace passage had no windows, the lamps needed to be constantly tended.

"Sorry," I said.

A door opened further along and Keren poked his head out to see what was going on.

"Syr-sylv, I was coming to see you," I lied, and turned to the guards. "Lady Lyssal is not feeling well. I need to fetch some herbs from a medicine shop down-level. Could you see that the trug is prepared, please?"

The guards went to do as I asked. I left the servant trying to clean up the mess on the floor and went to speak to Keren. Even through a haze of sylv, he looked tousled with sleep, but his drawled comment was keen enough. "Making medical decisions now, Tadpole?" His illusion-face kept moving, morphing in and out, neither one person nor another, but I glimpsed a sharply arched eyebrow. Sometimes, I thought, it would be better not to be Aware, at least in my case. I'd rather just see the illusion and be done with it. Anything would be better than faces that melted and reformed behind a mist of silver-blue.

"There's nothing wrong with Lady Lyssal," I said quietly, so that the servant would not hear. "I just need to get down into the port quickly. I am sorry to have awakened you."

I went to hurry by, but he reached out and brought me to an abrupt halt, gripping my arm. He was a strong man. "Wait. I'll come with you."

"I don't have time," I protested.

"Don't move," he said.

He disappeared inside his apartments to dress; I hurried off towards the palace entrance. He caught up with me, still tucking in his shirt and tying back his hair, just as I stepped into the trug.

One of the guards closed the gate for us. "Ready?" he asked.

Keren had his cloak with him, slung carelessly over one shoulder with his fingers hooked into the hood, but didn't put it on even as we started to descend. I thought it a little odd, because it was cool out there. A brisk wind whipped across Hell's Vat and swept up the cliff. The trug ropes sang, pulleys rattled and clinked. I swallowed hard as the contraption swayed when the wind caught us.

As we descended, Keren leaned back against the railing and regarded me speculatively. "So," he said, "suppose you tell me what all this is about."

"It's private," I snapped, only half listening. I hated being up so high when I had no wings. "I didn't ask you to come along."

"My apologies." His tone was as dry as a sand dune in the sun.

We eyed each other warily, distrust and an odd feeling of kinship warring in us both. The farther down we traveled, the more the powerful aroma of sylv that usually swirled around him lessened.

"I think it is time you and I were honest with one another," he said at last.

I looked away so that he couldn't see my face. "I can't. I'm sorry. Some secrets are not mine to disclose."

"I would endanger both Trysis and Devenys by divulging my own," he said. "Yet I am willing to take the risk."

I shrugged. "Go ahead."

"Without a guarantee you would be as forthcoming?"

"What guarantee would you have that I would keep a promise of secrecy anyway?"

"True." He pursed his lips, considering.

"Oh, this is ridiculous!" I exclaimed. "Neither of us trusts the other. Where can this possibly go?"

He changed direction. "Where are you going now in such a hurry?"

"To the ghemphic enclave."

"The *what* enclave?"

My wretched accent again. I enunciated as clearly as I could. "Ghem-phic."

"Why?"

"Because I have reason to believe there might be a raid on them."

He looked blank. "Ride?"

I sighed. "Raid . . . raid . . . by the guards. On them. Aimed at getting rid of them from Brethbastion."

He stared at me as if he could not believe what he was hearing. "Ordered by the Bastionlord?" he asked finally.

I nodded.

"Or by his wife?"

I was silent.

"Why do you protect her? You *must* know what she is. She doesn't coerce you."

Skies, I thought, he knows she is a dunmagicker. I was trembling and gripped the railing to hide my fear. He had to be a Keeper. Nothing else made more sense. And then it struck me. That night in the Securia's office: one sylv light, two people. One of them had to be able to see the light created by the other . . .

The trug arrived at the change platform, and spared me the difficulty of answering. A guardsman came forward to open the gate. "We are going all the way to the bottom," I told him. He nodded and indicated where the trug for the next section, attached to a separate block and tackle, was already waiting.

Keren and I didn't speak until we were on our way down, alone again. "Answer my question," he said.

"What makes you think she's a dunmagicker?" I countered.

He didn't answer.

I stared at him, trying to penetrate the sylv with only the dimness of a single oil lamp to help me. "Awareness," I said, sounding stupid. "Trysis is Aware?" Only Awarefolk could see another's sylv light. *They must have known I was Aware.*

He was silent, and we remained unspeaking until we reached the next relay platform. I was thinking furiously, trying to work out what I was missing. We changed trugs again, after a brief argument with the guardsmen over whether we had to pay or not.

"You're right," I admitted finally as we started on the way down once more. "We need to be honest with each other. But not now, not here. When we go back to the palace again. Right now my problem is to warn the ghemphs they may be in trouble. I suspect that—if they weren't hassled last night—it will be today at dawn."

"Don? Oh—dawn. Yes, common procedure with guardsmen. Dawn attacks are demoralizing. What exactly are the orders?"

" 'To eliminate them from the city by whatever means necessary.' "

"Trench below! *Why?*"

"At a guess? It might be money. Sylvs use gold, silver and precious gems in their citizenship tattoos. Or it might be because ghemphs are the means by which islandoms maintain their nationhood. Their identity. Breth plans to subdue the whole of the Middling Isles, make it one nation under the Breth banner. Tattoos are a reminder of divisions Breth wants to eliminate."

He was silent again, thinking about that. "We have a lot to discuss, you and I, Tadpole. And that's not your name, surely."

"No," I said. "My name's Ruarth."

"Wrath?"

I nodded. It was close enough.

CHAPTER 20

NARRATOR : RUARTH

ONCE OUT OF THE TRUG ON THE BOTTOM level, I started jogging off towards the mouth of the Scour. I wanted to get there as soon as possible, but there was little point in racing: we would just end up exhausted. It was something like three miles to the river mouth.

Keren left his cloak with the guards at the bottom trug, and it was then I realized why he had brought it in the first place. It had concealed a sword and harness. Like Blaze, he preferred to carry the large sword in a hinged scabbard on his back. He was fit and had no problems running while wearing the thing, and I was glad to see all my weeks of stair-climbing exercise enabled me to keep up.

Even so, by the time we arrived at the enclave, the sky had lightened—and the guards were there before us. We came around the corner and ran into two men whose job it was to stop anyone going any farther along the path. Ahead of us were the ghemphic house-holes. Even as we arrived, we heard a scream and then a gray shape ran from one of the houses and dived into the river. Beside me, Keren tensed. That did not go unnoticed by the guards, who eyed the healer's sword and went to draw their own weapons.

Hurriedly I stepped in. "I am equerry to Lady Lyssal," I said, "and this man is the personal healer of the Bastionlord and the court. We are here to oversee the—operation and make sure there are no casualties." The last word came out sounding like causalities. I attempted to repeat it and only managed to mangle it further.

"Casualties," Keren said quickly, as the men looked mystified. "Lady Lyssal wants no one hurt."

One of the men laughed. "Then you are too late, I imagine. Our orders were to see the ghemphs out—and not before time, if you ask me—and if they are stupid enough to resist . . ." He shrugged. "Then they get what they deserve."

Keren gave me a look that said half a dozen things all at once, then brushed past the guard and started to run towards the huts. The guard reached for his bow, which was propped up against the cliff. "I wouldn't, if I were you," I told him mildly and wondered at Keren's certainty I would be able to stop the man. The healer was a gambler. "Lady Lyssal is due to give birth soon. I suspect your Lord would take it amiss if the healer were to die just before the birth of the heir."

He hesitated, then shrugged. "You'd better make sure he doesn't interfere then, Syr," he said.

I went after Keren. He had entered the first of the householes, and was kneeling alongside an elderly ghemph on the floor. The creature was dead.

"Do you always turn your back on guards with bows?" I asked, nettled.

He shrugged, apparently unconcerned. "I knew you'd stop him. Besides, there was no way he'd have had time to aim before I got in here." He stood up, shaking his head. "This fellow is dead."

In the windowless inner rooms of the house, some soldiers were poking around, looking for hidden people and valuables. Under some bedding they found another ghemph, and dragged the creature out. A female, or so I guessed as she was young. One of the guards said, "Well, what have we here, d'you think?"

"Someone with something to hide perhaps?" another replied. "Shall we give 'em a lesson to remember us by?" And he tucked the tip of his knife under the ghemph's chin. "We told you all to get out and line up in front of the houses. We don't take kindly to disobedience from you gray-skinned scums of wood-lice."

Keren had his weapon out in an instant. The calm, gentle healer vanished, but the guards did not appear to notice. Their mistake.

"Cut off his ears," a third guard, oblivious, suggested.

"Good—" the first began. He never finished. Keren burst on them like a wind squall. He flattened one man simply by hooking his leg behind the fellow's knee and giving him a good push. The guard ended up on his back, looking astonished. Keren elbowed another man hard under the ribs so that he collapsed with a whoosh of air. The last fellow, the one with the knife, found a sword at his own throat. He faltered and dropped his weapon. The ghemph scrambled to her feet.

"Run," Keren advised her, and she didn't wait for a second invitation. She was out of the house in a second, heading straight for the river. Keren looked around at the three soldiers. "The Lady of Breth did not want the ghemphs hurt," he lied. He dropped his sword from the man's throat and ran it down along his uniform buttons to the ties of his culottes, where the tip hovered, horribly suggestive. With his free hand, he indicated the body in the other room. "It seems you have already displeased her. Take care not to compound the error."

I expected them to fight back. They were soldiers, after all. But they exchanged glances and did nothing. "That wasn't our orders," one of them mumbled. He seemed embarrassed. "No one said we wasn't to kill any of them critters."

"Well, someone is telling you now," Keren said, and turned his back on them to go to the next house. "We fixed that fellow's pox the other day," he said to me by way of explanation as we left, and I heard rather than saw his amusement. "Marvellous how grateful that makes a man."

In the next house-hole we found three more dead, gutted like plucked waders prepared for the pot. And there was a child in the fourth house. She looked as if she'd been trampled. There were no more bodies that we could find, nor any more living ghemphs. Presumably they hadn't waited for whatever fate the soldiers had planned for them, but had disappeared into the river. By the time we reached the last house-hole, the soldiers were piling a few pitiful belongings in a heap outside the first door. Apart from the tattooing gemstones and instruments, there was hardly anything.

"Four adults dead," I said to Keren, "and one child. All for a few precious stones and metals." I was thinking of Flame. Of how she would ever learn to live with this, if we managed to rescue her.

Keren said nothing. He left the house and crossed the road to the edge of the river. He knelt there and dipped his hands into the water to wash them. He rubbed his right palm hard, and I thought I saw a flash of gold. I went to stand behind him. There was a soft swirl in the water, and a single head emerged, a gray face poking up through floating strands of kelp. I thought it might have been the first of the ghemphs I spoke with on my initial visit to the enclave. He and Keren gazed at each other. "I am so sorry," Keren said. "We were too late to warn you."

"The bodies," the ghemph said. "Give us the bodies."

Keren nodded and went away, leaving me there with the creature.

"Why?" he asked.

"Dun." I crouched to speak to him. "The dun of a subverted sylv who has come to power . . ."

"It must be stopped," he said.

"It will be. I swear it." The words almost choked me.

He nodded. "A contract has been broken here today, between your people and mine. The time has come for change, Ruarth Windrider."

"We have both suffered from dun excesses," I pointed out, more than a little riled that I—a Dustel—should be lumped together with these Brethian bullies.

Keren came back with the first body. A guards officer was shouting at him, but he took no notice. He stripped off the clothes, and gently lowered the dead creature into the water. The ghemph received it and sank out of sight.

"*Hey!* What the Trench do you think you're doing?" The officer strode up, his face glaring with fury. "You are inter-fering in Securia business here!"

Keren stood. "No. It is you who interfere in the busi-ness of humanity. What you have done here today is against all the accepted practice of the Isles of Glory." And he brushed past the guard to fetch another body.

"Syr," I told the officer, "it is best you do not involve yourself. If you value your position."

The man hesitated. He was dubious, though he must have known who we were by this time. He also knew what he had been ordered to do.

I played on his doubt. "If I were you, Syr, I would not draw attention to yourself, or to the fact that people died here."

He stared at me, then turned on his heel and stalked away. One by one Keren and I carried the other bodies to the water's edge and released them into the hands of their people. The child was last, and the ghemph who came to re-ceive the body was, I suspected, the mother. I will never for-get the look on her face as she took the dead girl into her arms.

Beside me, Keren said, "And to think I once thought their faces had no expression." He sat down on the bank and watched as the swirls in the water flattened and vanished, and broad brown leaves of kelp closed over the surface gaps. The sylv that had enshrouded him ever since his arrival in the city was thinner now. I sat beside him and took his right hand in mine. I turned it over, palm upwards.

The gold gleamed at me: a curled M with a line behind it. I traced out the shape with a finger. Tears pricked at the back of my eyes. "I knew someone once," I said, "who had that mark on the palm. Only that person wasn't a man, or a healer, or a Brethian, or a sylv." I reached up and touched Keren's ear, where a tattoo melted in and out of my sight. My fingers found an empty lobe. I sought his eyes, striving to penetrate the sylv. It teased out into strands and softened. "Her name was Blaze," I said.

Anyara isi Teron: Journal entry
16/1st Single/1794

I'll admit, I never guessed that Keren was Blaze. Silly
of me, I know. I think perhaps I fell victim to my
Kellish upbringing. The idea that a woman would
pretend to be a man is so foreign to me, it is almost
unthinkable. Almost as unthinkable as the idea that a
boy would pretend to be a girl.

And yet, why not? It worked, did it not? They
deceived everyone. They manoeuvred themselves into
the ideal place to be—healers at Flame's side when
the baby is born.

How straight-laced I am still! How bound by the
rules of the world I was born into! Ladies must be
ladylike. We do not wear men's clothes, we do not behave
like men or talk like men, we do not pretend to be men,
and we certainly must not aspire to a man's ambitions.

Nathan laughed at me when I admitted that I was a
little—well, shocked. You are naive, he said. Well, I
said, that kind of thing never happens back in
Postseaward. He started laughing. I pressed him to tell
me what was so amusing. Finally he told me there are
indeed women who dress as men, and men who dress
as women, yes, back in Postseaward too. There are
even women who bed women and men who bed men.
He didn't want to talk about these things at first, but I
would not relent, and I can be a determined lady. In
the end I learned so much. Indeed, I learned how
much I didn't know, how much I didn't understand
about the nation I lived in. About human existence.

My overall feeling is not now one of shock, but of
outrage. Outrage that—because I am supposedly a
gentlewoman, an unmarried one at that—I am judged
to be too delicate, too sensitive to be exposed to
reality. I am still outraged, yet somehow there is
something a little, well, absurd about it too. Women,

who are destined to give birth and often to suffer in the process, are judged too weak to be exposed to reality. Does it never strike anyone as even faintly ridiculous? Let alone preposterous?

If Shor were to hear this conversation, Nathan remarked, he would probably call me out on the grounds of shaming you. Of showing the utmost disrespect to a woman of breeding.

Pah! I said, and I say it still. I have extracted a promise from Nathan that if I have any further questions about anything I see or hear or read, then I am to feel free to ask him to explain. I shall hold him to it too. He doesn't always find it easy to be frank with a gentlewoman, of course, but at least he lived much of his life in the Isles of Glory, where people are not quite as hypocritical as they are back in Kells. I am grateful for that, at least.

I have come a long way, and I have started to wonder now about wearing trousers, as traveling women do as a matter of course in the Isles. It would be so much more sensible than these ridiculous skirts and petticoats that are so difficult to launder. I wonder what Shor would have to say about that.

In fact, I wonder about a lot of things, these days.

There is always time to indulge in idle thought aboard ship, and I have been giving much consideration to what I want to do with my life after this voyage is over. The only thing of which I am certain is that I do not wish to return to the same life I led before. I must have more purpose. I need—not fame, or money—but validity. At the end of my life, I need to be able to look back and see that I accomplished something.

The seas are rough tonight, and my nib dances over the page as the ship tosses. I shall go to bed and puzzle some more over why being a woman of means seems to preclude any sort of accomplishment beyond the production of neat needlework, the execution of pretty watercolors, the possession of a passable singing voice and the birthing of a great many children.

CHAPTER 21

I LOOKED AT HIM, STUNNED, THEN shocked, then a mess of emotions. "Wrath," I said. *"Ruarth?"*

I couldn't believe it. *He wasn't Aware.* But Ruarth *was* Aware, therefore this person could not be Ruarth. I stared at him. It was possible that he could have been a Dustel bird once, I supposed. Like most Dustels, he was short and he spoke in a sort of thick-tongued way that distorted some sounds. But he had muscles in his legs, a tanned skin—and yellow hair. No Dustel I'd ever seen had yellow hair. They were Souther people! His tattoo was Cirkasian.

I said, suspicious, "But you are not Aware. If you were, I would know it. And why did you not recognize me? Us? This mark on my hand?" I shook my head. "You aren't Ruarth."

"Yes, I am. The same Ruarth who flew into that blowhole the day Eylsa gave you that gold bouget. I'm just not . . . the same. Magic blinds me. Sylv stifles me. Dun suffocates me. I hear differently, see differently, smell differently. I don't even recognize your voice. The whole world has changed for me. The worst is my Awareness. It is oversensitive. All I see of you is this . . . this cloud of sylv. Whose is it? Where does it come from?"

I paused to sieve through all that information. Only Ruarth could have known about the blowhole, surely . . .

I said, still cautious, "Trysis. She's a sylvmaster healer from Keret. Very strong in power. She made all the illusions because we didn't want Flame to recognize us. She even changed my voice. And she does all the healing, of course. Prove to me you are Ruarth."

"I saw you search Ransom Holswood's room back in that inn on Gorthan Spit, The Drunken Place. I was sitting on the window ledge, and you read his name written on the flyleaf of his breviary . . ."

Now that was definitely something that only Ruarth could have known. Ransom Holswood, the heir to the Bethany Islandlord, had run away to the Spit because he had wanted to be a patriarch rather than a ruler. I'd only realized his identity after I'd searched his room and found his breviary.

I said aloud, berating myself, "How daft can you be, you shrimp-brained halfbreed?" I grinned and pulled him into my embrace, swamping him with the fierceness of my hug. "Trench take it, Ruarth—I am so *glad* to see you! We thought you were dead!" I released him and took a hurried glance behind to see if anyone had noticed the odd sight of the healer embracing the Brethlady's equerry. Fortunately, none of the guards appeared to have any further interest in us. They were already carting away their loot. I turned back to him. "Crabdamn, Ruarth, you have one Trenching load of middenshit to explain here. How can she have done this?" I was talking of Flame, of course, and I didn't expect an answer. I already knew.

"It's our fault," he said quietly. "Not hers. You promised to kill her. You've had the opportunity. And so have I. We've allowed this to happen, Blaze. We are just as much to blame. I didn't do anything for exactly the same reasons *you* didn't do anything."

I gave a sigh. It was true . . . we were to blame. And I had reneged on my promise to her. "Not so easy, is it?"

"No."

For a moment we just looked at each other in silence, sharing so much. "We've been waiting. Waiting till the baby is delivered. Then . . ." I shrugged. "We thought once the child was dead, maybe she would have a hope . . . Oh, Ruarth, it's so hard to give up hope."

"You know it's Morthred's? And the child is the one responsible for her subversion?"

"Yes."

"And you will kill it."

"Oh yes; that I will do without a qualm," I admitted.

"If you want her to live—*Flame* to live—don't tell her what happened here. Not ever."

I thought about that, wondering what he meant.

He waved an arm at the house-holes. "Blaze, she will have so much to learn to live with, if she is ever cured. Don't add to it."

"She may hear it now from the guardsmen," I warned. "Ruarth, you had better tell me what happened. All of it. How come you look like a Cirkasian? You even have a real tattoo! And you don't—well, you don't look much like some of the other Dustel bird people I saw after . . . after what happened. I did think there was something unusual about you at first. I caught a feeling of Awareness once or twice, but when I homed in on it, what I felt was so odd, I dismissed it. I thought it must have been all the dun confusing me. There's so much of the sodding muck about. It didn't occur to me you were Ruarth. I *was* curious; I couldn't understand why you—alone of all the court—were not coerced. I was suspicious."

"That's putting it mildly," he said. "I couldn't walk into the room without raising your hackles."

"Sorry." Then my grin faded. "How—how is she, really?"

"Blaze, you know as much as I do. She's been subverting sylvs," he said. "Or trying to. I'm not sure that she is being very successful."

I laughed. "Oh, yes, she's been successful, all right. But Trysis has been walking behind her, so to speak, curing them as fast as she's been doing it."

He gaped at me, almost too scared to hope.

"We arrived the same day as the first of the sylvs—remember? Trysis blurred herself and sneaked down into the cells every night, to undo whatever Flame did during the day. Dun subversion is easy enough to heal if it's done immediately. Of course, Flame's been reinfecting them as she realized things weren't happening as she wished, but Trysis has been attending to that as well. So far Flame hasn't an inkling of what has been going on. She thinks it's the failure of her dun to work as quickly as she would like."

He looked as if a huge burden had been lifted from him. "Thank you," he whispered. "Feathers 'n' pox, Blaze—" He was so overwhelmed, he couldn't finish.

"Thank Trysis." I clapped him on the back. "You look as relieved as a boat just cleaned of its barnacles!"

He smiled weakly. "Something like that."

"We've promised to get them out of there eventually." I stood up. "Let's get back."

"Your sylv illusion is wearing off. You are beginning to look more like Blaze, and there's less blue fog around."

"That's the disadvantage of this. I can't be away from Trysis much, or my voice begins to sound like me, and I lose this handsome face. And as for Dek—" I laughed. "The need for illusions is driving him crazy, as you can imagine."

"Dek?"

"Devenys. Didn't you guess?"

He stared. "Charnels! How ever did you get Dek into a *dress*?"

"With a great deal of trouble! He hates it, but I just couldn't run the risk of Flame guessing it was us. It seemed the best way to disguise him. I thought she might be on the lookout for me in the company of a sylv for illusion—but that she would be less suspicious of a couple with a daughter."

As we walked back towards the trug, I told him the whole story, from when Morthred was killed and Tor and Kelwyn decided to go to Tenkor to find a cure.

As for Dek and me, when we left Xolchas, we'd headed not for Brethbastion, but for the south-west Brethian port of Kovo. I needed to find a sylv, because I wanted to disguise us both with illusion. I already knew from a past visit that there were no sylvs in Brethbastion, and that the Bastionlord didn't like sylvs, so I thought I had a good chance of finding a disgruntled sylv healer somewhere in Breth, someone who wouldn't mind taking part in a deception. I wasn't worried about any Awarefolk I might find at the Brethian court—it was just Flame I wanted to fool. So I went to Kovo, disembarked and sent the ship, the *Petrelwing*, on its way to Brethbastion without us. Eventually I had found Trysis. She was not only a sylvmaster in healing skills, but she had a deep hatred of dun, having lost several sylv friends to subversion. We then set off for Brethbastion on one of the riverboats down the River Scour. The *Petrelwing* had to beat around the southern cape of Breth so it arrived two days after we did.

When I finished the tale, Ruarth asked, "What made you come *here*? I mean—how did you know that's where Flame would go after Morthred died? I did ask the ghemphs to tell you—"

"I didn't see any ghemphs till this morning. No, it was an assumption we made once we realized Flame was pregnant with Morthred's child. How did *you* find out that the baby was Morthred's?"

"You'd better hear the whole thing. It's not much of a story. I—I'm not much of a hero."

I don't think there was much he left out of his tale, except for details. It was an appalling story: a recounting of a tragedy that left me feeling ill. Ruarth believed himself inadequate and cowardly, but to me, what he'd endured showed his courage, and the extraordinary depth of his love for Flame, not his cowardice.

When he finished, I told him as much. "You know," I added, "once, when Flame and I were talking, about the two of you . . . I thought to myself that . . . well, to put it frankly, that she loved you more than I loved Tor. The depth of what she felt . . ." I cleared my throat. I never found it easy to speak of love. "I don't know if it helps, but the way you felt

about one another: it was strong enough to surmount diffi-
culties that would have made most people throw up their
hands and walk away. You will surmount this too. Because
of who you are, and what you had."

He gave a strange sort of shrug, like a bird ruffling its
feathers, but he didn't say anything. I don't think he could.

By the time we reached the trug platform, the top of the
cliffs was already lassoed by sunlight. The lower cliffs and
the Vat were still shadow-dark however; the surface of the
water appeared brown in the gloom, brown and oily.

"Seeker—where's Seeker?" Ruarth asked suddenly. I
knew he had ambivalent feelings about that halfbreed fen-
lurger of mine. There were times when even I thought
Seeker eyed birds with the speculative air of a predator contemplating its next meal.

"He's on the *Petrelwing*. And probably furious with me
for leaving him behind. I've heard him howling for me a
couple of times in the middle of the night, but I could hardly
arrive at the palace with that barnacle-brained mutt in tow."
The trug creaked down onto the platform and, as there were
other people going to ascend with us, we let the subject
drop.

As we rode up, I couldn't help but feel cheered that I had
made contact with Ruarth at last. Still, the day had begun
badly with the ghemphic deaths and, from then on, it just got
steadily worse.

I STOOD ON THE BALCONY OUTSIDE MY
room and looked at the ship entering the Vat. Dek, still in a
muddle of delight that Ruarth was alive and dismay that the
Dustel had seen him wearing a dress, had just drawn my attention to the new arrival. I didn't need to read the name to
know it was a Keeper ship, one of the Council fleet. Their
ships were all built along the same design: raked masts and a
high poop deck. Besides, sylvmagic clung to it like steam
wisping around a pot. I sighed. It was just confirmation that
we had run out of time. Perhaps, I thought, it was for the
best. Ruarth knew he was not going to live much longer if

Lyssal had her way; she could no longer allow the residue of her compassion to protect him.

"It's a Keeper Council ship," I said to Trysis, as she came to see what Dek and I were looking at. "We have to act now, I'm afraid. No more waiting. Prepare the medication, Trysis. We will give it to Flame this morning."

The healer nodded and withdrew into the bedroom. Kelwyn had given us all the ingredients; it was just a matter of mixing them up and brewing the concoction. I could tell from the rigid straightness of her back that she hated what she was about to do, but we had long since made up our minds. There was no point in further discussion.

I'd come to like Trysis, as well as respect her skills as a healer. She could be acerbic at times, and there was a hint of steel in her character, but mostly she was a gentle lady, doing her best to alleviate illness and help others. An additional virtue, as far as I was concerned, was that she had an abiding hatred of dun.

Dek interrupted my train of thought. "What's the matter with the water?" he asked.

I leaned over the balustrade to have a look at the surface of the Vat. The sea was a dark green-brown, a strange, unnatural color. I remembered the kelp that I had seen when we had given the ghemphic dead to their families. "Weed," I said. "Seaweed. Trenchdamn it, that would happen now."

"What?"

"I've heard about this. When the winds come from a certain direction and the tides are right, you get these great rafts of kelp and other flotsam being washed into the Vat. Really jams the bay up tight and it's the very devil for a ship to get in and out. Dek, you'd better get a message to Captain Sabeston. Get him to anchor the *Petrelwing* out in the middle of the Vat before the weed really gums things up. We may have to leave in one whirlstorm of a hurry, and I don't want the ship stuck at the wharf."

I went inside to write the captain a note, and sent Dek off with it. He was glad enough to go; he hated being cooped up inside the Lord's Lode all the time. A few minutes later, Trysis gave me the prepared concoction for Flame. "Make sure she drinks it all," was the only comment she made. "Shall I pack our things?"

I nodded as I took the bottle.

I WENT TO THE BRETHLADY'S APART-ments. Lyssal was in her reception room, attending to some paperwork the Steward had brought around. The remains of her breakfast was still on the table in front of her. "I've brought your tonic, Syr-lady," I said cheerfully. I handed it to her with a bow. She drank the liquid, pulling a face, and waved me away. I left the room by the main entrance, and knocked at the door of the connecting room from the outside—Ruarth's bedroom.

He was standing out on the balcony when I entered, and I went through to join him there. He was holding a spyglass in one hand.

"I always started my day out here," he said quietly. "To check if Scurrey's schooner arrived during the night from Xolchas. Even once I decided that it wasn't coming, I still would come out here and watch." His lips twisted, as if he didn't quite know how to smile. He glanced towards the nextdoor balcony, but the doors to Flame's reception room were closed. "Charnels, Blaze, I've been sodding lonely."

The poignancy in those words brought a lump to my throat, and I wasn't used to feeling that way. Blaze Half-breed didn't get maudlin, or she wasn't supposed to. "You have a spyglass," I said. "Can I look?"

He handed it over with another attempt at a smile. "I obtained it by the simple method of remarking in the hearing of a group of courtiers that I would like to have one, and then watching them fall all over themselves to please the Brethlady's equerry. Extortion by fear has its uses—I learned the theory of that technique at court in Cirkasecastle. It has been a new experience to apply it in practice."

I scanned the bay. The Keeper vessel was not attempting to reach the docks; it was already anchoring out in the middle of the Vat. I steadied the spyglass along the balcony railing till I could finally read the name: *Keeper Fair.* Duthrick's ship. The harbourmaster's boat was already tied up along-side. I straightened. "Well, well, well," I said. "Now that *is* interesting."

"Blaze, is there something *else* wrong with my eyes?" Ruarth asked. "The water looks odd."

"It's filled with tangled strands of giant kelp, but that wasn't what I was talking about. That vessel is the *Keeper Fair.*"

"*Duthrick* is here?" He took a deep breath before adding, "I can't even begin to think of all the implications of that!"

I continued to scan the ship with the spyglass. "I can't see him, but I do recognise one of the sylvs on board. His daughter, Jesenda. And that is interesting, because she's not an Academy graduate, or even a student. I always thought she was just an ornamental."

"Ornamental?"

"Yes, you know. One of those women whose job it is to look pretty and be admired. Useless females."

I was utterly dismissive and he raised an eyebrow. Oddly enough, he then forgot to lower it. "Sorry," he said when he realized I was staring. "I am just beginning to find out how useful eyebrows can be, but I don't think I've quite got the hang of it yet."

"Er, no. But perhaps I'm wrong about Jesenda. In fact, from time to time I had wondered if I was."

"Why?"

"She seemed too intelligent to be satisfied with the kind of life she leads. And occasionally she used to say something remarkably astute. What troubled me most, though, was the amount of sylv she always used."

"Making herself pretty?"

"No, not at all. She doesn't need to. She's beautiful . . . in a sort of full-bodied way. Like matured brandy. But she always stank of sylv anyway. And I am usually very cautious around people who stink of anything . . . especially sylv-magic. It invariably means they are not what they seem." I took another look through the spyglass, then snapped it shut and handed it to him. "There are another two Keeper ships out there. One is just about at the entrance to the Vat; the other much farther out to sea."

He started staring at his feet as if they were the most fascinating things he'd ever seen.

"Ruarth?" I asked tentatively.

He wrenched his eyes away and raised them to meet mine. "Yes? Oh, sorry, Blaze. *Three* ships? What do you think has brought them here?"

"Not just any three either. I know the first two are armed with cannon-guns, and I wouldn't mind betting the third is too. My guess is the Keepers have been getting as uncomfortable as sailors with sand in their underdrawers about what has been happening in Brethbastion."

"How would they know?"

"Ruarth, The Hub has a network of spies from Spattshield to Fen. There's nowhere in the Glory Isles they don't keep a watch on. They've come to see what the Bastionlord is up to. They've come to find out if Lyssal is subverted, because they heard she was with Morthred on Xolchas. And they will know about the wedding by now." I gave him a look that must have told him he wasn't going to like what I was about to say next. "I'm sorry, Ruarth. But time's up for all of us." I paused, then added, "If there is anything I ever believed about you, it is that you are . . . astute. That you see things the way they are, with all the ramifications."

"Small drab birds that everybody overlooks have access to everybody's secrets."

"It has made you wise."

He grimaced. "A repository of knowledge, no more than that. What it did *not* make me is a man of action. Dustels observe; they don't fight. I've been the watcher on the window ledge, a bystander to life, since the day I was born."

"Today, that changes."

That half-smile again. "Blaze, blunt and to the point, as ever. You know, I feel a strange relief. No more waiting, no more inaction. I knew that anyway, after last night . . . She will kill me today," he added matter-of-factly, "if I don't leave."

"Flame takes a harmless tonic every day. One that is good for pregnant women. Today we substituted it with something else. It should bring on the labor."

"But—she's not ready—she's not nine months—"

"I know. We hope it won't harm her . . ."

"*Hope?* You don't know for sure?"

"Not absolutely. But Gilfeather gave it to me," I said gently. "He told me to use it only if we had to, and I think we have to right now. He would not have given me anything he thought would kill Flame. Listen, Ruarth, the Keepers are sitting down there in Hell's Vat, looking up at the cliff here. And they will have Awarefolk with them. At least one, possibly more. And you *know* what one of the Awarefolk will see. This whole lode is saturated with dun. They are going to act on that knowledge, and act soon. We have to move before they do, and to do that we have to kill Flame's baby. Once that happens we might have a chance to get Flame out of here. This is the only chance we are going to get."

"How long—?"

"An hour or two before it starts to work. Go to her, Ruarth. She will be calling for me a little later. And don't worry: Trysis is the best I could find."

"And afterwards . . . charnels, Blaze, we have to take her all the way to Tenkor in order to find help, and even then, there might not *be* a cure . . ."

We stood like that, sharing memories with a look, two people who loved someone in our different ways. There was such pain in him then—in his expression, in the way he held himself—that I found myself telling him something I didn't think I would ever tell anyone.

"There's something you should know," I said, and I heard the muted ache in my own voice, symptomatic of something felt so deep it could hardly surface. "Trysis can pinpoint how old the child is, and therefore when it was conceived." I had to force myself to go on. "This baby was not a product of Flame's first abduction by Morthred in Gorthan Docks. It was conceived in Creed, when she voluntarily went back to him . . . to save me. Because of me, she suffers all this, Ruarth. She made a sacrifice so huge, so tragic, just the thought of it takes my breath away. I—I cannot imagine what I ever did to deserve that. Flame *knew* she would be raped and subverted again. She did not deserve consequences so appalling."

My voice dropped to barely more than a whisper. "Since Trysis confirmed what I had already guessed, every day I have lived has been more than just harrowing; it has been my own personal hell. And now? Now, every day I see her, I also see the anguish that gives the lie to the words she utters . . . Flame is there, Ruarth. She's still there, still in hell. Because of *me*." I had to look away from him, so I studied my fingernails instead. "I suppose what I am trying to say is that I will do anything to get Flame back. And if I can't—then, I will keep my promise."

I raised my eyes to meet his again. He managed a husky, "She would thank you, if she could."

I gave a more businesslike nod. "Go in to her now. Let us know when she asks for Keren."

He nodded and went to the connecting door. I added, "It's good to see you, Ruarth. As a man, I mean. I like . . . hearing you *talk*."

"You have no idea how good it is for me just to know you are here," he said, and I had rarely heard anything said with such a heartfelt emotion. Ruarth truly had been very lonely.

"I'll leave the door open a crack," he added, "so that you can hear."

I nodded and waited. A moment later I heard Flame say, "I expected you to have gone this morning."

"I know," Ruarth replied. He sounded resigned.

"It's your funeral."

"I know that too. And it *is* my choice."

I moved so that I could peer through the crack of the door.

She waved a hand in irritation at the dishes on the table. "Get rid of this stuff, Tadpole."

"Are you aware some Keeper ships have arrived?" He crossed the room to ring for a servant.

She looked up quickly. "More than one?"

"Three. The first one is *Keeper Fair*."

She shrugged. "My old friend Duthrick: yes, I saw. What of it? This time we will be evenly matched."

"Three ships, probably all with cannon-guns," he pointed out.

"And I have a whole city's army led by coerced officers. Anyway, this time he is after something from me. Or from Trigaan. He wants to buy saltpetre."

"Will you sell it to him?"

"Of course not. We shall need it ourselves."

"Keeper ships are bound to have at least one of the Awarefolk with them. They won't even have to come ashore to get a whiff of dun."

"Yes, but they won't know its origins if they don't see me, will they?" She was calmly unworried.

He paused a moment. Then, "What have you done?"

"Told the harbormaster to keep them anchored in the middle of Hell's Vat until the weed clears, and to delay landing approval."

I frowned. It seemed obvious that Keepers would not care about protocol or proper procedures where dun was concerned. It worried me that, as time went by, Flame appeared to be losing some of the sharp edge of her intelligence. In a perverse way I grieved over that. Every time she showed a lack of her former acumen, my heart sank, even when I knew it was to our overall advantage.

Ruarth asked, neutrally, "And what do you hope to gain by the delay?"

"Time for my subverted sylvs to be sufficiently . . . enslaved."

He looked as wary as a sparrow asked to enter the open door of a cage, and she caught the expression. There was a long silence when they just stared at each other. Then she said, "Go down to their cells, Tadpole, and tell me what you see. I'll write you a note of clearance to enter the place." She sat down at the writing desk and dipped her quill into the ink.

He asked, "You intend to take on three armed ships, probably with a full complement of Keeper sylvs on board, with a handful of subverted sylvtalents?"

She nodded calmly. "Subverted sylvs and a Brethian army with coerced officers. There is much that can be done with stealth and illusion. They won't know what is happening until it is too late. And by then, I will be the one with armed ships . . ."

She handed him the note and he went to do as she asked.

As a servant entered to clear the breakfast dishes, I unobtrusively closed the connecting door and slipped away.

CHAPTER 22

NARRATOR : RUARTH

THERE WERE FORTY SYLVS THERE NOW. Forty. She could have brought the whole of Breth to its knees—if they were subverted.

But they weren't. Not even the two middle-aged ladies who had been first to arrive. I went to their cells and they just sat there, looking at me. One of them had a sylv light shining and it was blue, untainted with dun. I saw no sign of dun marks on their skin. There was no sign of the women's previous anger either. They were watchful—and silent. Accompanied by a guard, I walked the rows, looked into all forty cells, and no one uttered a word. A faint trace of dun drifted by, a soft mist of reddish-brown—but it was almost banished by a gentle all-pervading flow of sylv.

"Thank you," I said to the guard. And I walked back up the stairs to the Lord's Lode.

When I entered the reception room again, Lyssal was still there, waiting for me. She lay on the sofa, propped up with several cushions. "Well?" she asked.

"They are a long way from subversion," I said quietly. "I assume that means Morthred was better at it than you are. He was, after all, a dunmaster."

She absorbed that, and stirred uneasily. I wished I could see her expression properly. "How does my dunpower seem to you, Tadpole, compared to his?"

"I'm sorry, I don't know," I said, in perfect truth. "I saw his power with the eyes of a Dustel bird. I see yours with damaged human vision. I see things differently—I see *everything* differently now."

She didn't reply. She looked pale, and I did notice she was sweating slightly. For a brief moment Flame was there in her eyes, vulnerable and scared. "Are you ill?" I asked. My mouth felt dry.

"Perhaps. I have cramps. Ask Keren to attend to me."

I nodded. I could have rung for a servant; instead, I left the room myself. Outside the door, I paused. Kelwyn Gilfeather, I thought, I hope you knew what you were doing.

I turned to the guards on duty there. "No one is to come inside except the sylv healers. No one, not even the Bastionlord. Do you understand?"

The guards exchanged a worried look at the idea that I would try to bar the Islandlord from his wife's apartments. I tried to look embarrassed. "It's her time," I said, "and keep that to yourselves. One of you go and get Syr-sylv Keren, quickly."

I slipped back inside, walked through to Lyssal's bedroom and locked the adjoining door to Trigaan's bedroom. I was under no illusions: once Lyssal realized her cramping was the beginning of labour, her first thought would be to coerce someone to kill me. She could not possibly risk me being alive to kill Morthred's child. And so I had to be sure she did not speak to anyone she could coerce . . .

Which left me with one problem. There was no way I could bar Trysis from the room. I was going to have to be careful the healer from Keret, gentle middle-aged lady as she was, did not suddenly stab me in the back with a surgical knife.

Trenchdamn you, Morthred, I thought. You were right about one thing: you left a legacy to haunt us.

* * *

WHEN BLAZE CAME IT WAS WITH BOTH Dek and Trysis. They were all carrying bundles.

"What's all that?" Lyssal asked irritably. "Keren, I have these awful pains. I think I have eaten something . . ."

"If you will go through into the bedroom, Syr-lady, I will examine you."

Lyssal, still unsuspicious, did as she was asked. Once on the bed, it was Trysis who examined her. The sylv healer looked up at Blaze and nodded. "Well on the way," she said.

"I don't want *her*," Lyssal said petulantly. "*You* are my healer, Keren. *You* examine me."

Blaze nodded and said soothingly, "Of course, Syr-lady, but I don't think there is any doubt Trysis is correct. Your baby is on its way."

Lyssal shook her head. "No, that can't be right. It's too early . . ."

"Sometimes babies have other ideas," Trysis told her.

"But I'm not ready yet. I have things to do—" She sat up.

"I'm sorry," Blaze said and pressed her firmly back onto the bed. "You must lie down."

"Then have a couple of my guards enter so I can give them orders; there are things that must be done!"

"Later," Blaze said. "Let me examine you first."

I stood in the doorway, and I didn't need to see properly to know that Lyssal glared at me. I stared back. She pointed a finger at me. "I don't want him anywhere near my baby, do you hear me? He wants to kill the child! He wants to kill the heir to Breth!"

Blaze looked at me and shrugged. "I think you had better leave."

I withdrew to the reception room. Dek was there, unwrapping the bundles they had brought with them. Two swords and some clothing were among the things that tumbled out. He blushed furiously when he saw me. "I'm glad to see you didn't die," he said. He tugged at the bodice of his dress and blushed some more. "We thought you'd turned up your toes."

"I'd what?"

"Y'know—lost your feathers. Died. Kelwyn was awful upset."

"Ah. I suppose he blamed himself." I sighed. We all had our burden of guilt, me included. All this time, and I hadn't managed to save Flame . . . I pushed the thought away and tried to lighten the moment. "I'll make a bargain with you, Dek. I shan't mention your dress sense, if you don't draw attention to the fact that you are already taller than I am. You have grown!"

He looked pleased. "I have, haven't I?"

Blaze came in from the bedroom, looking worried. "What was all that about, Ruarth?"

"Probably Lyssal wants to coerce someone to throw me over the balcony railing. She thinks I will kill the child."

She looked at me curiously. "Would you?"

I nodded. "Of course. If it was born a dunmagicker. As we all know it will be. She's probably coercing Trysis to kill me right now."

Blaze's eyes widened and she dived back into the bedroom.

I WAS CALLED TO THE AUDIENCE ROOM that afternoon. I didn't want to go, but when the Bastionlord made a request for your presence, you didn't refuse, not even when you knew he was the coerced eggshell of the man he once was.

Lord Rolass Trigaan was seated on his throne when I entered, flanked by several of his favorite courtiers and a whole phalanx of guardsmen. As I'd expected, the Keepers were not as obedient as Lyssal had expected them to be; I didn't know whether they had used illusion or more conventional methods, but they had gained entry to the palace. Trigaan had evidently acceded to their request for an audience, as they were now drawn up in front of him. They stood below the dais, resplendent in their robes and chasubles, yet being treated like a bunch of naughty school children in front of the schoolmaster. The only trouble was Trigaan now seemed unable to deal with them on his own.

"Ah," he said as soon as I entered. "Spindleshanks—I sent for you. What is this message I had about the Lady of Breth? She is unwell? Why is she not here? The delegation from the Keeperlord is here!" He sounded petulant.

I bowed deeply to him, then politely to the delegation, which consisted of one of the Awarefolk and nine sylvs, including a number of Hub Academy graduates, all now working for the Keeper Council. I was not raised in the palace of Cirkasecastle for nothing: I could recognise the insignia of rank. It was also easy to spot Duthrick's daughter, Jesenda. She was the only sylv who did not use her talent to enhance her appearance, and the only one who did not wear the chasuble of a Keeper Council employee. Because of the amount of sylv around her, I couldn't tell if she was beautiful, as Blaze had said, but she moved with a grace and assurance that spoke of a well-trained body. No soft drawing-room miss, this one. I suspected that her gaze in my direction was calculating, rather than dismissive.

"Forgive me, my lord," I said, "Lady Lyssal is indeed indisposed. I am sure she will be devastated to have missed the audience."

"Indisposed? In what manner?"

Once again I feigned embarrassment. "My lord, she is, er, about to deliver."

Trigaan seemed to swell in size, if that was possible—his body already overlapped the throne on all sides. He beamed. "Why, that is good news indeed! Ladies, gentlemen of the Keeper Isles, you must stay to celebrate the birth of a Brethheir! We cannot discuss business at a time like this, can we?" His eyes wandered back to me. "Spindleshanks—organize something."

I bowed and withdrew, cursing to myself. All I wanted to do was get back to Flame's apartments; instead, given such a public directive, I had to make some attempt to attend to the needs of the visitors. I cornered the House Steward and passed most of the duties on to him, but he wouldn't allow me to go. "You're from the Cirkase court," he said. "I'm sure you know more about the needs of Keeper Councillors than I do. Keepers don't come here very often." I suppressed a sigh and answered a string of questions as best I could. Every time I turned around and headed back towards the royal apartments, he—or one of his underlings—would think of something else to ask. I found myself responding to inquiries as to whether Keeperfolk ate sea-snails, or if they would expect to be accommodated in palace rooms or would be willing to return to their ships. I had to give an opinion on the appropriate seating arrangements for dinner and which music the musicians should play. It was frustrating.

I was still with the House Steward when the royal audience finally finished and the Bastionlord escorted Jesenda Duthrick down to the dining hall. Fortunately, by then the servants had laid out the beginnings of a feast, although the kitchens still worked furiously to supplement what was already there. Eventually I found an opportunity to slip away to find out what was happening to Lyssal.

When I reached the door to her reception room, I glanced behind me. It was more a habit than any premonition; as a bird I had become used to being able to see behind, and I still liked to know what was at the back of me, even if it now meant I had to turn my head.

There was someone there, wrapped in sylvmagic. They stood watching, secure in their belief that I could not see them. They cloaked themselves so heavily in sylv I wondered they could still breathe. For a moment I stood still, and tried to peel the layers of magic away to see the original below. And the person, made uneasy by the intensity of my stare, stirred a little. Her skirt swirled and I caught a glimpse of gold sandals on feet she had not sufficiently shielded. Jesenda. I had not the faintest doubt she had deliberately followed me. I turned away and entered the room.

I stood there with my back to the door, breathing heavily. And then I heard her ask the guard on the other side of the closed door, in a soft, gentle voice, "Are these the apartments of the Brethlady?"

The guard gave an affirmative reply, then there was silence. Presumably she had moved away.

"What is it?" Dek asked.

"Lad, I think it's time you changed those frills of yours for trousers. We may have to leave in a hurry."

The relief on his face said more than any words.

I went to knock on the door to Flame's bedroom. It was Blaze who answered. On the other side of the door, Flame was moaning. Blaze stepped out and pulled the door closed.

"She's too preoccupied to think about you at the moment, Ruarth, don't worry. And she's doing fine. Trysis says it will be a quick birth, in all probability, because the babe is small. Another couple of hours."

That didn't seem quick to me. No Dustel bird took more than a few minutes to lay an egg. "There's a Keeper delegation here," I said. "Trigaan is attending to them, but Duthrick's daughter followed me back here. I heard her ask the guard whose apartments these were."

She digested that, troubled. "What do you bet she sends her Awareman along to have a look. Who is it?"

"The Awareman? He was introduced to me as Satrick Matergon."

"Don't know him."

"Young fellow. We're in a middenheap of shit, aren't we?"

Being Blaze, she didn't preen her words. "Yes. We have to keep them out as long as possible. Ruarth, go back to Lord Trigaan and tell him I don't expect the birth until, um, tomorrow morning." She crossed to the writing desk and began scribbling. "Dek, get the guards to take this note to the captain of the *Petrelwing*. It's to tell him to expect us tonight some time."

"Ruarth says I should change," Dek said, his tone hopeful.

"Yes, I agree, but after you've sent off this note."

"Will I be able to wear Dunslayer?" he asked.

"Wear *what*?" she asked.

"Dunslayer. It's, er, what I've called my sword."

"Oh." She hid what could have been the beginnings of a grin and added solemnly, "I shall insist on it." She walked out onto the wooden balcony and beckoned us both. We all looked down over the railing. Far below, the ships tied at the wharf looked like toys bobbing on a puddle. The wind was strong, sweeping in through the harbor entrance, the flow di-

verted upwards when it met the granite cliffs on our side of
the Vat. It scoured the rockface with salt-laden air, and
brought with it the muddled sounds and tangled smells of
the port. I glanced to the side where the closest of the trug
stations was bolted to the rock near the palace entrance. The
chains and ropes whipped against the block and tackle,
clinking and twanging in frenzied music.

Down in the Vat, the surface of the water looked smooth.
The wind had not kicked up waves; there were no white
caps. The Vat was sealed tight with a lid of weed. "Do you
think it will be possible to get a message out to the *Petrelwing*?" I asked. "There doesn't appear to be any of the usual
bumboats out there . . . nothing's moving."

Blaze pointed far off to our right. "There," she said,
"See where the Scour flows into the Vat?" I took up my
spyglass and looked. There was a boat there, a flat-bottomed
punt, and the boatman was poling it along by pushing at
the floating weed. "Apparently there's some open water,"
Blaze explained. "Not much, but the river forces a bit of a
flow, called a lead, through the weed. One of the guards
was telling me about it this morning. They do manage to service the anchored ships by using the leads." She leant over
the balcony to look at the street below. "We may have to
escape this way. We need a rope . . ."

Dek's eyes went round.

Blaze didn't seem to notice. "But I don't want to arouse
suspicion by asking for a coil of climbing rope. Ruarth, ask
one of the servants to bring a pile of clean bed linen. That
wouldn't be odd." She smiled at Dek. "That can be your task
when you get back—to make us a rope."

Dek's eyes widened still further. "To reach the *ground*?"

She ruffled his hair. "No, lad, just long enough to get to
the street immediately below us. We can go the rest of the
way by trug."

I thought of what Flame was enduring. I thought of what
we were going to ask of her immediately after her child was
born. And I turned away with a shiver that would at one time
have raised every feather on my body.

CHAPTER 23

NARRATOR : RUARTH

JESENDA DUTHRICK APPROACHED ME
across the reception hall, where the delegation was now
freely mixing with Brethian courtiers. I thought she was
smiling, although I couldn't be sure. "Syr Tadpole," she said,
"surely that cannot be your correct name."

"I was named Ruarth at birth," I said.

"Then that is the name I shall use. I do not like inappro-
priate nicknames. They are demeaning."

"As you wish, Syr-sylv. That is kind of you."

She inclined her head, and her whole stance seemed surprisingly intimate, excluding the rest of the room, as if we
shared a secret.

I peered hard to penetrate her aura of sylv and hunted
around for something to say. "I hope the meal was to your
liking? We had little time to prepare, as we had no warning
of the arrival of your delegation."

I caught a glimpse of her nose wrinkled up in an expression of disarming ingenuity. "No. It seems there was some

miscommunication. The harbormaster was even reluctant to let us leave our ship. It was quite troublesome for us to arrange it."

"I understand there is a problem with weed blocking the port. I also understand that conditions in Hell's Vat do indeed become quite hellish once the weed rots."

"Ah. Perhaps that explains it." She looked at me with an odd expression on her face. Perhaps she found my accent hard to understand.

I said, "Forgive my curiosity, Syr-sylv, but I notice you do not wear the chasuble of Keeper Council agents as the others do. Might I inquire what your position is with this delegation?" My pronunciation might have been awkward, but at least my Cirkase upbringing had included an incidental education in the conversational maneuvering of court diplomacy.

"I represent my father, the Keeperlord."

I must have looked startled. "But are you not the daughter of Councillor Duthrick?"

"Yes, I am. He is now Interim Keeperlord."

I digested that, with a sinking heart. "Indeed? Forgive me if I have been less than respectful, Syr. I did not know this."

She inclined her head again and I glimpsed a delightful smile. "You have never been less than charming. The Lady of Breth, Syr—is the birthing a difficult one?"

"It is a first child. I'm told such deliveries are often long." I was cautious. All my instincts warned me to be careful. She was as acute as a sharpened quill, and probably a great deal more dangerous. A heron, I thought. A heron that shadows the water to see better.

She waved a hand at the room. "I have eight sylvs with me, and many more down on our ships. Any one of us can also heal. Indeed, there are some among us who are healers by both inclination and experience. If there is a problem, I am sure that we can help."

"That is a kind offer. However, the sylv healer in attendance does not seem to think there is a problem—I have just spoken with her. Him."

"That is encouraging. However, the offer stands. In fact,

the Bastionlord has suggested we stay overnight in the palace, just in case we are needed. We have one of the Awarefolk on hand, as well."

"Awarefolk?"

"Yes. I understand the Castlemaid—pardon, the Lady of Breth—is sylv. She will want to know whether her child is sylv, won't she? Especially as the Bastionlord is not."

My heart jerked. I had to think of a way to keep the Awareman away from Lyssal. It was one thing for the Keepers to guess she was the source of the dun they saw, quite another to have it confirmed. My mind raced, and refused to disgorge answers.

She leaned in to me, placing a friendly hand on my arm in a gesture of intimacy while she spoke. "But then, I suppose you could tell her that anyway, couldn't you?"

"Me?" I stuttered.

"Yes, Matergon tells me he thinks you might be Aware too. Doubtless that explains your position as equerry to the Castlemaid?"

I resisted yet another overwhelming desire to stare at my feet. "If you will excuse me, Syr, I believe I must return to my Lady. As you can imagine, I do not like to be away from her apartments for very long. Just in case there is something she might require."

I bowed deeply and scuttled away like a crab from a hungry sand plover.

A few minutes later I was recounting the conversation to Blaze and Dek. "She's suspicious as hell," I concluded.

Blaze was thoughtful. "I'll bet her tame Awareman has already taken a look at this passageway on her instructions and made an assessment of the dun. And what about the sylvs down in the cells on the Buccaneer's Lode? When we were in the trug on our way up here this morning, I smelled them then. I think most of them use sylv lights in their cells."

"I can smell it too," I admitted, "from the street level."

"Then I think we can assume the Keepers know there are sylvs down there. Whether they realize they are prisoners is another matter. Do you think she has other Awarefolk down on the ships?"

I shook my head. "That wasn't the impression I had. I think there's only Matergon."

"Probably. If there were others, she would have brought them up to the palace as well. I don't like the way this is going, Ruarth." Her tone seemed worried as she turned from me to the lad. "Dek, I want you to sit out on the balcony with Ruarth's spyglass. I want to know if you see any sylvs leaving the Keeper ships under the cover of illusion."

Dekan Grinpindillie nodded. The sulky girl had vanished. He was wearing his own clothes, with a sword at his side, and a gleam of exuberant joy in his eyes. Now that Trysis had let the sylv illusion fade away, I noticed he'd broken his nose since I saw him on Porth, and he had a partially gold tooth; that was something new too. It was unusual, melded to a broken tooth in a way I had not seen done before. When he saw me looking at it, he tapped it proudly and said, "A ghemph did it."

"Ah. Sometime you will have to tell me how that came about. How's Flame?" I asked, looking at Blaze.

"Enraged," she answered, with a sigh. "She is adamant that you are not to be allowed anywhere near the baby once it is born. Damn it all, I feel as low as a lugworm myself. There I am pretending to be a sylv healer when all the time I am planning infanticide."

"It's Morthred's Trenchdamned legacy," I growled. "Sometimes I think we will spend the rest of our lives repairing the sodding damage the bastard left behind. Tor was right, Blaze. We have to rid the world of dun, and if that means sylv as well, then so be it."

Just then Trysis called her into the bedroom, and Dek and I were left once more to wait and worry.

IN THE RED WASH OF SUNSET, WE SAW boatloads of sylvs head towards the shore, using the open lead to the Scour. They obscured their passage in sylv, which was enough to tell us their intentions were not friendly. We lost sight of them when they landed. I went to tell Blaze, but there was little we could do right then.

The baby was born about an hour later. A boy, as Lyssal had predicted.

Blaze beckoned me into the bedroom. Lyssal was lying in the bed, her eyes closed. The stench of dun permeated the air of the room, the red-brown of its color seeped deep into the bedding like blood. Trysis had the child in her arms, wrapped in a blanket. It was tiny, and its mewling was almost inaudible.

Blaze jerked her head at the healer, indicating she should leave the room. She left, carrying her burden, without speaking. Lyssal's eyes sprang open, almost as if she sensed the baby's departure.

"Flame?" I whispered, my heart tugging unbearably.

"What have you done with my child?" she asked, and struggled to raise herself from the pillows. Lyssal, not Flame.

"Nothing," Blaze said, soothing. "Trysis has taken him into the next room to wash him. Here, you must be thirsty," she said, and handed her a glass.

She took it, and sipped while Blaze supported her. And then, in an abrupt gesture of rage, Lyssal sent the glass flying across the room, its contents showering the bed and floor. "You sylv bastard!" she screamed at Blaze. "What was in that?" She grabbed Blaze by the arm and a stream of dun—matched by a flow of foul-mouthed vituperation—poured out of her. Blaze gagged, and staggered back.

"Stop it! You can't subvert her, Lyssal," I said. "Trysis—!"

The healer poked her head in the door.

"Remove your illusion," I said.

Trysis glanced at Blaze, who nodded.

Flame—or was it Lyssal?—gaped as the face that was Keren vanished, revealing Blaze's features. She closed her eyes briefly, as if it was just too hurtful to acknowledge what she was seeing. When she opened them again, it was as if she was at war with herself. I glimpsed a flash of hope from Flame but it was quickly swamped by Lyssal's hatred. *You halfbreed scum!* she screamed at Blaze, and launched herself out of the bed.

None of us expected it. It was an explosion of rage and

violence from a woman who, moments before, had been exhausted. She went for Blaze's throat, but having only one arm, she couldn't choke her. Instead, she attacked Blaze with fingernails and teeth. Dun exploded around the room, shards of it splintering against us all in bursts of a red stench as vile as a long dead whale beached in the sun. The destructive edge of it started a fire in the bedding. Porcelain panelling shattered from the walls. Blaze went over backwards under the impetus of Lyssal's physical attack. Lyssal, tangled in bedding, tumbled on top of her. Nails scarified furrows down Blaze's cheek. Dek came flying in, took one look and grabbed the water jug on the night stand. Blaze rolled Lyssal over onto her back. Dek emptied the jug onto the burning bedding. I sat on Lyssal's feet and Blaze managed to pinion her to the floor. Dun still poured out of her. The child was screaming in Trysis's arms. I'd never heard a baby sound so unnaturally furious; it was as if adult rage had somehow been reduced down to a newborn's vocal cords. Dek shook out the blankets to make sure the fire was out.

"Ruarth," Blaze said, her voice remarkably calm, "I've got her now. You get me that brown bottle on the bedside table."

I scrambled up to fetch it. "What is it?" I asked. I removed the top and sniffed at it.

"The same thing I put in her water. A sleeping draught."

"You are going to kill my baby!" Lyssal shouted. She was looking at me, her desperation so intense she was almost lifting Blaze away from her. "Charnels, Ruarth—he's my child! How can you let her do this? Dear sweet heaven, please, Ruarth—not my child. Not my son. *Please*. He's just a baby . . . Ruarth, if ever you have loved me . . . I've never even held him in my arms. *Please*, I beg of you. I'll kneel at your feet. I'll do anything. We can go away together, do all those things we once dreamed of . . ."

Blaze, white-faced and brutally abrupt, interrupted. "Dek, hold her nose so she has to open her mouth."

The lad paled, but he obeyed without a word.

"Pour some of it in," Blaze said to me. "A capful. Quickly."

Lyssal moaned. "No, please don't. I love you, Ruarth. Don't do this to me."

I refused to look at her and poured out the dosage. A foul outpouring of dun hit me in the face and I gagged—but I kept my hand steady. I knelt by her side on the floor and waited for the worst of the dun color to clear so I could see what I was doing.

Dek gripped her head as she struggled to twist her face away. Blaze kept Lyssal's upper body flat to the floor and her remaining arm in a tight clasp. Lyssal kicked; Blaze shifted her body weight to trap her legs as well. Lyssal tried to keep her mouth closed, but Dek tightened his grip on her nose and she was forced to gulp in air. I tipped the liquid in. I was crying.

She spat out the first dose, and we had to do it all over again. The look of betrayal she gave me when we succeeded was enough to cut flesh from bone.

Blaze continued to hold her until her eyes closed and her body relaxed. We all stood up, stepping back, yet unable to look away, unable, even, to look at one another. We were deeply shamed, yet knew of no path to follow other than the one we took. "I'm sorry, Ruarth," Blaze whispered.

Trysis stood in the doorway looking at the wreckage of the room, and at Flame lying amid a twisted mass of wet and smoking blankets. "God in heaven," she said, the words rattled out of her, "what kind of people *are* you?" I don't think she expected an answer. I don't even think she meant it as an accusation, but I know I felt it as one.

"Check that Flame is all right," Blaze told her, and took the baby from her. She unwrapped the child, laid him on the bed and said to Dek and me, "I want you both to look at him and tell me what you see."

We looked. The baby may have been small and underdeveloped, but he radiated dun, rich and red and powerful. Already he was using it to strengthen his body. He had stopped screaming. His eyes opened, and he turned his head to look at us all, one by one. The focus of his eyes was real, intent and so unchildlike that I shivered, my breath caught somewhere inside me. I was glad when dun swirled, obscuring him, and I could break away, start breathing again.

"Dek?" Blaze asked. The lad also had trouble wrenching his gaze from the child, and she had to repeat his name twice before he looked at her. His face was white, drained of all color. When he finally spoke, it was to say something I had not expected. "If you don't kill it, I will." He did not look back at the baby, but held Blaze's gaze. I was suddenly reminded that he had killed his father, executed him for the murder of Dek's mother. There were depths in Dek that were easy to overlook.

Blaze put an arm around his shoulders, which was something she didn't do too often, not to anyone. "Dek, go watch the Vat and the trug some more. See what those Keepers are up to."

He left the room without looking back at the baby.

Blaze turned to me. "Well?"

I tried to meet her eyes, and couldn't. "He is dun," I said, even though I knew she didn't need telling. "And strong with it."

"We have no choice," she said gently.

But I couldn't speak. This was Flame's child. Once, we had spoken of her children as being mine too. Once, we planned our family and had dreams of joy.

Blaze took a vial out of her pocket and when the baby opened its mouth to cry, she tipped in a few drops. He knew, I swear he knew. He looked at her with such hate and fear, and his little hands waved in ineffectual protest. He hiccupped once, and died. His eyes remained open, staring at us, blank in death—yet somehow managing to be accusatory. Almost immediately the dun started to fade. Hands trembling, Blaze replaced the cork in the bottle. It was Trysis who moved forward to close those tiny eyelids. "God forgive us," she said. "God forgive us all."

Of one accord, we looked at Lyssal. Lying there, her face serene in her drugged state, she seemed all Flame: vulnerable, gentle Flame. We exchanged glances, three people linked by the horror of an act we had been raised to believe was heinous. Scarred forever by a guilt-seared memory.

Someone was knocking at the outer door. Blaze ignored

it and turned to Trysis. "I am sorry to have involved you in this. And I thank you for trusting me."

The healer had emerged from the fog of her magic as a middle-aged, graying woman, dumpy, short and plain. Her eyes were anguished, her expression rigidly set and her voice as harsh as crow song. She said, "I may not be Aware, but there are times when a healer can see the evil of a disease. You did something here that needed to be done. Please God that you can cure this woman now."

"How is she?" I asked. The knocking at the door became more insistent.

"She's fine. Physically anyway."

"We have to get you all down to the *Petrelwing*," Blaze said. "We need your power of illusion, Trysis. That outer door *is* locked, isn't it, Ruarth?" The knocking had gone from insistence to hammered urgency.

I nodded.

The healer glanced uneasily at the door. "I can disguise us, but I can't blur other people into invisibility—it's not something I have ever been good at. I couldn't get us past the guards."

"They are doubtless aware there has been some dun activity in here," Blaze said calmly. "They will have heard it, if nothing else, which probably explains that knocking. We're going over the balcony. The difficulty will be to take Flame with us—"

She didn't complete the sentence. Dek came rushing back in from the reception room. "They're comin' up in the trugs at the far end of the Lode!" he said. He meant the Keepers, of course. "They're tryin' to hide that with illusions and it's growin' dark, but I can see enough to know they have swords 'n' pikes. They look like they're gonna attack somebody!"

"Did they stop on the street below us?" Blaze asked.

Dek shook his head. "Nope. They're goin' straight on up to the other entrance on our Lode."

"Dear God," Trysis exclaimed. "Are they mad? This is the Bastionlord's palace!"

"No," Blaze said quietly. "Not mad. What better time to

attack a dunmaster than when she is giving birth? Keepers
are just as vulnerable to dunpower as you are, and if they
only have one of the Awarefolk with them . . . Here, let's get
Flame out onto the balcony of the reception room. We'll
have to lower her down. Take her feet, Dek. Ruarth, go and
tie the rope to the balcony railing. Trysis, speak to whoever
is at the door. Delay them—but don't open it." She got behind Flame and hefted her shoulders as easily as lifting a
child. I went out onto the balcony. Dek had made a good job
of the bed-linen rope. His knots were those of a sailor; the
lad's time aboard ship had been well spent.

I didn't hear what Trysis said, but the knocking at the
door ceased and she joined us on the balcony. We rigged up
a sling with a crossover harness, suitable for lowering
Flame. "You go down first," Blaze said to me, her eyes as-
sessing, sizing me up. "You'll have to swing into the road
below. Trysis, can you at least do your best to make both him
and the rope hard to see—?"

The healer nodded, her eyes troubled. "I don't think I can
climb down a rope, though. I don't have the strength in my
arms to do that sort of thing any more. And it's dark and the
wind is gale force—"

Blaze interrupted. "We'll lower you after Ruarth. Flame
next, then Dek. Get going, Ruarth."

It didn't seem to be the time to tell her I had developed a
reluctance to tackle heights, so I flung the rope of sheets
over the balcony and climbed up onto the balustrade. At
least, I thought, I have strong arms. Slowly, I began the descent. Even with the weight of my body, the rope moved in
the buffeting of the wind, and I ended up spinning like a
seagull caught in a whirlstorm. I clung tight and didn't look
down. Above me, Trysis leant over the balcony, concentrat-
ing to control her illusion. Unfortunately, the mist of her
sylv made it hard for me to see again and I almost descended
past the street and down to the Buccaneers' Lode. Then the
silver mist cleared a little as Trysis focused her power better,
and I saw I was dangling next to the street balustrade. I
swung a leg over and dropped onto the roadway. I leaned
against the stone and started to preen as I always did after

being frightened out of my wits. I stopped, feeling ridiculous, when I realized I was nuzzling at my shirt.

The rope disappeared upwards. I heaved in a deep breath and looked up and down the street. The only person visible was the single guardsman manning the trug about thirty paces down. He was standing next to the wall, propped up in such a way that I suspected he was dozing. I padded across to the wall niche opposite me and snuffed out the lamp there; anything to make Trysis's task easier. The guardsman didn't stir. There was no sign of any Keepers.

A minute later Trysis was lowered down. I helped her out onto the roadway and we waited for Flame. "Will she be all right?" I asked, trying to keep my anxiety under control. "To move her like this when she's just given birth—"

There was horror in the healer's voice as she replied, although I wasn't sure if it was the memory of what we had done to the baby, or what we were doing to Flame, that put it there. "There's a risk," she said. "There are always risks." She touched my arm. "Even if you manage to cure her, there's a risk she will never forgive you, you know that. There will have to be so much forgiveness: for killing her child, for not killing her when you knew that was what she wanted, or just for seeing her as she has been—subverted and cruelly indifferent to the world, cruelly savage to you. There will be little you can do about it."

I tried to force down an urge to vomit. "I—I know."

"You must love her very much if you can rise above the taint of all that has happened."

I nodded dumbly and threw up over the balustrade.

Flame's unconscious form dropped out of the darkness above and we gently lowered her to the roadway. We released her from the rope and I gave it a slight tug to tell Dek and Blaze to descend.

"Is she all right?" I asked Trysis, as she knelt in the roadway to examine her patient.

"As far as I can tell. She's not bleeding any more than is normal."

I glanced at the rope. It whipped away in the wind, writhing like a living thing, but no one pulled it up. As Trysis cradled Flame, I leaned out over the balustrade and craned my head upwards. The top of the rope was lit by the light from the lamps of Lyssal's apartments, and there was no one there. I didn't dare shout, fearing I would alert the guardsman. I turned back to Trysis. "There's something wrong. I am going back up to see what's happening."

Fear flared from her, disturbing the trail of healing sylv that fingered her skin, but she nodded. "We'll be safe here. I'll continue to maintain an illusion."

It took me a while to grab the rope on its wind-born dance. When I finally had it in my grip, I climbed up, refusing to think about my lack of wings. Refusing to remember this would once have been so easy . . .

When I arrived back in the apartments, Blaze and Dek were pushing the desk in the reception room in front of the wooden door to the outside passage. The door, massive though it was, juddered under blows. One of the molded porcelain panels decorating the wall beside it splintered with an audible crack, and pieces of the naked nymph it portrayed shattered. The inverted breasts, now jagged cups, rocked gently on the floor.

"A slight problem," Blaze said. "We are under attack. Take Dek and get out of here. No, wait, before you both go, help me move the beds against the doors in the bedrooms— someone is bound to tell them all these rooms are connected."

"I'm not leaving you," Dek protested as we heaved the heavy bed in my room against the outer door to the passage. In the reception room another porcelain panel succumbed to the vibrations of the battering.

"Yes, you are," Blaze told him as we ran to Flame's room and did the same there with her bed. We then pushed the night stand in front of the connecting door to the Bastionlord's chambers, and added a footstool and the wash stand for good measure. "The most important thing is to get Flame to the *Petrelwing*. While they think we are all trapped in here, they may not think to block the trugs or the stairs or the ships in Hell's Vat. I'll follow you if I can."

We retreated back to the reception room, and locked the two doors to the bedrooms. A thundering blow from the outside made me wince. "Blaze, they'll claw you to pieces. There's a whole pecking *army* out there."

And indeed that is what it sounded like. They had not yet found something heavy enough to splinter the door, but they would soon enough. I wondered—as we shoved a tallboy in front of the door to Flame's room and a heavy sofa in front of the one to my room—if the Keepers had managed to enlist the aid of the Bastionlord's guards as well. With Lyssal drugged and her baby dead, her coercion of them may have weakened.

When we finished blockading the doors, Blaze put her hands on Dek's shoulders, saying, "Lad, I know you want to stay with me and fight this one out. But I'm relying on you to get Ruarth and Flame and Trysis to the ship, because you are the only one with a sword. I hope you won't have to use it, but who knows. Now get over that balcony, right now!"

Dek gave a sigh and nodded. "Syr Gilfeather said summat like this might happen."

"And I'll bet he said you were to go if it did," Blaze added.

He nodded miserably.

"I'll lower you," I said to Dek. "Quick, let's not delay. As soon as you get down to Trysis, you help her carry Flame to the trug, and get started on your way down. I'll join you via the stairs, if I don't catch you up before then."

Dek was born in a house in the mudflats of Kitamu Bays and he'd never seen a hill until he was thirteen or fourteen, let alone a cliff. It was no wonder he didn't look too happy about swinging out over the Vat on the end of the sheets, but he did it.

When he'd reached the roadway safely, I turned back to Blaze. She had tucked her hair up under a bandana to keep it out of the way and was examining a silver-plated cake dish. She tipped out the cakes, slipped the handle over her left forearm and jammed it on tight with a napkin. I gaped. "A shield," she explained. "Of sorts."

Now that all the sylvmagic had gone, it was good to see her familiar features again. She looked at me wryly. "You'd only hamper me, you know, Ruarth. You have to go too."

The sound at the door changed. They had brought in something heavier, and the wooden panel above the lock began to crack. "I know," I said. I flapped a hand at the door. "Blaze, they are sent by the Keeper Council. If you kill them, there will be no way back. Come with us. We'll take our chances together."

"I want to save Flame, Ruarth. And this is the best way to do it—and I think you know why." She smiled at me, a smile of gentle tenderness. Once I would have said such a smile was foreign to her essence, but I knew better now. "It's been a long time since I underestimated you, Ruarth," she added.

For a moment I couldn't speak. Yes, I knew why she had to stay behind and I knew what that decision was going to cost her, even if she—by some miracle—escaped. I sometimes think we define ourselves by our choices, and the one she made then marked her forever. I had the perfect way to say goodbye, to say thank you. To honor her. "That citizenship," I said. "It's yours, any time you want it. For the Dustel Isles—believe me, I can arrange it. Any time." I had enough connections in the world of Dustel Islanders to know that was possible.

She nodded in appreciation and bent to kiss me on the cheek. Then she added softly, "If you ever do get back to Tor and Kelwyn, tell them—tell them—oh, just that I cared. Now go, you lousy pile of feathers, before I start bawling like some snotty-nosed brat of a street urchin!"

I climbed over the balustrade once more. My last glimpse as I lowered myself was of her pulling the shutters closed, that ridiculous cake plate still on her arm.

CHAPTER 24

WHEN DEK REACHED THE STREET, IT WAS
to find Trysis had already woken the guardsman on duty at
the trug station and ordered him to bring the contraption up
from the lode below. Trysis, with a cheekiness I later realized was characteristic, asked the man to help them carry
Flame to the trug. She used illusion to make Flame appear to
be a rather drunken palace manservant. "He's been summar-
ily dismissed; I have to take him home, the poor sot," she
told the guardsman chattily, while Dek—or so he told me
later—gazed at her in a mix of jaw-dropping horror and
open admiration.

By the time I arrived on the street, all I could see were
the ropes slipping downwards from the pulleys. I raced for
the stairs while the guardsman's attention was still fixed on
the manipulation of the windlass, and went down them two
at a time. I didn't stop at the Buccaneers' Lode, but kept on
going. At the next street I simply jumped on as the trug
passed by. It bounced alarmingly, but stayed level. I picked

myself up and tried to stop my heart banging away like the drumming of a woodpecker in breeding season.

By the time we reached the first change, I had calmed down—until we heard a commotion above. Someone was shouting, several people, in fact. We made for the second descent, carrying Flame, trying to look unconcerned. The guardsman there, though, was gazing upwards, trying to catch what was being yelled down to him. I looked up and saw torches flaming on the palace balcony and the street below it. I could not see Blaze.

"She's dead, isn't she?" Dek whispered, his voice wavering as he tried to come to terms with the possibility.

"She's a damned hard woman to kill," I said. "She has the bloody-minded tenacity of a seagull. Right now, Dek, we are going to concentrate on ourselves." I raised my voice to the guardsman. "Come on, good fellow, we have no time to waste."

The guardsman had better hearing than I did. He said, "They want me to stop you, Syr. If you wouldn't mind stepping out from the trug—"

"Oh, if you like." I told him affably, even though my heart was again thundering inside my chest. I knew then I really could no longer be the watcher on the window ledge. I had to act. I had to be a human, not a bird.

I made a gesture to tell Dek and Trysis to stay where they were. I stepped off the trug. When the guardsman raised his head to look up at the lodes above again, I grabbed him from behind and put my knife to his throat. He struggled of course, equating my short stature with weakness—a mistake. I might not have known the first thing about combat, but I had a torso developed by a lifetime of flying. I pulled one of his arms up behind his back with one hand and used the other to hold the knife. He jabbed the fingers of his free hand at my eyes. I jerked my head away, and he whammed me on the nose instead. My eyes watered. He bashed my cheekbone. I bit his thumb, hard. He yelled. I choked off the cry, afraid he would rouse one of his comrades. He slammed a heel into my knee, and I fell. I managed to drag him down with me. My knife sliced a shallow cut across his neck as we went down, but I lost it altogether as my elbow hit the winch.

Dek bounded from the trug to my aid and, to my utmost relief, grabbed the man's flailing arms. Together we forced him onto his back. I knelt on his arms and Dek pinned his legs down while I relieved him of his weapons. The cut at his neck oozed, and I started to shake just thinking how close I had come to accidentally killing him.

I spoke into his ear and tried to sound viciously calm. I was nowhere as good at it as Blaze was. "Now listen, you carrion-eating crow: you can stay alive and winch this trug down. Or you can die now and I will winch it down myself. Which is it to be?"

"I'll do it," he said sullenly.

"Good decision." I jerked my head at Dek. "Back on the trug and down to the bottom. Once there, you know where to go. Now move!"

Dek, somewhat to my surprise, obeyed without argument.

The guardsman worked the windlass—actually a capstan meant to be operated by two people—while I stood behind him, pointing his own sword at his behind. The trug carrying Dek and Trysis lurched out of sight. When it halted at the bottom, I used the blade to slash the main rope connected to the capstan so that it could not be winched upwards again. The four corner ropes that passed through the framework of the trug to stop it from spinning were, however, still in place, attached to the frame of beams that held the block and tackle.

I looked at the guardsman. "Take off your coat and give it to me," I told him.

He glared at me but handed it over.

"Lie flat on the street," I said. "Turn your head away and cover your eyes." He did as he was told, even as he smoldered with a resentful fear. I stuck his sword into my belt. "Don't look up," I told him, "or you're dead." It was just as well he obeyed, because it wouldn't have done for him to see me shaking with my own terror and disbelief at what I was doing.

I tied the coat sleeves around my waist and climbed to the top of the beam—still steadfastly refusing to look down, refusing to give in to the instinct that said I could open my wings and fly. I reached out to take hold of one of the farther corner ropes. I grabbed it, and swung myself down under the framework. Once there, I gripped the rope with my legs and I hung by one arm while I untied the coat and inserted my hands, one at a time, into the sleeves—but without pushing them all the way through. With my hands protected inside the sleeves, I gripped the rope and began the long slide to the trug station far, far below. The wind played around me in a heavy-handed game that shook the rope and tugged at my clothing. About halfway down I was suddenly enveloped in sylv; I sent up a silent prayer that it came from Trysis. I stared hard at the illusion that now surrounded me, and decided she was making me look like a guardsman wearing an officer's uniform.

By the time I arrived at the bottom, the others were in the final trug, waiting to be lowered. The attendant guardsmen—two of them this time—were more intent on finding out how the pulley rope on the middle section had been severed, and why. They had spotted me descending, of course, and waited until I hit the ground before bombarding me with questions. I answered none of them. "Emergency!" I yelled at them. "Get me down to the Scums immediately. Move!" There was more shouting from above, but the wind whisked the meaning away. I jumped into the waiting trug and tried to look as if I expected to be obeyed.

They didn't pause to think but grabbed the handles of the capstan and we started on our way down. When I had my breath back, I said to Trysis, "That was good thinking. You are quite devious for a healer."

"And you are remarkably innovative for someone who was a Dustel bird only two or three months back."

I shrugged. "Dustel birds knew more than most people thought."

She considered that and nodded. "Do you know," she said slowly, "I think the rest of the Isles had better watch their step around the Dustel Isles from now on."

I found myself grinning at her. Another new experience, and one I found I enjoyed. "D'you know, I think you are right."

"That was awe-makin'!" Dek told me. "Slidin' down the rope like that! I would of been petrificated!" Then he added with rueful disappointment: "But in the fight—I forgot to use Dunslayer. Can you believe that? I just pummelled the fella instead."

I laughed. And then sobered. "How is Flame?" I asked Trysis.

"As well as can be expected. Still drugged. I don't expect her to wake for hours."

I looked out over Hell's Vat but could see little. Riding lights gleamed from ship masts, stitching a few lines of yellow into the black surface of the Vat. The wind continued its howling, yet the water of the bay was lifeless and as thick as oil.

Finally we were safely at Scum's Row—but our troubles were far from over. We had to find a way to get out to the *Petrelwing,* still anchored in the center of the Vat. Quite apart from it being night time, with few people around to help, it was impossible to row through the mess of weed in the bay. As a sailor on watch duty on a berthed coastal jobber put it: "You may as well try to milk a ship's rat as move a rowboat through that tangle of kipper-stinking weed. As thick as a grave is deep, that is. You have to go to the Scour and get a punt if you wanna get out there."

I thanked him and moved away. "We'll never get to the Scour ahead of the pursuit," I told the others. "Not carrying Flame. It's miles."

"So what do we do?" Dek asked.

They were both looking at me, waiting for *me* to supply an answer. That was almost as unnerving as the thought of guards coming after us. "Let's have a look at the water," I said and walked down to the lowest stair of the dockside water steps with Dek. Trysis stayed with Flame. It was too dark to see.

"Wait a tick. I'll, er, borrow that lamp over the chandler's door," Dek said. He was back in a minute, grinning and swinging the lamp as if he had every right to it. He held it out to cast light on the water, but in truth there seemed to *be* no water. Just a brownish-green surface that glistened wetly back at us. I took off my shoe and poked at it with a bare foot. It was slimy to the touch and barely even undulated when I tried to dig a heel into it.

Dek looked at it dubiously. "Careful, Syr Ruarth. If you go down through that lot, you'd never get up to the surface again."

"I wonder if we could walk across it."

He looked even more alarmed. "No one's been doin' that. One of the palace servants told me nothin' crosses the Vat till the wind and tide stops bringin' the weed in. Then the muck rots and stinks till the riverwater manages to wash it out, but that's not gonna happen while the wind blows like this."

"If we stay here, we get captured. Sometime very, very soon."

Dek prodded at the weed with a hand, still cautious. "There was lots of mud round where I was born, in the Kitamu Bays. We used to cross that sometimes. On a slide."

"What's that?"

"A flat plank of wood. You sit on it, put one leg in the mud and sort of push off with that foot. You get real mucky, like, but you can move. We used to pick up cockles and stuff when the tide was out."

"Right. Something flat to lie Flame on, to spread the weight," I said. "And a rope. Look around, lad."

He scampered off and I returned to where Trysis was kneeling on the wharf alongside Flame. She had wrapped the guardsman's coat around her patient. "She's all right," she said, anticipating my question.

Dek came back. "Reckon we could wake the chandler? There's some crates outside his place, and they've got real big lids but they are nailed on. If we had one of those—you got any money, Syr?"

I nodded. "Plenty. Put his lantern back and then we'll wake him."

He obliged with irrepressible good humour, climbing on one of the crates to do it, and I then banged on the door. The man who answered was as irate as a nesting magpie—until I showed him a handful of setu coins. I told him what I wanted and allowed myself to be parted from a scandalous sum. In return, we had a crate lid, which he'd levered off for us, along with some extra wooden slats, a plank or two and some short lengths of rope and cord. We hurried back to the water's edge.

I put the crate lid down on the surface and gingerly stepped onto it. Water swilled up into the cracks, but no more than that. Dek and Trysis handed Flame to me and I laid her down on the rough wood. Even under her extra weight the lid hardly made a dent in the entanglement of kelp and bladder wrack. Carefully I stepped away from the lid onto the kelp. I immediately started to sink, until I was knee-deep. Then I stopped. I felt like a stork standing in a swamp. There was no way I was going to be able to walk like that, let alone pull the crate lid with its load behind me.

I thought of birds. Long-toed jacanas and large-footed lily-trotters on ponds. Pigeon-toed, web-footed ducks waddling across mud. I struggled back to the steps, where I sat down while I strapped a slat to the sole of each of my shoes. Then I tried again. I didn't sink this time but it wasn't going to be easy.

"You too, Dek," I said. "It is going to take the two of us to move the crate lid."

He nodded and copied me. Trysis looked appalled. "I can't swim," she said, giving me an apologetic look. "Can you pull both Flame and me?"

Just at that moment, we all heard shouts in the distance. Guardsmen, I guessed. They'd used another one of the trugs to descend . . .

I handed an extra wooden slat to Trysis. "Use this to help push us along. Let's go." She scrambled onto the crate lid. Dek and I tied two lengths of rope to two corners of the lid. He took one of the ropes and I took the other, and together we took one ponderous step, then another, pulling the heavily loaded lid behind us. Trysis pushed at the back. When I stumbled on my elongated footwear, I knew I had to do more than just remember to pick up my feet; I had to swing them sideways first, then forward. A duck. Like a duck. Dek attempted to imitate me. "I can swim," he said. "But there's really nothing to swim *in* here, is there?"

He was right at that. "I've actually no idea if I can swim or not," I told him. I lurched another three steps and tripped over a lashing of weed that had wound itself around my footwear. On my hands and knees, I shivered as the water ran into the hollows I made in the kelp. "Let's hope I don't get to find out," I added in a mutter.

Each arduous step sounded like the glug of water poured from a narrow-necked jar. We splashed and wallowed, slipped and fell and sloshed. Trysis kept her lips pressed tightly together, but Dek cursed ripely, using words he could only have gleaned from his time as a guardsboy in Lekenbraig. Fortunately, the wind still keened and howled, slapping the shrouds of the ships anchored along the quayside. We caught snatches of shouted orders and the sounds of planks rattling as men ran along the wooden boardwalks of the wharves. We could see lanterns swaying as they ran. In the darkness of the night, we were—I hoped—invisible against the blackness of the weed-clad surface of the harbor.

When I look back on that appalling journey across Hell's Vat, I remember the fear most. Not fear of those behind us, but of the water and weed beneath us. Every step we took was another stab at disaster, another temptation of fate, another risk of death. Another chance to sink below that slimy mass, knowing there would be no way up again.

And then there was the sheer labour of it. Every new step meant a foot had to be dragged out of the hungry weed, with the tentacles of it still clinging, still trying to slurp us back into the morass. It was like a living thing, a beast spread out over the bay to suck in the unwary. We hadn't covered more than thirty paces before we were exhausted, yet we had to go on..We had to be off the surface of the bay before sunrise.

I was thinking all the time: what if the Awareman is here somewhere. He will see Flame as a dun glow . . . a beacon to his Awareness, screaming her presence as clearly as if she shouted out to him, "I'm here! I'm here!"

We staggered on, lurching like drunks, trailing our burden, never far from collapse. Guessing that the captain of the *Petrelwing* would not have anchored close to the Keepers, I selected the set of riding lights that seemed to be more on its own, and we headed that way. As we neared the lead where the flow from the river pushed its way through the weed, the kelp thinned. My footing became more treacherous. Dek trod on what looked to be solid weed, and one leg disappeared into a hole. Inexorably, he began to slip under. I dropped the rope and flung myself flat in his direction. Just as his face went under I grabbed a fistful of his hair. Trysis leant over and together, inch by tortuous inch, we pulled him through entwining weeds onto a thicker mat of kelp. After he was beached we lay exhausted, panting. Flame, fortunately, slept through it all.

We backed off a little, and reached the ship by a more circuitous route. It was too dark to read the name on the prow, but the sailor on watch assured us we had found the *Petrelwing*.

If we thought our troubles were over, of course we were wrong. The captain, an elderly bearded Xolchasman named Sabeston, had been expecting our arrival, but he wasn't at all happy Blaze was not with us, and even less pleased when we said we had to leave without her. And then, as he pointed out, how were we going to leave anyway? It was one thing for a river punt to reach the stranded vessels, quite another to ask a brig to sail out of a harbor clogged with weed.

I waited until Flame had been taken below under Trysis's care, and Dek and I had managed to scrounge some dry clothes and warm up, before I tackled the problem with Sabeston again. He still wasn't happy, and the ship had still not moved. "If we don't leave," I told him, "you are going to have Keepers searching the vessel for us before the day is out."

He swelled up like a courting pigeon. "They wouldn't dare! This is *my* ship! And this is Breth, not the Keeper Isles."

"Do you think they care for that?" I asked wearily. "With their sylv and their cannon-guns they think they have the right to rule us all to suit themselves. Power has its own legitimacy; it doesn't have to rely on being made legitimate by others. Disbelieve that, Captain, and we could all be in trouble."

My eloquence was spoiled by having to repeat everything twice before Sabeston understood my accent. Then he merely reiterated, "No Keeper is going to set foot on this ship!"

"Then you may find you will go down in history as the first vessel to be blown out of the water by cannon-guns." Puffed-up pigeons, I thought, often seem rather ridiculous.

"Let them come and search us," Dek said. "Syr-sylv Trysis can hide us with illusion."

"Not from the Awareman," I pointed out. "If that man is still alive and if he comes anywhere near this ship, he will know we harbor someone who reeks with dun. That's all he needs to know. And no illusion will hide it . . ."

"Then what are we gonna do?" Dek asked, his eyes widening as he realized our predicament was just as dire as it had been when we were out on the weed.

"Well, we could gamble that the Awareman is dead, I suppose. Which is certainly possible—even likely. Safer, though, for the captain here to sail us out of the Vat. Somehow. Now, That's his job. I am quite certain that in her instructions to him, Blaze indicated we may have to leave her behind."

Sabeston said nothing to that.

"Now," I repeated, staring at him. "*Before* the Keepers decide otherwise. I am sure the captain is a fine enough sailor to get his ship out of this place, weed or no weed. Maybe he can try piling on the sail."

"With winds like this pushing us farther into the bay?" Sabeston asked in withering tones.

"All right then, try kidging!"

"*Kedging*," he growled. "If you are going to use nautical terms, at least learn to say them right!"

I thought I had; but I refrained from saying so.

Inevitably, Dek asked, "What's kedging?"

"Taking out a special kind of anchor in a small boat,

dropping it, and then pulling the ship to the anchor. Then you have to haul it up and do it all over again. It's a slow way of moving, but one that might work." Sabeston gave a grunt in reluctant agreement, then left us to issue orders to his crew.

Dek grinned at me. "Where did you learn so much about sailing?"

"I traveled a lot when I was your age, sitting up in the rigging on inter-island ships." Flame had hated me doing that, though, because she never got to go anywhere.

Fifteen minutes later, the kedging was well under way and the *Petrelwing* was moving—at about the speed of a leg-less duck, but it was moving. It was still dark, and I doubted any of the Keeper ships had yet noticed our departure.

I went to lean on the rail, Dek at my side. Ahead of us, the gap to the ocean was still invisible; behind us the cliffs of Brethbastion were sprinkled with bobbing lights, many of them a sylv blue. As we slowly made our way up through Hell's Vat, the two of us stood there in silence. Both of us were thinking of Blaze. Both of us were waiting for some re-action from the Keeper ships, those black shapes in the gloom still ahead of us. Gradually the vessels took on sub-stance and detail, becoming recognizable silhouettes, then sleek ships caught in the first morning light. And slowly, so very, very slowly, they dropped behind.

"I don't unnerstand," Dek said at last, his misery drag-ging at his voice. "Why couldn't Blaze come with us? She didn't delay the Keepers for very long. How could she? She's only one person and once they broke through that door . . ." He shook his head, as though the weight of his grief were a tangible thing.

"That wasn't the reason she stayed back," I told him. I'd known that from the beginning.

"Then *why*?"

"She had to kill the Awareman."

I heard his abrupt intake of air. Felt his horror.

"But . . . Awarefolk are kin. Sort of. Y'know that. You feel it too; or you used to." His shock was palpable; this didn't fit into Dek's world of honor.

I nodded. "Yes, I did. But if the Awareman left the palace he would have been able to follow us like a dog following a scent. And he would have been able to tell those Keeper ships we are on board this vessel. By now they would have opened fire . . . But, you see, they don't *know* where we are. They may have guessed, but they can't know for certain, and that stays their hand. Not even the Keepers can blow us out of the water simply because we are leaving the harbor. So to give us a chance to escape, the Awareman had to die. That's why Blaze stayed."

"And you think she did it. Killed him."

"Yes." I waved a hand at the Keeper ships. "I haven't heard them run out their guns."

"Oh." He thought about that. "She—I don't think she would of liked killin' one of the Awarefolk very much. I don't think she would of liked doin' that at all."

Dek, I reflected, was growing up. "No. You're right. She wouldn't have liked it one little bit."

"And we left her behind there. She could be dead. Or a prisoner."

"Yes."

He looked at me, his eyes bleak, as the day brightened and we kedged out through the blocked entrance to the Vat into the open ocean. "Was it all *worth* it, Syr Ruarth? I mean, Flame's still dun, isn't she? Was it all worth it?"

It was an effort to reply. "I don't know, Dek. I simply don't know."

CHAPTER 25

I ONCE TOLD YOU THAT DURING THE course of my life I killed two people whose deaths seared me. One was Niamor, back on Gorthan Spit. He had been dying anyway, rather horribly of a dun sore, and I put him out of his misery. And yet, as my sword slid in . . .

I hadn't known him very long, but he'd been a friend. And I saw something of myself in him; in some ways we were two of a kind—self-serving rogues, living on our wits and trying not to hurt too many good people while we were at it. The look in his eyes as he died haunted me for years.

Killing dunmagickers, on the other hand, never bothered me too much. Poisoning Flame's baby was not exactly pleasant, but it didn't keep me awake afterwards. The child was a monster, conceived in rape and deformed with dun from that moment on. He was a disease, not a human being. What he did to Flame was justification enough for his death;

what he would have done with his life made it imperative. His wasn't the second death that has tormented me.

The second was the Awareman, Satrick Matergon.

I CLOSED THE SHUTTERS TO THE BAL-cony the moment Ruarth left. I didn't want anyone to start thinking about the balcony immediately when they entered the room. I wanted those people who were battering down the door to think that the Brethlady was still in the adjoining bedroom.

The next thing I did was to make things as damn difficult as I could for them. The first ones through would be scared, I knew that. You are always scared when you don't know what lies behind a closed door. They would believe they were about to face the destructive force of dunmagic. They could be killed, burned, subverted or maimed by a blast of dun. They would come in fast. The Awareman would be with them, probably right in the center. It would be his job to tell them the source of the dun, his job to tackle that source. None of them would be looking at the floor.

I scattered a number of small obstacles across the room: cushions, a hassock, a low table, a chafing-dish, a drawer taken from the sideboard. I memorized where they were—I didn't want to trip over them myself. I scattered a few other objects around the room in places where they might come in handy: some more dishes, a poker, a bowl of ashes I raked out of the fire. I held my sword in my right hand; in my left—which I shielded with a cake dish—I gathered up one of the sheets that Dek had not used for the rope. I put a knife in my belt. Nothing like being prepared for anything. I had one advantage over Hub Academy graduates. *I* didn't follow any rules.

When they finally broke in and pushed away the desk that had been reinforcing the double doors, I wasn't the first thing they saw. I was under the desk. The first wave—five of them—came rushing in to find no one there, or so they thought. As they went past, I managed to hamstring two of them with sword slashes to the back of the knee. Then

I rolled out from under the desk, on the far side. One of the sylvs leaped towards me, put his foot in the chafing-dish, skidded and hit the back of his head on the desk as he went down. I trod on his chest and broke a couple of his ribs as I lunged for the man behind him.

By that time I had sorted out what I was up against. There must have been twenty sylvs, every one of them armed. Jesenda was the only person I spotted without a sword, and she didn't enter the room, but stayed in the doorway, watching. I singled out the Awareman right away, of course. He was the only one with no hint of sylv floating around his body.

I threw the sheet over the sylv who was about to attack me, and jabbed his thigh with my blade as I slipped past him towards the Awareman. The room was beginning to fill up, and there wasn't much space to fight.

"The other room!" the Awareman was shouting. "The worst of the dun smell is through there—" He was pointing at Lyssal's bedroom. Some of the sylvs began to clear furniture away from the blocked door. I couldn't get to the Awareman; there were three sylv swordsmen between us. The first was a brash young man who apparently thought a woman with a sword could not possibly present a challenge. He threw himself at me in an ill-considered frontal attack. I deflected his first lunge, and hit him in the nose with my makeshift shield. After that it was the work of seconds to disarm him and open up a nasty gash on his hand as I did so.

The other two were more cautious—and there was no shortage of armed Keepers to back them up. I lunged at one, forcing him to take a backward step that had him stumbling over the drawer on the floor. As his sword went up, pointing uselessly at the ceiling, I placed my hand on his chest and pushed. At the same time, I was warding off an attack from the other with my own sword. Crabdamn it, I thought, this is not going to work. There's too sodding many of them.

The Awareman turned his back, heading for the door to Lyssal's room.

I danced sideways, scooped up the bowl of ashes from the tallboy and flung it in the face of the man duelling with me. I slashed another man who came at me from the side thinking I had not noticed him. Then I did the only thing I could think of to salvage the situation: I threw my sword at the nearest sylv, wounding him, vaulted up onto the desk, pulled out my knife, took two strides across the top and launched myself at the Awareman's back. He crashed face down and we both went sliding head-first into the wall. Luckily for me, his head took the brunt of the impact.

The sylvs, of course, did not stand around waiting to see what happened next. They all came at me, sword points lowered at my back. I had a split second left. I was still lying on top of Matergon, and I still had my knife in my hand, resting beside the man's neck. I didn't try to lever myself up. I used my left hand to grab a fistful of Matergon's hair. He was groggy, and barely protested. I pulled his head back towards me, and slipped the knife into his throat.

And then I surrendered. Most of the sylvs didn't even know what I had done until they pulled me off Matergon and realized he was gasping in a growing pool of blood. He was Aware, and could not be healed, of course. All they could do was watch as he died.

As I said, it was not something I am proud of, and it haunts me still.

They tied my hands and feet while others searched the apartments. By that time some of the Bastionlord's guards had arrived, looking vaguely troubled and at a loss. I wondered just how long it would be before the effect of Lyssal's coercion disappeared now that she was unconscious.

Jesenda came to stand over me where I sat leaning against the wall. My bonds were tight and uncomfortable.

"Halfbreed," she sneered. "I'll have you executed for this."

"Nice to see you too," I replied. "You know, I would have thought not even a Councillor's daughter could usurp the prerogative of a Keeper court."

"My father is Interim Keeperlord now," she corrected me. "And you will be hung."

"Hanged," I said.

She looked blank.

I explained. "Clothes are hung; people are hanged. Just a small grammatical point."

She stared at me as if I were mad. Perhaps I was. "You are going to regret that you crossed my path," she said.

"I already do," I agreed.

"Nobody makes a fool of a Duthrick and gets away with it."

"Heavens, Jesenda, I've *already* made a fool of your father and got away with it."

She almost spat at me. "You are going to have a very uncomfortable trip back to The Hub. You'll wish you'd never been born."

She wasn't quite right in that. I never regretted my birth, but there were a number of days on that interminable journey when I wondered if I was going to make it off the *Keeper Fair* alive. For a ship of the line with some of the best-appointed cabins I'd ever seen on a vessel, it was surprising just how bad the ship's brig was. Dark, squalid, damp, cold, vermin infested, far too small—and I was manacled.

It was a long, long journey.

Anyara isi Teron: Journal entry
15/2nd Double/1794

*We are anchored in Metan Reach between Calment
Minor and Calment Major! What a wild and rugged
land this is. Tor Ryder once fought here, as the Lance
of Calment, to aid peasants against the cruelties of
those that ruled them. I wonder how they fare now,
those peasants, for the rebellion failed. It was a long
time ago, of course, back around 1732, I suppose.*

We lose several of our ships after this—the KN
Warrior *and the two merchantmen with their cargo of
aetherial nuns—they will go first to the Keeper Isles.
Our two research vessels will continue on down to the
Souther Isles. I will be sad to say goodbye to part of
our fleet; it has been a great comfort to have their
presence somewhere on the horizon over the months of
the voyage. The first thing I did each day when I went
up on deck was to look for their sails, to make sure we
had all made it through the night together. And only
when the prerequisite number of ships was counted,
did I feel all was right with the world! Silly, I know, but
the vastness of the ocean is intimidating to a
landlubber like me.*

Later:
*Shor and I argued today, in a way we have never done
before. He found out—from an innocent remark made
by Sister Lescalles—that I had copies of the last of his
Glorian interviews. He was furious, and gave me a
dressing down in front of Nathan, Dr Hensson and
Captain Jorten. So* humiliating . . .

*He had no right to say some of the things he did. I
am neither his sister nor his betrothed, and I am of age.
He was younger than I am now when he first went off to
the Glory Isles! And yet I lowered my eyes and said
nothing in my defence. Why? Because I know he could
make things awkward for me when we disembark.*

I shall be so dependent on his good offices, and so I bite my tongue and play the dutiful woman.

In my heart I want to be like Blaze or Jesenda, a woman of substance and determination and bravery, able to make her own decisions.

In fact, I think I will read some more of the papers. It will cheer me.

CHAPTER 26

I EXPECTED TO BE CONFINED TO A ROOM in the Synod for two days until the three Keeper ships made their way down the Hub Race and sailed away. Instead, I was kept there for two weeks. By the time Garrowyn came to release me, I was so furious I could barely speak.

"Two *weeks*?" I asked. "My God, Garrow, you are not going to hear the last of this. This was kidnapping, pure and simple. The unlawful imprisonment of a Keeper citizen."

"Aye," he agreed amiably. "Probably. Though I am no lawyer, ye ken. But I wouldna make a fuss if I stood in your shoes, laddie. Your father approved it. The Synod knew and said naught. Complain and ye'll only end up looking a fool."

I took a deep breath. "Why so long?"

"Seemed better. To make sure The Hub dinna get to hear of things too soon."

I glared at the Plainsman. "Am I free to go now?" I asked, my tone as brittle as sun-bleached seashells.

"Aye," he said.

I picked up the few things they had brought me to occupy my time—a few books, some scrolls, quills and ink, a prayer book—and turned to leave.

As I brushed past the Plainsman, he asked, "*Are* ye going to tell the Keeperlord about this?"

I hesitated, all too aware now that I could not lie to this man. "Not at the moment," I said, through almost clenched teeth. "There's no point. The Hub is not going to send reinforcements to Breth. The Keeper Council has brought back all its fleet so as to outfit each ship with cannon-guns, but there is no more black powder for them. Jesenda and the rest are on their own."

"And ye would look right daft if ye told Duthrick ye were caged when ye should have been warning the lassie," he added, grinning.

"Oh, shut up, you crazy old fool," I said. I sounded as savage as I felt.

"I do have news for you," he said, quite unruffled, "if ye can bide a wee bit to listen to this ancient gowk of a selver-herder."

I took a deep breath. "That was rude of me. I shouldn't have said that. You cannot help either your age or the chaotic state of your mind."

He laughed. "Ach, lad, ye have a sharp tongue in you, indeed. I just wanted to tell you we have the cure we sought."

I suppose it should not have been such a surprise, but I was shocked to the core. We had been walking side by side, about to go downstairs and leave the Synod, but now I stopped dead and stared at him. I knew then I'd never expected them to be successful in their quest to find a cure for magic. I had thought it all a stupid dream of impractical men, with their magniscopes and separators, their talk of vapors and ichor and clotting blood.

"I don't believe you," I said at last.

He shrugged. "I can prove it. By giving it to you as a cure for that sylv of yours."

I opened my mouth, and closed it again. "I'm not interested."

"Nay, laddie, ye're just in too much of a quiver I might be

right!" He continued to grin at me. "Come, I'll buy you a cup of chocolate at that shop opposite the Synod. That braw nevvy of mine introduced me to the stuff, and now I canna do without it. It's a sinful beverage, to be sure, and it's a wonder the Patriarchy doesna declare it so."

He took me by the arm and pulled me down the stairs.

We didn't speak again until we were in the shop, the cups of hot brown liquid steaming in front of us. "What have you done?" I asked. I still wasn't sure I wanted to know.

"Put simple-like, for the layman, ye ken, we found ye have sylv in your blood. It's there whether ye use your sylv or not. When ye *do* use it, we found it in other places too, like your skin. But even in your blood it is not concentrated and is difficult to detect if ye dinna use your talent. However, when we drained the blood from the placenta and umbilical cord that linked a sylv mother and her sylv child, there was a thumping lot of it. There are lots of factors we don't understand—for example, why a sylv mother doesn't necessarily pass on her sylv to the child if the child's father is a nonsylv. There must be something present in the child too, perhaps, for him to be able to receive his dose of sylv.

"Anyway, we found the sylv was a component in what we call the ichor—the clear part of the blood that can be spun out from the red part. And it's almost as though a sylv mother manufactures the stuff and sends it to her child in large amounts, particularly around the time of birth. Are ye with me so far?"

I nodded, interested in spite of my anger towards him.

"And then we did the same thing with Aware mothers who delivered Aware babies. Of course, we had no way of seeing or smelling Awareness, so that made it all doubly difficult. We hoped if sylv was found in abundance in the ichor of the cord and placenta—afterbirth, ye ken—from sylv mothers, so would Awareness be in Aware mothers."

"And was it?" I asked.

He drank some of his chocolate, and gave a contented sigh. "Delicious stuff. Yes, but we found the presence of Awareness wasn't as predictable as sylvmagic. Some Aware mothers seem not to pass on Awareness even if they wed

Awaremen. But when we did find Aware mothers who had Aware babies, we could take a few drops of this Awarefolk placental ichor and mix it with the ichor we collected from the placental blood of sylv mothers—and the sylv would vanish within hours. Just like that. Tor couldna see it and Kel and I couldna smell it. It was gone like it never had been."

"So what did you do then?" I asked.

He dropped his voice as several people came to sit at the next table. "We tried doing the same thing with ichor from ordinary mothers and bairns—and nothing happens to the sylv: it just continues to be as strong as ever. But when we make the cure from Aware mothers who have Aware bairns, it works every time."

I found what he said oddly unsettling and sipped my drink to cover my unease. "So you have a cure for sylv in a glass tube. How do you turn that into a cure for dunmagickers?"

He heard my sarcasm, of course, and looked more than a little uncomfortable. "Well now, there's the rub. We dinna have too many dunmagickers to experiment on."

"So what are you doing?"

"We've tried giving it to animals—both orally and introduced into the blood—and naught's died yet."

"Wonderful. There are no dun animals that I know of."

"We just wanted to make sure the concoction is not poisonous. We tried distilling it, but the cure distilled out along with all the other impurities, so that is not a verra good solution. Then we tried boiling it, and the cure was still there, and it still worked. We hope the boiling will destroy any impurities, if there are any. Just a precaution, ye ken."

"So what's next?"

"We already had a couple of folk lined up—in fact, more than a couple, seven to be exact. Sylvs who want to be nonsylv. We gave a couple of them a drop or two in their drink and we put the liquid into the blood of others, through the skin. Naught's happened to the first clutch, at least not yet. The second clutch, four sylvfolk—they all had trouble getting their magic to work the following day. And now they are beginning to see sylv when others magick it. Of course, we dinna ken how long the effect will last. Whether it will be forever. Anyway, laddie, if ye want to rid yourself of your sylv, ye have only to ask . . ."

"I like being sylv," I snapped. Inwardly, I was relieved. If they had to introduce this cure into the blood, then it was unlikely they would be able to change sylvs to Awarefolk without their consent.

He shrugged. "As ye wish." He looked unbearably smug. And those fire-flecked brown eyes of his were far too knowing.

I looked at him with loathing. "How much of this stuff do you have?" I asked.

"Of the cure? Ach, we will have ample in time," he replied.

I had an odd feeling there was something I was missing. Something he wasn't telling me. "Are you going to ask me to keep this a secret from the sylvs in The Hub?"

"Nay, lad, dinna fash. Ye are welcome to tell them. In fact, I think the High Patriarch will send word to them himself when we are a wee bit more certain about some of the variables. The Keeper Councillors will be after having some in their pouches for the next time they meet a clan of dunmagickers, surely, and we'll be right glad to oblige."

I nodded. "Then I'll mention it next time I see Syr-sylv Duthrick."

"Aye, ye do that, laddie."

"But you haven't proved a thing about the cure and dunmagic yet, have you?"

"Not yet. But Kel and I both feel dunmagic is just an overdose of sylv. No more than that. Dinna be looking so dour, laddie. Here, have some more chocolate." He poured me another mug before I could refuse.

I sat back in my chair and took a look around the room. The drinking shop attracted a wide range of clients, from elderly scholars to students who hardly had two setus to rub together in their pockets. That day, there was even a ghemph there. I looked at him idly, and then remembered something. The face I had seen in the tidal bore that night I rode my waverunner: it belonged to a ghemph! Why had I not realized that? A ghemph, riding the wave naked in the surf, in the middle of the Race . . . the idea was preposterous, yet I knew I was right.

I DID GO TO SEE DUTHRICK NEXT TIME I was in The Hub. I thought it might be difficult to make an appointment now he was Interim Keeperlord, but that wasn't the case. He seemed delighted to see me and invited me into his office. After some polite inquiries as to my health and that of my father, he turned the subject to the reason for my visit. As briefly as I could, I told him all I knew. He listened gravely, according me respect by taking all I said seriously. When I finished, he nodded and then sat still for a while, deep in thought, before saying, "Jesenda asked me about the name Flame before she left. I was able to tell her Flame and the Castlemaid are one and the same person, so you need not worry. She is forewarned. She knows what she could encounter in Brethbastion." I breathed a sigh of relief, but I don't think he noticed. He went on, "I fear the Lady Lyssal is beyond help now; there is a limit to what sylv healing can do. Jesenda has her instructions with regard to her . . . future. And as for you, Elarn," he added, "you have done well. I will admit to doubts when Jesenda first spoke to me of you, but I can see she was not mistaken. You have great potential."

I felt a surge of warmth. "Thank you, Syr."

"One question: you say this Garrowyn Gilfeather man seemed to think obtaining more of this cure for magic would not be a problem in the future."

"That was the impression I had, yes. I wondered if perhaps he was thinking that Menod sylv women who opted to be cured would add to the numbers of Awarewomen willing to donate their, er, afterbirth. As a consequence, there may be greater numbers of Awarefolk born in the future."

He frowned, then said, "At least we can be glad the oral administration of the cure does not seem to have worked. If there is any change in that—any change at all—let me know immediately. If it was that easy . . ." He shuddered. "All it would take to destroy the sylvs of the Keeper Isles would be a few cups of the stuff spilled into the water storage tanks of the city. And Ryder would do it too. That's the kind of man he is. Utterly ruthless and without scruples."

I blinked. That didn't quite match with my idea of Ryder. To me, he seemed to be someone who agonized over his decisions, who was being torn apart because he despised the dun within him and fought it at every turn. "Did Jesenda tell you I found out he was contaminated by dun?" I asked.

"Yes, of course. But that does not excuse him. He was always unscrupulous; I met him in Gorthan Docks, you know, when he was helping that renegade halfbreed bitch, and he had no taint of dun then or Blaze would have told me. The man has always been corrupted." He was dismissive.

I thought he was wrong, but lacked the courage to contradict him.

"I want you to go back and work for them again," he said. "I want a list of the names of the people who were given the cure, all seven of them. As soon as possible."

"I'm not sure that is possible," I said. "The Gilfeathers seem to be able to see right through me. I can't deceive them . . ."

"Elarn, so much depends on this, you have no idea. Think about it for a moment. Do you know what the bane of our existence as sylvs has been? Always, ever since there first were sylvs?" He didn't wait for my answer. "The Aware! We can't make an advantageous deal when there is one of the Awarefolk present. We can't have a proper election if there is one of them about. We can't make an illusion without them seeing through it. Every decent sylv loathes the sight of an Awareman. Or woman. If it wasn't for them, we'd rule the whole of the Isles by now, bringing our vision of prosperity to all. But no—we have to pretend to conform to the damn rules because the Aware are there. We bring so much to the Isles—healing, beauty, culture, theater, rule of law and order—and what do we get in return? The Awarefolk being flung in our faces!"

His rant made me increasingly uneasy. Was he condoning any kind of trickery, as long as it was by a sylv, as legitimate?

He did not notice my unease. "You still don't see the danger, do you, lad? You forgot to ask Ryder and Gilfeather one all-important question: is it possible to turn ordinary people into Awarefolk with this 'cure' of theirs?"

The question plunged into my conscious mind like a boulder into a pond. My thoughts, suddenly churning, couldn't keep up with one another. The implications were too vast, too all encompassing, too world shattering.

"I need that list, Elarn," he said. "I need it soon, before this whole thing gets out of hand. We have to strike back."

ON THE LONG RIDE BACK TO TENKOR, I thought over all Duthrick had said. Of course, he was right: I'd missed the obvious. Missed the reason for Garrowyn's smugness. This liquid of theirs was more than a cure for sylv: it was an elixir of Awareness. Anyone given it would be Aware . . . which is what had made Garrowyn so smug. He envisaged a Glory Isles where anyone—as long as they were prepared to forego the possibility of being sylv healed when sick—could opt to be Aware. Awareness would protect them from sylv illusion and trickery, and it would protect them from dunmagic. The Menod would be happy to spread Awareness throughout the Isles at no cost, anything to break the stranglehold the sylvs had on economic and commercial life. The sylvs would then have only one avenue to use their skills to make money: sylv healing. Yet fewer healers would be required because most people would now be unable to benefit from such healing. Sylvpower was doomed to wane.

And so I went back to the Gilfeathers and Ryder, although it almost choked me to do so. I didn't want any more to do with them, I was so angry at their high-handedness over my imprisonment.

I found Ryder in a foul mood, at loggerheads with the Plainsmen. Apparently, he wanted to take the cure himself, thinking he could rid himself of dun, and offer proof it worked against dunmagic. The Gilfeathers thought it might prove fatal as Ryder was already Aware. Sort of like having a double dose of medication. Ryder took the problem to the High Patriarch, who promptly forbade him from experimenting on himself. Ryder submitted, of course, but his irritation was visible to us all just in the way he held himself.

Getting hold of the list of the seven sylvs who had been given the cure in one form or another was simple; the names had been written down and the list left on Ryder's desk. I copied them out and Duthrick sent word to me to pass the names on to a man called Varden, who was apparently a Keeper Council agent in Tenkor.

I didn't like the fellow, on sight. He was a lean, narrow-eyed man of about forty, with the physique of a swordfighter. I guessed he was a sylv, although he did not use the prefix. When I gave the list to him, he glanced at it, nodded, and said—in an offhand manner that chilled me—that he had already received his orders concerning these people. All he had been waiting for was the names. The whole transaction, quickly over, left an unpleasant taste in my mouth.

Two days later, when I arrived at the Synod rooms used by Ryder and the Gilfeathers, I found the three of them seated at one of the tables, looking like I felt after a bad night out on the town.

"What's the matter?" I asked, joining them.

"One of the seven who took the cure died last night," Ryder told me tersely.

I was stilled. There was no particular reason why I should instantly suspect Duthrick and Varden had something to do with this, but it seemed logical. Why else ask for the names? I just hadn't wanted to think about it. Hadn't wanted to know. I went cold all over. *Murder.* Dear God. "Died? Of what?" I asked, forcing the words out.

"We think it might be some form of blood poisoning," Kelwyn said. "Unfortunately, the family are so fashed with us they will not allow us to do an autopsy."

"A what?" I asked. My mind was reeling, not taking things in properly.

"A study of the body to determine the cause of death. We do that as a matter of routine up on the Sky Plains."

"And there's another one of the cured who is ill," Ryder added. "We have to face the fact that our cure does more than cure—it kills."

"It doesna make sense," Garrowyn muttered, "and I dinna believe it. If what we took from the afterbirth was poisonous, how could the mother survive it, let alone the bairn?"

"We contaminated it somehow?" Kelwyn suggested. His face was ashen, his freckles standing out like blotches, his hair even wilder than usual from his habit of running his hand through it.

"That's not possible," his uncle growled. "Think of all the precautions we took. Nay, there was no contamination. Maybe it's just coincidence."

I sat there in silence and listened as they debated the cause. I was having trouble breathing. I had never felt worse in all my life. A man was *dead* because I identified him. He had been *murdered*. Murdered on the authority of the government I professed to respect and serve. And I was so stupid I hadn't seen it coming, although all the signs were there. I licked dried-out lips. And the other six . . . ? If I admitted what had happened, would that save them?

My thoughts churned on, making me feel even more ill. If I told the truth, then sylvmagic—and with it, much of the prosperity of the Keeper Isles—was doomed. If I kept quiet, then Ryder would stop the experimentation, believing the cure killed people. Did I serve my country and my kind—and condone murder? Or did I serve my religion and what was morally right, thereby bringing down a whole way of life? I knew what Jesenda would say. And I loved her. If I betrayed the Keeper Council, and her father, then I could hardly expect her to love me. To marry me.

If Kelwyn and Garrowyn had not been so upset themselves, if their own emotions had not swamped their nostrils, they would have smelled the stink of my guilt.

LOOKING BACK, I WONDER AT THE LAD I was then. How could I have made the decision I did? There seems no moral justification. I allowed a further six people to die, one by one, over the next week, because I dreamed of a woman, the tempestuous, sensual, unpredictable woman I wanted so desperately to wed. Because I wanted to be respected by her father. Because I thought that as a sylv I had to be loyal to sylvs. Because the Keeper Isles was my islandom, and its Keeperlord asked it of me. Islandom guards killed in the service of protecting their nation, I reasoned. This was no different.

Of course it was different. It was as different as rape is different from an act of consensual lovemaking. From the wisdom of my present years, I don't know why I couldn't see that then.

Kelwyn Gilfeather said that the lacerations of guilt leave their mark on your path through life. He was right. I have paid for my blindness. And to this day, I believe I will pay for it again, when I finally meet my maker. It is only just.

AFTER I LEFT THE SYNOD BUILDING THAT day, I did not return. I spent my time with Marten and the more disreputable of my friends. I gambled away my pay, drank myself into a sottish stupor every night, indulged in stupid antics like walking the ridgepoles of the Matriarchs' Bureau for a dare or climbing each of the university's various towers, on the outside, in the dead of night, for a bet. I rode my runner with a recklessness that deserved to be punished—but never was. The more risks I took, the luckier I seemed to be. And every day I heard of another death of one of the seven until there were no more to hear about.

THE WEEKS DRAGGED BY. I LOST WEIGHT, but gained a reputation for being a nasty man to cross. My friends began to avoid me, although Marten stayed loyal, even when I pushed his friendship to the limit. I came close to being suspended from the Guild for behaviour unbecoming to a Syr-tiderider; they meant my constant drunkenness.

Ryder, when I glimpsed him up in the city, looked haunted; Kelwyn haggard. Only Garrowyn seemed to be the same. Kelwyn cornered me one day and told me Garrowyn wanted to continue the experiments because he didn't believe it was the cure that had killed the seven. Kelwyn and Ryder, though, were adamant the experiments be halted. Looking at Kelwyn, seeing his distress, I felt my guilt like a burden, a weight that settled inside my chest and wouldn't go away. By this time, of course, Kelwyn sensed my guilt, but he just thought it had the same roots as his own culpability. He was too good a man to dream I had condoned murder.

I continued to avoid all three of them.

And then, just before the festival of the Whale-king tide, almost two months after Jesenda left The Hub, everything began to unravel.

CHAPTER 27

NARRATOR : ELARN

IT STARTED WITH THE ARRIVAL OF THE three Keeper ships from Breth.

I happened to be in Tenkorport when someone mentioned Keeper ships were on their way in. I climbed up to the top of the Guild Hall tower on the waterfront to have a look. The view north towards The Hub was obscured: it was raining inland and brassy flashes of lightning periodically splashed towering storm clouds. To the south, out towards the ocean—well, there can be no grander sight than three Keeper Council ships under full sail entering the Hub Race, proudly riding the tidal bore, all flags flying against the backdrop of an angry sky. They were magnificent.

Usually, Keeper ships were so anxious to ride the bore tide as far as they could that the signal flags went up calling for pilots the moment they passed the standing wave. Our pilots—all retired sweepmen—would be rowed out and taken on board without the ship ever losing the bore. I expected that would happen this time too, so it was with surprise—and a racing heart—that I noted only two ships called for pilots. I used the farscope mounted on a stand in the tower to see their names: *Keeper Pride* and *Keeper Just*. The third, *Keeper Fair*, indicated her intention to anchor in the area known as the Roads, where ships usually waited if there was no berth available.

It was Jesenda, I decided. She wanted to see me, she couldn't wait to see me again . . . so she had devised some excuse to make a temporary stop.

There is no fool like a young man in love. No one so naive, so able to believe what he would like to be the truth, rather than what is. That Jesenda would—or could—persuade the captain of a ship of the line to lose the tide so that she could dally with her lover was ludicrous, and I should have known it. Instead, I swelled with pride and arrogance; Jesenda was back, and she wanted to see me. Soon everything would be all right again; she would tell me that what I had done was right and wise, a decision that would save lives in the future . . .

I was about to leave the tower when, to my surprise, Kelwyn arrived. "What are you doing up here?" I blurted out. "The tower is out of bounds to non-guildsmen."

"I brought him," Tor Ryder said, and mounted the ladder to emerge from behind the Plainsman. "We have permission." Whose permission he didn't say.

He went straight to the farscope to take a look at the ships.

Gilfeather didn't wait for his comment. "Which ships are they?" he asked me.

I told him, and added the information that one of them was coming in to anchor. He stood there, his hair raked by the breeze, and watched as the *Keeper Fair* separated itself from the tidal bore and approached Tenkor bow on. Once, whenever I'd thought of Kelwyn it had been with a tinge of—well, not contempt exactly, but of superiority. I was a Tenkorman, and he was some sort of backward tribesman, a clumsy buffoon—until the day he defeated me so easily and laid a knife at my throat. Now as I looked at him, I saw other things: a steadfastness, a handsome profile beneath that wild hair. Paradoxically, the fact that he could physically best me made me see he was a man who preferred to use his mind.

"She's there, on that one," he said quietly to Ryder, and pointed to the *Keeper Fair*.

"Who is?" I asked.

"Blaze," he said.

"How in all the Isles could you possibly know that?" I asked.

"I can smell her," he said.

I thought: he's joking, of course. He must be, surely. And then: Trenchdamn it, he can't *really* smell that well, can he? Inside my head, a small voice answered: you know that's how he tells when you lie, you dolt. And he smelled Garrowyn all the way from the Synod the day he arrived.

"Flame?" Ryder asked.

Gilfeather shook his head. "Not there. Nor Ruarth, nor Dek. But Blaze—she's confined somehow, Ryder, I can tell. She—well, she smells."

Ryder stiffened, and right then he was more warrior than priest. I almost felt his blast of rage. And then he was in control once more, the Patriarch Councillor, the prospective leader of the Menod. "They are coming in to the dock."

"No, just to the Roads," I said, referring to the offshore anchorage. "Which probably means they have nothing to offload or take on. They want to make a brief visit for some reason." I looked back at the ship, now beginning to furl sails. Beyond the vessel, the sky lowered with dark clouds and the gray ocean was white-capped and wild-tempered. Bad weather was on its way.

"We will go back to the Synod and wait," Ryder said. "If they want to see us, they will have to come to us."

"Blaze—" Gilfeather began.

Ryder interrupted. "We cannot have an incident here. Let us find out the facts first," he said. I might have thought him calm if I hadn't seen the way his hand tightened on the railing. "Nothing will happen to Blaze in the next few hours that has not already happened to her."

With that, the Plainsman had to be content.

We left the tower together, but they returned up the hill while I went down to the dock to await the boat from the *Keeper Fair.* It was not long in coming. Even before the ship's anchor chain rattled out, the boat was on its way. As it drew close to the wharf, I could see Jesenda there, and several of her sylv attendants. I expected her to acknowledge me—of course I did. I was grinning all over my face as she climbed out onto the water steps.

However, there were others, more important, to greet her: the harbormaster himself came down from his office, and the Hubbian Ambassador to the High Patriarch was there too. I hung back, suddenly aware that, as far as they were concerned, I had no status. What I didn't expect was that, once the initial protocol greetings were over, Jesenda would sweep past with no more than a gesture that I was to follow.

"I wish to see the High Patriarch immediately, and this assistant of his, this Tor Ryder," she was saying to the Ambassador. "Is there no one here from the Synod to greet me?"

"Syr-sylv, how were they to know you were here?" the Ambassador asked, placating. "Allow me to find you a sedan chair—"

And so I trailed up the hill behind a swaying sedan chair that contained Jesenda and the Ambassador. I felt humiliated, even though I knew the thought was silly. She would not want to draw attention to our relationship, of course she wouldn't. I was being a dolt.

Although I'd dropped back behind the others, I found myself the object of scrutiny of one of her entourage. He wore the chasuble of the Hub Academy, with the trimming that told me he was a sylv graduate. That in itself meant he was one of The Hub elite. He was older than I was—by a good five years, I suppose. He wore a sword and carried himself with arrogant belief in his own superiority, yet he dropped back to speak to me. "I suppose you're the tiderider Jesenda took up with," he drawled.

I tried to match his cool confidence. "I beg your pardon?"

"Lose yourself, lad. This is a matter for grown men of substance, and I don't believe you are invited."

"Perhaps you might do better to let me be the judge of that," I told him. "I am the recipient of the invitation, after all." Inside, I felt a moment's doubt. Had that slight hand signal from Jesenda really been a request to follow her?

The man fingered the hilt of his sword, not with any hostile intent, but rather to emphasize his status, and perhaps his maturity. He was a trained warrior, a traveller; to him I was a mere tiderider of no import and no experience. I ignored him and looked away.

At the entrance to the Synod, we were directed to the audience room. No one commented on my presence, but Jesenda did not acknowledge me either. She continued to talk quietly to the Ambassador. Refreshments were brought, but it was a full half hour before Ryder swept into the room, wearing the ceremonial chasuble of his office. I had never seen him dressed that way before. He was making a point, obviously. He was followed by the High Patriarch's secretary, twelve Menod Councillors, Kelwyn Gilfeather and—even more surprisingly—Garrowyn. The High Patriarch was nowhere to be seen.

Garrowyn winked at me, and then his gaze homed in on the swordsman who had taunted me. He looked the man up and down as if he didn't think much of him, and snorted. The man reddened with anger and his hand fell to his sword hilt. Garrowyn raised an eyebrow in utter astonishment, thereby reducing the man's anger to the status of childish temper. I almost laughed out loud. But how had Garrowyn known? It was almost as if he'd sniffed out the few words I'd had with the man on the walk up. Smells again. My amusement died; these Mekaté Plainsmen were scaring me.

While this byplay was going on, Ryder bowed low over Jesenda's hand, saying, "My apologies, Syr-sylv. It seems Lord Crannach is indisposed. He wishes me to attend to your needs instead. How may I be of assistance? But first—won't you be seated?"

He waved a hand at the overstuffed chairs grouped in a

circle at one side of the room, but Jesenda, holding herself rigidly straight, refused the offer. "I have not come for social pleasantries, Syr-patriarch," she said coldly. "And in fact, my mission concerns you. I have a formal letter of complaint to deliver."

Ryder looked surprised as she handed him a small packet. He did not open it, but gave it to the High Patriarch's secretary. "To *me*, Syr-sylv? Forgive me, but to the best of my recollection, we have not met. How, then, can I have offended?"

"While I—as the representative of the Keeperlord—was at the court of the Bastionlord, I was attacked by a swordswoman whom I believe was there at your instigation."

Ryder was politely bemused. "You are mistaken. I am a Menod patriarch, Syr-sylv. I do not send swordswomen out to do the work of the Patriarchy. Diplomacy by swordplay sounds more like a Keeper Council indulgence. In fact, I seem to remember one Keeper Council swordswoman of note whose activities extended from one side of the Isles to the other. What was her name now? Kelwyn, do you remember by any chance?"

Gilfeather didn't blink. "Blaze Halfbreed, I believe, Syr-patriarch. She was, as I understand, on the personal staff of Syr-sylv Duthrick."

"Ah, yes, that's the name," Ryder agreed, smoothly urbane.

"Do you deny this is your sword, Syr?" Jesenda asked. Her eyes flashed fire as she held out her hand and one of her entourage gave her the sword he was carrying. It was a huge thing, but—from the way she handled it—seemed to weigh surprisingly little. "And before you answer, let me point out that your name is etched into the hilt."

He took the weapon from her and examined it. "Then doubtless at one time it was indeed mine," he conceded. His face was as inscrutable as a death mask. "However, as a Patriarch Councillor, I no longer regard the possession of such a weapon as appropriate. I gave it away."

"You were recently seen on Xolchas Stacks, in the company of Blaze Halfbreed."

He arched an eyebrow. "Are you telling me the swordswoman who attacked you *is* one of your father's own agents?" With seeming disinterest, he handed the sword to one of his assistants.

"A renegade agent, sent to Breth at your instigation, Syr! On behalf of the Menod."

"You are on dangerous ground," Ryder said, and his tone would have chilled most people into an inarticulate stutter. "The Menod Patriarchy does not use sword-wielding agents to achieve its aims. Whatever Syr-aware Blaze did was of her own volition, on her own decision, as I am sure she would tell you if you were to ask her. I do not give orders or instructions to those who are under neither my pastoral nor my spiritual care."

"Yet I am sure she went to Breth with your knowledge and blessing, Syr."

Ryder frowned in apparent puzzlement. "I am at a loss to explain your ire, Syr-sylv Jesenda. As far as I know, it is not a crime to go to Breth, and I bless a great many individuals in any one year, as do most patriarchs. As I was completely unaware that you, or any Keeper Council ship was going to Breth, how I could have been to blame for any attack on you, I am unable to say. Perhaps you can tell me what happened in more detail—?"

He made Jesenda look a fool, and I felt for her. She'd somehow found out the extent of Ryder's involvement in the intended rescue of Flame, but she was on slippery ground if she thought to blame him for whatever it was Blaze had done.

"Blaze attacked me in the Brethbastion palace," Jesenda told him, "in the Bastionlord's very apartments. She killed an Awareman in my employ, and slaughtered the Lady of Breth's newborn child, heir to the crown of Breth. She was instrumental in the kidnapping of the Brethlady. I am taking the halfbreed back to The Hub to stand trial for these crimes."

"You are courting a dubious legality," Ryder snapped at her. "If she committed a murder on Brethian soil, then she should be tried on Brethian soil. And as the Lady of Breth was dunmagicked, and bearing the dun-tainted son of Morthred the Mad, some would say Blaze did us all a favor. Somehow I think the Bastionlord would be more inclined to reward her, not try her."

"You obviously know more about this than you are saying," Jesenda snapped back. "I returned via Xolchas Stacks, and they make no secret of your involvement there. This is not Menod business, and never was."

"A crime committed in Breth is not your business either. I suggest you put Blaze Halfbreed ashore here, Syr Jesenda, and go on your way."

"She killed one of the Awarefolk under my command. She will stand trial for that in The Hub. And I have come here today to warn you to keep out of this."

Ryder's mouth was pressed into a thin line.

She continued, "Do not think to intervene, Councillor. My ship is armed, remember. And I believe you know what an armed warship can do."

"Oh, yes," he snarled. "I was standing next to Patriarch Alain Jentel when he was cut in two by your damn cannon-guns. Can you tell me why the master of the *Keeper Fair* should not stand trial for that crime, Syr?"

Trembling, she lost her composure altogether. "If he were to stand trial it would be for killing the wrong man, Syr!" She spun on her heel and went to leave the room. There were two bright spots of color in her cheeks as she passed me by, her entourage hurrying to keep up.

I hesitated, torn. I was embarrassed for her, not knowing why she'd been so foolish as to accuse a Menod patriarch of things she could not possibly prove, for all they may have been true. I wanted to go after her. But I also desperately wanted to know what Ryder had to say. So in the end, I stayed.

The tension in the room shattered into a buzz of bewildered questions as the door closed behind the visitors. One of the patriarchs turned to Ryder, asking the question that must have been on everyone's mind: "Just what did she think she was *doing*? Is she saltwater mad?"

"I think Syr-sylv Jesenda is far from mad," he said. "That

was a warning, addressed to me, nothing more. Telling me not to intervene."

"But you weren't likely to do that anyway, were you?" the man asked, more puzzled than ever. "Intervene because they want to try a halfbreed citizenless agent of theirs who used to be—from what I've heard—one of their paid assassins?"

"Hardly likely, as you say," Ryder said, his reply so brittle that the patriarch blinked, astonished his innocent question had induced such a cold reaction.

I slipped out of the room and ran after Jesenda. She had not bothered with a sedan chair on the way down, and it was surprising how much ground her party had covered by the time I caught up with them. When she saw me, she barked an order. "Get your tiderunner and paddle out to the ship. I want to talk to you."

She was still fuming, so I nodded and scurried to do as she asked.

BY THE TIME I REACHED THE SIDE OF THE *Keeper Fair*, the Tenkor pilot was on board and the vessel had shipped anchor. I had to scramble up netting slung over the side, while the ship heeled as sails unfurled and caught the first wind. Sailors hauled the tiderunner to the deck with scant concern for its surface. A seaman saluted me the moment I arrived on board, and conducted me directly to Jesenda's cabin.

When I entered, she turned towards me, still furious. "God, I could kill that man! The Souther upstart! Just who does he think he is?"

"The next High Patriarch, I imagine. And he's hardly used to being accused of conniving at murderous attacks on Keeper agents. What in all the seas were you thinking, Jes?" I wanted to take her in my arms and tumble into bed, but even I was wise enough to see that would not get me anywhere just then.

"I wanted to warn him off," she said. "Father told me Ryder was planning to set Blaze up as his mistress when they left Gorthan Docks. The man was apparently besotted with her. Blaze freed Flame from the *Keeper Fair* there—so Ryder must have been involved as well, but Father could not prove it. Then they turned up on Xolchas together. Whatever Blaze was doing, Ryder *must* have known and consented."

For a moment I was shocked into silence. Ryder being attracted to Blaze was one thing, but her *lover*? And working with her against Duthrick and Keeper interests? It was almost too much to swallow. They seemed such an unlikely pair, for a start, and Ryder was not far away from becoming High Patriarch. Such a man should have been, well, both virtuous *and* circumspect. I said slowly, "He had a point, though—he can hardly have known you would turn up in Brethbastion. What happened anyway?"

"The bitch barricaded them all in the Brethlady's bedroom while the woman gave birth, then they spirited her away. The baby was murdered."

"Was it really Morthred's get? Was it dun?"

"How should I know! The brat was dead by the time we broke in. The Bastionlord kept on saying it was his—that he bedded Lyssal in Cirkase, but I don't think that can have been true. So yes, it probably was dun."

"What happened then?"

She flung herself into a chair. "Blaze stayed behind to give the others time to escape, or so I thought. The Bastionlord and his court, even his guards, were so damned befuddled with dun they weren't much good, so I took control. We battered down one of the doors to find just Blaze there, swinging that damn sword. Trench take the bitch, but she's *good*." Her fingers drummed on the arms of the chair. "Her real aim was just to kill the Awareman. So I had no one to tell me where the others went, no one to follow Lyssal's dun trail. They could escape—and did."

"Lyssal escaped? But what happened to her? Ryder and Kelwyn Gilfeather have been expecting her to turn up here, but she hasn't."

"A ship left the port, a Xolchas vessel. When I couldn't find Lyssal anywhere, I guessed she must have been on board, but by the time I woke up to that, it was too late. She's somewhere in Xolchas, I suppose, although I couldn't get that damned Xetiana hellhag to admit it." She took a deep breath and tried to calm herself. "Sorry, I am not myself. I shouldn't be too angry, I suppose. The trip was not a total disaster." She managed a smile.

"What happened?" I asked.

"The Breth Bastionlord was like a lost child wailing for his mother—didn't know what was going on. I waved the contract to buy unrefined saltpetre under his nose and he signed it like a baby, at a price that will have my father thinking the sun shines in my smile. I sent the *Just* and the *Pride* to collect the first consignment in Kovo, while I chased down the Xolchas ship. Unfortunately, I lost it on the second night out. I sailed on to Xolchasbarbican, but I didn't see them there either. They could still be on their way here, I suppose. That tub of theirs is not a patch on any in our fleet. Or maybe the dun bitch blew them up with her perverted magic." She continued to tap her fingers impatiently on the arm of her chair. "While I was waiting for *Pride* and *Just* to catch up with me in Xolchas, I questioned Lord Xetiana and heard the whole story of the death of Morthred. Did you know it was Kelwyn Gilfeather who actually killed the dunmaster? Blaze and Ryder were in it up to their necks, though, working together."

I gaped. *Kelwyn* killed Morthred? Killed the dunmaster who had sunk an entire islandom? The thought was too bizarre. In fact, the whole story seemed bizarre. I asked, "You really want to try Blaze for murder?" The thought upset me, not because of Blaze, but at the idea of how much her death would upset Kelwyn. I realized then, with some surprise, that I actually liked the man.

"Of course!" Jesenda replied. "She killed the Awareman— I saw her do it."

"You were attacking her at the time."

"She was conniving at the escape of a dunmagicker in the form of the Castlemaid."

"Make up your mind—you told Ryder she was kidnapping the Lady of Breth and killing the Brethheir a moment ago."

"What does the particular slant on it matter? The important

thing is that she is going to be tried and hung—hanged, as she deserves."

I frowned. Something about Jesenda's passionate dislike of Blaze made me uneasy; it was too close to irrational. "Does she deserve it? Seems to me she was either killing a dunmagicker—the baby—or trying to bring an islandom's heir here for a cure. Neither of those things sounds like a crime to me."

"She killed one of my men!" Then, quite suddenly, her anger evaporated and she added casually, "Would you like to see her? The great Blaze Halfbreed is not nearly so great now that she is chained in the ship's brig. I go down to take a look at her every once in a while. She stinks."

"No, thank you," I said. Blaze had never been anything but polite and pleasant to me, and I found I had no wish to see her humiliation.

"As you please. Elarn, tell me what has been happening here in Tenkor with Ryder and Gilfeather."

I swallowed my impatience, pushed away my thoughts of bedding her and gave her an outline of events instead. I tried to sound neutral when I described the deaths of the seven Menod sylvs. She didn't seem at all fazed—nor did she doubt just who had caused the deaths. "Varden?" she asked. "I know of him. Very good with poisons, my father once told me. Clever of Father to think of him." I found I couldn't look at her face and hurried on with my tale.

When I finished, she laughed, a full-throated laugh of appreciation, and clapped her hands. "That's *wonderful*! Elarn, you are not only the strongest sylv there's ever been, you are so clever." She kissed me full on the mouth, and then said, "All their plans are nullified. They are sitting there with their success in their little bottles of curative and they don't know it—they could wipe sylvs from the face of the earth, and they have no idea." She started giggling again, and pulled me down on top of her on the bed. Her amusement was infectious, and we ended up rolling around with laughter.

When we'd recovered, I asked, suddenly curious, "What d'you mean, the strongest sylv there's ever been? You making fun of me again?"

She shook her head. "No, of course not. You'll see. You just need more training, that's all. You are behind the rest of us because you weren't properly taught as a child, that's all."

"What makes you think I am any better than anyone else?"

"Because your puppy squashed my kitten, you fool." She nuzzled my neck. I looked at her blankly. She laughed and explained further. "I didn't think anything of it at the time, of course—it wasn't till years later that it struck me and I began to wonder. I even thought my memory must have been at fault. Think about it, Elarn! How can an illusion—which is not real—interfere with someone else's illusion? It's impossible. Or it should be. Yet you did it, aged four. And you saw my sylv light that night in the Basin."

"But that was you," I protested.

"No, it wasn't. It was you. I can't make anyone else see my sylv light."

"I've never seen anyone else's."

"Have you looked? Bet you could if they wanted you to. That's what my father thinks, anyway. It's why he wanted me to get to know you. But let's not talk about such serious stuff now. I haven't seen you for two months!"

I stared at her, unsettling questions wanting to tumble out of my mouth and change the way I felt about her. But she took my hand and placed it against her breast, and then leaned towards me, lips parted—and everything I had been about to say vanished from my mind. Unfortunately, just when we were settling down to more serious passion, she suddenly leaped out of the bunk and held out her hand to me. "Come, Elarn, I'll show you something that will really make you laugh."

I wanted to protest, to undress her, to feel her body, her fire, under me, on me . . . But Jesenda always led, and I followed.

She took me up on deck and headed towards the afcompanionway. There should still have been light in the sky but bruised storm clouds were layered thick to muffle the dusk and the first glow of evening stars. She scampered along the deck like a child, and I followed in her wake—

embarrassed—loving and yet wanting to disengage from the childish antics. I had to pass under the scrutiny of the pilot, whom I knew well, and my embarrassment grew. Worse still, he was bound to tell the tale back in Tenkor, which meant my father would eventually hear of this.

She took me to the ship's brig, guarded outside by a sailor. Puzzled, I could not imagine why she had brought me here. I even wondered fleetingly if she wasn't a little mad. The place was foul, a single cell deep in the bowels below the waterline. It contained only a slops bucket. And Blaze. It was so small she could not stand, nor lie full length. There was no blanket and it must have been cold because the inner hull seeped moisture. Her wrists, neck and ankles were manacled and linked by chains. The door was made of iron bars, to ensure she had no privacy.

Jesenda dismissed the guard. She made a sylv light and sent it into the cell so that I could see Blaze better. The woman was filthy, and the cell stank—of bilge, of bodily wastes, of rats.

"Nothing of the proud Aware bitch now, is there?" Jesenda asked me. "She is watched around the clock by men forbidden to talk to her. She has no private moments. I have the only key to those manacles in my cabin." She addressed her next words to Blaze. "We are in Tenkor," she said. "Another few days and you stand trial before Keeper justice. And we know what the outcome of that will be, don't we?"

Blaze smiled. "Indeed we do," she said. Her voice was calm and steady. "The outcome decided beforehand ... Keeper justice indeed." She transferred her gaze to me. "Syrsylv Elarn. By the amount of sylv around you, I see you must have finally decided to acknowledge your heritage. But what have tideriders to do with this?"

I was startled, and not just because she recognized me. "You knew I was sylv?" I asked.

"Oh, yes," she replied, offhand. "Saw you once as a child, leaking sylv all over the place."

Excluded from the conversation, Jesenda immediately directed attention back to herself. She insinuated her arms around my neck and pulled my face down to hers. Her lips clung, rapacious, demanding all my attention, all of me. I couldn't give it, not with Blaze watching. "Let's go back to the cabin," I murmured in her ear.

"No," she said, her voice full of malicious mischief. "I want her to see. I want her to want . . . I want her to know all that she is about to lose . . ."

But it was more than that, I knew. I recognized her building excitement as a further extension of what we sought when we flirted with discovery back in The Hub. It wasn't me she wanted; it was the thrill of the possibility of discovery and, in this case, of having Blaze there, of knowing how much the Awarewoman would hate her inability to walk away, to escape.

Jesenda's kiss deepened, her tongue probed, she fumbled with the ties on my trousers. My body responded, as fickle to my wishes as ever. And I broke away, only just stopping myself from retching. "The smell," I mumbled, "I can't take the smell."

She stared at me, furiously angry. "No one turns me down, Elarn. No one."

The words lay between us, hovering on the verge of irrevocable. I knew I could still step back from them, do what she wanted, and things would still be the same. But if I turned her down, there was no going back. The thought was appalling.

I watched her, the way the silver gleam of sylv light made her skin glow, made her eyes seem soft and inviting as her anger segued back into seduction. I still had my arms around her, her breasts were still warm against my chest, the curve of her lips and the tip of her tongue still issued their invitation to mine. The moment hung in the balance, the temptation potent and sensual, offering the possibility of sensations we had only touched upon, and satiation we had barely skimmed. I knew I would never quite find the wonder of it again if I were to turn away.

I tilted my head slightly to look at Blaze. She was barely an arm's length away, and the look on her face was not for me, but about me, and me alone. I could have expected many things: hatred, revulsion, scorn, indifference, pity even. But it was none of those things: it was concern. Just that.

I released Jesenda and stepped back. "I can't," I said. "Not here."

My tone begged for her understanding, but she turned without a word and left me there. Her sylv light winked out, leaving us in the dim light of the one candle in the guard's lantern. I conjured up my own sylv light.

I took a deep breath and turned to Blaze. "Thank you," I said.

"For what?" She was amused now.

"For—I'm not sure. For saving me from making more of a fool of myself than usual, perhaps." I surprised myself by the depth of the bitterness I heard in my own voice. I took my coat off and handed it to her through the bars. "Here, take this. I'll tell Ryder and Gilfeather you are here."

She didn't bother to ask how I knew of her connection to them. "Thanks. Although I imagine Gilfeather already knows."

"He does. He said he smelled you."

She laughed. "Poor man. The stench must have knocked him endways."

I fumbled in my belt pouch, pulled out my purse and gave that to her as well. "Maybe you can use this to bribe a jailer for better food or something. It's not much."

She took the purse, and it vanished into her clothing. "Ask Ryder to pay you back," she said. "I'm unlikely to be in much of a position to oblige . . ."

God, I thought, she can still joke.

"Flame Windrider, the Castlemaid—has she turned up in Tenkor?" she asked.

I almost said no, then realized her position. She was going to die because she had tried to rescue her friend. To tell her she had not succeeded would have been cruel. So I said instead, "I don't know. I'm sorry."

She nodded, philosophical. Just then the guard came back into the area, and gave a jerk of his head to say I had to leave.

Just before I turned to go, I asked, my voice suddenly husky, "I wasn't the first she brought down here, was I? Not the first she—" I made a vague gesture with my hand.

She pulled a face. "Er, no. You were the fourth actually. She gets around."

CHAPTER 28

SHE GETS AROUND.

And fools like Elarn Jaydon believe her.

I walked away from Blaze's cell, incapable of saying another word. I left my sylv light behind. I didn't know how long it would last once I was gone, but I gave it a boost anyway.

Back up on deck, I asked a sailor to put my tiderunner over the side while I climbed down the netting. It was awkward, because the ship was under full sail now, and the Race was rough. Floodwater pouring down from inland rains met the incoming tide and stiff winds from the south, to stir up a maelstrom of foam and choppy water. It would not be an easy passage up the Race for the three Keeper ships.

It was certainly a hard paddle back to Tenkorport for me. I guided my tiderunner over to the calmer waters along the bank as soon as I could, but I was working against the tide and the wind, and it was rough. Worse, of course, was how I felt about myself. I'd been such a fool. Such a weak, gullible, purblind, besotted fool. How was it possible for one person to be so completely, criminally stupid?

When I thought back on everything, it was hard to believe I did not see through her manipulation. All those tales of me supplying information for her personal use—twaddle, of course. Every word I said went straight to her father. Her own father used her as he would use one of his agents, and she used her body, her beauty, her seductiveness with his full knowledge and blessing. She knew I had reservations about Duthrick, she knew I had a background steeped in Menod morality, so she tailored her words, pretended she was a breath of fresh air that would change the nature of Keeper government. She'd separated herself from her father in my mind. All that business of spying on Duthrick—that was all hogwash and fish scales. She spied *for* her father, not *on* him. She had played me like a fish on a hook, a salmon given its supposed freedom to run, then gently tugged this way and that . . . They wanted me because of who I was, because of what I had access to, because I was—they believed—a powerful sylv tiderider who would one day be an asset to Keeper Council strength.

My shame filled my body, heated my skin. Seven innocent people died because of my infatuation. Seven people, sacrificed on the pyre of a young man's pride and erotic need. There was nothing I could do to undo their fate. For them, it was over. And I hadn't even known them. Were they family men, breadwinners, mothers? Were they young, or old, upright citizens or lying hypocrites? Were they grandparents—or children, even? I had no idea.

I thought of Cissy. Of how she must have felt in the minutes before she died. Bitter, betrayed, fooled. Bearing the child of a man she could no longer respect or even like. And for the first time I understood what I had done to her. For the first time I felt more than pity, more than relief. I felt grief, not because I had loved her—I hadn't and that could not change—but because I'd betrayed her and she hadn't deserved that.

By the time I crawled up onto the wharf in front of the Guild Hall I was cold, shivering, seeping guilt from every pore.

Denny was there to help. He must have been waiting and watching in the tower, even though he was under no obligation to do so, as I had not been out on Guild business. I told him as much, and he just grinned at me and took charge of the tiderunner. I returned to the Hall, washed and changed and then donned my oilskins for the trudge uphill to the Synod. It was close to midnight by then, and the rain was heavier, the wind wilder, the cloud thicker. The guard at the gate was not keen to let me into the building at that hour, but it was hard to say no to the son of the Guildean, I suppose, especially when I told him it was an emergency.

I tried Ryder's room first; he wasn't there. And Kelwyn wasn't in his either. Eventually I tracked them both down in Garrowyn's room. They were drinking, but the alcohol did not seem to have lightened the atmosphere. Three lobsters morosely contemplating the boiling water in the pot would have looked more cheerful than these men did.

It was Kelwyn who opened the door to me. "Well?" he said, pulling me into the room as if he was worried I'd change my mind. "What have ye found out?"

He'd known it was me, I thought. He'd known I was at the door. What the hell was it with these two Plainsmen and their noses? Were they bloodhounds?

I'd left my oilskins downstairs, of course, but water still dripped from my cap, to runnel down the creases of my face like tears. And suddenly they were all quiet, looking at me. For a moment I felt they read me like a book.

It was Garrowyn who spoke first. "Sit ye down, laddie, by the fire." He picked up a glass and poured something into it; Quiller brandy, if I wasn't mistaken. "Here, drink this. It'll put flame in your belly and curl your hair." He whipped the cap from my head and hung it on the mantelpiece where, still dripping, it steamed gently. "And now," he added as I did as he said, "ye can tell us just why you look like you've been smacked on the jaw by a wet trout."

I cleared my throat, sick with embarrassment. "You know I've been taking whatever I learned here and telling Jesenda. Or the Keeperlord."

"Aye," he agreed. "Ye wear your passion in your smell, ye ken. And treachery, well that has a smell all of its own . . ."

"You don't know it all," I told them. "You don't know half of what I have done. And I can't tell you now—not tonight. Tomorrow . . . I'll come and see you tomorrow . . ." I had intended to tell them the whole story, but suddenly I couldn't, not then. My realization of the extent of my foolishness was too fresh, too raw in my mind.

"Then what *is* it you want to tell us tonight?" Ryder asked. "Is Blaze on that ship, as Kel and Garrow say?"

I nodded. "Yes. Jesenda showed her to me. She's manacled, and chained—" I told them all I'd seen, and all that Blaze had said. All that Jesenda had told me about the half-breed's probable fate. "They are taking no chances with her," I finished.

Ryder snorted. "Duthrick's daughter has learned a thing or two about Blaze from her father, it seems. She knows Blaze is a hard woman to keep in a jail."

"We'll see about that," Kelwyn said. There was an anger in his tone that was uncharacteristic and we all looked at him. "I lost one woman I loved to the nastiness of an illogical legal system," he said by way of explanation. "There is no way I am going to watch another be slaughtered by a court that has decided its verdict before it ever sits."

By the way Ryder blinked, I suspected this was the first time Kelwyn had spoken openly of his love for Blaze. I stood up, a little unsteadily. "Those ships won't get to The Hub in a hurry, in spite of the fact there's a lot of water in the Race," I said. "The weather is sodden and the conditions appalling. It'll take them two or three days at least to arrive, unless the weather changes, which I doubt. And now, I'm going back to the Hall. To sleep. If I can. Tomorrow— tomorrow I'll tell you all you need to know."

I took my cap and jammed it back on my head. It was still damp.

It was Ryder who opened the door, and stepped outside after me. "Don't be too hard on yourself," he said. "If God can forgive you, you can forgive yourself."

"And what about the dead?" I asked. "How do I get the dead to forgive me?" I walked off; left him standing there, watching.

I HAD FORGOTTEN I WAS ON DUTY THE next day.

It may have slipped my memory, but it hadn't slipped Denny's. He woke me before dawn, in plenty of time to dress, have breakfast and catch the bore. The weather was foul, and it was just two days before the Whale-King tide was due, which meant the bore was going to be large and tricky as the two moons began to align with the sun.

I had the most God-awful trip to The Hub and an even worse one back to Tenkor. Usually, I would have rested overnight and come back the next day; but I had made a promise to Ryder and the Gilfeathers that I intended to keep, so I took the next ebb back down again. It rained all the way, driving cold rain. After a few minutes of being relentlessly battered and blinded, I knew I would either have to turn back, or think of a better way of doing it. After a few experiments, I found I could build a ward over my head to keep the rain off. It was harder to keep it moving with me—every time I relaxed my vigilance, I left it behind. Still, an instant deluge of cold water was an immediate reminder, and I soon learned to manage it better.

Worse, perhaps, the ebb tide was so swollen with water it was more like a storm-affected bore tide. It was full of flood debris, much of it hidden by the mud and silt in the water. I had several narrow escapes, and one harrowing moment when my tiderunner capsized and I only just managed to upright it and hold to the wave at the same time—by sheer force of will, I think. After that, I built a second ward of filigreed rakelike tines that I used to comb the water for debris just ahead of my runner.

I arrived back in Tenkor, shivering and blue and so exhausted I could scarcely stand, let alone move. In fact, I considered myself lucky to have made it back at all. I climbed out onto the wharf, blessing Denny, who was there to greet me with a warm blanket and a hot cup of chocolate, ready to hustle me away to the Hall and a hot bath. He had yet another commendation coming up from me; at this rate he'd be entering the tiderider training school soon and I'd lose the best tide boy in the Hall.

I paused a moment under the shelter of the harbormaster's veranda to drink the chocolate, and glanced at what was happening at the neighbouring section of the wharf. A ship had just berthed and there was the usual crowd of officials, hucksters and chandlers soliciting business. I wouldn't have thought anything of it, if I hadn't caught sight of the red and green tagairds of the two Gilfeathers in among the crowd. A moment later, I saw Ryder as well. They were part of a group of people who were carrying someone away from the ship on a litter. They came by me a moment later and I looked down on the face of the supine woman as they passed. She had her eyes closed as if she was sleeping. Even though she was pale and thin, she was still one of the most beautiful women I had ever seen.

As Kelwyn passed me, I clutched at him. "Who is it?" I asked.

He paused to answer the question. "Flame Windrider," he said. He looked upset. "Severspit, Elarn," he added, "it's horrible. She is riddled through with dun, like—like mold through cheese. And now we dinna have a way to help her . . ."

He shook his head in sorrow and hurried on after the litter. A large dog with feet the size of chafing dishes loped after him. I looked at the ship: *Petrelwing,* out of Stabbing Stack, Xolchas. All I could think of was that this was not going to be another death laid at my door. I wouldn't let it happen.

Wearily, I returned to the Hall, had my bath and changed. Then I gobbled down a meal in the warmth of the Hall kitchens and reported in to the duty officer. By then my feet were beginning to feel as if they belonged to me again. Denny had long since dealt with the dispatches I brought from The Hub, so, after I filed a blistering report on the Hub Race conditions, I went on up the hill to the Synod.

The closer I came to the building, the slower I walked. Anything to delay saying what had to be said. It was still raining, and even sheltering under oilskins, I was damp around the ankles by the time I arrived at the gates. I soon found out the Castlemaid was lodged in the Synod; not in its infirmary, but in its jail. The same room I'd occupied when I'd been held against my will.

The anteroom was crowded with people. Some I knew: the Gilfeathers, of course, the High Patriarch Crannach and several other Aware patriarchs. Still others were strangers to me and had apparently been on board the *Petrelwing*. They included a middle-aged Brethian woman dressed in the garb of a sylv healer, a young Mekaté lad who responded when someone called him Dek, and a short young man with a Cirkasian tattoo and extraordinarily knowing eyes of a brilliant blue. The dog was there too, lying in the middle of the floor and forcing everyone to walk around him. He gazed at me with doleful eyes.

The door to the inner room was open, so I slipped past all of them, unnoticed except by the dog, to where Ryder sat at the woman's bedside. He held her hand, his head bowed in prayer. I approached on the other side of the bed and studied her. She was so young, so lovely.

Ryder stirred and raised his gaze to meet mine. My breath caught when I glimpsed his pain. I wanted to say something, but didn't have the words. He was a senior patriarch, and I was just a not particularly pious young man. "You want to hear something curious, Elarn?" he asked. He didn't wait for an answer but continued, "Blaze stayed behind to give Ruarth and Dek a chance to escape with Flame. And now she is a prisoner bound for a trial that can only have one conclusion. I can't even *try* to rescue her because I am a Menod Councillor, bound to uphold the law of the Keeper Isles. Bound to condemn murder, which apparently she has committed. She sacrificed herself to save this woman. More than that even; she sacrificed her integrity by killing a fellow Awareman, someone doing the same job she herself once performed. And now I will make that sacrifice useless by killing Flame because she is a dunmagicker and I cannot cure her. How is that for irony?"

"Kill Flame?" I echoed stupidly.

"She is strong in dun," he explained. "We can't allow her to be undrugged. She'd just blow out the wall and escape." He looked back at the woman in the bed. "She's been kept sedated all the way from Breth . . ." He swallowed. "We have to kill her."

"Oh God, no," I blurted out. "Not another murder. That won't be necessary."

He glanced up at me in puzzlement. "Another?"

I stood there looking at him. Looking at her. And knew that no matter what it cost me, no matter what it cost a whole land, I could not be the direct cause of another death. I *couldn't*.

I licked dry lips. "Syr-patriarch—I have committed a terrible sin."

He frowned, dragging his focus away from his own misery with an effort. "This is something you need to deal with here and now?" he asked.

"Yes. It concerns—concerns the seven who died. It is my belief they were murdered by an agent of the Keeperlord's, a man called Varden. Apparently he has some skill with poisons. He did it so that you would think the cure was toxic."

His face changed and I knew he'd seen the point immediately, although it took him a while to speak. Rage flashed and was buried. Finally he said, "And it was you who told this Varden who the seven were."

I nodded. I don't think I could have spoken right then.

"Ah, Elarn. That will be a heavy burden."

I nodded again.

"You don't know this for sure, though? That they were murdered, I mean?"

I shook my head and cleared my throat. "But why else would he have wanted the names? Duthrick told me to give them to Varden. And I preferred not to think about what he would do with them . . . I didn't ask. I didn't ask . . ." My voice trailed away and I hung my head like a shamed schoolboy.

He came around the bed and laid a hand on my shoulder. "God has a generous spirit, Elarn, never forget that. We will speak of this again, but just now it is more important we put things right." He went to the door and called in the two Gilfeathers and the man with the blue eyes. "This is Elarn, a tiderider," he said to the latter, and quickly filled them in about what I had done. Kelwyn—with one pitying glance in my direction—went off to fetch some of the cure.

Garrowyn gave me a speculative look that brought the deep red of my shame into my face. The man with the blue eyes stared at me too, cocking his head at me in an odd fashion. Then he said, in a thick accent that told me he had once been a Dustel bird, "I'm Ruarth Windrider. Thank you for being honest in time to save Flame."

If anything, I went an even deeper red. "We don't know if it will save her," I warned him. "Maybe the cure is really poisonous. Maybe the effect of it doesn't last."

"We could still try it on me first," Ryder said quietly. "Which is what we should have done in the first place."

Ruarth shook his head. "No. Let's face it, Tor. Flame either has this cure, or she has to die. We all know that—and so did she. We have no other options."

"Aye, but we do," Garrowyn contradicted. "The Hub and the Keepers and sylv healing. That has ever been an option, no?"

"Jesenda's instructions were to kill her," I said, "not to bring her back to be sylv healed."

They all looked at me. I couldn't meet their eyes, none of them.

"She told you that?" Ryder asked.

"Yes. So did Duthrick. Or he implied it. He also said he doubted Flame could be sylv healed." None of them commented, and they refrained from looking at me, but their condemnation hung in the air. No, perhaps that's the wrong word. It was more . . . disappointment. They had expected better of me. And, in a way, that was worse.

"Then we have our answer," Ruarth said.

Kelwyn returned just then, bearing a small medical bag. We watched in silence while he washed his hands and

Flame's upper arm first with soap, then with distilled alcohol. He placed a few drops of the cure on the cleansed arm, then pricked her skin several times with the point of a sharp medical knife.

"Is that all?" Ruarth asked, amazed at the simplicity of the action.

"That's all," Kelwyn said. "There won't be any change for a day or two, apart from a red patch on her arm. Her recovery from dun—if it occurs at all—will be gradual. We thought—think—the Awareness somehow spreads and multiplies in the blood, and attacks the magic already lurking there."

They started talking about why sylvhealing had not helped the seven poisoned Menod sylvs—because they had, perhaps, already become Aware. But I didn't want to hear about that. I slipped out as quietly as I'd entered.

THE FOLLOWING MORNING IT WAS STILL raining. I woke late, to the news that the last longboat for The Hub had overturned a few miles up-Race. The cargo was lost and two of our guildsmen drowned, along with several passengers. The Guild was in an uproar. Some said the Race should have been closed to water traffic, especially after my report of the day before. Others thought it was the fault of the traders who had overloaded the boat because they feared the Guild would stop the service on account of the bad weather. Still others blamed the guildsmen who had allowed the overloading, or faulted the weirmaster in The Hub, who had released too much water at the wrong time in order to save the city from flooding. Either way, a huge ebb wave had been on its way downstream when it hit the incoming bore . . .

There were always arguments like this, every time something went wrong; I supposed it was human nature to want to find someone to blame and to look for ways to stop a tragedy from happening again. Normally, I would have expressed my opinion as vocally as the rest; this time I was silent. I'd narrowly escaped disaster on the Race myself the day before, and my reaction was to try not to think about it too much. I'd made it back safely when others did not. I didn't want to think about those lost; I just wanted to feel glad I had survived. Besides, I had other things to think about. I was consumed with guilt.

I decided to climb up the Hall tower to take a look at the weather, but Marten accosted me on my way across to the foot of the stairs. "Hey, Elarn, where were you last night?" He clapped me on the back. "I heard you had a real bumpy ride in yesterday—someone said you looked like a blue lobster with your eyes out on stalks."

"Yeah, good description. It was crudding cold, I can tell you. Came close to losing the wave, you know."

He made some remark about me being, as usual, the luckiest tiddler in the rock pool. Then he added, "You know they have closed the Race? All tiderides by boat or tiderunner have been suspended till further notice."

"I'm not surprised. Marten, it is goddamned awful out there—there were times when I felt like an ant caught in bathwater when the plug is pulled."

"Yeah. But even so, it won't be long before people drag out that old superstition about how riders tame the waves when they ride, and if we suspend tideriding, the waves will get bigger."

I grunted. "As long as no one asks me to do the taming. Let 'em try riding it like it is today!"

"They are talking about cancelling the Whale-King Festival, did you know?"

I didn't, and I was startled. That was unheard of . . .

Some said the festival had pagan origins, and it ought to be banned, but most people thoroughly enjoyed the day. Everyone who had a runner or a boat decorated it elaborately and paddled out onto the Race to wait for the bore tide. They wore colorful costumes to match their craft, and the surface of the water was strewn with flower petals. The High Patriarch was rowed out in one of our longboats to sprinkle holy water on the bore wave and bless the tide. Those who didn't take part watched from along the wharves and the shore. The rest of the day was spent feasting and dancing. A young girl and a young man were crowned as Tide Lord and Tide Lady for the day, and they paraded through the streets, waited on by others dressed as the Silver Moon, the Blue Moon and the Sun. Everyone usually ended up sopping wet, as it was traditional for young children to wield water-soaked sponges in the crowd, and for lads to pour water from balconies down onto unsuspecting spectators. The latter then had the added incentive of enjoying the way wet clothing clung to the girls' figures . . . Not only children enjoyed the Whale-King Festival.

But not, I thought, this year. If the High Patriarch was calling for it to be cancelled, he was right. People would be killed if they paddled out onto the Race with the weather like this.

I climbed up the Hall tower, to find the top level was occupied. My father was there, and so were three other men: the High Patriarch, the Chairman of the Chambers of Commerce and Tor Ryder. Embarrassed at intruding on such a high-powered gathering, I was about to retreat as unobtrusively as I could, when the High Patriarch spied me and beckoned me up the last few steps. I thought he looked old and ill. His palsied hands shook, and I realized Ryder had not been lying when he'd told Jesenda that Crannach was sick. "Elarn," he said, "come on up. I hear you were the last one to have ridden the Race safely. What is your opinion? Should we go ahead with the Whale-King Festival tomorrow?"

I glanced out towards the ocean. The whole of the Race was churned up brown, the curled tops of the waves stained and dirty. The backdrop was a sky turgid with storm cloud. "Not," I said, gesturing at the view, "if it's like *that* tomorrow."

"You can make the blessing from the shore," Ryder told Crannach.

"The rest of the festival can go ahead as planned," the Chairman added. I could almost see him doing sums in his head, toting up how much the various Guild members would lose if the festival was cancelled altogether. My father did not look in my direction once.

The High Patriarch thanked me, and they all left, resuming their discussion of what was to be done as they descended. Except for Ryder. Ryder remained, leaning against one of the corner posts of the tower, his arms folded, his expression as troubled as I'd ever seen it.

"How is she this morning?" I asked when the others were out of earshot.

"We are keeping her sedated," he said, "so it's hard to say. There don't appear to be any problems as yet." He shook his head. "Poor Flame. She didn't deserve this fate."

"To be dunmagicked? No one deserves that," I shuddered. "But still . . ." I took a deep breath and gathered my courage. I needed to say something, and I wasn't sure how he would react. "Syr-patriarch," I began, "although to kill those seven people was wrong, and something I should never have lent myself to—I don't know if I have done the right thing by telling you about the reality of their deaths."

"What do you mean?"

"I, er, I have enabled you to use the cure however you like—and you want to wipe all magic from the face of the Isles. You can, can't you? You can give this cure to people who have no magic, and they will end up Aware. And that will mean it will be pointless to be sylv . . . the only people they will be able to magick will be their fellow sylvs."

"That's right," he said. "Sounds like poetic justice, doesn't it?"

"Perhaps. But it also means the end of sylv healing. And theater. The Keeper Isles will be vulnerable in ways it never has been before. The Keeper Council as we know it will not be able to exist. So many things will have to change . . . We will probably end up having a hereditary royal line like everyone else, and I can't believe that's better than what we have now."

"We don't have to turn to an hereditary Islandlord! What would be wrong with having an honestly elected government?" he asked. "Where the leaders told the truth instead of fudging it deep inside illusion?"

"Ordinary people *like* the illusion," I said. "They feel safe with handsome, strong, confident people in charge. Now they will see them as they are—just like the rest of us. Just like *them*. And ordinary people will think that if our rulers aren't special, then maybe anyone can rule . . . a, um, fishmonger from Milkby perhaps . . ."

"Or a tailor from Magreg," he added, smiling slightly as if he remembered something. "And maybe, just maybe, that's no bad thing."

I stared at him, wondering if he was serious. And he was, of course. In the end that's exactly what happened, and no bad thing it was too. But with the youthful arrogance I had at twenty, I lacked the vision to see it.

"To change the subject a little, did you find out anything about saltpetre from Jesenda?" he asked.

"Oh—oh, yes. I forgot to tell you. *Keeper Pride* and *Keeper Just* are carrying cargoes of the stuff. Jesenda got the Bastionlord to put his signature to a long-term trade contract, while he was still half muddled with dun."

"Clever of her, although perhaps not very ethical." He sighed and leaned against the railing to look up-Race. "We need to get to The Hub, Gilfeather and I. We have to do our best for Blaze at the trial."

"Kelwyn won't stop at that," I said, certain I was right.

"Perhaps not, but first we will try legal means . . . the problem is that there are no boats going up-Race."

"Are you asking me to take you? I can't do that. I'd have to steal a longboat. I would never be allowed back in the Guild. And you and Gilfeather would have to do the rowing—"

He interrupted. "No, I'm not asking you to do that. I wouldn't have you risk your life, and we both know it would be a risk in waters like these. I was just going to ask you how long you think it will take the Keeper ships to arrive in The Hub."

"The day after tomorrow perhaps."

He thrust his hand out into the wind. "It's a southerly gale. Won't it blow them all the way to The Hub in hours?"

"Ah, but the outflow of water is carrying them down-Race."

"And how long is the Race likely to be closed to water traffic?"

I shrugged. "How can I say? We just have to wait and see what the weather does. Our weather and tide specialists up in Tenkorhaven might have a better answer for you."

He changed the subject again. "Have you been to the Worship House to pray yet, Elarn?"

I shook my head miserably.

"It will help. If you need to discuss it, well, I am alway available."

He meant it too.

CHAPTER 29

YOU WANT TO KNOW ABOUT THE WHALE-King bore tide? The one that killed so many people back in 1742? Then you should ask Elarn Jaydon, not a Sky Plains-man who never dipped a hand into the sea until he was a grown man. Elarn was there, after all, and he knows more about tidal bores than any man living. He was a fine Guildean in his day, you know; he was elected to the post when he was in his early forties. A great improvement on his father, who was an unpleasant, unbending bigot of a man.

Me? Well, aye, I was there in 1742. On the bore, I mean. Under it too. And I suppose if you want to know what it was like for someone like me, a fellow who can't do more than dogpaddle across a calm mountain tarn . . .

I first heard about it from the ghemphs.

I'd sought them out, of course. It was the only way I could think of to help Blaze. No boats were leaving for The Hub, and the roads were in terrible condition because of the rain. Either way, I was stuck in Tenkor. But the ghemphs weren't. They were creatures of the sea, and Eylsa's pod was duty bound to give Blaze aid. So I went to the Tenkorhaven ghemph enclave. The moment I entered the tattoo shop, I sensed that the ghemph behind the counter knew exactly who I was. He ducked into a back room, and a moment later ushered me through into a sparsely furnished parlor. Several elderly ghemphs sat around a fire. On such a wet, blustery day, the room was a pleasant place to be.

"You have need of a ghemph?" one of them asked, in that stilted fashion of speaking they had.

I nodded, and sat down in the chair he proffered. "Aye. For Blaze Halfbreed," I said, and told them all I knew.

They listened in silence, but their hands and fingers fluttered in commentary even as I spoke. When I finished, one said, "And you want us to render her aid?"

"I thought Eylsa's pod might."

"There are rules governing our behavior in all our dealings with humankind."

"Your people helped us on the Floating Mere." I refrained from mentioning they had actually disposed of a number of subverted sylvs in an orgy of slaughter. By comparison, it was hard to imagine they may have a problem with saving someone they had pledged to help in need.

"That was a remote place with no witnesses except a few befuddled magicked slaves," he reminded me. "You say Blaze is aboard the flagship of the Keeper Islandlord. To rescue her from there would be an act that we could not afford to be seen undertaking."

"Aye, I understand that."

"She has a way to call her pod to her for help."

"She is not free to do so." *Her* pod? They thought of Blaze as a pod member?

More flutterings of their fingers.

"We will inform her pod of her need, but be warned: they will not help unless they can do so undetected." The firmness of his tone indicated the subject was closed. "And now," he added, "we have a matter we wish to convey to you. The bore tide tomorrow, due here around the middle of the day, the one they call the Whale-King—it will be the largest and most destructive in living memory. The force of it will sweep into The Hub with a power that will smash the city and kill much of its population. We have warned the ships on the Race and the Keeperlord of this. Even here in Tenkor, the merchants along the waterfront should vacate their shops and warehouses."

I frowned. "But—why? What is special about this one? It happens every year, surely!"

He nodded and launched into a lengthy speech. I hadn't known they could be so articulate when they wanted. "Yes," he said, "when the moons and the sun are aligned. But there are two other factors that will play a part in the tide tomorrow. It has been raining heavily and incessantly in the high country of the Keeper Isles. Unfortunately, over the past ten years or so, the hillslopes and valleys there have been denuded of the forests with which they were once clad, in order to provide the Keeper Isles with the timber needed to fuel their burgeoning shipbuilding activities. Water now runs off these naked hillsides in quantities never seen before. Every river that feeds the River Hub and the Hub Race is in full spate, and the worst of this flood will hit the Race tomorrow. In addition, a typhoon is forming out to sea, and it is moving north. The winds are heaping up a storm surge against the coast, and the tide that will meet the force of the downstream water tomorrow will be beyond imagining.

"Do not come down to the sea tomorrow, Syr Plainsman."

DO NOT COME DOWN TO THE SEA.
Sensible advice, and I couldn't keep it. How could I? Blaze was out there somewhere, on a ship that might or might not make The Hub harbor in time.

After talking to the ghemphs in Tenkor, I found Elarn Jaydon and asked him to come to the High Patriarch's office with me. When we arrived, however, it was to be told that Crannach was ill again, quite seriously this time. Ryder was dealing with all affairs of the Patriarchy in his stead. I didn't join the queue of people waiting to see him; instead I sent in a message saying merely: "Urgent I see you now." It had the desired effect. Elarn and I were ushered in immediately; Ryder may not have liked me much, but he did trust me.

And he trusted the ghemphs. No sooner had he heard what they'd told me than he sent off messages to the Guildean, the Chairman of the Chambers of Commerce and the harbormaster.

"And what about The Hub?" I asked. "And Blaze?"

He was quiet for a moment, then said, "The *Keeper Fair* may not get to The Hub in time. If it is caught in the Race . . . who knows."

"If the ghemphs are right," Elarn said slowly, and he sounded as though he wasn't convinced they were, "any ship in the Race will be wrecked. The Race gets narrower as it nears The Hub, the inrush of water becomes higher, the outflow is faster . . . a ship would be flung against the banks. They have to be warned."

"They have been," Ryder pointed out. "The ghemphs said so. But maybe—just maybe—this will offer Blaze the only hope she has of escape."

I exploded. "Creation take it, Ryder! Ye heard what Elarn told us. Blaze is chained and manacled. If the ship goes down, so does she!"

"Then we have to hope the ghemphs help her," he said. "Gilfeather, just what can we do anyway? There's no way we can get to her in time. With the state of the roads at the moment, a journey to The Hub by land would take seven or eight days. And the Tideriders' Guild has quite rightly stopped all longboats."

His tarn-blue eyes were cold, but it was pain and despair that made them that way, not a lack of emotion. We stared at each other, and each knew how the other felt.

"The Hub should be warned again," Elarn said.

"The Hub has been warned. Your Guild members should not risk their lives on these waters the way they are now," Ryder said, and his voice sounded dangerously taut. "And why should you anyway? The ghemphs have told them what to expect!"

"But don't you see?" Elarn asked. "They won't have believed it! Would Duthrick ever listen to ghemphs? I don't think so. Syr-aware, you've been to The Hub. You know how flat it is, except for Councillery Hill and Duskset Hill. Surely you can imagine how many people will die if a tidal wave swept over the harbor breakwater." His odor was pungent: a mix of fear, excitement, anxiety, and a sort of appalled grief. "I have sylv skills . . ." he added quietly. "I think I could make it. There's a tide tonight, at midnight . . ."

"No, you wouldn't make it," Ryder said. "The last long-boat that tried didn't, remember? And things have worsened since then. Don't even think it, Elarn. Now, listen you two, I have a lot to do. The people who have been moved out from the wharves have to be housed somewhere . . ." He expected us to leave, and when we didn't, he said irritably, "Well?"

"Tor," I said, "ye used to care about other folk."

"I still do, Gilfeather. But I have to think of more than just friends." He stared at me, then added, "You still don't understand it, do you? Every single ship in the Keeper Council fleet is in the Basin of The Hub at the moment. According to our intelligence, they are being, or have just been fitted with cannon-guns—triple banks of the monstrous things. And the *Keeper Just* and *Keeper Pride* are carrying saltpetre to make more black powder. Jesenda has told Elarn here that the Keeper Isles have signed a treaty with Breth to buy as much unrefined high-quality saltpetre as they need in the future. Do you know that most of the skilled sylvs of the Keeper Isles—the agents and the merchants, the ones who work hard at deceiving the whole of the Isles of Glory—are in The Hub right now because their ships have been called back? Do you know that ranged along the wharves of The Hub are the bronze foundries and ironworks, churning out more cannon-guns . . .?"

I swallowed, finally assimilating what he was trying to tell us. The chill that followed the realization was the cold fingering of guilt, touching my soul. A ghemph warned me once: *We did more evil than we knew tonight, Gilfeather.* He had been talking about Tor Ryder and our accidental dun contamination of the patriarch. *You will have to learn to live with that,* he'd said.

"It is God's will, Gilfeather. It has to be. Just as I knew you crossed my path for a reason—to find a cure for magic—there is a reason for this storm."

Until then, I'd not understood what made him so certain we would find the cure. Now I knew: he thought it was God's will. God's will that his path had crossed mine. God's will that a storm surge was going to wipe out the cannon-guns and fleet and sylvs of The Hub. I said, "I thought your God was a—a *caring* deity."

"He is. This *is* the kinder way. If the Keeper Council and Duthrick have their way, people will live under the Keeper thumb from Fen Island to the Spatts, and through the years, how many countless thousands would die? This way, Duthrick and his guns and most of his sylvs will be wiped from the face of the world. The Hub will be broken by this time tomorrow. God sent his warning to them; they chose not to listen. In the end we will have a better, more equitable world."

I didn't know what to say. I could smell the dun on him as he uttered those words, and I knew in my heart there had been a time when he would never have given voice to such sentiments. And for that, Blaze and I would have to accept responsibility. "I think it's time ye took the cure for magic yourself," I said quietly.

"I already have," he said. "This morning, after I saw that Flame's improvement was so substantial. The High Patriarch is dying, Gilfeather. I never wanted to stand in his shoes, never. But it seems it will happen, and soon. It wouldn't be a good idea to have a new High Patriarch carrying a taint of dun in him, I think. In time the magic inside me will succumb to the added dose of Awareness I've given it." He smiled slightly. "Either that, or I'll die from an excess of Awareness. But right now the dun is still there, and I have to believe that its presence is God's will too. If it weren't there, then maybe I'd encourage you to go, or even go with you, but it *is* there. And so, as your spiritual advisor, Elarn, I must ask you not to go. It is not God's will. Let it be."

Elarn spun on his heel and walked out.

"Keep an eye on him, Gilfeather," Ryder said.

I nodded and left him. I found Elarn leaning against the

wall of the passageway, taking deep breaths. "It's not like that," he said. "It's not."

"What isn't?"

"Our faith," he said. "Being Menod. He's mad."

I shook my head. "Nay, just conflicted. He carries a contamination of dun inside his body. It has changed him. Twisted him."

"And that is *God*'s will?"

I shrugged. "Ach, how can I answer that? I dinna even believe in your God!"

He started to laugh. "Oh, we're all mad, Syr Plainsman! Ryder *knows* it is the dun speaking, that if it weren't there, he would do everything to rescue Blaze. And then there's me . . . I'm going to ride a midnight tidal bore in a typhoon—how mad is that?"

"Why go?" I asked, interested in his reply. "Ye have been made a fool of by those fancy sylvs there in The Hub. What do ye owe them?"

"Nothing! But what Ryder is advocating—I *know* that's wrong. I *know* Menod folk should not behave that way—that our doctrine teaches us to care for our fellow men. The people of The Hub—my aunt and her crazy maid—none of them deserve to drown. Not even Jesenda."

"Will ye take me along too?" I asked.

He threw back his head and laughed some more. "Yes! Why not? A selver-herder who can scarcely row a boat—what can be madder than that?"

I smelled his fear, and it was potent.

WE STOLE THE BOAT OUT OF THE boatshed—Elarn, Marten and me. Elarn had asked Marten along to manage an oar, and Marten obliged with an amiability I found puzzling. Apparently he had so much faith in Elarn's judgement that going out onto the Race during the worst storm in living memory didn't faze him. "Crudding cold," he told me happily as we forced open the boatshed door. "Elarn says you're not much good with an oar—is that right?"

" 'Fraid not. But I'm thinking that if we each only have one oar, I might be able to manage . . ."

He looked at me as if I was mist-mad. Which I was, I suppose.

The wharves were deserted, so there was no one to notice when we levered open the lock on the Guild boatshed and entered the darkness beyond. Elarn didn't even bother to use his sylvmagic to cover our theft. "We'll take that one," he said, and pointed to the smallest of the boats. It seemed ridiculously flimsy. He handed us both a bundle of gourds wrapped in netting as we seated ourselves in the craft. "Tie one of these floats to your waist. Then if you go overboard at some time, you have a chance." He sounded remarkably matter-of-fact.

Outside, waves crashed over the boards of the wharf. As we paddled out of the doorway into the chopped-up water of the Race, the spume in the air was so thick I could not tell if it was raining. Cold and wet and wild, the menace of the night hung in the smell of the storm, in the tang of ozone, salt, seaweed.

"Put your backs into it!" Elarn roared at us as he pulled at the sweep—we were already in danger of being thrown against the pilings and splintered into firewood before we even began. It was a maelstrom, and we were still in the shadow of the island. The center of the Race was like a mad washerwoman's tub—a swirl of foam and water going in every direction imaginable.

I smelled the strong sweetness of sylv, and the rain stopped. Or so it seemed.

"What the hells—?" Marten asked, and almost dropped his oar.

"Magic!" Elarn yelled over the sound of the wind. "Warding . . ."

He had built a ward on all sides of us, shutting out the rain and spume. When I glanced over my shoulder, I realized he'd extended the magic out in front of the prow so that it combed the water like the tines of a fork. I couldn't see it, but I could smell it, and I could see its effect. He must have been using sylv lights as well, I suppose. My own vision was confined to moments when lightning lit up the sky and sea. I wondered dubiously if the warding would protect us from a lightning strike, and reflected on the strangeness of magic. The ward stopped the rain, but the Aware—and me, presumably—could have walked through the very same warding.

I should have been sick. It was rough enough to make even a seasoned sailor throw up, but it didn't happen. Perhaps I was too scared. Perhaps it was having to concentrate on pulling at the oar that kept queasiness at bay. I struggled to face the blade the right way, to keep my strokes in time with Marten's even as the waves and wind wanted to wrench the oar from my control.

Elarn brought us to the center of the Race, bow pointed upstream, while we waited for the bore to catch us from behind. We had to work just to keep the boat correctly oriented.

I heard it first. Even above the crash of waves and the howl of wind, I heard it.

A roar, unearthly, seemingly unnatural. A swathe of sound that silenced the storm. This was a barricade of water on the move. A wild piece of the ocean, ripped from its place and sent forth as a curtain wall, bearing down on us from shore to shore, sweeping all before it. I glimpsed it as lightning flashed, a tantalisingly frightening second of impending disaster, seen and then obliterated from sight by the blackness of that turbulent night.

"My God," I heard Marten mutter. "The *speed* of it."

"Row!" Elarn screamed at us, and we obeyed, our terror as potent a force in our bodies as the tide was in the ocean.

Marten and I faced backwards, watching for that horror to rise up out of the darkness. And when it came, it was even larger than I thought was possible. A leviathan that towered over us, impossibly huge, its curling top lace-edged with spume, its face tear-streaked with foam, its heart alive with sound and power. I thought: we are dead. There was no way we could match its speed. It was going to churn over us, reduce us to splinters.

And then there was an intensified smell of sylv and the boat leaped forward in the seconds before the wave hit, giving us the extra impetus we needed to match the speed of the bore. Elarn had used a ward as a lever to impel us onwards.

And then we were moving upwards on the bore, racing upwards towards that crest. I thought we would take flight, that we would shoot out into the air, a wingless shearwater bound to drown. Elarn was yelling, but I didn't know what he was saying. My oar would no longer dig into the water. In fact, there seemed to be no water under us. It was all behind Elarn, or teetering over him, on the verge of falling, of wiping us from existence. It seethed, hissed, threatened. It was surely alive, intent on devouring the mortals who dared to challenge it. We were insects on the skin of an animal we could not control. An irritation to be brushed aside.

But the water never fell. We were there, suspended, hanging in the wave, hooked—or so it seemed—only by Elarn's sweep. Beside me, Marten was praying, his lips moving, the words whisked away on the wind. We were racing forward on the bore tide, on the Whale-King's eldest child, the precursor of his even larger and more ferocious father due in just twelve hours.

Elarn grinned at me. The man was exhilarated, made more alive by the danger. "Now you know that life is real, Plainsman," he shouted. "This is a ride you will never know again."

Aye, I thought. Because I'll never live through this one.

I REMEMBER THE INTENSITY OF THAT night best, I suppose. When you are living every second on the edge of death, knowing all it takes is the smallest of slips and your life ends, everything takes on a purity of focus and etches itself on your brain. I can relive that night, every second of it. The aromas are with me still: the sweetness of the sylv, the death around us—seaweed ripped from beds, cattle drowned, sea creatures battered. The smell of flood, of a turbulent ocean. Rain-drenched air, saturated clouds, crackling lightning. A world in turmoil.

The Race narrowed and widened and narrowed again; sandbanks and hidden pools and rocks, the bends and curves—they all served to change the nature of the tide, of the very speed of the wave. We would seem safe and then the bore would collapse around us with frightening suddenness, into churned-up white water, a boiling madness. There were moments when only the strength of our arms and backs saved us, and Elarn's sylvmagic, keeping the boat straight and still part of the wave. Sometimes it seemed there was no single wave—but rather a field of waves, each agitated, enraged, wanting to swamp us. And just when I thought we had found the right combination of brawn and skill and position, everything would change again.

If it had been anyone else manning the sweep, we would have failed a hundred times before we did. Elarn, inexperienced as he was, could lace his instinct with magic, and it was his instinct that saved us, again and again. As I watched him, I knew this man was not the youth I had met a few months earlier. Then he was callow, self-absorbed, thinking with his loins, aggrieved at the world, easily swayed by a woman's smile. When he had been betrayed, he could have become embittered, cynical. He could have chosen to use the betrayal as an excuse not to trust, not to care. Instead, he matured with a rapidity most young men could never have matched. His decision to warn The Hub, to go against Ryder himself—it was his attempt to atone for the deaths he had caused, of course, but I didn't think the less of him because of that. Nor did I think the less of him because he revelled in the danger; I could also smell his fear. He feared, and he faced his fear again and again on that wild ride. And not once did he ever regret his decision. His resolution was as strong an aroma as the storm itself. In a way, I think he found absolution that night.

Dawn came, pewtered with cloud, obscured with rain. And an hour later, out of the river ahead, came a surge of storm floodwater. I smelled it first, and warned Elarn, but bore and flood met in a confused twinning that birthed a chaos we could not even try to tame.

The prow of the boat shot up, the oars probed in vain. Elarn leaned into the sweep, struggling for purchase—and the shaft snapped. He tumbled overboard. The impact of two waves meeting shot a spume of water into the air, and somehow I was spinning into it, helpless and screaming.

We had lost not just the wave, but the boat as well.

CHAPTER 30

NARRATOR: ELARN

MY FIRST THOUGHT WAS: I'VE KILLED US all. Myself, my best friend and Kelwyn Gilfeather. All because I had an insane idea that I could take a longboat through to The Hub in weather like this. No one could survive a sea like that. It was too rough, too cold, too powerful.

The plunge into the water was terrifying. Within seconds I lost all idea of which way was up, or how to get there. The gourd floats were as much use as a pocketful of stones. I was tossed, tumbled, beaten. The cold was numbing. My helplessness was terrifying. My struggles made no impact on anything. Normally, the bore would just have spat me out of the back of the wave, and that would be that. Not this time. This was the Whale-King's child fed on a typhoon, meeting a Race that had devoured a flood. We were just food for the beast born of the union.

The breath was pummelled out of me and I knew what it was like to drown.

Then I felt arms around my chest, hugging me to a muscled

body. I thought it was Marten, trying to save me. Or Gilfeather clutching me in his desperation. But these arms had a strength Marten could never have mustered, not in that maelstrom. And the grasp contained none of the frightened last hope of a drowning man. Their owner had a purpose and direction no human could have called on in that gyration of water gone mad.

I surfaced, and gulped in air. Water broke over my head, but I was more or less floating, and strong hands held me there. I summoned up the last vestiges of my sylvpower to create a sylv light—a dim, pitiful thing, but enough to see who had rescued me.

A ghemph.

I didn't even try to make sense of that. Half drowned, half stupid with fatigue and shock and cold, I did no more than watch as ghemphs dived and surfaced, pulling both Marten and Gilfeather up from the depths. Then they hauled us to where the longboat floated, upside down and water-logged. Ghemphs were everywhere. They set to work to right the boat and empty it out.

I let my sylv light fade.

THEY PULLED US ALL THE WAY INTO THE Basin. The oars were gone, and without the ghemphs there was no way we could have reached shore. We were too exhausted anyway. Gilfeather was throwing up over the side. And it was bitingly cold. We think of the southern Keeper Isles as having a balmy climate, washed as it is by the warm southern currents, but, believe me, that night the sea was icy and the lashing wind and bitter rain had us huddled together, shivering. I had no sylv reserves to call on, and so we had no shelter except Gilfeather's tagaird. I asked him, much later, how it was he managed to hang on to that absurd garment when we had all been dumped into the sea. He informed me no Plainsman is *ever* parted from his tagaird. When I pressed him, he admitted, with a sheepish grin, that the confounded thing had been wrapped around his neck and had damned near choked him as the weight of the wet material dragged him down.

Sometime after sunrise we passed the *Keeper Fair*. We weren't far from The Hub by that time. Gilfeather suddenly roused himself to lean over the prow and talk to one of the ghemphs, and I knew that even through all that rain and wind he had somehow smelled Blaze again. The wind snatched his words away, and I did not hear what they replied either, but the answer seemed to satisfy him. He flopped back into the boat.

By the time we clambered out onto the wharf opposite our Guild Hall in The Hub, the sky was about as light as it was going to get that day. It must have been about ten in the morning. We barely had time to say thank you to the ghemphs before they were all gone, vanished back into the water. To this day, I don't know why they helped us. I do know that without them we would all have died.

We made straight for the warmth of the Guild Hall and a hot bath. There, we had a stroke of luck: the guildsman in charge of Guild affairs in The Hub, Syr-tiderider Leviath, happened to be in the building. In Guild hierarchy he was second only to my father, and his authority in The Hub was respected. He listened to our tale while we ate breakfast. And he believed us. I suppose it would have been hard not to—only someone who had an urgent story to tell would have been mad enough to tackle the Race in that weather. Before we even finished our tale, he was calling for guildsmen to send messages to everyone in positions of power in The Hub, including Interim Keeperlord Duthrick, with the warning. He counselled abandonment of the Whale-King Festival, for a start. He was furious, and it didn't take much to realize why. Until we told our story, Leviath had been unaware the tidal bore was going to be any larger than usual. Duthrick had neglected to mention it . . .

We parted after that; Marten stayed behind to help the Hall guildsmen carry longboats and tiderunners to safety. Gilfeather and I chose to see Duthrick. "I want to meet the bastard," Gilfeather said, by way of explanation. That was unusually strong language for the Plainsman.

We found the Keeperlord in his office on Councillery Hill. His secretary was not keen on letting us in to see him without an appointment, but eventually relented. I'm not sure whether it was because I was so insistent and I was the Guildean's son, or whether it was because Gilfeather fixed him with a penetrating stare from under those wild eyebrows.

Duthrick was less impressed by the Plainsman. When I introduced the two men, his eyes slid over Gilfeather as if he wasn't there at all and homed in on me. "Yes, what is it, Elarn? We are very busy this morning; the storm last night did quite a bit of damage and the tidal bore destroyed a section of the breakwater. We have to make sure it is mended before the next bore. And I have already received word from Leviath on why you thought it necessary to risk your life in the Race last night."

I tried for calm. For dignity. "The tide last night was only a precursor to what will happen today. We expect the worst to hit The Hub about three this afternoon—"

" 'We' being—?"

"The Tideriders' Guild."

"And your information comes from—?"

"Our own knowledge of tides. And warnings from the ghemphic community. The height of the tide is going to flood the lower areas of the city, Syr, and it is possible the force of the bore will destroy waterfront buildings."

"We have the breakwater. And you can hardly expect me to take any notice of anything ghemphs say. They are halfwits at best, and superstitious non-humans at worst."

"They are an aquatic race, well acquainted, ye'd think, with the vagaries of tidal surges," Gilfeather said mildly. "Ye would do well to listen. It would be unwise for there to be anyone at all in waterfront buildings this afternoon."

Duthrick ignored him. "Elarn, I am cancelling the festivities. However, this city has stood here for hundreds of years, and it's never been flooded by a tidal surge. If I move everyone out of their homes, if I ask all the foundries to close down and shift what they can to higher ground, and it is all needless, can you imagine what my credibility would be afterwards?"

Oh God, I thought. That's what all this is about . . . Duthrick is afraid he will lose the election. He thinks Fotherly will make him look a fool if the tidal bore doesn't flood the place.

"Can ye imagine what your credibility will be if ye dinna move everyone out and there *is* a flood?" Gilfeather asked. "Especially when it is known you knew beforehand. Fotherly could win the election without making a single speech. If the two of you happened to survive, of course."

Duthrick did look at him then, with an angry, contemptuous stare. "I don't know who you are, but this is none of your business, Mekatéman." He looked back at me. "Who sent you here? The High Patriarch or that interfering fellow, Ryder? Because I am damned sure it wasn't your father! What is this—some sort of plot for us to abandon the wharf area so the Menod spies can have a free rein to see what we are doing there?"

I gaped at him. "Syr, I would not risk my life for something so . . . so ridiculous. Nor do I deserve to be accused of disloyalty to the Keeper Council."

"No, of course not. I did not mean to imply you would knowingly take part in a conspiracy. But you are young and easily duped."

"As you and Jesenda duped me?" I asked with a barely controlled rage. I forgot everything I ever learned about caution, about respect for those in positions of power. "Yes, I can be a fool, I'll grant you that. But this is a larger matter than any of us. The Whale-King bore is going to come rampaging down the Race a few hours from now and do untold damage to our city—"

I never finished. The secretary ushered in one of the Keeper Councillors, an impatient man who didn't wait for Duthrick's reply to his perfunctory greeting before he launched into his news. "Syr, the Menod are telling people to move to higher ground, and the Guild is emptying their Hall on the waterfront! Fotherly is down in the town telling everyone you have lost control of the city, that you are letting every second-rate functionary give orders to townsfolk. He is saying you are hiding the truth from everyone. People are angry, Syr. They don't know who to believe!"

Duthrick looked as thunderous as the sky outside and I was

the immediate target of his anger. "See what you have done with your foolishness, boy?" he asked. "Had you come to me *first* with this idiotic tale of yours we might have been able to contain this. Instead, it is becoming a shambles, fuelled by that idiot Fotherly, for his own ends." He turned to his secretary and began snapping orders. "I want a proclamation read out in every marketplace saying there is little likelihood of any flooding or danger to property or person. Have it state that although the bore tide will be higher than usual, the city will be protected by the Interim Keeperlord and sylvtalents."

The secretary bowed and withdrew; Duthrick turned to the Councillor. "And you, Sutherby—I want you to be in charge of getting every single Hubbian sylv over the age of ten down on the waterfront by one o'clock. I don't care who they are, I want them down there. We are going to raise a ward that will circle the Basin and go part of the way up the Hub River. From the weir, along the wharves, to the end of the residences. A long line of sylvs. Understand?"

"Yes, Syr . . . but that's, that's got to be at least ten miles!"

"And we'll have thousands of sylvs to man it. What with all the sylv agents back in port with their ships—yes, I would say we have enough skilled sylvs in The Hub right now, wouldn't you, Sutherby?"

"If you say so, Syr."

"Then go and arrange it, man."

Duthrick turned his attention back to me. Gilfeather he continued to ignore. "We may be able to turn this mess around to our advantage, no thanks to you, Elarn. If the tide really is high, we can persuade the gullible that it was my foresight in arranging sylv warding that saved the city from catastrophe."

Gilfeather and I exchanged glances. We both remembered the bore rising up out of the darkness of the Race. And that had not been the Whale-King. The moons and the sun were not in true alignment when that tide had formed. What was coming could only be larger, more rapacious. Gilfeather said quietly, "No sylv ward is going to stop this tide, Syr. Ye will just kill your sylvs—and yourself."

Duthrick looked him up and down as if he was a sand tick. "And who are *you* to tell me what I can and cannot do?"

"I am no telling ye what ye can do—merely what will happen if ye do it. And I? Well, I am the man who killed Morthred the Mad."

It was unlike Gilfeather to be theatrical, but that was good theater. However, if he hoped it would give Duthrick pause, he was wrong. The Keeperlord was shocked—the way he stared at Gilfeather you'd have thought the Plainsman had just announced he was God—but in the long run it didn't make him hear what Kelwyn was trying to tell him.

There was a long pause. Then Duthrick said to me, "I trust you will be down on the wharves, Elarn, with the rest of us at one o'clock."

"It would be better if we did nothing," I said. "Then at least some of us would be alive at the end of today. This way we are all going to die."

"Don't be ridiculous. You can't base belief on the words of a ghemph!"

"I don't, not entirely. I *saw* last night's bore. I *rode* it. Dear God, what do we have to do to convince you?"

"Nothing. Leave me. I have work to do."

When I opened my mouth to protest, he went to the door and pointedly held it open.

Gilfeather and I left. Outside in the street again, wearing our oilskins in the drizzle, Gilfeather asked, "You won't really be mad enough to be down on the waterfront anywhere near three o'clock, will you?"

I didn't reply.

"Sometimes, Elarn," he said softly, "the most courageous thing ye can do is live."

GILFEATHER WENT TO SEE IF HE COULD find Blaze. I detoured to make sure my aunt and Aggeline were safe, then went to tell Syr-tiderider Leviath all that Duthrick had said. I found him deep in discussion with the weirkeeper, deciding how to manage the weir barrier to make the amount of water in the river as manageable as possible. I passed on all Duthrick had said, and left to help the sylvs organize the warding. I knew the danger, yet I could not walk away. They were sylvs, and so was I.

Their task was hopeless, doomed long before they even started, but I was the only one among them who realized it. They were already dead, we all were, yet I was the only one who understood the poignancy. I'd never felt so helpless.

Around one o'clock, I saw Duthrick again. He was scrupulously polite and asked me if I would mind taking charge of the warding in front of his house along the western edge of the Basin. He wanted someone to help his wife, as he had to command the more important area around the wharves and foundries. Polite in my turn, I said I would do my best. In my heart I wondered why he asked. He must have known I was good at warding: Jesenda would have told him. Did he perhaps—somewhere inside his arrogant soul—have a speck of doubt? Perhaps part of him wondered if the ghemphs were right, and he thought I might be the best person to take care of his wife, and his property?

Shortly after I arrived at the Duthrick house, I saw the *Keeper Fair* enter the Basin with the *Keeper Pride* and *Keeper Just.* They all went to tie up at the wharves. The ache inside my chest—it had been there ever since I had last seen Jesenda, I realized—took on a new dimension. I wanted desperately to see her again, to have all the things she had said then be some kind of terrible mistake. I wanted to warn her about the bore. At the same time, I never wanted to see her again, ever. But then, today she was going to die, and there was nothing, nothing I could do about it.

I tried to organize the sylvs in the area near the Duthrick mansion into some kind of order, but they would not take it seriously. Many were society matrons, plump, lazy and complacent. They all hated being out in the rain and cold, even though their servants rigged up shelters for them along the beach. When I attempted to have them practise their ward-making, one gray-headed man made a snide remark about children who wanted to teach their elders how to suckle. I tried to explain how difficult it would be to ward properly: a sylv, after all, could not see someone else's warding, only his own, yet it was imperative each ward join seamlessly to the next. It should have been possible, but people kept wandering off each time there was a squall of rain. I wanted them to erect the wards and leave them there, strengthening them every now and then, so when the bore arrived they would be more solid. Some of the sylvs said that took too much energy and they would build their wards if and when the tide came. I lost my temper and raged at them. I pointed to the debris line left by the last tide; in many cases it had encroached on their gardens or heaped flotsam against their boundary walls.

And that was when the explosion came.

The noise was unbelievably loud, and I swear I felt the ground shiver beneath my feet. We all turned towards the docks to look. It wasn't easy to see what had happened. The curve of the bay partially blocked our view of the wharves and it was raining, but somewhere along the quayside, something was burning. Sparks shot up in bloodied gouts and burning material showered down with the rain, like the abandoned debris of a dying whirlwind. Fingers of flame stroked up a mast to cup the crow's-nest.

"Oh my God," someone said, "the ships are burning!"

We stood there watching, shocked, unable to think what could have happened. I know some absurd ideas rushed through my head: perhaps the making of sylv wards was to blame, perhaps joining wards together had led to an explosion that set the ships on fire. My rational mind told me it couldn't happen, but I thought it nonetheless.

I tried to get everyone's attention again, to return them to the problem of warding, but there was even less interest now. They grouped together in knots under the shelters and ignored me. Two of the men said they were going to the wharf to help. I protested, and one of them told me bitterly that there was no way he was going to listen to the idiocy of a tiderider still wet behind the ears when Hubbian commerce was going up in smoke. He stomped off with his friend. Several others followed.

A minute or two later, more spears of red-hot debris shot into the air on a sheet of billowing flame. The blast of it hammered at us, made us stagger. The noise left me momentarily deaf, and made my chest ache with its power. We stood there, staring at what had once been a port. My incomprehension was total.

Someone gave a moan. *God*, I thought, most of these women—their husbands were there, at the docks. Their sons and daughters . . .

I gave them no time to think. "Quick!" I yelled. "It's almost time for the bore. Everyone—erect your wards *now*!" This time—in a state of stunned disbelief—they did at least oblige. I began to check whether they had each connected up properly to their neighbors' wards on either side. I couldn't see their wards of course, but I could see raindrops run down them, like water streaking invisible window glass. For the first time that day I blessed the slanting, gusting rain. I ran down the line of wards along the beach, correcting problems, telling almost everyone to make their wards taller. They grumbled, but they did as I asked. Perhaps they did at last hear the desperation and despair in my voice. Perhaps it was the sight of the number of ships that had left the dock, even before the fire, to anchor in the middle of the Basin. Perhaps it was Duthrick's wife, who suddenly took it into her head to support me and gave the grumblers the sharp edge of her tongue. Perhaps it was the sight of burning ships and the sound of several more shattering explosions that at last sobered them, hinting that The Hub was on the verge of a catastrophe they could not understand, telling them people were dying or already dead.

In spite of the rain, the fire along the wharves burned fiercely, obviously out of control. And that was when I heard it: the roar, like low-level thunder approaching.

The tidal bore was on its way.

I flung up my own ward, placing it in front of everyone else's, as a first bastion, but I could only extend it several hundred paces in length. If I made it any longer, it would be too strung out to be effective against the power of the wave.

And then we saw it. By some oddity of nature, an errant shaft of sunlight lit up the juggernaut and rainbows played along the crest. I had never seen anything so large. I had never heard anything so frightening. We saw its curling top over the banks of the Race. We saw it ignore the breakwater as if it were a line of beach pebbles. It engulfed everything and came on straight at us. It was a living monster and there wasn't one of us who thought our flimsy ward would hold against power like that.

It flung ships about like wooden toys. It swallowed a pinnace, and the people on board disappeared into the foam, their cries and their struggles so puny they lost all meaning. I heard screams around me, and the sylvs fled, racing for the shelter of the houses. They could have left their wards still standing behind them, but in their panic almost all of them forgot: I saw the stain of raindrops disappear and fall to the ground.

It was strange; minutes earlier I had been almost sick with fear, but faced with the certainty of death, I found a clarity of thought and a cold calm. I remember thinking: why am I doing this? My ward is about to be whacked flat to the sand, and no power boost I give to it is going to make one whit of difference. And anyway, one ward is not going to do the job . . . I remember looking far to my right, where the wave struck shore, and seeing the first of the houses engulfed like paper cut-outs.

And in the split second that was granted to me, I made the decision to live. I withdrew my ward in towards myself, I shrank it, arced it, pulled it in around me until I was standing inside a filigree ball seamed with the curved blue ward poles. I closed my eyes and thought of nothing except keeping the surface of the ball strong. My last glimpse of the bore was the face of the wave, churned brown with floodwater, as it blotted out the sky.

I DON'T REMEMBER MUCH OF WHAT HAP-pened next. Sometimes I was upside down. Sometimes I was slammed from one side of the ball to the other. Sometimes I was rolled along inside. I was bruised and battered, but I was alive, and I stayed that way.

I opened my eyes only when I felt that the ball was at last stilled, and the world around it was at last silent. I allowed the ward to unfold like an opening bud, and found myself lying on a sea of mud on what had once been a street. It was eerily quiet, apart from the sound of trickling water. No screams. No cries for help.

Around me the lower city had died.

Sylvmagic also died that day, and the world was a different place.

Anyara isi Teron: Journal entry
36/2nd Double/1794

The Dustel Isles. I can hardly believe I am here.

We called into a deserted bay this morning to fill the water casks. A river spilled into the ocean from a rocky ledge and all the men went swimming. How I envied them! Lescalles and I had to be content with a walk in the heat.

When I watched the men from a distance, Lescalles was shocked and tried to hustle me away. Is there anything that does not shock the dear sister of God? (If she knew the thoughts I have as I write this and remember the glimpse I had of Nathan, his body wet and glistening, wearing only his underdrawers as he dived from the rocks . . . I am wanton, of course. I must be. Even worse, I revel in it. Oh, how I have changed!)

What a strange and wonderful landscape we have found; a surreal world that could perhaps be the invention of a fevered mind—except that it exists, and I have been there. The bleached white plants that appear in groves are not plants at all, but the remains of corals. They are sacred to the Dustels, and it is considered a sin to break them, so we had to be very careful. I understand that when the Dustels came back to the islandom, they survived by trading the red and black corals, popular for making expensive jewellery. To live they had to destroy something extraordinarily beautiful; so now, in compensation, they have made it a crime to touch any that remain.

We on the RV Seadrift sail on to Arutha this afternoon. The two botanists on board are particularly interested in Arutha because of its orchids.

RV Windrift, on the other hand, is heading for one of the other islands of the Dustel Group—where Morthred, fleeing from his uncle, once took refuge with the Menod. The scientists on board are anxious to find out if there is any truth to the story of a great Menod center of learning once existing there; they want to excavate the place, if they find it.

Shor is interested in interviewing the people who now live in the area. Apparently they are all Dustels who say they were never birds, but fishermen from South Sathan in the Straggler group. He's heard there is actually someone who saw the islands emerge from the sea—a fisherman's daughter with the lovely name of Waveskimmer—and so he sails with the *Windrift* to see if he can locate her. She will be quite elderly now, of course. Our two ships will meet again there and then we will sail on to The Hub in a few weeks' time.

I am almost light-headed at the thought of being free of Shor's censorious gaze. How can I ever have contemplated marriage to such a man?

Three more days and I will be in Arutha. Three more days and I will meet Blaze.

CHAPTER 31

NARRATOR : BLAZE

I THOUGHT IT WAS RATS, YOU KNOW, AT first. Gnawing the wood somewhere above my head in that hellhole of a ship's brig. A constant *scrrtch, scrrtch, scr-rrrrrtch*. Wood dust shimmered down to cover my shoulders. The guard on duty at the time didn't notice.

I kept silent. You never know what you can turn to your advantage later . . . even a rat.

Then I realized the scraping was too regular, too effective. A hole was being made in the decking above my head. It had to be ghemphs. I smiled to myself: Gilfeather had not failed me. Strange that; the way the mind works. It could have been Tor who had gone to the ghemphs—Elarn was going to speak to him—but I *knew* it had been Kelwyn. Last time Tor rescued me, he'd paid too a high price: dun contamination. Sometimes there are things that you know in your heart, and in the end, those are the things that should guide you. Tor would never rescue me again.

By the time I heard the scratching, I guessed we were

almost in the Basin. It had been a rough trip up the Hub Race, but now there were subtle differences in the sounds of water under the keel, in the way the ship's timbers creaked. The hole above my head grew larger and I could see ghemphic claws, then a face. Still the guard did not notice. From where he sat, he could not see the decking above me, but he would surely notice if I suddenly disappeared through it. "The only key to my manacles is in Jesenda's cabin," I whispered to the ghemph when I saw the guard was looking the other way.

Her eyes twinkled and she dangled a key through the hole.

My smile broadened to a grin as I took it. It seemed I owed Elarn Jaydon something too. The key fitted, and in less than a minute the shackles were hanging loose. I flexed cramped muscles and tried not to scream.

The guard noticed something wrong then. He stepped up to the bars of the door and peered inside, trying to find out what I was up to in the gloom. Before he could react, I reached out, grabbed a handful of his hair and yanked hard to jerk his temple against the bars, hard enough, in fact, to daze him. I held him there by the hair while he made ineffectual tugs at my hand and groaned. Then I wrapped the manacle from my neck around his instead, and locked it to the bars. It was a tight fit.

He started yelling. I grabbed him by the nose and twisted. "Shut up," I hissed, "or I will poke your eyes out. Understand?" That silenced him, at least temporarily.

I looked up. The ghemphs—there were more than one of them—had managed to remove several pieces of planking. I hoisted myself up through the hole, to find myself on the storage deck. It was dark, and there was no one around except for four ghemphs, none of whom I recognized. One of them grabbed me by the arm and hustled me up a companionway to the lower gun deck. It was raining—I could hear it drumming against the side of the ship—and some light filtered down from the deck above. There was still no one about; doubtless they were all occupied.

I grinned at the ghemphs. "Where are we?" I asked.

"Just sailing into the Basin," one replied. "But you have to get out of here now. Once ashore, you must go uphill.

When the bore comes, in an hour or so, there is going to be a
tidal surge. The Hub is going to be underwater soon."

I blinked. I don't think I took it in, not really. I understood
he was telling me there was going to be a flood, that there was
some urgency, but I had no conception of what was to come.
Right then I was much more concerned about how to get off
the ship without being observed. The guard was already
yelling again, but fortunately he wasn't easily heard over the
sounds of the rain and the waves and the creaking timbers.

I asked the ghemphs how best to leave.

"Through these here," one of them said, and indicated the
hatches along the sides of the ship. They were, I realized,
the holes where they ran the guns out when they were fir-
ing them. She opened up the nearest one and I squinted
through, towards the shore. We were approaching the docks,
still three hundred paces or so out. There was a line of
Keeper Council ships tied up there, more than I had ever
seen before in The Hub at any one time. We were at the eastern end of the harbour, near the foundries and the shipyards.

"Someone might see us," I said. "If not from the ship,
then from the shore . . . we need a diversion." I cast an eye
around. There was a lantern and its flint lighter hanging
from a beam near the companionway. I piled up a few dirty
wads of tree-cotton from a tin near the cannon-guns, spilled
the oil from the lantern out on top and sparked them alight
with the lighter. So easy.

I didn't intend to burn the ship to the waterline. I thought
someone would find the fire before it spread too far. Besides,
the constant rain had soaked the decks; hardly good conditions to burn a ship. I didn't know much about black powder,
you understand. I didn't even really stop to consider what
was in those barrels behind each of the cannon-guns. I piled
on a few more cotton wads to make more smoke, and we
wriggled through the gun ports to plunge into the sea.

It was a shock to realize how turbulent the water was.
There were sizeable waves in the Basin. But it was too late to
turn back. I changed all thought I had of swimming somewhere less public before climbing out; once I hit the water I
knew it would be all I could do just to get to shore by the

shortest route there was. The water was cold and rough. If I spent too long in it, I'd die.

The ghemphs swam beside me, urging me onwards, pulling me, until we reached some water steps. I crawled up onto the stone stairs out of the water, then turned back to say thank you. And they weren't there any more. I was about to turn away when they erupted from the bay, spiralling upwards in perfect unison, water spinning from them in necklaced lines of droplets. Once high enough to be free of the surface, they threw themselves backwards onto it again, bludgeoning hollows in the water with the force of their fall. Then they sank back under the waves and vanished.

"We will breach for you," Eylsa's pod-sister had told me once. I had misunderstood. I'd heard the word as "breech" and hadn't known what she meant—but now I knew. They were breaching, as whales and dolphins breach, to honor me.

I took a deep breath and brought myself back to my predicament. I was hardly free yet. I was in the heart of the Keeper sylv territory; I could even smell sylvmagic around me. I was saved only by the fact that it was raining and most people out and about were too preoccupied to take note of their surroundings. I squelched across the wharf and hid under the canvas that covered some barrels, to give myself some time to assess the situation. The wharf bustled, more than was usual in such awful weather, surely. People were shouting, giving orders. There seemed to be an inordinate number of sylvs around: the smell of magic was thick in the air. To both the right and left of me I could see wards being set. Nearer to me, lugboys pushed several laden handcarts past. Farther along the wharf, a few of the larger ships, all merchantmen, were leaving the dock and heading out to anchor in the middle of the Basin. Evidently their captains deemed it safer not to be battered against the docks.

The *Keeper Fair*, on the other hand, was just being maneuvered into the dock a couple of hundred paces away, the fire apparently still undiscovered. Perhaps the flames went out, I thought, but it didn't matter anyway. I had escaped undetected. A few moments later the gangplanks rattled down and Jesenda came onto the docks with her sylv companions.

They hurried straight into the Keeper office across the wharf. She was met by a group of people, but I was too far away to work out what was going on, and the rain was making too much noise on the canvas over my head for me to hear anything.

I was just about to peer out in the opposite direction to see if I could slip away from the area unobserved that way, when—without warning—someone grabbed me by the arm, pulling me upright into the rain. I jumped, and whirled around, ready to fight.

"Whisht," he said, admonishing, "ye *are* a bonnie sight for sore eyes, for all that you are ever wanting to attack first and talk later."

For once I couldn't think of anything to say. But then, he never needed words.

And he didn't waste the moment, or what his nose told him of it. He pulled his tagaird over our heads to ward off the rain, then raised his face a little to kiss me on the lips. And it wasn't a brotherly peck either. I think I opened my mouth to make a halfhearted protest, and he took advantage of that too. And I suddenly found I was damned if I wanted to protest anyway. I grabbed him so tight, I probably came close to cracking his ribs.

And that was when the *Keeper Fair* exploded.

We both turned our heads as we collided with the barrels, staggering under the concussion, jaws dropping, kiss forgotten. Neither of us had ever heard a sound so loud, or looked on a fire so intense, or seen flames shoot so high. It created its own wind, a gust that skewed the rain and sent the wet tagaird flapping hard against our bodies.

The *Keeper Fair* disintegrated before our eyes. Burning pieces of canvas and planking flew across the wharf to land on other ships. Several bodies cartwheeled through the air to land in the sea. Even as we watched, the upper gun deck blew out with another massive explosion. A cannon-gun shot across the wharf and embedded itself in the wall of a cooper's shop. The main mast shivered and toppled, flames licking the shrouds, in spite of the rain.

Kel, wide-eyed, still not looking at me, managed to murmur, "Sweet Creation, ye *are* a bonnie kisser, to be sure!"

Unable—for once—to laugh, I muttered, "Trench below, I think I did that."

"Ach, I dinna have the slightest doubt of it," he said. "Who else? Ye have to live up to your name, after all."

"I didn't *mean* it," I said in a small voice.

"Nay, of course not," he agreed amiably. "It's just that things tend to happen around you, I know. Like things fall off tables and break when I walk past. I think it's a birth defect." He gathered in his tagaird and used it to shelter us once more. "Listen, we have to get out of here. Elarn and I have been trying to get it into the thick skulls of these gowks that the Whale-King is going to dump half the southern ocean on The Hub in less than an hour, but we haven't had much success. Duthrick even decided it was some kind of Menod–Fotherly plot on our part to make them leave the ships unguarded." He gave a sudden chuckle. "He'll be more convinced than ever now, I fear."

"The place is alive with sylvs," I said.

"Aye. Duthrick decided they can raise a ward against a flood. Well, he doesn't really believe it's coming, but he thinks he can persuade folk afterwards that sylvs were the ones who protected the city with a giant sylv ward, stretching all the way along the waterfront . . . like a sea wall."

"It may just work," I said.

"Elarn thinks it'll fail. And he knows more about the sea and sylvmagic than we do. Unfortunately, he feels honor bound to be part of the warding." There was a reason for that obviously, but it wasn't the time to explain it. "Come on, lass, let's get out of here."

I looked around and hesitated. What was left of the *Keeper Fair* was burning fiercely now, and the ships on either side—*Keeper Pride* and *Keeper Just*—had both caught fire as well. Some of the crews were fighting the flames, but most seemed to have abandoned ship, fleeing in all directions. Which seemed an extravagant reaction to fires that had not yet truly spread that far, especially in wet weather. I

thought of the fiery belch of cannon-guns heaving balls at
Creed. I thought of the size of the explosion we had just witnessed. "Um," I said tentatively, "Kel, d'you know, I think it
might be an idea to *run*?"

And I took off up the wharf, with him pounding after me.
At the first street I swung left. A few seconds later another
explosion shook the ground. "This way," I called over my
shoulder, without looking back. I guided Kel upwards to
Duskset Hill, in the poorer section of the city, where I had,
as a child, once lived among the crumbling tombs of an
abandoned cemetery. There were other people making their
way upwards too—ordinary folk, carrying their most precious possessions. Obviously some people did believe in the
coming flood. No one took the slightest notice of us.

We were almost at the gateway of the old cemetery when
the *Keeper Pride* simply vanished in a flash of flame. I was
looking back over my shoulder at the time and saw it happen: a cataclysm beyond my comprehension, followed a moment later by a roar thunderous enough to be the voice of
some outraged god. We stopped there, speechless, looking
down on the harbor.

Four ships were now burning like hilltop bonfires; and
there were two gutted hulks listing, half sunken at their
moorings. The wharves themselves were a long line of fire.
Buildings behind the docks seem to have been flattened. As
we watched, the *Keeper Just* rose up out of the water and
then burst into a ball of rolling flame. The sound when it
came left our ears ringing. *"Shit,"* I muttered. "What have I
done?" I felt sharp regret. It was a sorry end to what had
been beautiful vessels. Worse still, people *died* down there.

"It looks as if ye have single-handedly wiped out the
pride of the Keeper fleet," Kelwyn remarked. He sounded
awed. "What in all the wide blue skies did you do, lass?"

"Something to do with the black powder, I think. And
fire. They had barrels of the stuff." I was shaking.

"Ah. Impressive. But I wouldn't let it worry you too
much." With his usual perspicacity, he homed in on the true
cause of my shock. "Dinna fret, lass. Those people—and
those ships—would have drowned anyway, in a minute or

two. In fact, I rather think you may well have *saved* lives by, er, persuading folk the dock area was unsafe. To put it mildly. Shall we move into the cemetery to wait this out?"

He helped me up onto one of the tombs, where we sat under the overhang of its decorative roof embellishments. The rain eased and then stopped, although the wind was still damp and blustery. Around us, crowds of people from the poorer quarters were milling, guarding their pitiful belongings, trying to rig temporary shelters among the gravestones and vaults. Menod priests moved among them, already distributing food and blankets.

Kelwyn wrapped his tagaird around me. It was too damp to do much good. Looking down on the conflagration he said, "Ryder will be delighted."

"Flame?" I asked rousing myself out of my shock. News of Tor could wait. "Have you seen Flame?"

"She's safe on Tenkor. On the way to being cured," he said, "as far as we can tell."

"You found a cure?"

He nodded. "Ryder took it as well. Though we are a bit uncertain yet as to just how good it is."

A patriarch came by, and offered us a blanket. We took it gratefully and wrapped ourselves up tight against the chill of the wind. I leaned against Kelwyn's chest. "Ruarth? Dek?" There was so much I wanted to know, and I didn't want to think about what had just happened down on the dockside.

"Dek and Ruarth are fine too," he added. "Ye did a grand job there on Breth."

"I killed an Awareman," I said and the remorse I felt was intense. "He was just doing his job too." I gave a snort of cynical laughter. "D'you know what, Kel? I decided afterwards he'd be the last person I'd ever kill . . . I just couldn't stomach another. And now look what I've done." I nodded at the wharves below. "I was just instrumental in killing a whole bunch of innocent seamen. By *accident*."

"Ach, we two have a fine record for that, it seems," he said. "Accidental deaths of innocents."

We exchanged a look that said much, and then I changed the subject. I would think about it later. "How did you get here?" I asked. "Elarn said you were in Tenkor. And it has been too rough, surely, for the ride longboats . . . and what's all this about a flood anyway?"

"Well, now . . . it was the ghemphs who told us about that. There's a typhoon out to sea, and it has created a storm surge at the very time of the year's highest tide. Elarn had a hankering to come this way to try to set things right—to warn The Hub. So I came with him. I couldna lose you too, the way . . . the way I lost Jastriá, ye understand."

"Ah." I thought about that. About the implications. It felt good to have his arm about me. He wasn't Tor, and I didn't mind. "The ghemphs got me out. Thanks to you."

"They came to our aid too, Elarn's and mine. And another lad, friend of Elarn's. We were upended in that broiling cauldron out there in the Race. I thought I was setting my feet on Creation's pathway then, I can tell you—it was a wild journey and an uncanny way for a Plainsman to die, drowning in an arm of the ocean."

"Why didn't the ghemphs warn the Keeper Council about the flood?" I asked, and winced as there was another explosion below us. I never wanted to go near black powder ever again.

"Ach, they did. But Duthrick wouldna take it seriously. Because they were ghemphs, I suppose."

"Trenchdamn the man. Will he never learn? And you—are you saltwater mad, coming up the Hub Race in weather like this? You are lucky to be alive!"

"Aye, probably. I wanted to stop when we passed the *Keeper Fair* just before the entrance to the Basin, but the ghemphs told me they had your rescue under control. So when we arrived we concentrated on trying to get the message across to Keeperfolk. That's what I was doing right up till the moment I smelled you on the wharves. Fortunately, the Guild believed us. And so did the Menod. The patriarchs started moving their Menod folk out right away. Duthrick, on the other hand . . ." He shook his head in disbelief. "Even Fotherly is down there on the waterfront, with all his numerous sisters and their offspring. The two of them—Fotherly and Duthrick—have turned it into some kind of political exercise to show who has the superior commitment to the well-being of Hub folk. People are going to die because of their—" He stopped. Then, "Oh, Creation, here it comes, lass."

By some freak of timing, sunlight pierced the cloud cover and for one brief, glorious moment it shone down on the Race as the tide rushed in, funnelled ever higher, ever faster by the increasing narrowness of the confining banks. We were so far away, yet we could hear the rush of it. The thunder of it. Rainbows streamed along the spume of the crest.

And along the water's edge, stretched from the wharves to the palatial homes on the other side of the Basin, a string of sylvs raised their wards and linked them. Or tried to. It should have looked like a silver curtain of filigree held in place by undulating blue poles: a gigantic sylv bastion . . . but my Aware eyes saw its weaknesses, not its strengths. There were gaps where some of the more inexperienced sylvs misjudged the distances to the next sylv in the chain and didn't build far enough sideways—and were unaware of the fault because they could not see their neighbour's ward. Some of the sylvs didn't make their barriers high enough; they had no idea of just what they were up against. I watched in growing horror, sensing what we were about to witness. The annihilation of Keeper sylvs. The death of an islandom's elite.

The end of a way of life.

The bore wave slammed into the breakwater with a shuddering boom we all heard a moment later, and simply passed across the top of it. Then more water, piled up behind by the tide, followed; and then came yet another surge, the splashback from the higher banks on the opposite side of the Race. The Basin filled with raging water. The bore picked up the anchored ships and tossed them away like leaves in a gale. It blasted across the bay and into the berthed ships and the wharves and finally into the sylv wards. Some wards collapsed even before they were hit as their makers panicked and tried in vain to flee. For all the effectiveness the others had, they might as well have been built of thistledown and cobwebs. The men and women who'd raised them vanished under the deluge as if they had never been. Ships were tossed inland like winnowed chaff on a wind. The lower city disappeared under an onslaught of water. Wharf buildings crumbled. The fires were doused and even the smoke vanished.

We clutched at each other, rooted in shock, unable to utter a word. We believed the ghemphs knew things, we were prepared to believe them—but we still had not expected this. Not such . . . devastation. Around us people stood frozen, silent, mouths slack, concussed by the sight of their city destroyed. Above it all, the public buildings on Councillery Hill still towered untouched in all their magnificence—the theater, the Worship House, the hospice, the University, the Chambers of Commerce, and of course the Councillery itself. But in the streets below, buildings were crushed and swept away; the rubble and ruin of ships and town and port inextricably mixed like some mad god had shaken up the world. When the water finally drained back to the Basin, dribbling through the channels that had once been streets in a slow reversal of the horror, most of what was left behind was unidentifiable detritus, now buried in mud. Out in the Basin, rooftops floated alongside the bobbing wreckage of ships and trees, dead ponies, bodies and planking.

"Skies," Kelwyn murmured. "Poor Elarn."

Behind us, one of the patriarchs began to lead the watching crowd in prayers, and one by one people sank to their knees. Someone sobbed quietly.

I turned to Kelwyn. "Why didn't Tor come? He would have had a better chance of persuading the Councillors this was going to happen than a Plainsman and a young tiderider."

I may not have had his sense of smell, but I knew he didn't want to answer that question. He struggled with it, and finally said, "Ryder believed the Council had their chance when the ghemphs warned them. They refused to listen. To Ryder, that was the warning sent by God, and they chose to ignore it."

I had a hunch there was more he could have said, but didn't. I felt my eyes fill with tears at the irony of it. "He never used to be like that."

"Aye, I ken." He added gently, "He has taken the cure. Perhaps he will return to what he used to be."

I shook my head. "Ah, Kel, none of us will ever be what we were. Never." I looked down once more on the ruined city, and thought of the dead. Of the people I had known. The people I had killed. "Kel—I am so tired of it all. Of all the deaths. Of all the killing. Of always living on a knife's edge. My whole life has been like that . . . and *I don't want it any more.*"

He read more into my smell, of course, than I had said. He touched my face with his fingertips. He waved a hand at the scene below and offered the only comfort he could give. "They would have died anyway in the tidal bore."

I bit my lip, incapable of speech.

"Ach, lass, ye'll have to ask me outright. I'm a simple man—I need things spelled out."

I smiled at him and shook my head. "You're not a simple man, ye great gowk, and well you know it. And you—of all folk—don't need it spelled out at all." He was silent still, so I added, "I'm asking you to take me away with you, Kel, wherever it is you're going."

"Why," he said, as if it was the most obvious thing in all the world, "the Dustel Isles, of course. Where else can I make amends?" He ran a hand through his hair and it bounced back up into its usual wild tangle. Then he added, "I'm going to build them a hospital with Menod money. A place to teach and heal. And one day . . . maybe even more than that. A physicians' university perhaps."

"Sounds like a damned good idea." And it did too. The chance to build something, instead of destroy something. "A place for the Dustel children. The orphaned ones. The crazy ones . . ." I added. I took his hand and turned to look at him.

He flushed an interesting shade of red. "Ye'd make me the happiest man alive if ye came along. If that's what you want. I love ye, you know that by now, I imagine."

"Yes," I said. "But it's nice to hear it."

For the rest of what he needed to know, well . . . his nose wriggled at the tip. I didn't have to tell him.

CHAPTER 32

NARRATOR : RUARTH

IT'S NO GOOD ASKING ME ABOUT THE Whale-King tide of 1742. I didn't see it. I was—as usual—seated at Flame's bedside, holding her hand. Waiting.

Dek came in to tell me about it, though, after the tide had passed. He chittered with the news like an excited fledgling. "Oh, awe-makin', Ruarth," he said. "The bore was like one of them mountains on the move! D'you know it washed away part of the Tenkorport wharves? A great big ship's got its prow jammed through the upper floor of a chandler's on the dockside! And a *huge* shark washed up on the beach, and a pile of weed at the foot of the main street 'ud take us five minutes to crawl over!" He prattled on, but it was hard for me to be interested in much except Flame, and he soon sensed my reluctance to keep up my end of the conversation. More subdued, he asked, "How is she?"

"Trysis keeps her sedated, but lightly now. She's sleeping better, I think." At least she no longer fought the sleeping draughts given to her.

He looked at her critically. "It's hard to say if she's cured," he said. "She didn't use no dun, nor sylv, not since we left Breth. So the colors and smell faded. I can't see nuttin' now. But I guess that don't necessarily mean she's better."

"No. We'll find out soon. We are going to let her wake up."

Ryder came in just then, and Dek slipped out. I already knew that the patriarch's robes—and Tor's stature on Tenkor—intimidated the lad. "All that black," he'd whispered to me once. "He looks like the Sea Devil himself." I'd laughed, but I privately admitted that I found it odd to see Tor Ryder dressed as a priest; odder still to know that he came to pray by Flame's bedside. I remembered him more as a man of action wielding a sword—and as Blaze's lover.

"I suppose Dek told you about the tidal bore?" he asked after a glance at Flame.

I nodded.

"It was bad," he admitted. "Worse than I thought it would be."

"Bad enough to wreck a Keeper ship?"

"Oh, yes." We exchanged glances and he went to stand at the window. "It's a mess down there." The look in his eyes was haunted. "I should have gone after her," he said. "In fact, I should have got her off that ship as it passed through Tenkor, and been damned to the consequences."

It was unlike him to speak of regrets. He gave one of those wry smiles of his, acknowledging my surprise. "I blame everything on the dun, Ruarth. It's the only excuse I have."

"It's disappearing, isn't it?"

"The dun in me? Yes." He turned back to look out of the window again. "I just tell myself everything is God's will . . . that, I have to believe anyway. I think Kelwyn and Elarn went to The Hub on last night's tide."

It took me a moment to understand what he had said. And then I went cold.

He elaborated. "They disappeared last night, and so did one of the Guild longboats."

"Oh, my blighted feathers. Could—could they have made it?"

"To The Hub? I don't know. But if anyone could get them there, Elarn could." I think in his heart, whether Blaze lived or died, Tor knew he'd really lost her this time. Pain sliced through his voice and it seemed to have folded rifts into his face overnight. "God forgive me if I made a mistake, because I never will."

I couldn't think of a thing to say.

Garrowyn entered, as garrulous as ever. He came to pester me into eating, into going for a walk outside now that the rain had eased. He reminded me sometimes of the male bustards we'd seen stalking the grasslands of the Sky Plains: large, curious and always chivvying the other members of their flock. "Tor will look after the lass," he said. "Come, let's get something to eat."

I paused in the doorway on our way out. Tor was still gazing out of the window, a faraway look in his eyes.

ON THE SECOND DAY AFTER THE WHALE-King tide had passed, Trysis eased up still further on the amount of the soporific and Flame began to wake properly, to take an interest in where she was and what was happening around her. She spent most of the day, though, just staring at the ceiling. It was not until evening came that she was prepared to talk. She turned her head towards me, looked me straight in the eye for the first time, and asked, "Where are we?" I could see no hint of Lyssal there. The sunken wells of her eyes contained an infinity of fear, and little more.

"In Tenkor."

"I feel . . . weak."

Garrowyn, who was on the other side of the bed, said, "Ye've been sedated for a long time. Y'need to get up as soon as ye can. Walk around. Regain your strength."

She digested that. Garrowyn gave me a meaningful look, and left the room. It's time, he was telling me, to explain things to her.

I said, "Gilfeather found a cure for dun. We gave it to you."

She was silent for a long time. I tried to take her hand but she moved it away from me. Finally she said, "There's something else that's wrong. I feel different. I *am* different."

I swallowed. "I—I think you, er, probably aren't sylv any more either. Um, in fact, you are probably Aware. Or will be soon."

I waited, but she didn't say anything more that day. After dinner, she asked to have a bath. A matriarch came to help her, and afterwards when I returned, she was already asleep. I slept in her room that night, curled up in a chair, my head half tucked under my arm. When I awoke in the morning it was to find her already up, seated at the dresser, looking at herself in the mirror. She was painfully thin, almost ethereal.

She didn't wait for me to speak. "I remember everything," she said. "At least up until the moment you all forced me to swallow that drug back in Brethbastion. What—what happened to the—the baby?"

I had to wrench my gaze away from my feet to meet her eyes in the glass. "We killed it."

"Are you *sure*?"

"Yes."

The expression on her face was encouraging. She was *relieved*. "I'm glad," she said simply. "It was a monster. It was eating me alive."

"Yes." I think we both wondered briefly, in that moment, whether the baby could have been cured too. But neither of us wanted to go to that dark place. The child was conceived in rape and violence; it was tainted from the moment of its conception. To contemplate now what we could have done differently would have been madness.

She took in a deep breath, and her voice trembled on the verge of disintegration. "I'm sorry, Ruarth. I am so, so sorry."

I took a step towards her. "There is nothing for *you* to be sorry about. It was the dun."

She started crying and I raised her up into my arms. We stood like that for a long time, with her head on my shoulder and me holding her, trying so hard to believe everything would be all right.

We were still like that when Dek brought in the breakfast

sometime later. He was his usual bright self, brimming full
of questions—and answers to my questions, even when they
were unasked. "We haven't heard anything from The Hub
yet," he told us. "We still don't know if Blaze and Kel are all
right. If they survived the flood—"

I glared at him. I hadn't wanted to worry Flame about
Blaze at this stage, but he was impervious.

"Blaze?" Flame asked, suddenly alert and sounding much
more like her old self. "She's in trouble? Why would she go
to The Hub? That thick-hided bastard Duthrick will skin her
alive! Does the woman have pickles for brains? And *what*
flood are you talking about?"

"She didn't have much choice about going to The Hub,"
Dek said. "She was manacled—"

I intervened hastily. "It's a long story. Kelwyn went after
her. I'm sure she's all right." There were so many things I
didn't want her to know yet. She knew that of course; there
wasn't much that Flame Windrider couldn't sense about me.
She gave me a look that stopped the words in my throat, and
turned her attention to the one person who was going to tell
it exactly the way it was . . .

"Start from the beginning, lad," she said. "And tell me
everything. From the time I left you all that morning on the
Floating Mere back in Porth. And don't leave *anything* out."

AFTERWARDS, WHEN FLAME STARED AT
me, stricken, I said: "It was because of what you did for her.
You went back to Creed, and that was when—when the child
was conceived. Blaze had to try to make it right."

THREE DAYS LATER, THE GUILD REOPENED
the Race to tideriders. Blaze and Kelwyn were on the first
boat down.

Ryder waylaid Kelwyn in the anteroom, wanting to know
what had happened in The Hub, but Blaze came bursting
into Flame's room in a rush. She paused in the doorway and,
for once, all her emotions were written there, on her face.

Hope, fear, delight—all the things she usually hid now warring for expression.

"Flame," she said. Just that.

And then they were in one another's arms, Flame weeping and Blaze patting her awkwardly on the back. I left the room, shutting the door behind me, and tried not to feel that pang of jealousy that slid into me then.

I'd seen something in the way Flame looked at Blaze that was not there when she looked at me. A lowering of her guard, an abandonment of barriers, a desperate cry for the comfort she needed. For the validation. It should have been me she had turned to for that.

I thought: happy endings are nest tales for fledglings.

THERE WAS JOY, OF COURSE. JOY IN THE days that followed, when we knew for sure that all trace of dunmagic was banished from her body. Joy as her strength returned. Joy the first time she laughed, at some mad thing Dek said. Joy that she didn't mind the disappearance of her sylv along with the dun. "Who the Trenchdamn cares?" she asked, sounding almost lighthearted. "It brought me more sodding grief than pleasure. I feel a whole lot safer being Aware. I love the way it makes me feel. The—" she hunted for the right word "—the comradeship. You've always talked about that feeling of kinship, but I never understood what it meant till now." She looked at me as she spoke, and with such love.

But there were other emotions as well.

Despair when I realized the depth of her trauma. Grief as I acknowledged her fragility, as I recognized her inability to forget what had been done to her, or to come to terms with what she had done to others.

There were too few secrets between us. I knew too much about her suffering. I'd seen too much of her humiliation, known too many of her crimes. She'd seen too much of my wretchedness, watched my ineptitude too many times. I could forgive her, and love her in spite of it all—in fact, love her more *because* of it all—but she was unable to forgive herself. All very well to tell her it was not her fault, that it had been the dunmagic . . .

I tried. God, how I tried. And so did she.

The simple truth was that our love was not enough. Worse, my presence seemed to make it harder for her, not easier. I was a constant reminder of all she had endured. *I had seen it.* Every time she looked at me, she remembered, she thought she saw her crimes reflected in my eyes. Days passed, weeks—and it didn't get any better. We needed to part so she could heal.

When our separation finally happened, it was no great surprise. The inevitability of it had been with me from almost the first. I came into the room one day and she was standing there with a letter in her hand. She waved it at me, saying, "From my father's Chancellor. Asking me to return home. They are willing to give me the governorship of all of south Cirkase, as preparation for what I will one day inherit. They are willing to make numerous concessions to see me back in Cirkase. Ryder has been organizing it."

I drooped, and stared at my feet. I said, flat-voiced, "And you are going."

"Yes." She struggled with her distress. "I have to make amends for all I did. Perhaps as the Castlemaid I can start to put things right." She moved to the other side of the room and fiddled aimlessly with the ornaments on the sideboard there. "I've seen enough to hate the Islandlord system. There's got to be something better than what I ran away from."

I nodded. "I always wondered," I said, "whether your sense of duty would get the better of you in the end."

She turned to face me. "They have agreed I can choose my own consort. Ryder insisted on that."

I said gently, "I think we both know it wouldn't work."

She cried, but in the end she left me. And, in the end, I sailed away to dig up some buried treasure—to use it to build a university for my people.

CHAPTER 33

NARRATOR : BLAZE

AFTER THE BORE SURGE DRAINED BACK
into the Basin, we searched for Elarn. I didn't expect to find
him alive, but we both owed him much, so we went looking.
And found him, sitting on a heap of wreckage, weeping.

"She's dead, Blaze," he said. His whole body was shivering, in shock. "Jesenda. And the others too—hundreds of
them. Duthrick. Fotherly. Wendon Locksby. All of them . . ."

We both stared at him, wondering how it could possibly
be Elarn sitting there, apparently unhurt. "Fogdamn,
Elarn—how is it *you* survived?" Kel asked.

"I wrapped a ward around myself."

I gaped. "Your ward *held*? Against that bore tide?"

"I made it into a ball, with me at the center. I let the water take it and I just went with it. Inside it." He took a
deep breath. "I saved myself; in the end that was all I could
do."

He seeped guilt. He had lived and so many others had
died, and he was going to find it hard to come to terms with

it. That sort of thing never bothered me at all once; now—
well, now I empathized.

Kelwyn said gently, "You did more than that, Elarn. If
you hadn't brought the warning, no one would have been
saved. Most of the nonsylvs—especially the Menod among
them—went up into the hills."

"Our warning brought the sylvs right down to the waterfront," he pointed out bitterly.

"No, it didn't. Duthrick did that," Kelwyn said.

"But the sylvs are dead. They died trying to save their
city, their people." The look he gave us both was stricken.
"It's the end of Keeper sylvs, Gilfeather. We can never
rebuild what they had. Never." He wasn't talking about
buildings.

I almost pointed out that the actions of the sylvs had been
more crabdamn *stupid* than brave, but I held my tongue.
Then was not the time to say it.

Looking back on that day almost fifty years later, though,
I know Elarn was right about one thing. Tolerance towards
magic may have received a fatal blow on the day of the Fall,
but sylvpower in the Keeper Isles was smashed irretrievably
on the day the Whale-King swept into the city, and Keeper
dominance of the Glory Isles vanished with it. Neither
would ever return. The Change may have started months
earlier, put in motion by all that happened on Gorthan Spit,
but it was the events in The Hub on the day of the Whale-
King that determined the politics of our new world.

The heart of the Keeper Isles died that day. Of course,
there were sylvs who survived, but the whole idea of sylv
leadership lost its credibility. Sylvs had failed to save the
city. They had not told the truth about the danger. What was
left of the glamour of sylvtalent, of being sylv, of being
somehow better than ordinary folk—it all vanished in one
afternoon.

As an almost natural result, political power in The Hub
passed to Menod laity, to men and women who preached
moderation and tolerance and equality. They preached it, but
sometimes I found the rhetoric they used in the preaching
was too potent for me to stomach. They said, in fact, that

with the Whale-King, God had spoken. And the message was that magic was not favored by God. God had made his displeasure known. He had sent warnings, but the warnings were not heeded by sylvs, in their arrogance.

Sometimes I wondered just who was arrogant, but mostly I kept that thought to myself.

WE WENT TO TENKORHAVEN AS SOON AS the Guild allowed tideriding again, of course. I was anxious to see Flame, to know if Kel's cure had worked. I needed to see with my own eyes that she was still alive.

I was shocked when I saw her. She was so thin, with large haunted eyes staring out at me, telling me of all she had suffered before she even spoke a word. My heart sank as I held her. She was too good a person to deal easily with all the things that had happened. She felt too much, cared too much—and she had hurt too many people.

"You killed an Awareman," she said when we were alone. We were seated side by side on her bed, and she rested her head on my shoulder. "Dek told me. I know how difficult that must have been. And you did it deliberately—for me. Charnels, Blaze, how can I live with what I have done?" There were tears on her cheeks.

"You can stop trying to blame yourself for everything, for a start," I said, trying to sound cheerful. "That's conceited, you know. You didn't kill that Awareman—I did. It was my choice. And he knew the risks of Council service. He was a Keeper agent, just as I was once. Believe me, you don't go into that business without knowing death is only ever a breath away."

She dried her eyes, gave a weak smile and sank back onto the bed. "You are always so sodding, um, *balanced*," she said.

"I had a hard life," I pointed out. "Makes for a practical nature and a damned thick skin. Flame, what you did as a dunmagicker was mild compared to others of that ilk. You kept part of yourself inviolate, when others failed. You were a bad dunmagicker, you know, and you can be *proud* of that."

She stared at me in disbelief, and then gave a chuckle. "And you are the only person in the world who could say something as outrageous as that and get away with it." Then she changed again, the sombreness returning. "There are too many memories, Blaze. Far too many."

I tried to keep it light. "So, you scratched my face. No scars—see?" But she wouldn't laugh, and I knew she was thinking of Ruarth. "He knows it wasn't you. He's known you all his life . . ."

"I see the memories in his eyes sometimes," she whispered. "And I see how he despises himself because he could not save me. How can he live, seeing me every day to remind him? It's not me he has to forgive, Blaze. It is himself."

That might have been correct, but I knew that the opposite was true too. She could not see him without remembering all she needed to forget.

When I left her to rest, I found Tor talking to Kelwyn in the anteroom, but their conversation died the moment I opened the door. "I'll go and see Flame," Kel said. He was jealous, of course, but being Kelwyn, he hid it well and would never let it influence his actions—or inhibit mine.

Tor had aged. It was suddenly hard to remember that he was only a year or two older than I was. As Kel went into Flame's room, I took Tor's hands and kissed him lightly on the cheek.

His lips quirked up in a half smile. "It's good to see you alive, free and apparently not in some sort of trouble, for a change."

"Believe me, it feels good too. I'm afraid I lost your sword, though."

"No, you didn't. Jesenda gave it back to me. I shall make a gift of it to you a second time, if you promise not to lose it again."

We smiled at each other, a comfortable smile, slipping back into friendship. "Come," he said, "let's walk in the gardens for a bit. We finally have some sunshine."

It was the High Patriarch's garden he meant, a walled flower garden with a pleasantly meandering stone path, a fountain and a few wooden benches. "Kel tells me Crannach is dying," I remarked as we strolled past some jasmine trees.

"Yes, I'm afraid so. An internal growth of some kind. And he is a stubborn man. He won't use sylv healing; thinks it's godless."

"And you—did the cure work?"

"Yes, thank God. My Awareness is more acute than it used to be. An interesting feeling. Did you know that we already have people lining up to become Aware? We are going to have a hard time producing enough of the cure to match the demand, at least at first. And we have a great many Menod sylvs wanting to rid themselves of their sylvtalent as well, especially now that the news has got about that the seven who died were murdered on Duthrick's orders."

I caught the faint uncertainty in his voice when he said that last bit. "Something worries you?"

"Well, yes. To rid the Isles of sylvmagic is one thing—to see a decline in sylv healing is part of that, but it is an unwelcome part. Without such healing how can we be certain there will not be terrible epidemics, for example? The Isles *must* have an alternative to sylv healing, and it must be something better than lugworm oil for stomach ache and crushed pearls to dissolve kidney stones. I want to set up a hospital for the study of Sky Plains medicine. Those two stubborn selver-herders are refusing to build it here, though. They want to go to the Dustel Isles." He took hold of my hand. "But why in all the blue seas am I speaking of such things when I want to talk about us? Blaze—"

I cut in hastily. "Tor, I'm not going to change my mind." Back on Gorthan Spit, I had told him that my lack of faith was incompatible with his beliefs. Nothing had occurred since to alter my opinion. We were not suited. And now—now there was Kelwyn.

He stood silent. Around us the rain-soaked garden seemed dank and cold. The washed-out jasmine had no scent, and the paths were sodden and slippery with fallen blossom. "No, I knew that, I think," he said at last. "And maybe yours was a good decision to start with anyway. It seems certain that I'll be the High Patriarch soon." He sighed. "It's not something I ever wanted, but there are so many things that need to be done . . ." He paused, cleared his throat and added, "Kelwyn Gilfeather loves you; you *do* know that?"

I nodded.

"Are you—are you going with him?"

I nodded again.

He looked a little puzzled, but said, "He's a good man."

"I know."

He smiled. "Come and see me sometimes. It will be good to talk over old times."

I thought I knew what he meant. There would be many times in his life when he would be lonely, surrounded by people who had no idea of the kind of man he truly was. But me—I knew. And once I had loved him. And that made all the difference.

We sat down on one of the damp benches, side by side, but not touching. He asked, "Have you given a thought to Dek's future?"

"No, not really. In the end he'll make his own choices. Somehow I don't think what Kel and I intend doing will appeal to him much."

"Let him go off with Flame. She'll need loyal support and he adores her."

I was silent for a moment. "Ruarth—? You don't think it is going to work out."

He shook his head. "I'm afraid not. I think she'll go back to Cirkase. One day she will rule there. And I suspect she will marry Ransom Holswood."

"That—that milksop?" I stared at him, remembering the young Holdheir of Bethany who had wanted to become a Menod patriarch and succour the poor and homeless—and who had been besotted with Flame Windrider. Then I made the jump. "Trenchdamn," I said finally, shaking my head in disbelief. "You've got it all worked out, haven't you? You want to reform the world!" I couldn't decide whether I was angry or impressed.

"I did try something along those lines once, on Calment, with the point of a sword, remember? And yes, I still want to change things. It's just that I am wiser now about how to do it. With the power of Keeper sylvs gone, with their fleet and their cannon-guns in ruins, we can indeed reorder the Isles. Perhaps all that happened is part of God's plan for the Isles of Glory."

"A lot of people died in The Hub that day, Tor. Please don't tell me that was God's will." When he was silent, I added, "It's a damned dangerous business to assume you know the mind of God, however much what happens seems to agree with your own view of the world."

He laughed softly. "Ah, Blaze, you always were good at keeping me on the straight and narrow. Let's just say then that the Isles will be a better place if we take advantage of the good that will come out of this. Flame and Ransom will play their parts. So will the spread of Awareness."

I was unbelieving. "You think nonsylvs will be clamoring to have the cure on all islandoms?"

"Most have nothing to lose. They never could afford sylv healing anyway, or even a night out at a sylv theater. But they have much to gain: they will never be deceived by a sylv businessman, or need to fear dun. The horror of the Fall brought the tragedy and cruelty of dun into the heart of towns and villages all over the Isles; it made folks fearful, even illogically so, and many are willing to do anything to free themselves of that fear."

He was right of course, although I didn't quite believe it then. Awareness spread as fast as the Patriarchy could supply the cure.

He continued, "The Keeper Council doesn't have a fleet any more, let alone one armed with those damnable weapons. We *can* change the Isles."

"Don't feel too damn pleased," I replied. "There must be people around who know the secret of the black powder and cannon-guns. You can't stuff a bird back into the cage once it has flown."

"No," he agreed thoughtfully. "You can't. But you can keep the birds in line by being the eagle . . ."

I didn't know what he meant.

I found out about a year later. By that time Crannach was

dead, and Tor was the elected High Patriarch. One of the first things he did was to declare the building and ownership of cannon-guns, and the manufacture of black powder, to be the sole prerogative of the Menod Patriarchy. True, the use of the cannon-guns was to be governed by the Synod in severely proscribed ways: they could be used to prevent others from obtaining the weapons, and they could be used to back the Patriarchy in their growing role of arbitrator in any inter-islandom dispute. But still, it was hard for me to believe Tor had lent himself to anything that involved the use of a weapon he so despised.

I sent him a blistering message, and his reply was calm, reasoned, logical—and disturbing, nonetheless, coming from a man who had once loathed everything those weapons stood for. He saw the Patriarchy as peacekeepers and defenders of the downtrodden. *If we don't control cannon-guns,* he wrote, *others will. If we alone have them, there will never be another Keeper Council with cannon-guns on their ship decks, prepared to bully the weak, or another Island-lord wanting to steal the knowledge. This way we, the Patriarchy, are the strength of the Isles, yet we represent no one islandom, no one ruler, no one citizenship. We represent the Menod who are of all peoples; we represent the voice of reason and peace.* The next sentence was more personal. *Blaze,* he wrote, *believe me, I am well aware of the terrible irony.*

Whenever we met, we carefully avoided the topic.

In the end, I suppose time has proved him right. The cannon-guns did serve a peaceful purpose. They made you Kells—with your own cannon-guns—take us seriously. They forced you to deal with us as equals, as people to be treated with caution. So in the end, Tor's placement of cannon-guns in the hands of the Menod from one end of the Isles to the other had an unexpected benefit. I'll bet that amused him.

I can't help but think, though, that sooner or later there will be a fool of a High Patriarch who will misuse both his power and the cannon-guns. Or some unscrupulous band of pirates will raid a Menod post and seize the weapons.

Perhaps I just have a more jaundiced view of the world than Tor Ryder.

Still, we Glorians owe Tor Ryder a huge debt of gratitude. Think of the Isles of Glory before the Change, when sylvs and magic ruled, when illusive power made men rich, when the deceit of magic governed who was wealthy and who was not. When what island you came from mattered, and the absence of a citizenship tattoo meant hell to him who lacked it. Think of someone like me, abandoned in an overgrown cemetery, forcibly rendered sterile at thirteen, doomed from birth to be poor and despised, simply because of a missing tattoo. I was lucky. Awareness saved me. Most other children like me died before they had a chance to grow up. Those who survived were exiled to Gorthan Spit.

Think of the Isles now, with citizenship tattoos a thing of the past; a system of hospices and physicians charging reasonable prices to whoever wants treatment for an ailment; a network of Menod establishments that dispense charity to those in need; a movement towards elected leaders rather than hereditary ones. The Change was a slow, steady alteration of the laws and attitudes that once divided the Isles, a relaxation of rules that had for generations fixed people in immutable poverty and powerlessness, in unchangeable citizenship, in rigid prejudices, in the hereditary hierarchy of privilege. By the time you Kells sailed into our world, you found a unity of kinship and no possibility to divide and conquer. In a way, the Change goes on: only last year, the new Islandlord of Quiller Island granted his land-owning citizens the right to vote for an Advisory Council to guide him. Bethany and Cirkase are now legally unified and governed by an elected Council, with the Islandlord hardly more than a ceremonial head. It is a start. Everything now is negotiable, adjustable, flexible.

The Isles of Glory is a kinder place, and much of what it is today was shaped by Tor. When Islandlords made treaties, it was he who handed them the pen. The ghemphs cooperated to make the Change possible, but it was Ryder who persuaded them to do so. When inter-islandom laws were agreed upon, it was Ryder who drafted the wording. And when you Kells came sailing into the Isles with your first exploratory vessels, it was Ryder who dealt with you, meeting you as equals, showing you that the Isles were not some weak backwater ready to be conquered by an outside power. It was Ryder who extended Menod influence and charity and hospices to every corner, so that no man can ever be so poor or wretched that he is without help. It was Ryder who had the vision of an Isles without magic, and he achieved that, even though it was Garrowyn and Kelwyn who found the cure, and Kelwyn who showed him the obvious way to halt the birth of new sylvs.

Me? What else is there to tell? Sometimes I think irony ruled my life. Consider this: by the time I had my citizenship, the Isles had changed so much, I didn't need it. Or even want it. I was proud to be a Dustel Islander—but I didn't require the symbol any more. And what about the irony of a swordswoman who fell in love, first with a priest, and then a pacifist physician? Or the childless woman who spent the last fifty years of her life looking after children?

I'm more than eighty years old now, still healthy, still loved. Most of the adventure in my life happened in the first thirty years and sometimes those years are the most vivid ones, the ones I remember best, the ones that seem more real. Yet if you were to ask me which were the happiest years, then I would have to say the ones I have lived since.

And if you were to ask which of the two men in my life I loved the most—I would not answer.

They both have a place in my heart.

Anyara isi Teron: Journal entry
39/2nd Double/1794

They both have a place in my heart.

Those are the final words in the files of Shor's last trip. They sound like the last line of a novel from the lending library, and in such a book it would have been a pleasing way to end a story. Here, I find the words less satisfying. There are so many questions still unanswered. Blaze knew that, of course, as did Gilfeather. Their omissions were their final laugh at Shor, at his prejudices, but he had not the wit to see that.

I think I understand how the islandoms could go so suddenly from being places of such diversity, where people deliberately maintained differences by their strict laws against inter-island marriage (except for the Islandlords themselves, of course), to nations that found it so easy to leave the prejudices of citizenship divisions behind them. Aware kinship resulted in inter-island unity being the norm, not the exception.

But why are there no sylvs on the Isles today? After all, there must have been some left. They didn't all live on the Keeper Isles; even those in the Keeper Isles didn't all die in the Whale-King bore. And they could have given birth to sylv children. Where are those children now? And why did the ghemphs leave and where did they go?

But Shor never asked those questions. To Shor, there is unity because they had to face an external threat—us Kells. There are no sylvs now because there never was any magic. They are no ghemphs because they never existed.

I have asked Nathan several times to give me answers, of course. I am sure he must have asked those questions. But he smiles, and tells me to be patient. You will be there soon, he says. You can ask them yourself.

And he will say no more. Oh, he is an infuriating man! I hate him.

I am going up on deck so he can point out more of the things we pass. There are strange fishing boats now, called dhows, with lateen-rigged sails . . . I am becoming quite nautical in my learning.

We are only a few hours out of Arutha.

Three buildings—the chirurgeon's school that was part of the Arutha University complex, the hospice and the orphanage—commanded the cliff top above a series of stone terraces, like sentinels watching over the ascent from beach and sea. The stucco buildings were dazzlingly white, as were the bizarre groves of coral that clad the terraces, all bleached by a hot Souther sun. Beyond the hospice with its breathtaking sea view, the university town clothed the slopes of the island with rough-stoned buildings and a tumbled riot of tropical flower gardens. The Dustels had built the town from scratch, with minds still full of the things that brought joy to the heart of a bird: nectar and wild thickets; angular roofs with nooks and protuberances; flowering vines and tangled creepers; dry-stone walls with cracks and crannies; reed beds and shallow ponds of clear water; roadside verges thick with meadow grasses.

Two men—one who was most responsible for building the university, and the other who was the architect of the hospice and the chirurgeon's school—sat in the shaded terrace of the buildings not far from the cliff top, and watched the seabirds soaring among the offshore outcrops.

One of the men had flown himself once. He knew what it was like to feel the wind beneath his wings, to have the air cream through his flight feathers and hold him aloft. Now he was just an old man, crippled with arthritis as many Dustelfolk were, those who had once been birds.

He still dreamed of flying.

He dreamed of Flame Windrider too, sometimes.

The second man on the terrace was no longer watching the birds. He was large, compared to his Dustel companion, even though he'd shrunk with the passing of the years. His hair, white and wild, surrounded his face like a teasel that had caught wool on its hooks. His eyes had faded with age, his skin coarsened under a tropical sun, but there was a kindness in his expression that people still trusted, although some Dustels from other islands—people who didn't know any better—still called him Gilfeather of the Massacre.

Right then, those faded eyes were interested in what was happening below in the bay, where a ship was anchoring offshore. A large vessel, apparently with a draught too deep for the pier. He couldn't see the name, but recognized the design. He was over eighty years old, but there was nothing wrong with his eyesight.

"Well, well," he murmured. "What d'ye think, Ruarth—there's a Kellish ship down there. By the arrangement of her sails, I'd say it was another research vessel from Postseaward; possibly the same one as before."

Ruarth sat up to have a look. "Ah—it's to be hoped it isn't that self-important fellow back again, with all his questions. What was his name again? Shoriso something-or-other?"

"Shor iso Fabold. The 'iso' means 'son of,' I believe."

"That's it. Never did like him much, although the translator chappie was pleasant enough. Nathan. But then, he came to the Isles as a mere fledgling. Almost as good as being Glorian." He shook his head, remembering. "Funny ideas, the Kells. Didn't ever believe I once had feathers and could fly . . ."

"Aye, disbelieving lot. But then, we never did tell them the whole story, did we?"

Ruarth chuckled. "Not entirely."

Kelwyn stirred as he watched the ship heave to and the anchor chain rattle down. Can't even sit comfortably these days, he thought. I hate being old. "Can an old man ask ye something, Ruarth?"

"Of course."

"Those times when ye used to disappear off-island for months at a time . . ."

"Yes?"

"Did you go to Cirkase?"

"What do you think?"

"I think," Gilfeather said carefully, "that the Flame I remember didna care too much for, um, conventions. And neither did the Dustels of my acquaintance, come to think of it . . ."

"You could be right at that. Opportunistic little beasts, birds, you know. And she was raised by Dustels, more or less." The words sparkled with the mischief of an old man's happiest recollections.

"Two ruling Islandlords wouldn't have many chances to get together in the same place at the same time, I suppose," Gilfeather remarked. "Not even when they were married to each other."

"Reckon not."

"And he died a good ten years before she did too."

"More, I believe."

"Ye're a rogue, Ruarth."

"Once," he agreed amiably, "once. Blame that woman of yours. It was Blaze who came and told me that it was time I stopped sitting on the window sill. And as that was right after one of her own visits to Cirkase . . ." He shrugged. "A wise woman. She understood that time bevels the sharp edges, until all things are possible."

"Ach, I might have known she had her hand in there somewhere." Gilfeather squinted down at the bay again. "The Kells have launched a boat from that ship. Looks as if we may have visitors. A woman among them too, by the smell."

"Ought we pretty ourselves, d'you think?"

"Nay, laddie, I think we are past the point where it would make a difference."

They grinned at one another companionably.

"Do you think you did the right thing, Kel? Ridding the world of magic?" Ruarth asked, more soberly.

Kelwyn considered that. "Well, there's never been another Morthred. With many more Aware, dunmagickers had no hope of escape. All who existed were rooted out and either destroyed or cured. There are no subversions now." He'd never really made up his mind about whether sylv and dun were a disease, or just transmitted in the same ways as a disease, but that question no longer bothered him. "Aye," he said. "It was a bonnie, braw thing we did, Ruarth." And yet the idea of all that healing power lost forever—it was an ache in his physician's soul. But the only person who had really understood that was Garrowyn, and he was long gone.

And now . . . now, below them, a foreign ship's boat arrived at the pier and the group of Kells started up the steps to the top of the cliff. Kelwyn recognized Nathan's smell among them, but he didn't comment. "Aye," he said again. "We did the right thing. It's a better world we have now." He smiled faintly. "Even though it was really just us dancing at the end of Ryder's fingers."

Ruarth laughed. "Still rankles, eh? She loved you best, you know."

"Perhaps." But she'd always thought fondly of the patriarch, for all that.

"You should feel sorry for him," Ruarth added. "You are the one who ended up with the woman he loved."

"Aye. His own gowking fault too, the dolt." Kelwyn's answering grin was fleeting, but Ruarth saw it. "Skies, Ruarth—how I miss her!" He sighed. "I try to be grateful that we had fifty years, fifty good years. Grateful that she stayed . . . I never expected it. Every time she went away, I wondered if she would come back. But she always did. And then I would have the joy of seeing her walk up that path from the sea . . . And every day she remained, I woke to the miracle that she was still here. Still *content* to be here. It seems so . . . so *bleak*, now she has gone." He paused for a moment, then added, "I dream sometimes of going home. I find myself hankering after the cool of the Sky Plains, the way the meadow blooms in the birthing season . . ."

"The Plains now would hardly be the place you once knew."

"Ah—but they would. That's the whole point about the Roof of Mekaté. It doesna change."

"Would they allow you to return?"

A slow smile spread over Kelwyn's face. "They are Aware now. That makes them friendlier, no? I have written a letter to Tharn Wyn, asking if they have a spare room for an old man . . ."

"I would miss you."

"I can't stay here without her, Ruarth. Two months now, and it seems like a lifetime." He waved a hand to encompass all the buildings behind them. "All this— our meager attempt at restitution," he said, "for all that we had done. But in the end, ye realize no one can atone for the past; atonement is no more than a religious conceit, without meaning. All ye can do is to soften the suffering of the present or try to shape the future to be a better place. The rest you have to live with, every day of your life. I could do that, and be content—more than content, in fact—because she was here.

"Ach, listen to me. Preaching to my friends now. But ye understand what I am talking about—ye've walked the same road. It's just that . . . that I'm finding out it is harder to do it alone. She had the knack of living in the present, of making every moment . . . joyous."

Ruarth nodded. "She was like that. We were lucky in our women, Kel. That's what makes it so hard when they have gone. It's different for me, though—Flame was never here, on Arutha. I don't see her around every corner. You go to the Sky Plains, Kel. Will do you good. But I'll lay a bet you'll be bored out of your mind in a month, and you'll be back here in two, giving your lectures and arguing with your students."

They grinned at each other, and for a moment all seemed to be right with the world.

They sat in silence, remembering, until the Kellish party from the ship reached the top of the path and came towards them. Nathan was there, but not Shor iso Fabold. And the woman: Kelwyn Gilfeather brightened. She had the same swinging stride to her walk as Blaze had at thirty, the same broad-mouthed smile. And her aroma—he scented it from where he sat. Like meadow flowers in the warmth of spring: honesty, belief, trust. She liked him already, she believed in him, and he had not even met her. The knowledge had the heady stimulus of wine on an empty stomach.

He levered himself to his feet, and wondered whether this time around he might not tell the whole of the story. Someone should know about what the ghemphs did, after all. Someone who wanted to know. Someone who was willing to believe they had once existed.

Anyara isi Teron,
Postseaward, 1799.

Anyara isi Teron: Journal entry
43/2nd Double/1794

I am penning this in the guest room of the hospice on Arutha.

Where do I begin? There is so much to record. So many answers to my many questions. It has been days since I put quill to paper; and there is far too much to say. I have been disappointed and delighted in turn. I have wept and laughed, and now I have to record it all.

Blaze Halfbreed is dead.

There, I have written it. Bald words, and it is strange how much they hurt. I came so far to meet her, and now I never will. She died just eight weeks before I arrived. I cried when Ruarth told me.

I have been here three days, and know now what happened to them all: Blaze, Kelwyn, Ruarth, Flame, Elarn, Dek. I know what the Change was. And I know, I think, the answer to all those questions which have puzzled me.

Why did Kelwyn Gilfeather tell me the final chapter, and not tell Shor? The answer is simple really: his sense of smell is as acute as ever. He can tell that I believe him, just as he could tell that Shor did not. He could tell that I grieved with him for Blaze Halfbreed. He feels the intensity of my regret that I will never know her.

It seems almost fitting that she died as she had lived: without any half measures. No lingering illness, or creeping decrepitude. She rose one morning and— died. Poor Kelwyn. He finds it hard to accept. I am glad to be here; I think he finds some solace in talking of her to me, sensing, as he does, how much I admire her. How much I want to write their story.

* * *

I TALKED TO HIM ABOUT THE CHANGE
first: what, I asked, do Glorians mean by it?

*Everything, he said. The change of the Dustel birds
to people and the restoration of the Dustel Islands.
The end of magic. The rise of Menod power and the
decline of Keeper Isles dominance. The disappearance
of the ghemphs. The end of citizenship tattoos and
the demise of the importance of citizenship. The decline
in the power of Islandlords. A Glory Isles united by both
Awareness and the spread of Menod belief . . . In fact,
the Change covered almost forty years, from 1742 until
the year the first Kellish ship arrived, 1780. In fact, he
said with smile, I suppose you could say it never really
stopped. We are still changing, after all.*

*And then I asked him the one question that had
puzzled me for so long above all others: how did you
stop more sylvs from being born? I thought for a
moment he wasn't going to answer, and in truth he
didn't, not outright—but in the end he gave the clue I
needed to answer it myself. He enjoyed doing that, of
course.*

*But more sylvs were born, he said. They continued
to be born as long as there were sylv mothers giving
birth. We never stopped that from happening; how
could we?*

*I thought about that. So, I said, you cured them
after they were born. You made them Aware. They all
consented to be cured? I was incredulous.*

*Awareness, he said, can be given to the non-Aware
through pricking the cure into the skin. Now tell me,
what does that sound like to you?*

*The simplicity of the answer was breathtaking.
Tattooing. Tattoos. Ghemphs continued to tattoo the
newborn until the Kells arrived. Ryder persuaded
the ghemphs to spread Awareness by administering
the cure through their citizenship tattoos. It was the
ghemphs who had made every single baby born in
the Isles from 1742 until 1780 immune to magic.*

And once those immune children grew up, whether

they were men or women, they would pass their
immunity on to their unborn offspring—or, at the very
least, have nonsylv offspring. For thirty-eight years
the ghemphs ensured no more magic came into the
Glory Isles.

I felt a pang of sorrow.

Surely, I said, there must be elderly sylvs left
somewhere. After all, a baby born in 1740 would only
be fifty-four years old now. And, what's more, such a
woman could have given birth late in life, after the
ghemphs left, to a sylv child, especially if she had a
sylv lover. Is that not so?

In theory, Kelwyn agreed. And if you search for a
sylv, perhaps you may find one yet. Of course, the
heart of sylv society died that day in The Hub. Young
Keeper children were left untrained because there
weren't enough sylvs to teach them, and they
gradually lost their ability to manipulate their sylv as
a consequence, or never learned how in the first
place. Many sylvs rejected their heritage, or became
ashamed to acknowledge it. Others envied the kinship
of Awareness, and chose to be cured of magic.

To tell the truth, he said, I have not met a sylv for
years.

I sighed at that, and his nose twitched. My
romantic soul hoped, I suppose, that there would be a
sylv left for me to find.

Just one, somewhere in all the Isles. I wanted to see
an illusion, just once in my life . . .

AND THE GHEMPHS, I ASKED. WHY
did they do it? Why did they add the cure to the
tattoos?

But neither Kelwyn nor Ruarth was certain what
the ghemphic motivation had been, because the
ghemphs themselves never explained.

Ryder believed it was God's will. Blaze believed
it was because subverted sylvs killed Eylsa, and

then another subverted sylv—Flame—devastated the ghemphic enclave in Breth. They knew while there was dun in the world, ghemphic folk were not safe. And so they decided to help end magic. Perhaps it was as simple as that.

I could see the logic in that theory, but why then, I asked, once all the magic was gone, at the very moment the Isles were made safer for them, did they themselves disappear?

One explanation, Gilfeather said, was that once so many people were Aware, there was less interest in maintaining citizenship. By 1780, no one cared to enforce citizenship laws any more. And once that happened, there was no point to tattoos. And without tattooing, how were the ghemphs to earn a living?

Do you think that is the reason? I asked.

Gilfeather gave me a smile. Maybe, he said, it was because they knew you were coming.

Knew the Kells were coming? I asked. I don't see how that could have been possible—and even if they did know, why should they fear us?

He said: Perhaps you should ask yourselves that question. All I know is that the last of them left just as your first ships arrived. And that they removed all trace of their presence. They wanted to be forgotten, and most people were willing enough to do so. Most people knew little of them anyway.

Where did they go? I asked.

Back to the sea. After that—who can say? One day, he added, perhaps you Kells will find them. And if you do, I hope your people will be more understanding than we were . . . we could have learned so much from them.

And then Kelwyn Gilfeather leaned forward, eyes twinkling, and murmured in my ear, as though it was a secret to share: Do y'know, lassie—I rather think Elarn Jaydon never took the cure. And to the best of my knowledge, ye'll find him in Tenkor still.

I have more to relate, but I shall not do it tonight. Tonight Nathan waits for me in the coral garden.

I know what he will ask, and how I will answer. There is nothing more for me here on Arutha—but there is a whole world out there to be explored. A whole lifetime to be lived. And I will live it my way, as I choose, not as is chosen for me—for that is what Blaze taught me.

GLOSSARY

Glorian terms and people extracted from a compendium compiled by Anyara isi Teron, 1794–95, with reference to the situation of 1742. Original lodged with the National Society for the Scientific, Anthropological and Ethnographical Study of non-Kellish Peoples.

Alain Jentel: Menod patriarch from the Spatts, killed in the bombardment of Creed. Friend to Tor Ryder *(see also)*.
Amiable: A ketch belonging to Captain Kayed *(see also)*, seized together with the crew by Morthred *(see also)*.
Awareness/the Aware: The Aware are born with the ability (Awareness) to see and smell magic. They cannot perform magic themselves, nor can they be directly harmed or deceived by magic.
Barbicanlord: Ruler of Xolchas Stacks. (*See also* Xetiana.)
Bastionlord: Ruler of the Breth Island group. (*See also* Trigaan, Lord Rolass.)
Blaze Halfbreed: A citizenless, half Fen, half Souther Awarewoman, born and raised in The Hub, Keeper Isles. Parents unknown. Worked for the Keeper Council as an assassin of

dunmagickers, and as a bounty-hunter. Has since left Keeper Island employ.

Castlelord: Ruler of the Cirkase Islands. One child, Lyssal, Castlemaid *(see also)*.

Castlemaid: Name given to Castlelord's heir, if female; title now held by Lyssal *(see also)*.

Crannach, Syr-aware: High Patriarch *(see also)* of the Menod *(see also)*.

Creed: Small village on Gorthan Spit *(see also)* taken over by dunmagickers under the leadership of Morthred/Gethelred *(see also)*, then bombarded by the Keeper ships and abandoned.

Dek/Dekan Grinpindillie, Syr-aware: Illegitimate son of Inya Grinpindillie of Mekatéhaven and Bolchar, a fisherman of the Kitamu Bays, Mekaté. Was a guardsboy in Lekenbraig, Mekaté, for a short time.

Devenys, Syr-sylv: Brethian girl aged about thirteen.

dun/dunmagicker: Red (or red-brown) magic and the person who uses it. Harmful powers include the ability to kill others, to destroy property with explosive power that varies from individual to individual, or inflict sores that are ultimately fatal. They can also heal themselves, disguise themselves with illusion and erect protection wards. Dunmagickers are born, not made, and generally are able to learn how to control and manipulate their powers even if they are not taught to do so. Dunmagic is only visible to the Aware, or to the dunmagicker using it, although the effects are obvious to all.

dunmaster: A dunmagicker who is particularly skilful and powerful in the use of dunmagic.

Dustel Isles: Vanished islands of the Souther group. Believed to have been submerged in 1652 by the actions of the dunmaster Morthred/Gethelred, when the non-Aware inhabitants were turned into birds.

Duthrick, Councillor Syr-sylv: Executant Councillor and later Interim Keeperlord of the Keeper Isles. In charge of much of the covert activities of the Keeper Isles outside of their own islandom, particularly when intervention is needed to protect Keeper interests. Given name: Ansor, rarely used. Married, one child, Syr-sylv Jesenda *(see also)*.

Elarn Jaydon: Tiderider. Only son of the Guildean *(see also)* and his late wife.

Emmerlynd Bartbarick, Lord: Keeperlord of the Keeper Isles in 1742.

Eylsa: One of the ghemphs, water bouget pod. Died helping Blaze near Creed in 1742.

Flame Windrider, Syr-sylv: Name taken by Lyssal *(see also)* after escaping from Cirkasecastle.

Floating Mere: A Porth Island lake with an island, home to a dunmagicking enclave set up by Gethelred/Morthred. Wiped out by Tor Ryder, Blaze Halfbreed and a ghemphic attack.

Fotherly Bartbarick, Councillor Syr-sylv: Son of the Keeperlord, Emmerlynd Bartbarick *(see also)*. Also known as Foth the Foppish or Bart the Barbaric.

Gabania: Sylvtalent who worked for Syr-sylv Duthrick and the Keeper Council before her subversion to dunmagic.

Garrowyn Gilfeather: A selver-herder physician from Tharn Wyn on the Sky Plains of Mekaté *(see also)*. Uncle of Kelwyn *(see also)*.

Gethelred, Syr-sylv: A sylv member of the Dustel royal family before the disappearance of the islands. Reappeared as Morthred *(see also)*, dunmaster, with a dunmagicking enclave in Creed, Gorthan Spit. Killed by Kelwyn Gilfeather on Xolchas Stacks.

ghemph: Non-human race. Responsible for tattooing the citizenship tattoos into earlobes of all Glorian citizens. Grayskinned, hairless, with webbed and clawed feet, but possessing no outwardly visible distinction between the sexes. (*See also* pod.)

Gorthan Spit: The only island outside of all the legally recognized islandoms, a place where the citizenless can remain without harassment.

Guildean: Head of the Tideriders' Guild of the Keeper Isles. Elected on a five-yearly basis by members of the Guild. The Guildean's office administers the whole of the main island of Tenkor *(see also)*.

High Patriarch: Head of the Menod and the Patriarchy. Selected by the Synod from among Menod Councillors. Appointment is for life.

Holdlord: Ruler of the Bethany Isles.

Hub Race: Narrow estuary of the Hub River, approximately 100 island miles long.

Hub, The: Capital of the Keeper Isles.

islandom: An island or group of islands that forms an independent administrative unit, or country.

Jesenda Duthrick, Syr-sylv: Councillor Ansor Duthrick's twenty-year-old daughter.

Kayed, Captain: Captain of the *Amiable*, a ketch seized by Morthred, forced to sail first to Porth, then Xolchas, and finally Breth.

Keeper Council: Elected body that rules the Keeper Isles under the leadership of the Keeperlord *(see also)*.

Keeper Fair: Name of Syr-sylv Duthrick's ship.

Keeperlord: Ruler of the Keeper Isles, elected by the Keeper Council from among their own members.

Kelwyn Gilfeather: Sky Plains physician from Wyn, Mekaté. Exiled for life, for killing his wife.

Keren Kyros, Syr-sylv: Sylv healer from Yebeth, Breth.

Korlass Jaydon, Syr-guildean: Guildean of the Tideriders' Guild and therefore chief administrator of Tenkor; widower, father to Elarn *(see also)*.

Lance of Calment: Rebel known for his daring during the uprising of the poorer landless people of Calment Minor in the 1730s. Still has a price on his head in the Calment Isles. Identity largely unknown. (*See also* Tor Ryder.)

Lyssal, Castlemaid of Cirkase, Syr-sylv: The only child and heir of the Castlelord of Cirkase. Raised in Cirkasecastle and ran away in 1742 to Gorthan Spit, where she had an arm amputated after contamination by the dunmagic of Morthred the Mad. (*See also* Flame Windrider.)

Marten Lymick: Tiderider, Elarn Jaydon's closest friend.

Menod: A contraction of Men of God, used to designate the religion as a whole, or all worshippers/believers (male or female) of their God. Centered on the Keeper Isles, but widespread on all islandoms and generally seen as the religion of choice for most islandom ruling houses.

Menod Council: A body elected at an annual Synod, comprised of patriarchs and matriarchs, which rules the Menod faithful of the Glory Isles through a network of patriarchs and matriarchs. Administrative center on Tenkor Island, Keeper Isles.

Morthred: Dunmaster believed to be responsible for sinking the Dustel Islands and changing the islanders into birds in the year 1652. Real name: Gethelred, of the Dustel Islands royal family *(see also)*.

Niamor: A Quillerman who formed a friendship with Blaze Halfbreed on Gorthan Spit that eventually resulted in his death.

pod: An extended family group of ghemphs.

Rampartlord: Ruler of the Dustel Isles prior to the sinking of the islands. The position was not revived among the survivors or their descendants, but Gethelred would have been the rightful heir.

Ransom Holswood, Holdheir: A Menod who came to the position of heir to the Bethany Islands when his older brother died, thereby thwarting his ambitions to be a Menod patriarch. Was in love with Flame Windrider *(see also)*.

Ruarth Windrider, Syr-aware: A Dustel bird born on the roofs of Cirkasecastle, where he lived most of his life until he left in the company of Lyssal in 1742.

Securia: Name given to the post of the head of security in several islandoms.

selver-herder: Any person born to a Sky Plains tharn.

Sky Plains: High plateau of Mekaté Island. Home to the Sky People, herders with an economy based on a domesticated animal, the selver.

Stracey: Sylvtalent who worked for Syr-sylv Duthrick and the Keeper Council before her subversion to dunmagic.

sylv: Blue (or silver-blue) magic that enables healing, and the construction of illusions or protection wards. Sylvmagic cannot be used for destruction or to inflict physical harm on people or things. Sylvs are born, not made, but have to be taught how to use their power, otherwise it can become permanently dormant. Sylvmagic itself is only visible to the Aware or to the sylv using it, although the effects are obvious to all.

Syr: Courtesy title given to anyone with status, usually qualified by the reason for that status; e.g., Syr-aware, Syr-sylv, Syr-patriarch, etc.

Tenkor: Referred to as Tenkor Island, but in fact is a string of

six islands. High Tenkor Island has the connected towns of
Tenkorhaven and Tenkorport.

tiderider: A man who rides the bore wave up the Hub Race,
and the ebb wave back again, either on a single-person tiderunner *(see also)* or as part of the crew of a longboat. Also a general
term for any member of the Tideriders' Guild.

tiderunner: A small wooden craft with a paddle. It has a slight
indentation for seating and wells for the feet. A watertight com-
partment behind the rider is used for the transport of letters and
packets.

Tor Ryder, Syr-aware patriarch: Menod patriarch Straggler-
man, one-time scribe, rebel and swordsman. Was an active
leader of the failed Calment rebellion. (*See also* Lance of Calment.) A councillor of the Patriarch Council who succeeded
Crannach as High Patriarch.

Trench/Great Trench: Believed by many to be a place in the
deepest parts of the ocean where all dead souls go; sometimes
thought of only as the final home for the soul of any sailor lost at
sea; equated by the religious with hell and the home of the evil
Sea Devil. Generally thought to be cold, dark and unpleasant.

Trigaan, Lord Rolass: Breth Bastionlord. Known paedophile.

Trysis: Brethian woman from the town of Keret.

waverunner: A flat molded board used to ride the bore and ebb
waves. Can be ridden standing, kneeling or prone.

Xetiana, Lord: Barbicanlord of the islandom known as Xolchas
Stacks.

Glenda Larke is an Australian who now lives in Malaysia, where she works on the two great loves of her life: writing fantasy and the conservation of rainforest avifauna. She has also lived in Tunisia and Austria, and has at different times in her life worked as a housemaid, library assistant, schoolteacher, university tutor, medical correspondence course editor, field ornithologist and designer of nature interpretive centers. Along the way she has taught English to students as diverse as Korean kindergarten kids and Japanese teenagers living in Malaysia, Viennese adults in Austria and engineering students in Tunis. If she has any spare time (which is not often), she goes birdwatching; if she has any spare cash (not nearly often enough), she visits her daughters in Scotland and Virginia and her family in Western Australia.

You can find out more about Glenda at her website
www.glendalarke.com